MIDWIVES ON CALL
AT CHRISTMAS

D1323718

MIDWIVES ON CALL AT CHRISTMAS

FIONA McARTHUR
JENNIFER TAYLOR
ABIGAIL GORDON

First Published in Great Britain 2017
By Mills & Boon, an imprint of HarperCollins*Publishers*
1 London Bridge Street, London, SE1 9GF

MIDWIVES ON CALL AT CHRISTMAS © 2017 Harlequin Books S.A.

Midwife's Christmas Proposal © 2014 Fiona McArthur
The Midwife's Christmas Miracle © 2010 Jennifer Taylor
Country Midwife, Christmas Bride © 2009 Abigail Gordon

ISBN: 978-0-263-93158-7

24-1017

MIDWIFE'S
CHRISTMAS
PROPOSAL

FIONA McARTHUR

To my son Scott, who gifted me my first parachute jump and the pictures that went with it. And to the experience that I knew I would put into this book.

And to Lawrence, my chute buddy from Coffs Skydivers, who made it such fun that I was never, ever scared.

Mother to five sons, **Fiona McArthur** is an Australian midwife who loves to write. Mills & Boon Medical Romance gives Fiona the scope to write about all the wonderful aspects of adventure, romance, medicine and midwifery that she feels so passionate about – as well as an excuse to travel! Now that her boys are older, Fiona and her husband Ian are off to meet new people, see new places, and have wonderful adventures. Fiona's website is at www.fionamcarthur.com

CHAPTER ONE

SIMON LOOKED AWAY from the road as he drove and across to his sister. Saw the tiny furrow in her brow even while she was sleeping. His eyes returned to the car in front. So she was still angry with him. Where had he gone wrong? All he'd ever wanted to do was protect his family. Protect Maeve from making the same mistakes their mother had made.

Maybe he felt more responsible than other siblings because the day he'd found out he was only a half-brother to Maeve and the girls had been devastating and he did wonder if he'd over-compensated.

But he was concerned about Maeve. About the way she'd been taken for a ride and she still couldn't see it. If Simon was honest with himself, he was just as hurt because he'd thought Rayne was his friend and he'd been suckered in as well. His sister's predicament had been all his fault.

Simon could feel his knuckles tighten on the wheel and he consciously relaxed them. He needed a holiday, and Maeve needed somewhere safe away from the baby's father if he ever came back, so maybe Lyrebird Lake was a good choice, like Maeve said.

And it was Christmas.

Two hours later they drove into the driveway of the Manse Medical Centre, Lyrebird Lake. The long day drive north from Sydney had been accomplished with little traffic issues or conversation. The last hour since they'd turned away from the coast had been unusually relaxing as they'd passed green valleys and bovine pedestrians. It was good to be here finally.

Simon felt that warmth of homecoming he'd forgotten about in the rush and bustle of his busy life—almost like he could feel one of Louisa's enthusiastically warm hugs gearing up—as he slowed the car.

The engine purred to a stop and Maeve woke. She smiled sleepily, then remembered they were at odds with each other, and the smile fell away.

He watched her twist awkwardly in her seat as she took in the dry grass and huge gum trees 'I've heard such a lot about this place over the years. Thanks for bringing me, Simon.'

The tension in his shoulders lessened. At least she was talking to him again. He should never have mentioned his reservations about her idea of giving birth at Lyrebird Lake. That had been his obstetrician's point of view. Life had compartments, or should have, and he usually kept everything separate and in control.

Look what had happened when Maeve had lost control.

Simon's eyes travelled over the familiar sights—the hospital and birth centre across the road from Louisa's house, the sleepy town just down the road, and the sparkling harp-shaped lake to the left behind the trees.

Unexpectedly, considering the mood he'd been in when he'd started out for here against his will, he couldn't do anything but smile as he eased his car under the carport at the side of the house.

'Curious.' Simon admired the old but beautifully restored Harley-Davidson tucked into a corner and then shrugged. He couldn't imagine Louisa on it but there were always interesting people staying at the manse.

It didn't seem ten years since he'd first come here with his new-found dad, Angus, but this big sprawling house Angus had brought him to all those years ago looked just the same. He'd arrived expecting awkwardness with his fledgling relationship with his birth father, and awkwardness staying with strangers in this small country town. But there hadn't been any.

He glanced at Maeve. 'Louisa will have heard us arrive.'

'Louisa used to be the housekeeper before she married your grandfather? Right?'

'Yep. They married late in life before he passed away. I stay with her when I come at Christmas.'

Simon climbed out quickly so he could open her door, but of course, Maeve was too darned independent. By the time they reached the path out front Louisa stood at the top of the steps, wiping her hands on her apron, and beamed one of Lyrebird Lake's most welcoming smiles.

Simon put his bag down and leapt up the two stairs to envelop the little woman in a hug. She felt just as roundly welcoming as he remembered. 'It's so good to see you, Louisa.'

'And you too, Simon. I swear you're even taller than last year.'

He had to smile at that as he stepped back. 'Surely I've reached an age where I can't keep growing.' He looked back at his sister, standing patiently at the bottom of the steps. 'Though with your cooking there is a possibility I could grow while I'm here.'

He offered a steadying hand but Maeve declined, made her way determinedly balancing her taut belly out front, as she climbed to the top of the stairs, so he guessed he wasn't totally forgiven.

He missed the easy camaraderie they used to have and hoped, perhaps a little optimistically, that Lyrebird Lake might restore that rapport as well. He guessed he had been out of line in some of the things he'd said about her choice in men and choice in birthing place.

'This is my youngest sister, Maeve. Maeve, this is my grandmother, Louisa.'

Louisa blushed with pleasure. 'You always were a sweetheart.' She winked at Maeve. 'Grandmother-in-law but very happy to pretend to be a real one.'

Maeve held out her hand. 'It's nice to finally meet you. Simon's told us a lot about you and everyone here. He says you're a wonderful cook.'

He saw Louisa's kind eyes brush warmly over Maeve and Simon relaxed even further. Of course Louisa would make them both feel wanted. 'Boys need their food.' He smiled to himself because he wasn't sure how he qualified for boy when he'd left thirty behind.

Louisa went on, 'You're very welcome here, dear,' as she glanced at Maeve's obvious tummy. 'It will be lovely to have a baby back in the house again, even if only for a wee while.'

Simon squeezed her plump shoulder. 'Dad and Mia not here?'

'They're coming over for dinner tonight. They thought it would be less overwhelming for Maeve if she had a chance to settle in first.'

She turned to Maeve. 'And we'll take it gradually to meet everyone else. There's a huge circle of family and friends who will want to catch up with Simon and meet you.'

Simon went back to pick up their bags and followed Louisa and Maeve into the house. The scent of cedar oil on the furniture made his nose twitch with memories—overlaid with the drifting promise of fresh-cut flowers and, of course, the tantalising aroma of Louisa's hot pumpkin scones.

His shoulders sagged as his tension lessened with each step he made into the house. He should have come here earlier. Leaving it until now had been crazy but his last two breech women had come in right at the last minute and he hadn't wanted to leave them uncertain about who would be there for them.

But enough. He needed to let go of work for a while and just chill, a whole month to Christmas and his first real break in years—and maybe the strain wasn't all on Maeve's side because he'd been holding on too tight for a while now.

This was what this place was good for. Finding the peace you were supposed to find as Christmas approached.

Behind a bedroom door in the same house Tara Dutton heard the car arrive and when, minutes later, footsteps sounded down the hall she rolled over in bed, yawned and squinted at the clock.

Two o'clock in the afternoon. She'd had six hours sleep, which was pretty good. Her mouth curved as she rolled back onto her back and stretched.

Last night's sharing of such a long, slow, peaceful labour and in the end a beautiful birth just as the sun had risen made everything shiny new. Babies definitely liked that time just before morning. Man, she loved this job.

She wriggled her toes and then sat up to swing her legs out of bed. Heard calm voices. Relief expanded, which was crazy when she didn't know them—but they were here safely. It would be Angus's son, Simon, and his sister. They arrived today and she admitted to a very healthy curiosity about the man everyone obviously adored, and even more so for his sister.

Simon's arrival had been the main topic of conversation for the last few days but Tara was more interested in Maeve.

Twenty-five, pregnant and a newly qualified midwife. Two out of three things Tara had been before she'd come here. Pregnancy wasn't on her agenda.

But that was okay. She breathed deeply and vowed again not to let the unchangeable past steal her present, and thankfully the calm she found so much easier to find in Lyrebird Lake settled over her like the soft quilt on her bed.

Clutching her bundle of fresh clothes, she opened the door to the hallway a crack to check the coast was clear, then scooted up the polished wooden floor to the bathroom and slipped inside.

Simon heard the bedroom door open from the kitchen and leaned back precariously in his chair until the two front legs were off the floor, and craned his neck to see who was in the hall. He glimpsed the back of a small, pertly bottomed woman in men's boxer shorts, one tiny red rose tattooed on her shoulder exposed by the black singlet as she disappeared into the bathroom.

His mouth curved as the years dropped away. He remembered arriving here with his father and their first sight of the woman who would later become his darling stepmother.

See! Always someone interesting staying in this place, he thought to himself again with a smile, and eased the front legs of the chair back on the floor.

When Tara stepped out of the bathroom thirty minutes later she felt nothing like the crumpled sleepyhead she'd been when she'd slipped in.

Her glance in the mirror over the claw-foot bath had reassured her. Blonde hair spikily fresh from the shower and her eyes confident and ready to meet the new guy and his intriguing sister.

Tara had experienced a lot of heartache and struggle in her life and it had made her wary of meeting new people. But the shadows of her past had made her who she was today—her T-shirt said it all: 'Woman With Attitude'.

As she walked back towards her room she passed the open door of one of the guest rooms. She couldn't help but have a tiny peek inside.

Simon's bag lay open on the bed, and she blinked at the neatly folded clothes in piles lined up in a row as she drew level, unlike her own 'bomb-hit' room, and she vowed she'd keep her door shut until he left.

Simon came into view, busily unpacking, and must have become aware of the eyes on him from the doorway. He glanced up, smiled, and she faltered. Man, that was some smile, like a warm breeze had blown down the hall and into her face, and Tara nearly tripped on the towel that slipped unexpectedly from her fingers.

'Hi, there. You must be Tara.'

She bent quickly to retrieve the towel. 'And you're Simon.' Tara moistened her lips. Louisa had said he was a bit of hunk like his dad but she'd put that down as favouritism for a relative. She certainly hadn't expected the fantasy that suddenly swirled in her head. Something like inviting him in two doors down for some seriously red-hot tumbling, but, *mamma mia,* he had a wicked bedroom grin.

Whoa, there, libido, where did you spring from? More to the point, where have you been?

Then he stepped closer and held out his hand and she forgot to think, just responded, and his fingers closed around hers, cool and surprisingly comforting, as he leaned forward with grace and unselfconscious warmth so that she couldn't be offended as he unexpectedly kissed her cheek.

'It's very nice to meet you.'

A cheek-kisser? Her brain clicked in. And nice to meet you, too, mister. There was nothing gushing or sleazy about the way he'd done the deed but she still wasn't quite sure how he managed to get away with it.

It was as if his whole persona screamed gentleman and usually the goody-two-shoes type turned her off. Though she was trying to change her tastes from bad boys to normal men after the last fiasco.

This guy made her think of one of those lifesavers

on the beach at Bondi—tall, upstanding, with genuine love of humanity, careful of other people's safety but perfectly happy to risk their own lives to save yours. She blinked. And rumour said that apparently this guy wasn't even shackled to some discerning woman.

She was not bowled over! Not at all! She liked Angus for his solid dependability but this Simon beat his father hands down on the warmth stakes, that was all.

He was still waiting for her to answer him. Question? 'Nice to meet you, too.' What else could she say except something to get her out of his doorway? 'I'd better leave you to unpack.'

He didn't look like he wanted her to leave but she forced her feet to move. By the time she made it back to her bedroom her neck was hot with embarrassment. With great restraint she closed her door gently and with a sigh leant against it.

Talk about vibration. So much vibration it was lucky they hadn't spontaneously combusted. Holey dooley, she was in trouble if they were both going to live in this house for the next few weeks and react like that. Or maybe it was one-sided and he was totally oblivious to her. She smiled at her feet. Somehow she doubted it.

Simon watched her go. Couldn't help himself, really. Not a beauty in the stereotypical sense, her face was too angled for that, but she was a sassy, sexy little thing, and she had a definite pert little wiggle when she walked. She reminded him a bit of Maeve's girlfriends with that bolshie, I'm-my-own-woman persona that young females seemed to have nowadays.

Lord, he sounded like an old man but, seriously, this generation made him smile. But, then, didn't all women make him smile? Which might be why he hadn't seemed to find himself tied to just one. Problem with growing up with four sisters? Or problem with him and commitment?

Not that he didn't plan to have a family, settle down and be the best dad and husband he could be, but pledging to stay with one woman had been a tad difficult when he really didn't believe the odds of finding his other half.

Maybe he would end up in Lyrebird Lake at some stage, though after this last horror year he couldn't see himself taking the holistic approach to birth that was the norm here.

He turned back to the unpacking. Lined up the paired socks in the drawer and placed his folded jocks beside them. His last girlfriend had said his fussiness drove her mad and he was tempted to mess the line up a little but couldn't do it.

His sisters had always thought it hilarious that he liked things tidy. Having lived briefly with all of them as adults at one time or another, being the only sibling with stable housing, it wasn't such a bad thing. They were absolute disasters at order.

But he wouldn't change any of them. After his mother and stepfather had moved to America someone had needed to be able to put their hands on a spare house key to help out the current family member in crisis. And mild, acquired OCD wasn't a bad thing to have if you were a big brother—or a doctor. None of his patients had complained he was too careful.

He wondered what traits young Tara had acquired from her life and then shook his head. He didn't want to know. Lyrebird Lake was the last place to come for a fling because everyone would know before you'd even kissed her. A little startled at how easily he could picture that scenario, he brushed it away.

This was the place you brought one woman and settled down for good and he wasn't sure he believed in that for himself.

Five minutes later Tara had herself together enough to venture out to the kitchen, where Louisa had set out a salad for post-night-duty lunch.

The older lady hummed as she worked and the smile when she looked up to see Tara shone even brighter than normal.

'Have you met him?' No doubt at all whom she meant and Louisa wobbled with pride.

Tara had to smile. 'In the hallway.'

'Isn't he gorgeous?'

Tara picked up a carrot stick and took a bite. Chewed and swallowed—not just the carrot but the tiny voluptuous shiver as well. Back under control. 'He's very handsome. But no ideas, Louisa. He's an up-and-coming consultant here for a couple of weeks. And he's far too nice for me.'

'Silly girl. Of course he's not, he's just what you need.' She turned and started humming again and Tara had to smile as she glanced out the window to the veranda looking over the lake. She wasn't sure what that meant but she couldn't get offended by Louisa's mutterings—wouldn't do her any good if she did.

Tara had never had the kind of hugging acceptance she'd found in the small semi-rural community and sometimes she had to remind herself it might even be okay to learn to care for these people.

Then reality would resurface and she knew it would be just like the past—something would happen, she'd have to leave under a cloud and she'd be forgotten.

But she'd always have her work now wherever she went, she reminded herself, the first stability she'd known since the orphanage, and attainment had been such a golden rush as she'd passed her last exam, and that was priceless.

While socially she might be a bit stunted, okay, she granted more than a little stunted, but the work side of her life here couldn't be more satisfying with the midwifery-led birth centre.

She could finally do what she loved and, man, how she loved doing it. Loved the immersion in a woman's world of childbirth, the total connection as she supported a woman through her most powerful time, and then the exclusion when that woman departed for home.

Just like a foster-family and she was good at saying goodbye. Except unlike where she'd done her training in the city, you bumped into the women again in Lyrebird Lake, and she wasn't quite used to that but it wasn't as bad as she'd thought it would be.

Technically she was autonomous in that she had her own women to care for, under the aegis of Montana, the most senior midwife, and they case-conferenced once a week so everyone knew what was going on. She was an integral part of the team of midwives and doctors who worked in the adjoining hospital as well on quiet days, and they were always happy to be back-up for any obstetric hiccough. So she felt supported in her role and that she contributed. It was a heady feeling and she still couldn't believe her luck.

Incredibly, everyone seemed as eager to learn new trends as she was, and everyone researched changes in medical practice and then helped others to learn too. There was also enough going on in the other half of the hospital to stay updated on the medical side. This place was a utopia for a fledgling midwife who planned to make her career her life.

In the six months she'd been here her professional confidence had grown along with her belief in women and her own attending skills.

The motto of the lake, 'Listen to women,' had been gently but firmly reinforced. Very different from her training hospital's unwritten motto of 'We know best for all women.'

She wondered what the gorgeous Simon's philosophy was but coming from a busy practice working out of a major city hospital she had a fair suspicion.

Steady footsteps approached down the hallway and the object of her thoughts strolled into the room—which inexplicably seemed to shrink until he owned the majority of it—and she found herself basking in the warmth of his smile again.

Another unexpected flow of heat to the cheeks. Man, she'd never been a blusher. Thankfully, he turned the charm onto Louisa and Tara wilted back into her chair with relief.

She heard him say, 'I might go for a wander along the lake, Louisa, and relax after the drive.' He eased his neck as if it was kinked. 'Maeve's putting her feet up for an hour before this evening.'

Tara saw Louisa's eyes glint with determination and not being known for subtlety, Tara's stomach tightened, but it was too late. 'Why don't you join him, Tara? You always say it's good to walk after a night shift.'

CHAPTER TWO

Now, THAT WAS sink-into-the-floor-worthy. Tara could have glared at Louisa except the older lady didn't have a mean bone in her soft little body. Instead she shook her head. 'No. No. Simon will want to reacquaint himself. He doesn't need me to hold his hand.'

'I won't hold your hand if you don't want me to,' he was teasing, but this time there was no hiding the connection and she closed her eyes.

When she opened them he was smiling quizzically at her, and grudgingly she accepted that as a recipient it didn't feel as bad as it could have.

'I don't bite,' he said. 'I'd like the company but only if you want to.'

Growth experience. He thinks you're a socially adept woman. That would be a first. She could do this. The guy worked with women all the time. Practise at least on a man who was skilled at putting women at ease. Made sense. 'Fine. I can't feel more embarrassed.' She glanced at Louisa, who apparently didn't bat an eyelid at putting her in the hot seat and was humming happily, satisfied two of her chickens were getting along.

She could almost smile at that. Tara picked up the sunglasses she'd left beside the window because she still suffered from that night-duty glare aversion that too little sleep left you with. Simon held the door open for her—something that happened a lot in the quaintness around here. A few months ago she would have been surprised but today she just murmured, 'Thank you,' and passed in front of him.

They'd turned out of the driveway before he spoke and surprisingly the silence wasn't awkward. Thank goodness someone else didn't mind peace and quiet. Years of keeping her own counsel had taught her the value of quiet time—but quiet time in the company of others was an added bonus she could savour. She didn't think she'd met anyone she felt so in tune with so quickly. Though the air might be peaceful, it still vibrated between them.

Stop worrying, she admonished herself, a habit she'd picked up in the orphanage and on foster-parent weekends. Just let it be.

She looked ahead to where the path curled around the edge of the lake like a pale ribbon under the overhanging trees, and the water shimmered through the foliage like diamonds of blue glass in the ripples.

This place soothed her soul more than she could have ever imagined it would. Until unexpectedly a creature rustled in the undergrowth and her step faltered as it swished away from them into the safety of the water's edge. Typical, she thought, there's always a snake in the grass.

She shuddered. Snakes were the only creatures she disliked but that was probably because someone had put one in her bed once. 'Hope that wasn't something that can bite.'

Simon glanced after the noise. 'No. Doubt it. Might even have been a lyrebird.' He grinned. 'Have they told you about the legend of the lyrebird?' There was definitely humour in his deep voice. The man had a very easy soothing bass and she found herself listening more to the melody of the words than the content. Tried harder for the words.

'Nope. You mean as in why they call the place Lyrebird Lake?' She shrugged. 'Not really into legends.' Or fairy-tales. Or dreams of gorgeous men falling in love with her and carrying her off. Pshaw. Rubbish.

'Ah. A disbeliever.' He nodded his head sagely and she had to smile at his old-fashioned quaintness. 'So you wouldn't believe that in times of stress or, even more excitingly, when you meet your true love, a real live lyrebird appears and dances for you.'

Now she knew he was laughing at her. She rolled her eyes. 'Well, I haven't seen one and I've been here six months.'

'Me either. And I've been coming here off and on for ten years.' The smile was back in his voice. 'But my father and Mia have.'

This time her brows rose and she had no doubt her healthy dollop of scepticism was obvious. 'Really.'

His eyes crinkled. 'And Montana and Andy. And Misty and Ben.'

'You're kidding me.' These were sane, empowering people she'd looked up to. Consultants and midwives. Icons of the hospital. Or maybe he was pulling her leg. 'Don't believe you.'

'Nope. All true.' His eyes were dancing but she could see he was telling the truth as he believed it.

Then he'd been conned. 'How many times has this happened?'

He shrugged. 'Don't know. You'd have to ask.'

Brother. 'I will.' She shook her head. He'd probably just made it all up. Men did say weird things to impress women. Though he didn't seem like one of those guys, but, then again, her sleaze detection system had never worked well. 'What else don't I know about this place?'

He glanced around. 'Well, half of that hill behind the lake...' he pointed across the water '...is full of disused gold mines and labyrinths of old tunnels crisscross underneath our feet.'

She looked down at the path and grimaced. Imagined falling through into an underground cavern. She'd always had claustrophobia—or had since one particular foster-sibling had locked her in a cupboard. Now, that wasn't a pleasant thought. 'Thanks for that. How to ruin a walk.'

'Well, not really under our feet. That might be

stretching it a bit far. But certainly all around the hill-side and a long way this way.'

'Okay.' She shook off the past and thought rationally about it. 'I guess half our hospital's business comes from the mines out of town so it makes sense we'd have some here.' She glanced at him as they walked at a steady pace around the lake. Maybe she could start fossick-ing for gold after work—above ground, of course—and make her fortune to pay off the debts Mick had left her with. 'Have you been in them?'

He laughed. Even looked a little pink-cheeked. 'Once. To my embarrassment.' Shook his head at him-self. 'I can't believe I brought this up.' He glanced at Tara ruefully and sighed. 'I had to ring Mia to get my dad to rescue me.'

She looked across at him and grinned. Good to see other people did dumb things. 'Ouch.'

'Not one of my more glorious moments.'

She looked at him, loose-limbed, strongly muscled with that chiselled jaw and lurking smile. A man very sure of his world and his place in it. She wished. Shook her head. 'I'm sure you have enough glorious moments.'

The quizzical look was back but all he said was, 'Yep. Hundreds.'

She had to laugh at that. 'I'm still waiting for mine.'

'My turn not to believe you.' So he'd noticed her scepticism. He tilted his head and studied her with lei-surely thoroughness. 'Do you enjoy your work?'

'Love it.'

'Then I'll bet you have lots of successes too.'

She thought about earlier that morning and smiled. 'I do get to share other women's glorious moments.' Changed the subject. 'Mia says you're running a breech clinic at Sydney Central?'

'Yep. Was converted by an amazing guy I worked with when I was a registrar. Had the motto "Don't interfere". Said most women had the ground work for a normal breech birth.'

She couldn't agree more but her training hospital hadn't subscribed to that theory. The only babies allowed to be born in the breech position were the ones who came in off the street ready to push their own way out. She'd never been lucky enough to be on duty for that. 'I've watched a lot of breech births on videos but I haven't seen one in real life.'

'You will. Hopefully trends are changing with new research. Women are demanding a chance at least. Maybe one of your glorious moments is coming up. You obviously love midwifery.'

'I was always going to be a nurse, because my mother was a nurse, even though I don't remember much about her, but then one of my friends lost a baby and I decided I'd be a midwife. It was a good decision.'

'I think it's a fabulous decision. Some of my best friends are midwives.' He returned to their previous conversation. 'But I can't believe there isn't more to your life than your job.'

'You're right.' She thought of her arrival here six months ago. 'I love my bike.'

'Ah. So the black monster is yours?'

'Yep. The sum total of my possessions.'

'University can be expensive.'

She'd only just started paying that back. It was the bills Mick had run up all over town that crippled her. More fool her for having the lease and the accounts in her name. They'd both been in the orphanage together and when she'd met him again she'd been blinded to his bitter and dangerous side because, mistakenly, she'd thought she'd found family.

But her dream of everything being fair and equal had been torn into a pile of overdue notices. 'Druggie boyfriends can be expensive too.' Unintentionally the words came out on a sigh. What the heck was she doing?

'Nasty. Had one of those, did you.'

She turned her face and grimaced at the lake so he couldn't see. She was tempted to say 'Dozens' but it wasn't true. It had taken her too long to actually trust someone that first time. 'Hmm. I'm a little too used to people letting me down. Don't usually bore people with it.'

'Don't imagine you bore people at all.'

She could hear the smile in his voice and some of the annoyance with herself seeped away then surged again, even though it was unreasonably back towards Simon. What would he know about where she'd been? What she'd been through?

Then, thankfully, the calmness she'd been practising for the last six months since she'd met these people whispered sense in her ear and she let the destructive thoughts go. Sent the whole mess that was her past life out over the rippled water of the lake and concentrated on the breath she eased out.

She had no idea where the conversational ball lay as she returned to the moment but let that worry go too. Took another breath and let her shoulders drop.

'That's some control you have there, missy.'

She blinked at Simon and focussed on him. On his calm grey eyes mainly and the warmth of empathy—not ridicule, as she'd expected, but admiration and understanding.

'I'm practising positive mindfulness and self-control.' She didn't usually tell people that either.

He nodded as if he knew what it was, probably didn't, then he surprised her with his own disclosure. 'I'm not good at it. But if it makes you feel any better I have hang-ups too. Luckily I have a very busy work life.'

She smiled at the statement. 'Funny how we can hide in that. I was studying like mad, paying bills for two in my time off, and he was gambling and doing drugs when I thought he was at uni.' She shrugged it away. 'Now I have a busy work life and a really big bike.'

'The bike's a worry.'

'The bike?' She shook her head and could almost feel the wind on her face and the vibration in her ears. 'Not if you have no ties. Always loved the spice of danger.

It would be different if I had someone who needed me.'
There was a difference between someone needing you
and someone using you. She'd agreed not to drag them
both through the court system but she would only keep
all the bills at the cost of his bike. Even though it had
only been worth a quarter of the debts he'd run up, possession of the bike had restored some of her self-esteem.
Mick hadn't been happy and sometimes she wondered
if it really all was finished.

'Ah. So you admit that motorbikes are the toys of
possibly "temporary" citizens?'

'Spoken like a true doctor.'

'Ask any paramedic. The stats are poor.'

She grinned at him—he had no idea. 'But the fun is
proportional. I could take you for a ride one day.'

He raised his brows. 'I'd have to think about that.'

'Sure. No rush. You have time.' She couldn't imagine
him ever saying yes. Which was a good thing because
she suspected the experience of Simon's arms wrapped
around her and his thighs hard up against her backside
would make it very difficult to concentrate. Instead she
looked up ahead. 'So how far are we walking? You'll
be at your father's house soon.'

He glanced up in surprise. Looked around. 'You're
right. I guess he'll be at work anyway.'

'Mia will be home. She was on duty the night before me.'

'I'd forgotten you were up all night.' His glance
brushed warmly over her and surprisingly she didn't

feel body-conscious. It wasn't that kind of look. 'You do it well. I always look like a dishrag for the next few days.'

She nodded wisely. 'That would be the age factor.'

It was his turn to blink then grin, and she was glad he had a sense of humour. Nice change. Not sure why she'd tried to alienate him, unless she'd wanted him to turn away so she wouldn't have to.

'*Touché*, young woman.' He looked ahead to the house they were approaching. 'Let's go and see my gorgeous step-mama and my second family of sisters. This old man needs a cold drink.'

CHAPTER THREE

SIMON'S STEP-MAMA, NOT all that much older than Simon, greeted them with open arms, her red curls bouncing as she rushed out to hug him. Her eyes sparkled as she stared up at Simon fondly, and Tara was pretty sure nobody had ever looked at her like that.

Two copper-curled miniature Mias tumbled out of the door, one more demurely because she was eleven, and the other squealing because she was eight, but in the end both threw themselves at Simon, who scooped them up one in each hand and spun them around as he hugged them. 'How are my little sisters today?'

Tara unobtrusively admired the stretch of material over his upper arms as with impressive ease he twirled the girls like feathers. He might be way out of her league but this Simon Campbell was certainly delicious eye candy. She could deal with just looking in. She did that all the time.

He kissed them both on the cheek and they giggled as he put them down.

'It feels like ages since we saw you, Simon.' The elder girl, Layla, pouted.

'Eleven months. Christmas.' He put them at arm's length and looked them over, nodded, satisfied they looked well, before he turned back and studied Mia again. 'And how is my gorgeous step-mama?'

'All the better for seeing you.' They embraced again and the genuine warmth overflowed to where Tara was standing. 'Once a year is not enough.'

Touchy-feely family or what! Tara pushed away the tiny stab of jealousy. So what if Simon had this whole network of adoring relatives and she didn't.

Simon grinned and stepped back so that Mia turned to Tara and leaned in for a hug. Tara tried, she really did, to hug back. She seemed to be getting better at it. 'Tara. Great to see you, too.' Mia nodded her head at Simon. 'So you two have met.'

Simon grinned. 'In the hallway. Made me think of you and Dad. Then Louisa nagged Tara into accompanying me on my walk.'

'Poor Tara.' Mia grinned and looked at her. 'Met in the hallway, did you? I hope you had clothes on, Tara. I was in a towel when I met his father and sparks flew even on the first day.'

Tara had to laugh. 'In that case I'm glad to say I was dressed. And had six hours' sleep under my belt.'

Mia's eyes sharpened. 'That's right. You were on night duty last night. How was Julie's labour? What time was her baby born?'

'Quarter to five this morning, on the dot. Sunrise.'

Mia shook her head with a smile. 'Babies seem to love sunrise.'

'I was just thinking that.' Tara soaked up the warmth she was getting used to from these people and then blinked as Mia spun on her heel. 'Come in. What was I thinking?' She waved a hand. 'Have a cold drink. Angus will be jealous I got to see you first, Simon.'

'But not surprised.'

Mia laughed. Then she sobered as she remembered. 'Anyway, how are you? You look tired. And how is Maeve?'

'I'm fine. Maeve's pregnancy has four weeks to go and the baby's father is still in a US penitentiary. I hope.'

'I'm sorry you've all had that worry. What did your mother say? It must be hard for her to be living so far away in Boston when her daughter is pregnant.'

'There's not a lot she can do. Maeve refuses to have her baby in America and Dad's unwell and Mum can't leave.'

'Then Maeve is lucky she has you.'

He shrugged. 'My youngest sister has me stumped the way she is at the moment. I can't say anything right. I'm worried about her.'

Tara wasn't quite sure if she was supposed to hear all this or whether she should drift away and look out the window over the lake or something, but she guessed everyone else would know the ins and out of it. She'd find out eventually.

Mia was talking and walking until she opened the fridge. 'So you could've brought her here earlier, even if you couldn't get away. She could have stayed here or with Louisa. You know how Louisa loves to have people under her roof. And Tara's there.' She turned to Tara and drew her back into the circle.

'Isn't that right, Tara?'

'I've never felt more welcome in my life,' she said quietly, and hoped the others missed the pathetic neediness in the statement.

Thankfully they must have because Simon went on as if all was normal. 'Well, now that I'm here I'm hoping I can manage a few weeks of relaxation till she settles in. Though I may have to do a quick trip back and forth in the middle. It depends when my next two private women go into labour, but they're not due till after the new year.'

Mia closed the refrigerator and returned with two tall glasses of home-made lemonade. 'So how are your training sessions going? Have you managed to inspire a few more docs to think breech birth without Caesarean can be a normal thing?'

He took the glass. 'Thanks. I'm trying. My registrar's great.' He took a sip and closed his eyes in delight. 'Seriously, Mia, you could retire on this stuff.'

She actually looked horrified. 'Retire? Who wants to retire?'

'Sometimes I think I do,' Simon said half-jokingly, and Mia raised her brows.

The concern was clear in her voice. 'You sound like your father when I first met him. You do need a break. Watch out or Angus will be nagging you to move here and set up practice.'

'Haven't completed the research I want to do. A few years yet.'

A vision of Simon with a wife and kids popped unexpectedly into Tara's mind. Made it a bit of a shame she didn't stay in places too long, then she realised where her thoughts were heading. That way lay disappointment. Didn't she ever learn? She'd rather think about Maeve. 'So has Maeve joined any parenting classes?'

Simon shook his head and his concern was visible. 'Wouldn't go to classes in Sydney.'

Tara shrugged. 'I don't think that's too weird. She's a midwife. She knows the mechanics. And sometimes women don't want to think about labour until right at the end. Or be involved in the couples classes without a partner. I get that.'

She could feel Mia's eyes on them and obviously she wanted to say something. Tara waited. Mia was very cool and worth listening to.

'Why don't you ask her if she'd like to be on your caseload, Tara? I think a younger midwife would help when she's feeling a bit lost and lonely.'

Tara could feel her chest squeeze with the sudden shock of surprise. That was pretty big of Mia to trust a family member to her. Her eyes stung and she looked away. Nobody had ever treated her as she was treated here. Or trusted her. She just hoped she didn't let them down. 'You know I'd love to. But I guess it depends who she wants.'

Simon looked at Mia too. He felt the shock and turned to look at his stepmother. He wasn't sure what he thought about that and saw Mia nod reassuringly. Someone else looking after Maeve, not Mia? He looked at the bolshie but sincere young woman beside him. Was she experienced enough? What if something went wrong?

Then saw the flare of empathy for his sister in Tara's face and allowed the reluctant acceptance that Mia could be right. Maeve wanted to run the show. Wanted to listen to her body without interference, if he'd listened at all to the arguments they'd had over the last couple of weeks, and he had no doubt young Tara was holistic enough for his sister to be able to do that.

Normally he would be right there with a woman, cheering her on, but he was having serious personal issues doing that with the sister he had felt most protective of all his life. Not that he'd actually be there, of course. But he was darned sure he'd be outside the door, pacing.

So maybe Mia was right. It could be harder for Maeve to relax with the connection so strong between her brother and his stepmother.

He found the words out in the air in front of him before he realised. 'We'll see what she says.'

He reassured himself that if Mia didn't have faith in

Tara, she wouldn't have suggested it. And despite the mixed feelings he was starting to have about this intriguing young woman he really did feel a natural confidence in her passion for her work.

He'd seen it before. How Lyrebird Lake could bring out the best in all of them. Maybe he had lost that since he'd been so immersed in the high-tech, high-risk arena of obstetrics he studied now.

He'd even seen it with his own father. From hotshot international evacuation medic to relaxed country GP.

Maeve and Tara did have a lot in common and would get on well, the dry voice in his head agreed—all the way to dropkicking past boyfriends!

No. It would be good. This was all going to turn out even better than he'd hoped.

CHAPTER FOUR

THE DINNER PARTY was a reasonable success. Maeve smiled and said the right things but still kept her distance and seemed a little flat to Simon. His stepmother was her own gorgeous self and treated both young women as if they were long-term friends of hers, and his father said very little but smiled every time his eyes rested on his wife or daughters.

Louisa was in her element because she loved dinner parties and seeing the family together. She was always happiest when children were around.

And young Tara, dressed in skin-tight, very stressed jeans that showed glimpses of skin beneath the ragged material moulded to her lush little body, drew his eyes like a magnet every time she walked past to the fridge on some errand for Louisa.

His father came to stand beside him. 'Mia says you seem to get on well with Tara.'

'She's easy to get along with.'

Tara laughed at something Louisa whispered as she walked past again with a platter of fruit for dessert and both men sneaked a glance.

Angus looked away first. 'I think our Tara's had an interesting life. She's a tough little cookie, on the outside at least.'

Simon glanced at his father's face. 'Lots of people have tough lives.'

'Guess so.' Angus took a sip of his beer. 'What happened to Julia?'

'Didn't work out. Said I didn't pay her enough attention. Let my work come between us.'

'Did you?'

'Maybe.' Simon thought about it. 'Definitely. Spent a lot of time apologising for leaving and heading into work. Started to enjoy work more than home and she found another guy.'

'Took me a while to find Mia. It will happen to you one day and you'll recognise it.'

They both looked at Angus's wife. 'If I find a woman like Mia I'll be very happy.'

'Would you settle here?'

'So this is a job interview?'

'Cheeky blighter. Would you?'

'Not yet. But in the future I'm not ruling it out.'

Angus nodded then added innocently, 'Can you do three days for me, starting Monday?'

Simon laughed. 'I knew this was leading somewhere. Why?'

'Seeing as you're here, and Mia's had a big birthday last week, I thought I might take her up to Brisbane to do Christmas shopping. She loves it. Take her and the girls for a mini-holiday.'

Simon laughed. 'Can't see you shopping with Christmas music in the background.'

He grimaced. 'It's only a couple of days. I'm going to sit back and watch my women. Need more of that when you get to my age.'

'Poor old man.'

'Absolutely. So, will you?'

Simon had done the occasional shift in the small hospital over the last few years when one of the senior partners had had to go away, and he'd enjoyed most of the small-town country feel of it. Angus knew that. 'Sure. Why not? Andy will be point me in the right direction if needed. Haven't done much general medicine for a few years, though.'

'You've got a young brain. You'll manage. And it's almost December. Louisa wants the decorations up.'

Simon laughed. 'Thanks. And no doubt you'll bring her back something new I'll have to assemble.'

Tara walked past again and Simon's eyes followed. Angus bit his lip and smiled into his drink.

The next morning Tara heard Simon go out not long after daylight. It would be pleasantly cool before the heat of the day, she thought as she pulled her sheet up, the blanket having been discarded on the floor, and she wondered drowsily where he was going.

And then, as her fantasies drifted, wondered what

he was wearing, wondered if he wore his collar open so she'd see his lovely strong neck and chest. Funny, that—she'd never had a throat fetish before.

She grinned to herself and snuggled down further. Nice make-believe. And Mia was amazing. They all were, and yesterday, as far as Tara was concerned, had been an intriguing insight into the Campbell family and Simon in particular.

Watching the dynamics between Simon and his father had been fascinating. She certainly looked at Angus differently after some of the exploits Mia had mentioned. Who would have known?

She'd never seen such equal footing between father and son but, then, her experience was limited to snatches of dysfunctional family life. Maybe it was because Simon had made it to twenty before he'd even met his biological father. Angus was certainly proud of him and the feeling looked to be mutual. And both of them obviously adored Mia and the girls.

She'd have felt a bit like the Little Match Girl looking in the Christmas window if it hadn't been for Maeve, who, despite looking like she'd just stepped out of a fashion magazine, had looked more lost than she had. Why was that?

Maeve was who she should be concentrating her thoughts on. Especially if she agreed to join Tara's caseload.

An hour later she wandered down to the kitchen and Maeve, immaculate in designer maternity wear and perfectly made up, was there, picking at a piece of toast as if she wanted to eat it one crumb at a time. Perhaps her pregnancy hormones still gave her nausea in the mornings. Tara had seen lots of women like that well into their last trimester of pregnancy.

'Morning, all.' Friendly but not too pushy, she included Maeve and Louisa in her smile as she sat down. Louisa liked to fuss and judging by the tension in the room Maeve didn't appreciate it.

'Hello, dear.' Louisa cast her a relieved glance. 'What are you doing today?'

'Have a young mums' class this afternoon but happy to do whatever if you need something, Louisa.'

'No. I'm off to bingo with a friend down at the hall and I wondered if you and Maeve could fix your own lunches.'

'No problem.' She smiled at the younger woman. 'We'll manage, won't we, Maeve?'

The girl barely looked up. 'Of course.'

'Still nauseous?' Tara could see she looked a little pale around the cheeks.

Maeve grimaced. 'Getting worse, not better. And I'm starting to get this insane itch that's driving me mad.'

Tara frowned. A tiny alarm pinged in her brain with the symptoms but she let it lie for a moment. 'Not fun. What have you tried?'

'Pretty well everything.' She shrugged. 'Pressure-point armbands. Ginger. Sips of cold water. Sips of hot water for nausea.' She absently scratched her belly through her shirt. 'And just calamine for the itch but

I only put it on the places you can't see. I never liked pink as a kid and it's too embarrassing to be painted pink all over.'

Tara laughed. 'That's the thing with midwives. We know all the things we tell other women and it sucks when it doesn't work.'

'Embarrassing really.' The young woman looked a little less tense now that Tara had acknowledged Maeve knew her stuff.

'I imagine being pregnant would expand your thirst for remedies?'

Maeve rolled her eyes and even smiled. 'You have no idea. I've read everything I can find on common complaints of pregnancy.'

'I'll have to get you to brush me up on them later.'

Tara was glad to hear that Maeve really did have a sense of humour. 'Makes you wonder what the women thought when it didn't work for them either.' They smiled at each other.

Maeve nodded. 'I'll clarify next time. Works *most* of the time.'

'Have you had a chance to sit down with someone and talk about the actual plans you have for labour?'

It was a reasonable question, considering she'd just moved to a new centre for care, but Tara felt the walls go up from across the table.

Maeve shot her a glance. 'You mean antenatal classes? Simon been talking to you?'

'I'm guessing Simon talks to everyone.' A little bit

ambiguous. 'But Mia asked, yes. I usually run a younger mums' class this week and I thought seeing as you were a midwife you might be interested in helping me—from a pregnant woman's perspective. But, then, you might prefer the idea of just a chat, and I'd be happy to do that if you did want one if you're not already teed up with someone else?'

'Sorry. I'm just a bit narky lately. Everything is a mess.'

Life. Didn't she know it could do that! 'Oh, yeah. It gets like that sometimes. I'm an expert at it. Plus your itch and nausea would impact on anyone's day, let alone someone carrying a watermelon everywhere.'

Maeve did laugh then. 'Feels like it. And it feels like this pregnancy is never going to end, but I'm going to be patient and not let anyone push me into something I don't want.'

'Good on you. Who were you thinking of seeing here?'

Maeve shrugged. 'Don't know. As long as it's low key I don't care. I saw the doctor Simon teed me up with a few times but last month he started talking about induction of labour and possible epidurals and maybe even Caesareans. I couldn't believe it, so I told Simon I was out of there. He wouldn't hear of a home birth and we compromised on Lyrebird Lake Birth Centre.'

'And the father of the child?'

Maeve looked away. 'Conspicuous by his absence. And I don't want to look back on this birth and regret it. I'm already regretting enough about this pregnancy. I need to have some control and I wasn't going to get it at Simon's hospital.'

Tara was a hundred per cent agreeable to that. 'Go, you, for standing up for yourself and your baby.' Tara wondered if she could offer without putting too much pressure on her.

'There's three doctors here who do antenatal care, and four midwives. If you think you'd be happy on a midwifery programme, you just need to pick someone. I've two women due in the next fortnight but apart from home visits I'm free to take on new women. You could meet the other midwives tomorrow but keep it in mind. You're probably due for tests around now anyway.'

Maeve looked across and smiled with a shyness Tara guessed was way out of character. 'Actually, that would be great.'

'You sure?'

Maeve looked relieved. 'Very. And we can talk about the labour then too.'

'Fine. We'll wander down to the clinic after morning tea, check you and baby out, and get all the papers sorted with the stuff you brought. If you change your mind after I've nosed my way through your medical and social history I can hand you on to someone else.'

'Lord. Social history. And isn't all that a disaster? Sometimes I feel like I'll never get sorted. I never used to be like this.'

'Sympathy.' Tara smiled in complete agreement. 'I

was pretty lost before I came here. The good news is that you're female so you'll still come out on top.'

Maeve blinked and then smiled. 'Okay, then. Must remember that for my clever brother.'

'He seems nice.'

'Too nice.' Both girls looked at each other, were obviously thinking of their previous boyfriends who had been anything but, and laughed. Ten seconds later they heard footsteps leaping up the back stairs and Simon appeared behind the back porch screen door. Of course both of them struggled to control their mirth.

'What's so funny?' The door shut quietly behind him and he looked from one to the other, brows raised, fine sweat across his brow. Obviously he'd been running.

'Nothing.' In unison.

He shook his head at them. 'Okay. Girl talk. You want to go for a swim, Maeve?'

Tara saw her face change. Become shuttered. 'No, thanks. I'm catching up on my emails.'

'Tara?'

She could just imagine Simon in swimmers. Wouldn't she just. 'No, thanks.'

'You sure?'

Maeve chimed in. 'Go. It's your day off. We can do that other thing when you come back. There's hours before then.'

Tara didn't understand the wall Maeve had erected between herself and her brother. If she had a brother like Simon she'd be all over him, but there was probably stuff she didn't know. 'Fine. Thanks. I love to swim.' She looked at him. Saw him glance at his watch. 'I'm guessing you want to go now?'

Simon nodded and he seemed happy enough that she'd agreed to come. She'd hate to think all these people were forcing her on him but what the heck. She'd enjoy it while it lasted.

'Five minutes enough time? Out the front?' he said. 'I'll be there.'

Simon watched Tara towel her shoulders vigorously and then rub shapely calves and stand on one leg and dry her toes.

He suffered a brief adolescent urge to metamorphose into her towel. Apart from her delightful breasts her body was firm and supple and he suspected she would feel incredibly sleek and smooth in his arms.

The swim had proved to a little more bracing than they'd both expected and he saw her shiver. He guessed she'd had a cold start. 'Sorry. I was hot from my run so it feels good to me.'

She shrugged. 'Hey, it's summer in Queensland. I can swim all year round.' The idea was sound but the rows of goose-bumps covering both arms and her delightful thighs made Simon want to bring her in close and warm her against his chest.

Or maybe it wasn't the goose-bumps he wanted to warm against him. It had been a while since the last time he'd noticed so much about a woman. Passing glances, inner appreciation, sure, but this little fire-brand had him constantly ready without any effort on her part. Danger. Alert.

Thankfully she remained oblivious to his shift in thoughts. That was a good thing.

He could see her mind was still on the swim. 'And Lyrebird Lake's too far south for crocodiles.'

Crocodiles. Now, there's a thought. He'd bet she wasn't afraid of any animal. 'Not sure why but I get the feeling it would take more than a crocodile to scare you off something you wanted to do.'

She grinned at him and that was an added bonus. Her whole face lit up and warmed him more than any towel could. 'Thank you, kind sir. I'll take that as a compliment.'

'It was.' And a bit of a surprise. He didn't usually go for the daredevil type. 'So you have an interesting bucket list?'

'I've always wanted to go skydiving. Birthday present for myself next week.'

Of course she was. 'Seriously?'

'Yep.' Her eyes shone at the thought.

Well it was the last thing he wanted to do. 'Birthday wish I wouldn't be keen on.'

She shook her head and her spiky hair flicked drop-lets around like a little sparkler. 'They say you're never the same after you do it. All to do with my belief to live life so I know that I've been here before I leave this earth.' She looked so intense when she said that.

There was something incredibly gloomy about such a vibrant young woman contemplating her mortality that chilled him.

'You planning to leave this world?'

She shrugged. 'Not planning to, but anything can happen. My dad and mum died when I was six. That's why I'm always glad when people driving arrive safely. I was made a ward of the state. I grew up in an orphanage.'

'I'm sorry about your parents.' Hard reality to face at that age. At any age. 'What about her mother? Your grandmother?'

'Died in childbirth. No siblings.' No expression. No plea for sympathy. And he was guessing not much childhood—which explained a lot. But there was a wall that said as good as a raised hand, 'Don't give me any sympathy.'

'Nasty family history.' Understatement. He seriously wasn't being flippant. It was a shocker and he could see how that could be a trigger for more risky, adventurous behaviour. 'My life is boring in comparison.'

'Tell me about boring.'

He shrugged. 'Nothing to tell except my mother didn't tell my biological father she was pregnant, a minor glitch I didn't find out about till after I grew up. That was as adventurous as I got.'

'That's adventurous. Especially searching him out as an adult.' There was wistfulness in her eyes when she said that and he knew she wished she had someone to search out. He'd never actually looked at it like that.

'So, anyway, maybe I should be up for exciting escapades.' His voice trailed off as she pulled her T-shirt over her head and it stuck, alluringly, in a few damp places.

He closed his mouth and glanced away. Regathered his thoughts with some difficulty. 'One day I will try being adventurous for a change.'

She looked him up and down and he sucked in his belly. Not that he was ashamed of his six pack, and not quite sure why he should even think about it because he wasn't usually a vain man, but he had no control over the reflex. She just did that to him.

'You could jump with me on Tuesday if you like.'

He knew the horror showed on his face.

To make it worse, then she laughed at him. And not even with him. Not sure he liked that either.

Tough. He wasn't jumping. 'How about I come and be ground support? Hold a glass of champagne for you.'

He could see she liked the idea of that and he felt he'd redeemed himself somewhat. 'Thank you. That'd be very cool.'

'Okay. We'll talk about it later when I get the picture out of my mind of you stepping out of a perfectly good plane.' They picked up the towels and walked back towards the path.

'So what were you and Maeve talking about doing later?'

'Antenatal clinic. I offered and she's accepted to go

on my caseload.' She sounded a little hesitant and he guessed it could be confronting to take on the sister of the consultant. He needed Maeve to see someone and he didn't have much chance of her listening to him at the moment.

'That's great. Really. I think you guys will have a great rapport.'

She flashed a grateful glance at him. 'Thanks, Simon. I'm looking forward to it. I'll take good care of her.'

CHAPTER FIVE

THE ANTENATAL CLINIC opened at eleven a.m. seven days a week. That way the morning midwife had discharged any women and babies who were due to go home. Plus the ward was often less busy so the women booking in could look around. Except when there was a woman in labour.

Tara had ten women on her caseload at the moment in various stages of pregnancy and two who had already delivered on the six-week postnatal check programme.

The first visit at least would be held at the clinic but most visits she would do at the woman's home. All the midwives took turns to carry the maternity phone in case one of the other midwives needed help in the birthing suite or two women went into labour at once on the same midwife's caseload.

Maeve looked very interested in the running of the unit, judging by the way her head never stopped swivelling, and Tara smiled quietly to herself. She'd bet there'd be some thought about staying on after Maeve's baby was born.

Even during the antenatal check Maeve was asking questions about the way they ran the caseloads, and the girls were firm friends by the time the official paper-work was completed.

Tara sat back. 'Okay. So your blood pressure is slightly elevated and your baby is a little under the normal size for thirty-six weeks but all of those things could be normal. It's nothing startling but we've done a couple of extra blood tests to rule out anything we need to watch for.'

'You thinking my blood pressure could go up more? So watch out for toxaemia?'

'We'll both have a good look at the results. At the moment you feel well in yourself, and baby is moving nicely, but I wonder about the nausea and the itch.' She looked at her. 'Don't you?'

'Yeah.' Maeve sighed. 'Of course I'm thinking it could need watching. That's why I'm glad we sorted out the caseload. In case Simon decided I was high risk and whisked me back to Sydney.'

'If you got a lot worse we are a low-risk unit. But being thirty-six weeks helps so we don't have to deal with a premature baby if things did escalate.'

'Don't tell Simon.'

Tara had wondered if this would come. 'If Simon asks, I'm not going to lie.'

'And if he doesn't ask, don't tell him.'

'As long as the tests come back normal, there's noth-ing to talk about. Sure.'

'You wiggling out of that?'

'You asking me for the impossible?' Tara countered, and she saw the realisation in Maeve's eyes that she wasn't a pushover. She couldn't be.

Maeve stood up and so did Tara. It was going to go one way or the other.

'Fine.' Maeve shook her head. 'Sorry. I don't know why Simon makes me so wild. He hasn't done anything wrong. I guess it's because I feel like I let him down when I made the choices I did.'

'Choices are there to be made and who knows what the end result will be? But, boy, do I know that feeling.' She handed Maeve her antenatal card. 'I'm trying to learn that blame and guilt are useless emotions. So is resentment. It's helped me. Hard to do but letting all that go has really made me start each day fresh.'

Maeve patted her stomach. 'A bit hard when the reminder is poking out in front.'

'Nah. Perfect time to be fresh with a new baby. I'll be there for your birth, Louisa will spoil you rotten, and Simon will be a doting uncle.' She looked at Maeve. 'You say the baby's father is out of the picture. Do you think he'll try to find you when he gets out?'

'I don't think so. As I said before, a crazy, stupid, one-night stand with one of Simon's old friends, a hunk I've always fancied, but he didn't think to tell me he was going to prison. He hasn't answered one of my letters. Or Simon's attempts to talk to him. So that just makes me feel even more stupid.'

'Nope. Silly would be if you were waiting for him with open arms and no explanations.' Maeve made no move to go now they were finished and Tara glanced at her watch.

'If you want to come and help me with the young mums' class, it starts around one p.m. In the mothers' tearoom behind the desk.' Tara pointed.

'Thanks. I'll think about it. I might go for a walk now after sitting for so long.'

'Sure. Or have lunch and come back. I'll go home soon and grab a bite.' One of the midwives signalled to Tara as they walked out the door and Maeve shooed her towards the midwife.

'I'll go for a walk and come back.'

Tara arrived back at the manse half an hour later and Simon was in the kitchen, making coffee. He'd been waiting for them to return and, to him, it seemed like they'd been gone for hours. Maybe Maeve did have something wrong. Maybe his niggling worries did have some foundation. By the time Tara arrived, minus Maeve, he could barely contain his concern.

He forced himself not to pounce on her and gestured to the pot. 'You want one?'

'Love one, thanks. Black.'

'No sugar.'

'How did you know?'

He had to smile at that. He'd asked Louisa yesterday. 'So how did the antenatal visit go?'

'Fine.'

'So everything's fine?'

'I could tell you but then I'd have to kill you.'

'Come on. Reassure me.'

'Sure. We did bloods for thirty-six weeks and baby is moving well.' She rolled her eyes. 'Nothing else to tell until the blood results came back or we'd be speculating.'

'Speculating about what?'

'Nothing yet.' She was squirming and he wanted to know why, though it warred with his sense of fair play, but then there was big brother mode.

He saw the way Tara straightened her back and he felt a pang of guilt. She shouldn't have had to gird her loins against him.

She sized him up. 'You know, you're the one who said we should have a great rapport, and I'm just wondering how you think that will be built if I run to you with results and private information. I'm assuming you don't discuss your pregnant ladies with their relatives?'

He paused. Looked at her. 'No. You're right. I take that on board.' In fact, he was ashamed of himself for leaning on her but the niggling unease about his sister's health was also a concern. 'But if you're keeping something from me about my baby sister, I won't be happy.'

He couldn't seem to stop himself.

Tara was up for the challenge. 'Thanks for that. Didn't pick you for a bully. Silly me.'

True, and he didn't know what had come over him.

Simon reached out, wanted to touch her briefly on her shoulder, but pulled back. 'Tara, I'm sorry. I have no right to harass you. Please accept my apology.'

Her phone rang and she glanced at the number. 'Now I know why you drive your sister mad. Good intentions and apologies. Would make anyone feel bad. But I'm not going there.' She answered the phone. Listened and then said, 'Okay.'

She glanced at Simon with a bland smile. 'No problems. Gotta go.' Pulled open the fridge and grabbed an apple before she sailed out the door. 'See you later.'

Simon watched her walk away and he knew he'd been in the wrong—but she still hadn't given him answers.

The problem was that the last few days he'd been aware that something was not quite right about Maeve. He hated it had been a month since she'd last been seen, and he couldn't put his finger on the symptoms. But pressuring Tara was unlike him.

He guessed on Monday he'd be in a position to access his sister's blood pathology files when he went to work but he'd try not to look. It wasn't his practice to second-guess a colleague and he shouldn't start now. But it would be challenging not to peek.

CHAPTER SIX

MONDAY MORNING SAW Tara scooting around the ward, tidying up after their last discharged mother and baby. The first thing she'd done was check Maeve's results and thankfully they were totally normal so it was fine she hadn't mentioned anything to Simon.

As she worked she was thinking at least if Simon asked she could say everything was fine. Funny how she wasn't looking forward to the next time she saw him in one way and in the other she looked forward to just 'seeing him'.

Before she could think too much of it a car screeched to a stop out front and a harried-looking man she hadn't seen before leapt from the driver's side before Tara could open the passenger door.

'Her waters broke. She's pushing.'

Tara sent a reassuring nod towards the strained face of the woman seated awkwardly in the front seat, and wished this had happened earlier at handover so at least there would be two midwives there for the birth. Judging by the concentration that had settled over the woman's face and the tiny outward breaths she was making, that wasn't going to happen.

The man said, 'It's breech and they said Susan had to have a Caesarean birth in Brisbane.'

Tara doubted a Caesarean would be possible in the minutes they had left. 'Okay. I'll grab a wheelchair while you stand Susan up and we'll get inside at least.'

She was thinking breech, Simon, handy, and before she spun the strategically placed wheelchair out the door she pressed the little green button they used for paging help so that someone from the other side of the hospital could lend her a hand, even if it was only to phone the midwife and doctor on call.

'It's okay, Susan.' She spoke in a slow, calm voice, because people arriving at the last minute in labour wasn't that unusual, and she smiled again as she eased the woman into the chair and began pushing swiftly towards the door. 'You'll be fine. Help's coming, and we've had breech babies here before.' Not in her time but she'd heard the stories and Susan's belly didn't look full term so baby might be a little early as well. All good things for a breech delivery.

The stress on the husband's face eased a little and Tara shared additional comfort. 'The more worried Susan is, the more painful the contractions feel. That seems a shame so if everyone takes a deep breath and just accepts that baby is going to do this his or her way, we'll work it out.'

'Thank God, someone with sense.' The muttered

comment from the woman who hadn't previously spoken startled Tara, and she had to bite her lip to stop a laugh, but then Susan was hit by another contraction and became far too busy to add further pithy comments.

The sound of footsteps meant help was almost here and by the time Tara had Susan standing up from the chair beside the bed Simon appeared at the doorway.

From worrying about when she saw him next to relief at his appearance. Another miracle. 'Simon. Great. This is Susan, who's just arrived. Waters have broken and she wants to push her breech baby out very soon.'

Susan glared at him and said, 'I'm not lying down to have this.'

'Sounds good.' Simon crossed the room quietly and shook the harried man's hand. 'Simon Campbell. Obstetrician.'

'Pete Wells, and my wife, Susan.'

Simon turned to Susan and touched her shoulder briefly while he glanced at her tight belly and then her face. 'Hi, Susan. First baby?' The woman nodded.

'And what date is your baby due?'

'Four weeks.'

'And breech, you think?'

'Was yesterday at ultrasound. We were on our way to Brisbane.'

'Unless you've noticed lots of movements since then, your baby probably still is breech.' He glanced at Tara. 'What's the plan?'

'The plan was a Caesarean in Brisbane, but Susan

wants to stand up for a vaginal birth. So I thought that seeing you're here you could check and see where she's up to, and baby will tell us what to do. Unfortunately, Susan has to lie down for a part of that.'

Simon grinned at her. 'Interesting take. And I concur with it all.' He looked at Susan. 'You fine with those plans?'

'Perfect. As long as you are quick. I never wanted the Caesarean.'

'Ah,' said Simon, as Tara helped Susan undress and reluctantly lie down for the examination. 'A rebel.' Simon quickly but thoroughly palpated Susan's belly, stepped aside so Tara could also confirm the position of the baby, and then washed his hands and pulled on the sterile gloves. 'Baby taking after the mum? I'll be as quick as I can so you can stand up again.'

One minute later it was confirmed. 'Yep, breech. In perfect position. And ready to come.' He nodded at Tara. 'Best get another person here for baby and we can send them away if we don't need them.'

Tara crossed to the phone and called the switchboard then dragged a sheet-covered mat to the side of the bed in case Susan wanted to kneel down at some stage, and prepared her equipment. She'd never opened up sterile packs or drawn up needles so fast and excitement bubbled inside her. She was going to see her first breech birth.

Then Simon made it even more exciting. He spoke to the couple. 'I guess I should tell you that my specialty is promoting vaginal breech births at the Central Women's Hospital in Sydney, and if you don't mind I'd like to talk Tara through this birth so she can practise her own breech deliveries.'

He looked at Susan and then Pete. 'Is that all right with you?' Susan ignored Simon but nodded at Tara while she pushed, and Pete reluctantly agreed. Tara slid the little ultrasound Doppler over Susan's belly and they all heard the cloppety-clop of the baby's heartbeat. Susan's shoulders sagged with relief and she bore down with a long outward breath now she knew her baby was fine.

Simon went on. 'If baby decides to do anything tricky, I'll take over.'

Pete still didn't look happy but Tara was beginning to think poor Pete didn't handle stress well. 'We'll have to take your word for it,' he said.

'I guess that's all you can do.' Simon smiled sympathetically as he pulled a chair across and sat down beside Tara, who was perched on a little wheeled stool, leaning towards Susan. 'Though I could give you my card and my phone to ring the Sydney ward but you might miss the birth.'

Because it was coming. A little pale crescent of buttock appeared as Susan breathed out and Tara felt the increase in her own heartbeat. OMG. She was going to cradle her first breech in a totally natural, peaceful environment and she didn't even have to feel terrified because Simon was right there beside her and she felt anything but.

'So Tara isn't going to touch the baby at all until the last moment. Your baby is nice and relaxed at the moment and we don't want to scare it by putting a cold hand on him or her unexpectedly. The heart rate is great and Tara will listen after every contraction to Susan's tummy.' Simon spoke in a very quiet conversational tone and Tara listened and obeyed every word without feeling like he was saying she didn't know what to do. It was obviously a skill he'd mastered.

Simon went on. 'Breech babies have the same mechanisms as head-first babies and once the hips are through it pretty well means everything is going to fit because the hips are roughly the same size as the shoulders.'

Tara hadn't realised that. Now they could see the little swollen scrotum and penis and Pete gasped and grinned when he realised what it was. Tara couldn't believe how fast everything was happening.

'You're doing beautifully, Susan,' she whispered. 'You're amazing. Not long now.'

'Okay.' Susan sounded strained but not frightened and Tara could feel the swell of emotion she felt at every birth at the miracles women could perform. It was all happening like clockwork. The pointy bottom seemed to be curving out sideways before it stopped and swivelled and Tara looked at Simon to ask if she should flick the leg out but he just smiled and shook his head.

The buttocks came down a little further and the foot

lifted and sprang free. The other soon followed until baby was standing on tiptoe on the mat as his mother followed her instincts and crouched. Now the whole belly of the baby and the stretched umbilical cord could be seen.

'This is where we make sure the baby doesn't decided to spin the wrong way, but most of the time they drive better than we do.' Sure enough, the baby's body straightened, the stretched little chest lengthened, until there was just the top part of the baby inside.

'I can't stand it,' muttered Pete, as he twisted his fingers together, and Tara cast him a sympathetic look.

'I want to kneel,' Susan panted, and Tara cast a look at Simon.

'Just hang on for one sec, Susan. I'll move out of the way. You're almost there.' Tara pushed the chair away and knelt beside Susan as she turned sideways and with her reduced height the baby settled into a strange sitting position but with the movement the head slowly appeared, the little face flopped forward as the baby was born and Tara reached out and caught him before he fell forward onto his tummy.

'Well done,' Simon murmured with a definite thread of exultation in his voice. Tara felt a rush of emotion stinging her eyes as she dried the little body until the newborn screwed up his face and roared his displeasure.

She could see Simon's satisfaction in her management and she'd never felt so proud in her life. There was time for one brief glance of shared excitement and then it was back to the job.

'I'm just going to pop baby through your legs and you can see what you've had, Susan.' There was a flurry of limbs and cord and then Susan had her baby in her arms as she knelt upright. The face she turned to the three of them was exultant with fierce pride and joy. 'A boy. My vaginal breech birth boy. I knew I could do that.'

'Magnificently.' Simon shook his head with a twinkle in his eye that said he'd never grow tired of these moments, and Tara felt like she wouldn't want to sleep for a week she was on such a high.

Pete was in shock, and a little on the pale side as he flopped back into a chair Simon pushed up to him, while Susan was helped back up onto the bed by Tara. The new mum lay back with a satisfied smile and baby was just plain curious about the world and maybe even a little hungry.

They thanked the other doctor who had quietly arrived as unneeded back-up and he left. A few minutes later, after checking that all was well with Susan and the baby, Simon left too.

Tara leant against the doorpost, keeping watch that all was well now that she'd backed out of the circle of mother, father and child, and just soaked in the magic.

She couldn't believe it. Couldn't believe the experience that Simon had given her. Not just with his innate love of teaching and promoting breech birth to his less-experienced colleagues, but the ambience and peaceful joy of the occasion, because everyone, including her, had felt safe, and imbued with the faith that they'd had everything needed for the occasion. Her glorious moment! Because Simon had been there.

She'd never experienced anything like it. How could one man make that difference? It was a gift she hugged to herself.

Two hours later Susan was tucked up into bed for a well-earned rest but her eyes were wide and alert, baby Blake was tucked up in his little cot sound asleep beside his mother, and Pete snored gently in the big chair beside the window.

Susan and Tara looked at each other and smiled.

'I wish I could sleep,' Susan said dryly.

'It's the adrenalin from the birth,' Tara said quietly. 'Your instinct is to stay alert so you can snatch up your baby and run. You'll slowly calm down and drift off to sleep soon.'

'Thanks, Tara,' Susan said sincerely. 'From the first minute I saw you I knew everything was going to be fine.'

Tara had too. But Simon had ensured it really had gone well. He'd been amazing and she'd tell him so. 'I'm so glad. And thank you.' They grinned at each other as Tara gently shut the door to keep out the noises that might wake them.

CHAPTER SEVEN

SIMON DROPPED IN before the afternoon midwife arrived to see how Susan was faring.

'She's great. Talking about going home tomorrow. You going in to see her? Baby is awake and Pete's gone home.'

Tara was at the desk, completing Susan's patient notes. She went to stand and he put his hand up. 'Stay there. I'm just saying hello and I'll pop out to see you when I've finished.'

Tara nodded and carried on, wanting to have it all completed before the end of her shift. There was a mountain of paperwork when a baby was born, let alone when the woman arrived not expecting to have her baby with them, and she was transferring all the information they'd had faxed after the event from Brisbane.

But she still had to thank Simon and she didn't want him to leave without having the chance.

When Simon reappeared he had Blake with him. 'Susan's gone to the loo and Blake was complaining.' He carried the baby like a little football tucked onto his hip and his large hand cradling the baby's head with relaxed confidence. There was something incredibly attractive about a man comfortable with small babies and Tara hugged the picture to herself. Not that she was doing anything with it—just enjoying it.

Simon bounced the little baby bundle gently, feeling his weight. 'He's heavy.'

'Seven pounds on the dot.'

'Impressive for a breech.' He smiled at her. 'So were you.'

Tara could feel the heat in her cheeks. She hadn't been the amazing one. He'd instilled confidence in all of them, even the nervous Pete, so what was it about this guy that made her blush like a schoolgirl? Seeing that even when she'd been a schoolgirl she'd never blushed? 'I didn't do anything except put my hands out at the end, but I really appreciated the chance to be hands on, hands off. Thank you. And Susan was amazing.'

'It's okay, Tara. You were good because you didn't do anything. You did so well.'

'I can see why it's hands off now.' She changed the subject. Had never had been able to deal with compliments. Probably because she hadn't received that many in her life. She inclined her head towards Blake. 'You always been this good with babies?'

He grinned and she tried not to let the power of the smile affect her. Losing battle. 'I was a couple of years older than the eldest sister and Mum had three more pretty fast. So I guess I did get good with babies. I enjoyed helping with the girls and Mum was pretty busy by the time she had Maeve. I wasn't into dolls but it was always going to be obstetrics or paediatrics.'

He looked at Tara. Tried to see into her past. 'Were you a girly girl?'

Hadn't had the chance. 'What's a girly girl?'

'Dress-ups. A favourite doll?'

There had been a couple of shared toys she'd been allowed to play with but not her own. 'After my parents died I never owned a doll. So I guess not.'

His brows drew together but thankfully he changed the subject. 'What time do you finish?'

'Three-thirty.'

'Fancy another swim?'

Simon studied the strong features of the woman across from him. He became more intrigued the more he saw her. His four sisters had all been spoilt by everyone, including himself, and secure in their knowledge of their own attraction. Even Maeve in her current circumstances dressed and acted like the confident woman she was.

But Tara favoured the unisex look of jeans and T-shirts and now he knew that at work, despite the choices of the rest of the staff, she even favoured shapeless scrubs.

But in her plain black one-piece swimsuit she couldn't hide the fact she was all woman. A delightfully shapely woman with determination to the little chin and a wariness of being hurt that seemed to lurk at the back of her eyes.

An orphan. And a loner perhaps? 'Tell me about your childhood.'

'Why?'

'Because I'm interested.'

A wary glance and then she looked away. 'Nothing to tell.'

'Are you always this difficult when people want to get to know you?'

A clash of her eyes. 'Yes.'

'So did you always live in an orphanage or did you have foster-parents?'

'Both.'

He waited and she gave in with a sigh.

'I preferred the orphanage because at least I knew where I stood.'

He would have thought an orphanage would be way worse but he knew nothing. Hadn't ever thought about it. Didn't actually like to think about it when he looked at Tara. 'How so?'

'Being a foster-child is tricky. You know it's not permanent, so it's hard not to be defensive. If you let people get to you it hurts too much when you have to leave.'

He knew he should drop it, but he couldn't. 'Don't some foster-parents stay with the same children?'

Her face gave nothing away. 'I seemed to find the ones who shouldn't be foster-parents.'

He felt a shaft of sympathy for a little lost Tara.

Found himself wanting to shake those careless foster-parents. It must have shown on his face.

'Don't even think about feeling sorry for me, Simon.' There was a fierceness in her eyes that made him blink. And apologise. 'Sorry. I think my sisters had it too much the other way with people looking after them. I've always been protective. If you ask Maeve, too protective, and I guess I got worse when the truth came out that I really only had half the right.' It wasn't something he usually burdened others with twice but maybe unintentionally he'd trodden on Tara's past hurts and felt he should expose his own.

Of course Tara pounced on the chance to change the subject and he guessed he couldn't blame her. Served him right.

'So how old were you when you found out you had another father?'

The way she said it, like he had been lucky, if you looked at it from her point of view when she didn't even have even one father and he had two. Even privately complained about it. Novel idea when he'd been a cranky little victim despite telling himself to get over it.

He brought himself back to the present. 'After my dad's first heart attack, that would be the man I thought was my real dad, I heard my mother question whether I should be told about Angus. Not a great way to find out. Nineteen and I hadn't been given the choice to know my real dad for the whole of my childhood. And to be still treated like a child.' He hadn't taken it well and had half blamed Angus as well for not knowing of his existence.

'So how'd you find him? Angus?' Tara had looked past that to the interesting bit. Maybe he should have done that too a long time ago. She made him feel petty and he didn't like it.

'It was more than ten years ago, but at the time it all seemed to move too slowly. Took six months. He was on some discreet medical assignment overseas and the government wouldn't let me contact him. Then he came to see me and brought me here to meet my grandfather. It must have been a family trait because he hadn't seen his own dad for twenty years.'

'Louisa's husband?'

'Yep. Apparently Angus and Grandfather Ned fought over my dad's relationship with my mother, and when they ran away together and it didn't work out, he never came back here.'

She didn't offer sympathy. Just an observation as she glanced around. 'It's a very healing place.'

'Well, Angus brought me here to get to know him. And this was where he met Mia.'

He wondered if that was why he hadn't been able to commit to a relationship in the past. To fully trust people because even his own parents had betrayed him. He shook his head. Didn't know where all that angst had come from, it certainly wasn't something he'd talked about before, and if he'd stirred this kind of feeling in Tara by asking about her past, he could see why she didn't want to talk about it. When he thought about her life he felt incredibly selfish and self-indulgent complaining about his own.

She'd said Lyrebird Lake was a healing place. Maybe it was. Did that mean his coming here with Maeve meant it was his turn to move on? He mused, 'I don't know if it's the place or the people, but whenever I visit it seems when I leave here I'm usually less stressed.'

She laughed and he enjoyed the sound. 'Even if you lose some of your holidays to fill in for your dad and unexpected breech deliveries.'

'They're the good bits.' And he realised it was true. He smiled at her. 'The really good bits.'

'Like today.' She smiled back and the way it changed her face made him think of a previous conversation. Tara's glorious moment. She certainly looked the part.

He caught her fingers. 'Today has had some very magical moments.'

He smoothed the towel out of her grip and let it fall and gathered up her other hand. He half expected her to pull away but she seemed bemused more than annoyed. He tugged her closer until their hips met. Liking the feel of a wet Lycra mermaid against his chest, unconsciously he leaned in and her curves fitted his like they were designed for each other. He looked down at her long, thin fingers in his bigger hands, stroked her palm and felt a shiver go through her.

'What are you doing?' she whispered.

He had to smile. 'Enjoying another magical moment.'

Looked down into her face and then there was no way he could stop himself bending his head and brushing her lips with his. Watched her eyelids flutter closed and the idea that this prickly, independent woman trusted him enough to close her eyes and allow him closer filled him with delight.

Lips like strawberry velvet. A shiver of electricity he couldn't deny. 'Mmm. You taste nice.'

Her turn to smile as she opened her eyes and ducked her head to hide her face but he couldn't have that. Wouldn't have that as he slid one finger under chin, savoured the confusion in her eyes and face and then leant in for a proper kiss. She was like falling into a dream, soft in all the right places, especially her lips.

As she began to kiss him back there wasn't much thinking in his mind after that but a whole lot of feeling was going on. Until abruptly she ended it.

Tara felt as if she was floating and then suddenly realised she was kissing the man everyone loved. Who did she think she was? She pulled away and turned her back on him. Picked up the towel she'd dropped. Didn't know what had happened—one minute they'd been flirting and teasing, probably to get away from the previous conversations, and then he'd confused the heck out of her with the way he'd looked at her—and that kiss!

She could still feel the crush against his solid expanse of damp chest and was surprisingly still dazed by a kiss that had gone from gorgeously warm and yummy to scorching hot in a nanosecond.

And she'd thought he was a little stand-offish! This wasn't going anywhere, except a one-night stand, maybe if she was lucky a one-month stand. Well, she'd been as bad as him. She sighed and turned back to him with a smile that she'd practised over the years that shielded her from the world.

'Guess we'd better get back.'

He narrowed his eyes and there was a pause when she thought he was going to get all deep and personal or apologise, but he didn't. Thank goodness.

She just wanted to finish drying off and walk back to the manse. Maintain the reality that she was playing with a toy that didn't belong to her and if she kept touching it she'd be in deep trouble.

Simon really wanted to hold her hand, it would have been…nice? But Tara had tucked her fingers up under her elbows in a keep-off gesture that he couldn't help reading. Maybe he had come on a bit strong but, lordy, when he'd kissed her the second time the heat between them had nearly singed his eyebrows off. The thought made him smile. And grimace because it obviously hadn't affected her the way it had affected him. Did she realise the power those lips of hers held?

When they arrived back at the manse the kitchen was in chaos. Simon figured out that Louisa had cajoled Maeve into helping her assemble the Christmas tree and mounds of tinsel and baubles lay scattered across the kitchen table and cheesy Christmas tunes were playing in the background.

The manse had a big old lounge room but he knew every year Louisa put the Christmas tree up in the kitchen because that was the place everyone seemed to gravitate to—and this year was no different.

Simon loved the informality of it, unlike his mother's colour-co-ordinated precision, and he enjoyed the be-mused expression, mixed with a little embarrassment left over from their kiss, on Tara's face as she looked round at him.

'Excellent timing, Simon,' Louisa said, as she handed him an armful of tiny star-shaped bulbs on a wire and a huge black plastic bag. She gestured vaguely to the screen door and he inclined his head to Tara and opened the door for her. The long post and rail veranda looked over the street and then the lake.

'Outside is where it really happens.' Good to have something to fill the silence between them. Awkward-R-Us. He waved the roll of bulbs at Tara and set about repairing the damage he'd done by kissing her.

'This is the start of the outside contingent. My job is to help Dad put these up when I'm home.' He pulled a little stepladder along behind him until he reached the end of the veranda and climbed up. Started to hang the tiny lights as far as he could reach before he climbed down again.

Tara was still looking bewildered and maybe still a little preoccupied from their kiss at the lake. He was sorry she was feeling uncomfortable, but he knew for a fact he wasn't sorry he'd kissed her. He wanted to do it again. Instead he carried on the conversation because she sure wasn't helping. 'These go along the top wooden rail. You can see them from down the street. Looks very festive.'

'I imagine it does.' She closed her eyes and he realised she was doing one of those breathing things he'd seen her do before and when she opened her eyes she was the old Tara again.

She smiled, so she must be okay, and he felt inordinately relieved. 'I'm not experienced at decorations. Put a few up in the ward last year when I worked Christmas week. Santa Claus was a big hit with the mums and their new babies.'

Now, there was a fantasy. Maybe he could dress up as Mr Claus and she'd sit on his knee. Naughty Simon. 'Santa has potential for lots of things.' He could feel the smile in his voice and packed that little make-believe away for later. Then he realised that, of course, she'd missed out on family Christmas for most of her life too. Not a nice thought. 'I'm guessing he didn't visit the home?'

She looked at him with disgust. 'Don't go there, Simon. I'm fine. They looked after me and I was never hungry. Lots of kids can't say that.'

Okay, he knew that, but there was more to being cared for than food in your belly, he thought as he hung each loop of Christmas lights over the tiny hooks under the eaves, and winced again at how easy his own child-hood had been.

He glanced towards the kitchen, where his sister stood watching Louisa tweak the tree.

Maeve had been loved and cared for and told she was wonderful since the day she was born. A lot of the time by Simon because he'd thought the sun shone out of his youngest sibling. Though that wasn't doing him much good at the moment.

He remembered his father saying Tara was tough. He guessed she'd had to be. 'Okay. Moving on.' And he tried to. 'As you are inexperienced I will explain. You, Mrs Claus, have to hold the big ladder while I put the star up.'

'Louisa has a star?' The look she gave him made up for everything. She appreciated him backing off. Okay. He'd avoid the orphanage topic but he still planned to make this Christmas special.

'Yep. In the bag.'

Tara undid the string and peered in. 'A blue one. Looks three feet tall?'

He was going down the stairs to the lawn. 'Goes on the corner of the roof.' He pulled out a large metal lad-der from behind a water tank stand, and the long ladder reached all the way to the top of the roof.

Simon sneaked a look at her face, saw excitement growing as they put up the decorations, no matter how hard she tried to hide it.

She was loving this!

The thought made his heart feel warm and a feeling of delighted indulgence expanded in his gut. 'Louisa has everything Christmas. It started after she married Ned. Grandfather discovered she'd always wanted Christmas decorations and each year he bought something even more extravagant for her collection. She has a whole nativity scene with life-sized people for the front lawn, and all the animals move.'

'Now, that is seriously cool.' Tara's eyes shone as she looked at the ladder. Then she frowned as she looked back at him. 'If you can climb that and not worry, then parachuting would be a cinch.' She crossed over to him, carrying the star, and waited for him to put his foot on the bottom rung.

He looked at her but ignored the parachute comment. 'Hmm. The decorations are cool, but not when you have to assemble them and put them up, then pull them down every year. I could live without the ladder climb.' He grinned at her and knew she could tell he didn't mind. 'Dad usually does it but he asked me to start. Louisa likes it up before December and that's tomorrow.'

He sighed, glanced at the ladder and held out his hand. 'Better get it over and done with. At least there's clips up here for the star. It just snaps into a slot and the wiring is already in place. It will be exciting for the little girls when they come home.'

She grinned. 'You're a wonderful grandson. And brother.'

He edged up a step at a time. 'Don't think so. Sometimes I only see them once a year at Christmas.'

She raised her voice. 'They said you write to them.'

He stopped. Looked down at her. 'I send a pretty card or a funny postcard every now and then. They phone me on Sundays if I'm not working.'

She couldn't imagine what it would be like to have someone do that. Imagine if Simon did that for her? Her whole world would gain another dimension, and then she stopped herself. Smacked herself mentally. He was just a nice guy. A nice guy who seemed to like kissing her?

CHAPTER EIGHT

THE FOLLOWING SATURDAY was Tara's birthday. She hadn't mentioned it, so he hadn't, but he'd quietly arranged a cake at the place where they were going to breakfast after the jump.

He'd learnt something as a brother of four plus two sisters. Women loved surprises.

He didn't even know why he was looking forward to Tara's adventure when he hated the whole concept of risk, except now he wouldn't miss it because it involved Tara. He hoped he wasn't getting too caught up in the whole Tara fantasy. It wasn't like it was a date.

She'd started off quiet, and he'd wondered if she was sorry she'd asked him. In truth, the discussion had been before he'd kissed her, but then as they drew closer to the jump zone she became more animated.

He glanced across at her face, eyes shining, a huge grin on her face, and she squirmed in her seat like the kid she'd never had the chance to be. This was a whole new side to the woman he considered the most self-sufficient young woman he'd met, and he savoured her little bursts of conversation in a new way from his previous lady friends.

She had her own ideas, often contrary to his, on work, on politics, on sport even, but was always willing to listen to another point of view.

He'd rarely enjoyed a conversation so much. He could have driven all day with her beside him instead of doing what he'd come to do. Watch Tara jump out of a plane.

When they arrived Simon followed Tara from his car and almost had to run to keep up. Now, that was what he called eagerness to embrace the experience. He might even be starting to get her interest, even if he didn't share it.

He'd read the skydiving webpage when he hadn't been able to sleep last night. It had been intriguing with the way they mentioned 'changing your life with a jump', though he couldn't see how Tara's life needed changing in that way. She was the most centred person he knew to be around.

Apparently, sky-diving freed you of the minutiae of the everyday that could cloud the joys of living.

Okay, rave on, yet the expression had resonated with him and made him wonder with a startling moment of clarity if that was what he did.

He organised and pre-planned as much as he could, as if he could keep all the facets of his world—in his mind he could picture pregnant Maeve, so that included his sisters—in order and safe from the possibility of harm.

He glanced up as another plane droned overhead

into a scatter of puffy clouds in the blue sky. Safe from harm? Well, that went out the window with sky-diving. Literally.

Simon shrugged and guessed he could imagine the small stuff didn't matter when you were hurtling at two hundred kilometres an hour through those clouds before your parachute opened. If it opened. He shuddered and increased his pace.

Inside the flimsy building—how much money did they spend on this operation anyway, and just how safe were they?—Simon's gaze travelled around suspiciously until he realised what he was doing and pulled himself up. Tara would be saying he could draw bad luck with negative thoughts, and despite his scepticism he refocussed on the woman he'd brought here, and just looking at her made his mind settle.

She was grinning like there was no tomorrow. He jerked his thoughts away from that one as she beckoned him over.

'Simon?'

Her expression puzzled him—eager, mischievous, with just a touch of wariness. 'They could squeeze you in if you wanted to change your mind.'

'And you're telling me this because?'

Her eyes glowed with excitement and for a minute there he wanted to take her outside this building and back her up against a tree and kiss the living daylights out of her. Then she said, 'Why don't you jump with me? Do it spontaneously.'

He blinked. One pleasant picture replaced with another he didn't fancy. 'Like spontaneous combustion. One whoosh and I'm gone?' She was dreaming. 'Then who would do all the things I do?'

Her voice lowered and she came closer until suddenly there seemed only two of them in the room. 'Stop thinking about everyone else for a minute. Do it for yourself. Be irresponsible for once and find out what it feels like. Change your life.'

There's nothing wrong with my life, he thought, but he didn't say it. Just stared into those emerald-green eyes that burned with the passion of a zealot. The woman was mad. 'Nope. But thank you. You go ahead and have your instructions for insanity and I will arrange breakfast for afterwards when you land on the beach.'

'They say it's the closest you'll ever get to flying on your own.'

'I read that.' He'd actually done a bit of almost-flying when he'd kissed a certain someone the other day. He was barely listening as he soaked in her features. How could he have ever thought this woman was average?

She looked at him for a moment and then leant forward and kissed him quickly on the lips. 'Okay.'

Then she was gone, leaving an echo of her scent and the softness of her mouth that vibrated quietly in the back of his mind and all the way down to his toes. And a tiny insidious voice poked him with a thought. Imagine if it did change the way you lived. Not his work but his private life.

His lack of trust in relationships. The business of assembling scenarios so he could be sure he had all his bases covered. The worry about minutiae, like it said in the brochure. Possibly left over from the time he'd realised his own father had been totally unaware of him—when he should have checked if he had a son!

No way. He shut the thought down. Not today. But unconsciously, as he leant against the wall and watched her follow the instructions of Lawrence, her 'chute buddy' coach, he paid more attention as they prepared her for the way she left the aircraft and the way she had to bend her legs and point her toes as they landed.

He watched her tilt her head back, exposing her gorgeous tanned throat. Apparently that was so when you hurtled out of the plane your head didn't slam backwards and knock out the person who was going to pull the ripcord. Good choice. Tilt head. He could just imagine her. Wished he could see her do it. He grinned and looked away. No, he didn't. At least he was calmer than he'd thought he'd be, watching all this.

Simon glanced at the cost of the extravagant packages that could come with the jump and doubted she had enough for the whole experience to be filmed, captured in photographs as well and saved in a bound volume. He wandered discreetly over to the sales desk, enquired, and hoped like hell she wouldn't mind if he paid for the video/album package to arrive in the mail.

He ensured Lawrence switched on his high-definition camera. It was the next best thing to being a fly on the wall without having to actually be there. And she'd have a permanent memento of the event.

She hopefully wouldn't take it up full time if she loved it. Simon found himself smiling as he drifted back to the doorway, where he leaned while he waited for her to finish her induction.

Then it was time for her to go. Go as in jump.

Tara bounced across the room with her harness all strapped between her legs and over her shoulders. Plastic wind protection goggles sat on top of her head and she radiated suppressed excitement like a beacon in a storm.

The two other people in her group seemed to radiate less exuberant anticipation. Right there with you, buddy, Simon thought with some amusement, and appreciated again that Tara did bring a sparkle into his day. As long as she didn't want him to join her he was quite happy to stand on the sidelines and enjoy the show.

Tara barely felt her feet on the floor. She couldn't wait for that moment when they tumbled out. She glanced back at her older instructor who carried the chute that would float them to the ground again and wanted to hug herself with excitement. Or have Simon hug her.

She glanced at Simon, who watched her with a whimsical expression on his face. It was so cool he'd come with her. Even if he didn't want to jump, and it had been a pretty big spur-of-the-moment ask, he still looked fairly happy. She'd been a little afraid of that. That he'd radiate stress vibes and doomsday foreboding but he'd surprised her with how calmly he was taking it and how supportive he was.

She had an epiphany that maybe real men didn't have to do crazy things to be in tune with her. Look at her last man. He'd been crazy and had turned out to be a loser of the highest order so maybe the opposite worked.

She knew for a fact that Simon was far from a loser but she also knew she wasn't looking long term for someone like him. People like him spent their lives with prim and proper doctors' wives, not someone who wanted to seek thrills and drift from town to town like her. People like Simon hadn't been brought up in orphanages and foster-homes.

But you could kiss those people. The ones you weren't going to marry. It was a shame she'd enjoyed it so much because the idea of kissing Simon again intruded at the wrong times—like that mad moment when she'd asked him to jump and then kissed him.

But she wasn't worrying about that now and peered ahead to the tarmac where their little plane waited patiently for them. Excitement welled in her throat as they all paused at the gate and the actual jumpers farewelled their ground crew.

'Good luck. You look beautiful.' Simon's words took her by surprise and she could feel the smile as it surged from somewhere in her over-excited belly.

'Thank you. So do you.' She grinned at him and he leaned in and kissed her firmly on the lips so that she knew she'd been kissed. For the first time the ground felt a little firmer under her feet and the haze she'd been floating in sharpened to reality. Luckily, that made it even more exciting.

The next fifteen minutes was spent crammed into the plane as they climbed in a slow spiral up to fifteen thousand feet. She sat perched on the lap of her chute buddy and surprisingly time seemed to pass very quickly with the hills towards Lyrebird Lake in the distance and the white sand of the beach underneath them.

They were going to land on the beach below the lighthouse and apparently Simon would already be there with the ground crew waiting for them to land.

Her chute buddy was fun and kept saying how relaxed she looked. But this wasn't something she was afraid of.

Finally they reached fifteen thousand feet, the roller door slid back along the roof and the cold wind rushed in.

He'd told her it was one degree outside but it would only take thirty seconds to get back to warm air, but she doubted she'd have time to feel temperatures as they hurtled through the clouds.

The boy next to her, now securely strapped to his chute buddy, cast an imploring look at the safety of the plane and then, with one wild-eyed glance at the occupants, disappeared.

'Let's go, Tara,' Lawrence shouted in her ear, and he edged his bottom and Tara as well, balanced on his lap, towards the opening and swung both their legs out until their backs were to the plane. Below them the ocean and the beach curved below under the scattered clouds.

She pushed her head back into Lawrence's shoulder and then they were out. Wind rushed past their faces, she had a brief glimpse of the plane above them in the sky and then they were facing the ground with the wind rushing into her face and her hands clenched tightly on the chest straps.

Funnily, even in that moment, she could see Simon's face. She grinned at the image and stared out into the vacant air in front of her. 'Woo-hoo.'

Simon had watched the plane disappear into the clouds.

Fifteen minutes later he watched the blue parachute as it came into view, imagined the grin on her face, the joy in her eyes and found himself very keen to see her feet touch the ground. Though no doubt she'd be wanting the descent to last for ever.

At the last minute he pulled his phone from his pocket and videoed her landing. She waved as she sailed past, and he chuckled out loud. This had been fun and he'd been dreading it.

She landed smoothly on her bottom with her feet out in front of her, strapped like a little limpet to her chute buddy, and with a couple of snaps of the buckles she was free to stand and twirl around with excitement. He grinned as he watched her.

Later when he took her to the little restaurant on the river for a late breakfast she couldn't stop talking, reliving the experience, and he watched her shining eyes blink and frown and widen as she told the tale of her tumble from the aircraft, the whoosh of the parachute opening and the moment when she'd seen him watching her land.

Then he watched her eyes widen wistfully when a birthday cake was carried across the room and she glanced behind them to see where it was going. But his breath caught in his throat when he saw her eyes fill with tears when she realised it was hers. What was wrong? Had he done wrong?

He'd upset her and he didn't know why. 'It's yours. For you. Happy birthday, Tara.'

She just sat there staring at the lit candles as they burnt merrily. The candles started melting and began to dribble wax down onto the cake. Spluttered and dripped. Still she didn't blow them out.

'Blow them out.'

She looked at him. Her eyes still looked haunted. Then she whispered, 'Are you sure?'

'Quick.'

The waitress and chef who had followed the cake out were looking at each other, not sure what was going on, as they waited to sing like they did every time a cake was ordered.

Then she blinked, shook her head and blew them out. Almost defiantly. Certainly with ample power. To her horror, she even blew wax onto the tablecloth. Blushed and glanced at the waitress and her 'Sorry' was drowned out by the lusty singing of 'Happy Birthday'. Then she did cry.

The waitress and the chef bolted back to the kitchen and Simon handed her a napkin. Tara hid her face in it.

'Don't ever do that to me again.'

With startling clarity he suspected what was wrong. 'Have you ever blown candles out on a cake before, Tara?'

She glared at him. 'Not since I was six. As if you couldn't tell.'

'No cakes at the orphanage?'

'A hundred children would be a cake every three days. I didn't even know it was my birthday half the time. You couldn't know—I understand that—but it's never been a big day for me.'

He didn't want to think about a hundred kids without birthdays because it hurt all the way down to his toes. 'So why the parachute jump this year?'

She shrugged. 'Coincidence and maybe Lyrebird Lake warmth. They had a birthday party for Louisa and it was very cool. Started me thinking about a new life and a celebration that I had control of and wasn't using.'

'So a present?'

'Yep. That's my present to myself. I can't really af-ford it but...' she shook off the melancholy and gave him a watery smile '…it was so worth it.' She straightened her shoulders. Smiled at him again, though still a little misty-eyed. 'Thanks for the cake, Simon, and sorry for the drama. It just took me by surprise. I blew some candles out once and they weren't mine. Got in all sorts of trouble so just had a bit of a time slip there.'

'Well that cake was a hundred per cent yours and even the singing was good.'

She glanced towards the kitchen with a little embarrassment still on her face. 'Very good. They must think I'm mad.'

'I'm sure they're thinking you must have a very good reason for acting as you did. Or they think I upset you.'

Her first cake with candles? Damn it, he wished he could turn up on her birthday and buy her a cake every year until she was so blasé about it she didn't notice. Then he listened to the wild thoughts in his head. How had he got to this point?

Because seeing Tara every year for the rest of his life didn't seem an unreasonable thing. But that was crazy.

After breakfast they went back to check out the beach. Simon kept saying she'd eaten and she wasn't allowed to swim for an hour but, seriously, she only wanted to splash in the waves anyway.

They stripped down to swimsuits and she kicked a skid of water his way.

After some serious splashing in his direction Simon stopped watching her with a smile on his face and started to chase her. She was pretty fast.

But he was faster. When he caught her and lifted her, spun her, held against his strong broad chest like a prize, it was as exciting as falling through the air this morning.

She'd always watched others do this, dreamt of doing it herself one day with some hero, and now here she was, with this gorgeous guy tossing her around like she was a lightweight as he shuffled on the sand and pretended to throw her into the water. She squeaked in mock terror, feeling like she was in a movie, a fabulous romantic movie, and while she knew it was just that, a fantasy that would stop when the hour or two was up, she was darned well going to enjoy every fabulous second of it.

Plus it was her birthday. She was the birthday girl and Simon would not let her forget it. That was very cool.

Then Simon walked purposefully forward through the knee-high waves until he sank into the surf with her still in his arms and the cold salt water foamed around them. She could feel the core of warmth where their skins still connected and she couldn't do anything except turn her face to him and lean in for a kiss. A salty, exuberant kiss that was her way of saying thank you.

He must have been waiting because his arms tightened even more firmly around her and the kiss spiralled into a hot, hungry, searing feast of strength and softness and sliding tongues that were as hot as the water was cold around them. She grabbed on tighter and jammed her breasts harder against his chest and they didn't come up for air until a bigger than normal wave smacked them

in the head and they broke apart coughing and splutter-
ing and finally laughing.

Phew. She'd needed that bucket of reality because
she'd been getting swept away in the fantasy of it all.

She swam away from him, bobbed with the waves,
their feet still touching the golden sand below their toes
but rising up and down with the cool green waves as
her heart rate slowly began to settle.

This had to be the best birthday ever.

CHAPTER NINE

BACK AT THE manse life carried on as usual. Maeve slowed down even more as her baby grew and weighed her down, but her nausea had eased, although her mood remained sombre. Tara suspected she held unrequited affection for the baby's father and wondered if maybe someone should try again to contact him by phone. But that was for Maeve and she had enough happening.

Last night another of Tara's caseload women had had her baby and Tara had been up most of the night, but when she'd woken after lunch she'd felt strangely unsettled so she'd come out to the manger on the front lawn to find her peace.

Everything was so…Christmassy. She felt like a minor character who'd forgotten her lines. Presents were appearing under the tree inside and she'd started to buy little gifts for everyone but lacked the experience to know how much to spend so had gone for quirky.

With combined family enthusiasm Louisa had managed to assemble her Christmas nativity scene on the front lawn. Tara had been surprised that the little straw-filled crib was empty despite the adoring looks and nods from the mechanical Mary, Joseph and the three wise men, until Simon had whispered that baby Jesus would arrive on Christmas morning.

There was something very centred about the anticipation of the baby that appealed to Tara. When she needed to get away to think she ended up on the garden seat that had a clear view of the people and animals in front of the manger. The whole concept of sharing their front lawn with the town took a bit of getting used to so she tried to come when it was deserted.

Those crazy manger animals nodded twenty-four seven and at night floodlights bathed the area.

During the day it wasn't unusual for children to drop by on the way home from school to check out the display and in the evenings families wandered down and oohed and ahhed and discussed what was new this year.

Angus and Mia had brought back an outdoor train set that ran on solar lights, and it chugged around the lighted Christmas tree on the lawn with pretend presents in the carriages behind. That one was a big hit with the little boys. Tara was secretly very impressed with it too.

Then she noticed Simon coming towards her with a determined stride and her pulse rate jumped at the grin he was sending her way. She'd been busy with her caseload women and hadn't seen him for more than a few minutes in the last few days since the parachute jump and beach. It was probably for the best because she was taking heed of her sensible side.

'There's a parcel for you, Tara.' He handed her a thick, flat package and she took it and turned it over in her hands but really she was absorbing the vibration between them as Simon sat down. There was a little gap between their bodies and the air seemed to be vibrating in the space. Very unsettling. He nudged her.

'Go on. Open it.'

Something was going on because there was definite mischief in his eyes as he waited for her to open the parcel.

She glanced down at the address. 'It's from the parachuting club.'

'Let me guess. You've become a life member.'

She had to laugh at that. 'Only if they want a resident midwife—but I don't imagine there's a lot of call for parachuting pregnant ladies.'

'Perhaps not.' He was still waiting for her to open it obviously.

'Aren't you going to leave me in peace?' She looked across and raised her eyes. 'Sticky beak?'

'Yep.'

She smiled and began to ease open the package, careful not to tear any of the envelope.

He huffed out his impatience. But he was pretending. 'Rip it!'

'No.' Shook her head. 'Envelopes can be re-used. And it's not like I get many parcels.'

He folded his arms and she could feel his eagerness. She began to suspect what it was. Oh, my. 'Did you buy me the package, Simon?'

She surprised a look of wariness on his face she hadn't expected. He didn't say anything, just waited for her to pull it out.

When she did she couldn't speak. It was a bound volume of at least a hundred photos from right at the beginning of her instruction session to the moment she actually launched into space and all the way down until they landed. And then she saw the DVD.

She'd seen the camera on Lawrence's arm but had assumed it was there for safety reasons and had been sort of aware they'd been filming some of the jump. Not the whole lot!

If she thought about it she'd guessed some people might change their mind and buy packages after the jump. She'd lusted after one but had decided it was an expense she hadn't needed.

And Simon had bought her the full extravaganza. How did she thank him for something so huge—it was too huge—but it wasn't the sort of gift you could give back and say, *You keep it*. He just kept taking her breath away.

His voice was worried when she didn't say anything. 'Hope that's okay? I know how independent you are. But I just thought everyone would like to see your adventure too—without having to jump,' he added hastily. 'I can afford it, you know.'

'I guess you can. And it was a lovely thing to do. Probably the loveliest thing anyone has done for me—except maybe the birthday cake the other day.' She leaned across and kissed his cheek but it was a dutiful kiss. 'But that's it. Don't start buying presents for me, Simon. I move a lot and can't build up possessions.' Or unreal expectations.

He shook his head. 'You don't *have* to move a lot.'

He just didn't get it. The world always moved you on when you started to love a place. 'Sure. Okay. And thank you.'

She could feel the tears pushing one way as she pushed them back the other but more than that she wanted to look at the pictures and re-immerse herself in the jump so she could forget the look in his eyes. The more she thought about it and the reason Simon had said he'd done it, the more touched she was.

She was an ungrateful wretch with no gift-receiving skills. Where the heck did you get those skills? She leant across and kissed him on the mouth this time. The anticipation was building. 'I'm sorry. Thank you. It is great.' She glanced at him under her brows. 'Wanna look with me?'

He seemed to deflate with relief and she realised he wasn't as calm as he looked. Maybe Simon was having a hard time dealing with the undercurrents between them too? An intriguing thought that could come back to haunt her.

He slid next to her until their thighs were touching, and she wondered what the passing manger lovers would think about Dr Campbell snuggling up to the midwife, but then she gave up and prepared to open the book. The relief in his face confirmed her suspicion. He'd been worried he'd upset her and she guessed she could get tetchy so he'd been brave to push ahead and buy it. The guy was certainly a keeper. Such a darned shame she couldn't.

Instead, she opened the album and the first picture captured the day. There she was, the plane disappearing above them, and an expression of sheer exhilaration on her face as they freefell into the clouds. She looked at Simon and there was a look of indulgence on his face that made her pause and then dismiss the ridiculous idea that he might care for her just a little more than she'd thought.

After a hilarious fifteen minutes sitting on the bench, poring over the album, they took the DVD into the house, where they dragged Louisa and Maeve into the lounge room to watch it on the old television.

During the ten-minute DVD Louisa gasped and covered her mouth and even Maeve laughed out loud and expressed her envy that Tara had done something she'd wanted to do. Then it was over and Louisa and Maeve went back to the kitchen and she had to go and check on one of her early labour mums.

'Thanks again, Simon.' She'd probably kissed him enough, she admitted with a definite tug of despondency as she turned away. 'I'd better get going on my home visit.'

Simon nodded and held the door for her and he didn't lean down enough for her to attempt any sort of cheek-kissing salutation like he did. But he did say, 'So when are you going to take me on your bike?'

That stopped her. She'd thought it unlikely this conversation would ever come up. And it wasn't like she could say no now. In fact, she owed him big time. 'Any time you're ready.'

He shrugged. 'I'm officially off call and ready when you are. Make a date and do your worst.'

She looked him over coolly but inside she was doing a little shaking and wondering if this would be a clever thing to do. Simon, pressed up against her, his arms holding on tight. Leaning into corners together. His strong thighs alongside her thighs. But there was barely a wobble in her voice when she answered, thank goodness. 'I don't have a worst. Where did you want to go?'

He shrugged. 'It doesn't really matter as long as I get to try the full experience.'

This was getting weirder. Whatever that meant. 'Fine. Then Saturday. We'll go up to the lookout, it's a nice drive through the forest and it's a great place to watch the sunset.'

'You're on.'

Almost enthusiastic. Her voice held a hint of indulgence. 'You'll be wanting to parachute next.'

'I haven't ruled it out in the far distant future.'

She looked at him and he was smiling but whether he was teasing or serious she couldn't work out. What she could read made her cheeks feel hot. She almost wished he didn't look at her like that because it was going to be incredibly hard some time in the definite future when the feeling it gave her was lost.

But then her sensible side, the one that said she would survive no matter what, decided that being with Simon was like parachuting—the rush was incredible but the reality was the ground waiting for you. But it didn't mean you shouldn't enjoy the ride. This would never last but it was wonderful while it did and from now on she was going to take what was on offer with open arms.

On Saturday Simon was waiting for her when she returned from an unscheduled home visit. One of her caseload ladies was having breastfeeding problems so Tara had sat with her for the last feed until mum and baby were back in sync.

She glanced at her watch. 'Do we still have time before sunset? Or do you want to wait until tomorrow afternoon?'

'I've been waiting all day to hang off the back of your bike.' The words were jaunty but the unease was not quite hidden on Simon's face and belied his statement as he picked up his backpack.

She had to smile at that. 'Liar.' She watched him slide his arms into the shoulder straps and hoist the pack onto his back in one adroitly muscular movement. Dragged her eyes away. 'What's in the bag?'

'Never you mind. You worry about me and I'll worry about the bag.'

Oh, she was worried about him all right. 'Sounds intriguing. You'll have to wait while I change.' She glanced at his long jeans and solid shoes and nodded approval. 'I don't ride in shorts either.'

'Tell me you come in leather.' A wicked wink suggested he was fantasising and hoping she'd come to the party.

'I can do.' She raised her brows suggestively, playing along with him, and couldn't believe how much fun this stuff was. 'But normally only for long trips.' She tossed over her shoulder, 'You'll just have to wait and see.'

Simon watched her scoot along the hallway and despite his misgivings about actually being a pillion passenger on a motorbike he had the feeling Tara would be worth waiting for. Ten agonising minutes later he wasn't disappointed. Sweet mother!

Tara's long sexy legs were encased in skin-tight, dull black leather trousers and high black boots. The material's softness curved around the cutest tight little butt, and his fingers curled in his pockets. Untucked, she wore a white shirt with a plunging neckline and a short, black, sleeveless leather vest was loosely laced over the top. Yep, that completed the outfit, and he had to jam his hands into his pockets. Now he really couldn't wait to get on her bike.

She looked like something out of a Hell's Angels fantasy world and he was glad they were going into the country and not on the main road. He was man enough to prefer to have her to himself like this and couldn't wait to have the excuse to hold her around her waist and snuggle up against her. Must have a latent dominatrix fantasy he hadn't known about and he grinned to himself as he followed her outside and around to the carport.

She pulled the cover off the bike and sat astride as she wiggled it backwards. No, she wouldn't let him help pull it out and face it the right way, so he did the next best thing and just stood there and enjoyed the show. He decided that Tara was a strong little thing, and the thought made him even hotter, in a non-weather-related way.

Tara set about checking everything was right and finally gave him the nod. She handed him her helmet and pulled her spare on.

'So have you ever been on a bike before?'

'No.'

'Okay. So hold on loosely around my waist, tighter on the corners. Sit up straight. Try and lean gently into the corners in the same direction as I do. If you find the corners too hard just don't lean the opposite way.'

'Yes, ma'am.'

'Good. Remember that. I'm the captain.'

The captain. He kept his tongue firmly between his teeth when he really wanted to say, *Aye, Aye,* and grin at her. Or kiss her. Definitely the last. He'd been waiting all day for this moment, the sliding on behind her thing, of course, not the actual motorbike thing, and as he climbed on and shifted in until his thighs were up against her leather-clad buttocks it was as exciting as he'd imagined. See. He could be adventurous.

Initially she took off slowly and rode along the back streets of the lake and Simon found that holding onto Tara while the big bike vibrated strongly beneath them was a very pleasant experience. He'd decided that worrying about accidents wouldn't help at all so tried conscientiously to focus on the other, more positive things.

Lots of delightful sensory input to distract him, especially the really tactile stuff, like Tara's waist was the perfect width beneath his hands, and he tried not to dwell on the fact if he reached up and spread his fingers he could span her rib cage and even brush the undersides of her breasts. Felt the uncomfortable tightness in his jeans and dragged his mind away from that scenario because it was just too uncomfortable.

Her buttocks pressed against him as they sped up an incline and if he tightened his arms his chest could stretch forward and lean into her back any time he chose.

'You okay?' She turned her head a little and he heard the words. She sounded strained but it was probably the wind snatching them away.

'Fine,' he shouted back. Conversation was impossible and he didn't even try. They'd picked up speed and were climbing a narrow tarred road that curved around the mountain towards the lookout. Heavy forest growth hid the thousands of cicadas that were humming as a quiet thrum under the rumble of the engine as they rode along, and every now and then a circling eagle would soar into view.

The wind rushed past and he enjoyed the sensation of the breeze along his arms. Even got some of the reasons Tara enjoyed the freedom of riding her bike so much.

They came to a long curve in the road and he'd learnt to lean the same way as she did and felt a little of the thrill of adrenalin she'd talked about. He could imagine it would be even better if he was the one steering and Tara was holding on—maybe something for the future to consider.

By the time they arrived Simon was so comfortable behind Tara he'd moved on to enjoying the view but couldn't help appreciate how comfortable and secure he felt in such a short time—testament to her skill and confidence. It still made him shake his head how she had so much control over the powerful bike considering it was bigger than she was for a start and had a whole lot more horsepower than she did.

He got off first and she propped it sideways on its stand. Flipped her helmet open to talk as she fiddled with the chin strap. 'Enjoy that?'

'Yes, thank you. I actually did. And I'm very impressed with your riding skill.' His helmet was off and he stepped forward to assist her. She let him, just— irritable little thing. She obviously didn't like asking for aid so it was nice she was learning to take some help from him.

The strap came undone and she lifted her helmet off. 'I gave you the easy one to undo.'

'Ah,' he teased. 'Of course. Thank you.' He looked around. They had the lookout to themselves. 'I came up here years ago but had forgotten how amazing the view is.'

They walked towards the grassy edge that disappeared into the valley below. There was a little secondary platform screened from the road and he jumped down to the next level and held out his hand. 'It's even nicer down here.' He couldn't help the satisfaction in his voice. This was an excellent place.

Hmm, Tara thought. Simon looked pretty darned hot down there. More than hot. And there was a little bit of heat singing her even up here.

A tall, tanned, smiling hunk of a man, one she admired privately and professionally, holding his hand out to invite her to join him. Though, having been sandwiched against him for the last thirty minutes, she wasn't sure that jumping into his arms would be safe at this minute.

Looked a bit of a set-up, Tara admitted with an inward jiggle of awareness, and couldn't help but remember what had happened after the lake, and definitely after the beach frolic, but she had way more clothes on this time. Note to self. Keep clothes on.

She shrugged mentally and took his hand as she landed beside him. Sucked in the fresh, cooler air and shaded her eyes to estimate how much longer they had to get back before dark.

'Probably two hours till sunset?' In the distance the lake sparkled in the afternoon sun, and the mountains behind which the sun would sink were already dusted with gold. Simon was also dusted with gold, everything felt golden, and she could feel the prickle of nervousness again. 'I like this road for a run on the bike. I've been here a few times.'

The air shimmered between them with a bigger thrum than three million cicadas and the awareness in the pit of her stomach growled like a nasty case of hunger pains. Maybe it *was* hunger pains. She glanced at his backpack as Simon put it down on the grass. 'So? What's in the backpack?'

'A picnic for the princess, of course. Louisa is renowned for her picnic hampers. And I'm not without a few surprises.'

Surprises. Yep, he liked surprises. The first time, with the birthday cake, she'd cried. She was not going to cry this time. 'Ooh. Picnic. Cool.'

'Prepare to be amazed.' He crouched down. Withdrew the tartan rug and spread it in the centre of the grassed area so they were facing the view. He patted the rug beside him. 'Come on. Down you come.' He undid the laces on his shoes and pulled them and his socks off.

She was distracted for a minute. He had very attractive feet. Long toes and very masculine-looking feet. He wiggled the toes and she caught his eye. He was grinning at her.

Maybe she could lose her own boots? She sat down, feeling a little heated, a little confined in her outfit, and before she realised what she was doing she'd removed her vest and was reaching down for her boots.

Simon was pretending not to look as he studied the hamper with only occasional sideways glances at her cleavage. Ogler. She laughed at herself. No use getting prudish about that. Why had she worn that shirt if she hadn't wanted him to appreciate? And she guessed she would have been miffed if he'd sat there and stared at the view and not her.

'Yep, that's more comfortable.' She stretched out her legs and leaned back, resting her weight on her hands.

'Non-alcoholic sparkling wine?' Simon held out a plastic champagne flute and Tara grinned.

'Classy.'

'Story of my life.'

'Not mine.'

'Some people are classy no matter what. You're one of them.'

Aw, he said the nicest things, and she could feel the prickle in her throat. Not crying. Ha, said a little voice, you said you weren't taking any of your clothes off either.

He leant over and dull-clunked their plastic flutes in a toast. 'To the classiest lady I know.'

'To the smoothest man around.' She took a sip and it wasn't bad for a soft drink.

He took a sip and then put his flute down on the lid from the container that held cheese, nuts, celery and carrot sticks, and in the middle was a big dollop of guacamole.

'You had that in the backpack?'

'I told you Louisa was the picnic queen. She has a whole set of bowls she uses for hampers.' He pulled out another that held marinated chicken wings.

By the time they'd picked and sighed over the food, laughed at how strangely hungry they were, and had eaten far too much whenever the conversation flagged, the sun hovered over the distant mountains like a gold penny about to drop.

Simon had packed the food back into the insulated backpack, Tara was gazing into the small pool of liquid in her glass, and the playful mood had deepened back into the awareness that had always been there but which now eddied between them like the afternoon breeze.

'It's been fun, Simon.'

'It has, Tara.' There was a tinge of amusement in his voice as he slid across next to her. When his hip touched hers he lay back on the rug, one hand behind his head and the other he used to catch her hand.

'Those clouds over there look like a castle with a dragon.'

She looked up, squinted and frowned. 'Where?'

'You'll have to lie down to see.'

'Ha.' But she lay down and he pointed and she could just see what he meant before the turbulence slowly rearranged the puffy paintwork in the sky into something else.

'I can see a dinosaur.'

'Where?'

'To the left of the dragon.' She lifted her hand and he followed where she pointed.

'That's not a dinosaur. More of an elephant.'

She giggled. 'That's not an elephant.'

He rolled onto his side and she could feel him watching her. So this is was what they meant when they said 'basking'. Tara felt herself 'basking' in Simon's appreciation and it was a feeling she'd never really experienced. Could certainly grow accustomed to it too if she had the unlikely chance of that.

He leant over and kissed the tip of her nose. It was unexpected and she sneezed.

Simon flopped back and laughed out loud. 'It's hard being a man, you know,' he complained. 'I have to make all the moves and then she sneezes.' He put his hand over his eyes. 'I had this fantasy that this incredibly sexy woman—dressed in black leather, mind you—would attack me and have her wicked way with me, or at least kiss me senseless.' He sighed again. 'But it hasn't happened.'

Tara rolled over to face him, with her arm tucked under her cheek. Then, with a 'nothing dared, nothing gained thought behind her eyes', she climbed on top of him until she had one leg on either side of his body and her weight resting on her hands. She leant in and kissed his lips, once—he tasted so good—twice—*mmm...yum*—and a slower third time that threatened to turn into something bigger until she sat up. Feeling pretty impressed with her own daring, actually. 'Consider yourself attacked.'

'Mmm.' His eyes had changed to sleepy sexy and his hands reached up and slowly pulled her face down to his. 'I could get used to this.'

The sun was setting. And she wanted nothing more than to lose herself with Simon in this private place above the world. But she wasn't quite sure this was the right time—goodness knew where that thought had come from. 'I think it wouldn't be as much fun in the dark.'

He smiled lazily and kissed her neck. 'You sure?'

'Mmm. Maybe it would be.' She had no doubt it would be. No, Tara. Stop it, the voice of reason nagged in her ear. 'But I don't make out on deserted roads with bikers.' She said it as a joke to lighten the moment, because Simon had been on his first bike ride now.

He pretended to be disappointed. He kissed her again. 'I should have known that about you.' He hadn't given up hope.

But then she thought of Mick. The picture of a dishevelled biker. And she guessed she had. But she'd never really seen that until the end. She'd seen the lost little boy from the orphanage. The brother of her best little friend who had died so tragically young and someone who had needed her. She shuddered to think what Simon would have thought of Mick.

Simon's face changed and obviously, unless he could read her mind, he thought it was something else. 'You okay? I didn't mean to upset you. Hell, Tara, I think you're amazing. You blow me away and yet you make me feel so amazingly good.'

He rolled her off him and sat up. Reached down and pulled her up to sit next to him, tucking her into his side with his arm around her shoulders. 'Not sure how you do that but it's a great feeling. There's no pressure for anything else.'

'Ditto.' This guy was too much. Too nice, too amazing—for her. He'd be gone in a couple of weeks and she'd look back and wish she had made love with him. It was a gift to be here with him, right at this moment, and she was throwing it back because she was too scared of the moment—or was she too scared of the emptiness later?

Simon was like the foster-home she knew she'd have to leave. It really was better not to suffer the separation. But it felt so good to be tucked into his side, his strong arm around her shoulder. Close to him.

'You could still hold me, Simon.'

He cuddled her into him, gave the impression he couldn't get close enough, then lifted her onto his lap. 'Can't think of anything I'd rather do.'

So they sat there. Tara was still on Simon's lap as

the sun set with a magnificent orange glow that turned to pink and purple in front of their eyes, reflecting off the lake, and she snuggled into his shoulder as peace seeped into her.

Then she heard the strangest thing. It sounded almost like her motorbike but distant. The throbbing roar of her Harley-Davidson. For a horrible moment she thought Mick had found her then remembered she had the bike.

Simon shifted her off his lap and stood up as she scrambled to her feet herself.

But when they looked her bike was there. Less than ten feet away from them and definitely still and quiet. Then the noise came again. The louder roar of the engine then the sound of a bike idling. It came from the bushes across the car park and Simon started to laugh.

'What was that?'

'If I'm not mistaken, that, dear Tara, was our lyrebird.'

'You're kidding me. How could a bird make that noise?'

'World's greatest mimickers. They can sound like babies, chainsaws…' he grinned '…and apparently Harley-Davidson motorbikes.' Simon slipped his hand into hers and pulled her into his embrace. Kissed her gently. 'I'll have to apologise to my dad. Lyrebirds make amazing noises. That's pretty special.'

Still distracted, she kissed him back but not with her full attention. 'Not possible.'

But the sound came again and closer to them. To the side there was a rustle of bushes, the crack of tiny twigs, and she twisted her head to see past Simon's shoulder and then she saw it. A small grey-brown bird the size of a chicken, his reddish-brown throat lifted as he gazed at her. But it was the two long feathers that hung each side of his tail that told her what it was.

She whispered. 'Simon. Turn slowly and look to your left.'

Simon turned his head and saw it. A slow smile curved his mouth. 'I told you!' He squeezed her. 'Our lyrebird.'

He'd said 'our' again. She hugged that defiantly to herself and ignored her voice of caution. 'Why doesn't it run away?'

He grinned cheekily. 'Well, it knows I don't want to move.' He squeezed her gently. Looked down into her face. 'I really don't want to.'

But the lyrebird could. He strutted across to a little mound of dirt about six feet from them and climbed to the top, where he spread his gorgeous tail. Swivelled his head to glance at them as if to tell them to pay attention, and the two long tail feathers spread like the outside edges of a fan and outlined the distinctive harp-shaped feathers in the centre that had given him his name. And then he began to prance.

Tara could feel the rush of goose-bumps that covered her arms. A shivering perception of something magical and mystical, totally surreal, and Simon's eyes never left the bird's dance until he felt her glance at him.

The lyrebird shook his tail at them once more in a grand finale and then sauntered off into the bushes.

They stood silently, watching the bush where it had disappeared, but it had gone. Job done. Simon looked amused and then strangely thoughtful. 'You know what this means?' Simon said quietly.

He watched her with an expression she didn't understand and she searched his face. Then remembered what he'd said weeks ago when he'd first arrived. But she wasn't saying that.

Simon sounded more spooked than excited. 'It's a sign.' He tilted his head. 'Which I didn't believe in before, I admit.' Then he shrugged and said lightly, as if sharing a joke, 'We must be meant for each other.'

She stared at him—couldn't believe that. More goose-bumps covered her arms at the thought. She and Simon? For ever? Nope. Couldn't happen. 'Or there's a gorgeous female lyrebird behind us that we can't see.'

He smiled but she had the feeling he was glad she'd poo-pooed it too. 'Could be that as well.'

Then he pulled her closer in his arms until they squeezed together and with the magic of the moment and the dusk slowly dimming into night, he kissed her and she kissed him back, and the magic settled over them like a gossamer cloud, but it wasn't quite the same, Simon wasn't quite the same, and when it was the moment that balanced between losing themselves or pulling back it was Simon who pulled back.

If she wasn't mistaken, there was look of poorly disguised anxiety on his face.

CHAPTER TEN

IN THE LAST glow of the dimming evening the motor-bike's engine thrummed beneath them and Simon held onto Tara on the way back to the lake. A single beam of light swept the roadside and the rest was darkness, a bit like the bottom of the deepening hole of dread inside him. That had been too close. He wasn't ready for that kind of commitment. Sharing a lyrebird was for those who knew what they were doing.

Thank goodness she'd had the presence of mind to see his sudden distance because suddenly he hadn't been sure he really wanted to step off the edge with Tara. When had it become more serious than he'd intended? Did she really feel the same and if she did could he trust himself to be everything she thought he was?

On the mountain, at the end, it had been Tara who had agreed they should go, agreed when Simon had said he was worried about hitting wildlife in the dark. But, despite the peculiar visions of lyrebirds scattering in the headlights, the real reason had been that he wasn't sure he was as heart-whole as he had been any more.

In fact, he'd had a sudden onset of the heebie-jeebies about just how deep he was getting in here, and none of this was in his plans—or his belief system.

And then Tara had agreed so easily that now, contrarily, he'd decided she didn't feel secure either.

But earlier, standing with her in his arms, losing himself in the generosity that was Tara, despite her fierce independence, he'd almost believed the sudden vision that he could hold this woman for the rest of his days.

But what if he broke her heart for ever if he had to move on?

Like his mum had moved on from his dad. Like Maeve's man, and his ex-friend, had moved on from them. The problem was that since the lyrebird, just an hour ago, Simon felt connected to Tara by a terrifying concept he hadn't expected but which was proving stronger than he had felt with anyone in his world. And he wasn't sure he liked it.

She made him feel larger than life, which he wasn't, exuberant when he hadn't thought he had an exuberant bone in his body. She made him want to experience the adventure of the world. And with Tara it would be an adventure. A quest towards the kind of life he had only dreamt of having for himself.

Except it wasn't him.

He wasn't quite sure who she was seeing in him but it wasn't Simon Campbell. He needed to get a little distance back while he worked through this.

Because he wasn't the adventurous, fun guy Tara

needed. She needed someone to jump out of planes with, fall head over heels in love with her, and be there for the next month, the next year, the next lifetime. He couldn't be sure he could sign up for that.

She deserved someone who would do that. So why did he have the feeling there was a great cloud of foreboding hanging over his head?

Next morning at breakfast Maeve wandered into the kitchen and ducked under a Christmas streamer before she sat down. 'What's wrong with Simon?' She absently scratched her tummy and inclined her head back towards the bathroom her brother had just disappeared into.

The door slammed and Tara winced. 'No idea. He's been acting strange since we came back from the picnic last night.' Maybe he was always like this and she'd been too blinded by his pretty face.

Or she'd said something that made him realise she was the last woman he wanted to get involved with. Suck it up, princess, you know this happens to you all the time. 'Is he usually moody?'

'Nope.' Maeve shook her head. 'He's the most even-tempered of all of us. The only time he gets techy is if he's worried about something big.'

Did she qualify for big? Did he think she was trying to trap him? Cringe. Cringe.

Lord, no. She'd never do that. She'd been told often enough by Matron to push herself out there and be a little more demanding but it just wasn't in her make-up. If the family hadn't seen how badly she'd wanted their life, she hadn't been about to tell them and get knocked back for her pains.

She guessed Simon was that all over again. 'He'll get over it.' And her. Already had, it seemed. It was probably all in her imagination anyway and he had just been amusing himself.

Well, problem was there was so much to admire about him, and he seemed to enjoy her company, plus he was a darned good kisser, and she'd practically thrown herself at him last night and he'd knocked her offer back, and that had left them in an awkward place, now that she thought about it. Thanks very much, Simon.

Time to change the subject. And the focus of her life. 'So how are you going, Maeve?'

Simon's sister shrugged. 'I'm fine. Feeling less nauseous and much heavier around the middle.' She sent Tara one of the most relaxed smiles Tara had seen from her. 'But I'd rather talk about you two.'

Darn! Lulled into a false sense of security. 'There's no "us two".'

Maeve raised her brows disbelievingly and Tara wanted to bury her head in her hands. Seriously. How many other people thought she'd fallen for Simon? Or he for her? Just because they'd hung out together a bit, and kissed a few times, that smug voice inside insisted.

Maeve wasn't having any of that apparently. 'Well, if there's not a "you two" he's been pretty hopeless at getting the message across. What with parachuting photo packages, and pestering you for a bike ride, and Louisa for a picnic hamper—and the rug!'

Lots of eyebrow waggling coming her way here and Tara could feel the heat creep up her cheeks. So this was what it was like to have a sister.

Obviously Maeve had no scruples in laying stuff out in front of her and teasing. Maybe she hadn't been so unlucky as an orphan to avoid this stuff. Apart from Mick's sister, she'd never really been one for girly relationships. Again the idea of becoming fond of someone when you never knew when they'd go away for a weekend and never come back. She'd decided a long time ago it was better to keep her distance.

But Maeve wasn't keeping her distance, neither had she finished. 'Seems a lot of effort for someone he doesn't care about.'

Tara had no idea how to deal with this. With her acquaintances she'd just tell them to shut up but you couldn't do that to Maeve—or she didn't think it would work anyway. 'Can we change the subject?'

'Not until I give you some advice.'

Oh, no. 'Do you have to? Please. I hate advice. Comes with having to sort yourself out all your life.' She said it but now she knew Maeve better she doubted anything would stop her when she was on a roll. She almost wished for the washed-out, droopy dandelion Maeve had been before she'd recovered her spirits.

She looked again at the new, brighter Maeve and she

knew she was happy her friend had found her equilibrium. Lyrebird Lake was doing its magic. So, no, she didn't wish for droopy Maeve back.

Over the last few weeks, gradually they had become friends, good friends, if she dared to say it. She and Maeve had found lots to smile about. Lots to agree and not agree about and quirky, girly conversations that had often little to do with Simon. And, at Maeve's request, nothing at all to do with Rayne, the father of Maeve's baby.

'Me? Not give advice?' Maeve laughed at her.

Tara sighed. 'But you're not having this all your own way. I'll listen to you if you tell me what you're thinking about Rayne.'

Maeve blinked in shock and Tara grinned. 'And if I have advice then you have to listen to me.'

Ha. Miss Bossy didn't like it so much in return. But to give Maeve her due, she sat back with a grimace. 'I was being pushy, wasn't I?' She shook her head and smiled wryly. 'You haven't seen this side of me yet but I'm not normally the pathetic wimp I've been since I came here.'

She looked around and then back at Tara. 'You know what? You're right. I do feel better since I came here. This place really is as amazing as Simon says it is.'

Tara looked around with fresh eyes. Made herself feel the moment. Smell the furniture polish. Taste the freshly brewed tea from the pot that Louisa had made before she'd gone out. Saw the little touches that spelt

people cared. A Christmas nativity scene tucked in behind the bread basket. The growing pile of gifts under
the tree. The photo frames of family that Louisa polished with her silver cloth every morning. 'I think it's
the people.'

And Tara didn't ever want to leave but she wasn't
expecting the world to be that perfect. 'Yep. It's amazing. And it is good to see you firing on all cylinders—
even if you are a bit scary sometimes.'

'Scary? Me? You should meet my oldest sister, Kate.'
Then Maeve showed she at least was focussed. 'Seeing
that you hate advice, I'll keep it simple—and let you
in on a secret.'

She sat forward, ready to impart her wisdom, and
Tara pulled a face as she waited. 'My sisters and I have
decided Simon's been hiding from a real romantic relationship all his life—he's terrified the fairy-tale isn't
real.'

'Um. I hate to tell you this, but it isn't,' Tara said,
but Maeve ignored her.

'Whether that came from our mother and his dad
not staying together or the fact that he never knew his
dad, we don't know.'

She lowered her voice. 'What we do know is that
the right woman can help him come out from the place
he's been hiding all these years—but she has to get
past the barriers.'

'Barriers?' Tara was lost. She had no idea what Maeve
was talking about. She hadn't noticed any barriers.

'Not when-you-meet-him barriers. He's too good a people person for that. It's later. Whenever a woman is getting close, he'd discover some other place that needed him more than he needed her and bolt. She'd try and hold him, he'd spend less time with her, and then she'd give up and drop him. I've seen it time and again. But you're different.'

Her? Tara? Different? She couldn't help the tiny glow of warmth the words left in her chest. Then she thought it through and decided there was another reason she was different. Maybe because she didn't expect people to want to look long term with her?

'He's scared of long term, Tara.'

Well, there you go. Maybe she was the right girl for him after all. She forced a smile. 'I'm not presuming long-term.' Had lost that expectation years ago.

'Might be the way to getting it.' Maeve looked at her.

That didn't make sense. 'You mean, actually say, *Hi, Simon, I don't expect long term*?' The fantasy was tragically attractive—but it was fantasy. But that didn't mean one day it mightn't happen. Did it?

Maeve waggled her brows. 'And that just might be the way to break through the barriers.'

Nope. Tara didn't understand and she backed away from reading anything ridiculously ambitious into Maeve's comments. 'Okay. I've listened.' And you are scaring the socks off me at the thought of having any such conversation with Simon. Although if Simon was scared she would try to trap him, he did need to know that wasn't in her plans.

But he had changed after the lyrebird, true, and he'd practically said he remembered what seeing the bird dance meant. True love and all that stuff. For a guy who wasn't thinking long term she guessed that could be scary. She wasn't scared, just didn't believe the hogwash. All too confusing for a conversation.

'Your turn.' She sat forward. 'Tell me about the father of your child.' She really did want to know. She couldn't imagine anyone leaving Maeve. She was gorgeous and funny, and she was classy.

Maeve's shoulders drooped. Her confident persona disappeared into the dejected woman Tara had first met. There was an extended silence and Tara thought for a moment Maeve was going to renege. Then she sighed. 'I fell for Rayne like a ton of bricks.' She lifted her head, her eyes unexpectedly dreamy, and remembered. 'He's a head taller than me, shoulders like a front-row forward, and those eyes. Black pools of serious lust when he looked at me. Which he did from across the room.'

Tara had to grin. Descriptive. 'Crikey. I'm squirming on my seat over here. So what happened?'

She shrugged. 'We spent the night together—then he went to jail.'

Tara remembered Maeve saying he'd omitted to tell her he was going to jail. 'Was he wrongly convicted?'

Tears filled Maeve's eyes. She chewed her lip and

gathered her control. Then looked at Tara with a wry and watery smile. 'Thank you.'

Tara wasn't sure what was going on but she seriously wanted to get to the bottom of it. 'Did he tell you about it?'

Shook her head. 'Didn't have a chance. And since then he's refused to see or talk to me on the phone.'

That didn't make sense. 'So when did this happen?

Maeve patted her stomach. 'Eight months ago.'

O-o-o-kay. Tara suspected Simon might have reason to worry. 'And how long were you together before you fell pregnant?'

She sighed. 'One night. But I've always loved Rayne. He was the bad boy all the girls lusted after. I always thought the problem was more his mum than Rayne— she was a single mum and couldn't kick her drug addiction—but despite our mum's misgivings he and Simon were always friends.'

And now he'd got Simon's sister pregnant on the way to jail. Probably why Simon wanted to wring his neck.

Maeve was still talking. 'Simon and he were mates through med school and then Rayne went to California to do paediatrics. And he was supposed to come and work with Simon at his hospital this year.'

She shrugged. 'Something happened when he was over there, and apparently as soon as he hit Australia alarm bells went off. Simon picked him up from the airport, and neither of us knew that the police would come for him as soon as he was back in the country. It seems he suspected it was a possibility and didn't tell us.'

'Wow. Seems a strange way to act.'

'I'm pretty sure he planned to tell but Simon got called out to a patient before he could, I think.' Maeve shrugged.

'Problem was, I've fancied this guy since I carried a lunchbox to school, hadn't seen him for eight years, and that night Simon left.' She shrugged. 'I was feeling low after a break-up, here was this guy coming I'd had a crush on since puberty and it all just happened. Except Simon has never forgiven him—when, in fact, the guy had little choice because I practically seduced him.'

Her face went pink and Tara could see a heck of a lot had happened. Wow again.

'Obviously I've thought about that night and I think Rayne's natural resistance was lowered by the fact he might be in prison for the next ten years and I was throwing myself at him.'

'Imagine?' Tara looked at Maeve. Gorgeous, sexy, and, she was beginning to suspect, wilful and a little spoilt, but in a nice way. A way Tara could quite easily be envious of except she'd shaken that out of herself years ago as a destructive waste of wishful thinking.

'And then the next morning the police came and took him away. It was a shock because we'd slept together and he just walked away without looking back.'

Absently she stroked her belly. 'Simon was livid when he found out that Rayne had suspected they might come. But I think he'd come to explain and get advice from Simon, except it hadn't worked out. And then I complicated matters.'

Wow. Maeve had certainly complicated matters. It was like an end-of-season episode of a soap opera. Tara had major sympathy for Simon. But Maeve had problems too. And then there was the mysterious Rayne.

'Do you love him?'

She spread her hands. 'I've had all pregnancy to think about it. About the fact that he might not be the guy I think he is. Or if he was he might change a lot in prison. So when I see him again he might not be the hero that I always imagined him to be and I fell for the pretty face I'd always fancied and created the energy between us by wishful thinking.'

Tara agreed with her there. It all sounded explosively spontaneous. 'It's a possibility.'

'I know. I know. It was a whirlwind event that will affect the rest of my life. But really I don't know. He doesn't care enough to answer my calls. Or answer my letters. Or comment on the fact that I'm pregnant and soon to have his child. That hurts.'

Yep. That would hurt. 'That is hard.'

Maeve went on. 'When I found out I was pregnant I thought Simon was going to have a stroke. We had a huge fight. I said I was old enough to make my own mistakes and he said he could see that was true but not under his roof. Then he absolutely tore Rayne's actions to shreds when I knew it was mostly me. So we really haven't made up since then. But I still live under his roof so we've had sort of a cold truce for most of this year.'

She sighed again. 'I know I let him and my parents down. Crashed off my pedestal and that hurt too. But I swear, one look at Rayne, at his need for comfort, and I was a goner, and seeing how it turned out I can understand his reluctance to let me into his life now. I can regret the timing but if I'm ever going to have a child the fact that it's Rayne's is no real hardship.'

A can of worms getting wormier actually. 'I'm not sure I have advice for you. Except to say that guys in jail, even innocent ones, do change from the experience. I've known people who have. I'm not saying it won't work out between you, but he might be a harder, tougher man than the one who went in. If you do meet him again, which I guess you will if you're having his baby, make sure he is the man you love before you commit to anything. You have your baby to think of as well as yourself.'

Maeve looked back soberly. 'I guess it has been all about the baby and me. I do need reminding that Rayne is in a different world right now and that he's having it tough too. Thanks, Tara.'

Tara wasn't sure that was what she'd been trying to say. 'And thanks for your advice, though I can't see myself starting a conversation like that with Simon.' She smiled and stood up. 'As for your story, you make my life seem pretty boring.'

'Simon doesn't think you're boring.'

And here we begin the conversation again. Enough. 'The good news is I have to go and do some home visits so I'm going to leave you.' She carried her cup and saucer and cereal plate to the sink and rinsed them. 'Catch you later.'

As she walked towards her room she mulled over the conversation. No wonder Maeve had been low in spirits when she'd arrived. And it explained the tension between Simon and his sister.

It was understandable Simon felt betrayed by his friend and to a lesser degree by his sister. She'd actually love to hear Simon's side of the story but couldn't see how she could ask without betraying the confidence that Maeve had spoken to her about it all.

And that it all happened under his own roof wouldn't have helped his overactive protective bone.

Maeve had been very generous with her sharing and her advice and it had been nice to talk like that. Exchange banter with her friend. She was getting better at relationships with other people. Letting herself be more open and looking a little more below the surface to try to connect to other people instead of being too wary.

She'd never had a friend like Maeve before and hoped she'd helped her. Maeve had certainly given her something to think about with Simon. Maybe she could have real friendship relationships with women apart from being their midwife. Though she guessed she was Maeve's midwife as well.

She pulled on her jeans to ride the bike and slipped

into her boots. Organised her workbag on autopilot and mulled over Maeve's words. Shook her head. He wasn't scared. Simon didn't care enough.

When they'd been together at the lookout he'd been a gentleman and not raised her expectations. She supposed it was a good thing but she really would have liked to lose herself all the way in those gorgeous arms. And he'd been such a good kisser. She shook her head. Come on. He was way out of her league. Get with the programme.

CHAPTER ELEVEN

SIMON STOOD IN the shower and could feel the edges of panic clawing at him. And he couldn't ease away by running back to Sydney Central work like he usually did because Maeve was getting close to having her baby. He had to be around in case anything happened.

This was certainly the time he usually left a relationship—way past it, in fact, as far as rapport between him and the woman went—except for the fact he would have been sleeping with her well and truly by now and that hadn't happened with Tara. How on earth had the emotional stuff happened when they hadn't even slept together? Everything was upside down. Back to front. And confusing.

Maybe it was proximity. Of course it was incredibly hard not to get closer than normal when you were living in the same house and working in the same place and associating with the same people.

Um, except he had lived with other women and not got too emotionally involved. And he had the horrible suspicion he'd miss Tara if he created the distance he needed—either mentally or geographically.

That was the scariest thing of all. It hadn't happened before. He'd always felt the relationship was well and truly over by the time he began to see the signs of long-term planning on the side of his lady friend. Which was a good thing because that way he wasn't responsible for hurting anyone.

But this was different. The unease fluttered again as he turned off the shower tap. Silly thoughts of birthday cakes in the future still made him smile but that was not the sort of thing to do if he was deep in a relationship with his next woman.

Listen to himself. He doubted he'd ever been deep into a relationship ever—more floating along the surface with good sex, and with women who were still his friends.

But right at this moment he was abstinent and sinking. No utopia after what had been a truly delightful afternoon yesterday with loads of potential—until that bloody lyrebird had said she was his true love and he'd panicked. Well, at least he had seen the danger before they'd completely consummated their relationship.

He combed his hair with his fingers and opened the steamy bathroom door. Oops. He'd been in here a while. But at least he'd come to some conclusion. All he needed to do was pull away. Create some distance and see how it felt.

His stomach rumbled and he headed for the kitchen as he continued to mull over his dilemmas.

He just needed to let Tara know subtly that he wasn't a long-term prospect and then maybe they could just be friends. As in platonic. Hmm.

That brought up a whole new set of unpleasant dilemmas. If he and Tara were just friends that meant she could have other friends who were men. Maybe a lover. Someone else to take on her adventures. Someone else to do what he had knocked back. Strangely, not funny, idea at all.

He needed to think about that one.

'Hi, Simon.' He looked up from his preoccupation and saw a jeans-clad goddess.

'Hi, Tara.' He felt a smile spread across his face and then fall away as his previous conversations with himself came back.

'You okay?'

'Sure.' Hitched his smile back up. 'Of course. You?'

'Fine.' He could feel her concern. Saw her shrug.

'Okay. I'm going for a ride. To see one of my clients. Then maybe further afield. See you later.'

'Be safe.'

'High on my list. *Ciao.*'

He called after her, 'I didn't know you spoke Italian?'

'I don't.' She stopped. '*Ciao* and food items. Pizza, lasagne, *boccioni.*' She shrugged. 'The extent of my Italian. Anyway. See you.'

'Bye. When are you back?'

She stopped again and sighed. 'No idea.'

He opened his mouth to ask something else and closed it again. What was he doing? He lifted his hand to wave and turned away.

Geez. He was hopeless.

'Simon?' He spun back and she was there. Just behind him. And she was chewing on those gorgeous lips in a way that he wanted to touch her mouth with his fingers to stop her damaging anything.

'It's okay, Simon. I'm not expecting long term, you know. I'll be moving on soon.' She shook her head. 'Just wanted to let you know.'

'Me too,' he said helplessly.

And then she spun on her heel and walked away quickly. He was still staring after her when he heard the bike start and the roar as she rode away.

So why didn't he feel better? Basically she was saying they could have fun with no strings. Right up his alley. And he'd told her he felt the same. Liar.

When Tara drove into the driveway late in the afternoon of the next day Simon was sitting out at the manger, watching the animals.

She swung her helmet on her finger as she walked across the springy grass Louisa loved to water, and the smile he gave as she approached made the slight trepidation she'd started with worth the effort.

'Looking particularly fetching there, Miss Tara.'

He sounded relaxed. Thank goodness for that. Until

she'd given herself a stern talking to she'd been replaying the video of the dumb things she'd said in her head before she'd left. Dumb because she hadn't needed to put them out there, though he'd agreed—not dumb because she hadn't meant them, because she had. She sat down beside him on the bench and looked at the manger. 'Hi, Simon.'

'And what did you do today?'

She opened her eyes wide. 'I've had a very nice day, thank you. I visited my two postnatal mums, then rode all the way to the lighthouse. Watched the parachutists float from the sky. It was very beautiful.' Politely. 'What did you do?'

'I did a couple of hours for Dad in the general hospital while he took Mia to the airport to go visit a sick friend, and I had a decadent snooze this afternoon because I didn't sleep well last night.' He watched her face. 'I guess you're tired now?'

She looked at him over the top of sunglasses. 'No, Mr Old Man. I'm not tired. I am young and enthusiastic for adventure at all times.'

'Goody.' He grinned. 'And for the record that's the second time you've called me an old man.'

'Well, stop acting like one.'

He didn't offer any answers to that one. 'Trouble is I'm wide awake after my nap and could party all night. Got any ideas?'

She shrugged. 'What sort of things? Nature? Dining? Dancing? Astronomy?'

'Ah. Astronomy has potential.'

'For what?'

'Seeing stars.'

'I could help you with that right now.' She swung her helmet thoughtfully. He was teasing and it was fun. Until he said, 'I wondered if you were into violence.'

She thought about some of the people she knew and the way their demons seemed to lead them to violence. The fun went out of it and she stood up. They were from such different worlds. 'Nope. Much prefer to just walk away.'

She saw him reach out to stop her and then drop his hand and his mixed signals only confused her more.

Then he said, 'Sorry. I don't know what I said but I don't want to ruin the mood. So, before you go, what I've really been doing is sitting here waiting to ask you to dinner. Louisa and Maeve have gone to Dad's to stay overnight and mind the girls. I'd like to get dressed up and go on a date with you to the new restaurant down by the lake.'

She sat down again. 'Oh.' She looked at him. 'A date?'

'A fun date with a lady I like spending time with.'

She thought about that one. 'Fun', meaning 'not serious'. Wasn't that what she'd said she wanted, too? Hadn't they both agreed on that yesterday morning? 'Sure. I'd like that. What time?'

'When you're ready. I made a booking for six-thirty for seven.' She raised her brows at his presumption but he was ahead of her. 'It's not heavily booked and they don't mind if I cancel.'

She grinned at him. 'You really are a thoughtful man.'

'We old guys are like that.'

'I don't really think you're old.' She looked him over with mischief in her eyes. 'Far too sexy for an old guy.'

'Keep thinking that way. I thought we could have a drink before dinner at the bar, if you don't mind walking there.'

'Thank you. Sounds nice.' She glanced at her watch. 'I'd better have a shower and get changed, then.'

'No rush.'

'Sure. But I like to be on time. I was brought up that way.'

Simon watched her walk away, that sexy, determined little walk that had him squirming on his seat. And the crazy thing was she had no idea what she did to him. He wasn't much better at guessing why she affected him like she did but tonight he'd come to the conclusion he was going to try to figure it out by taking it to the next level. Regardless of the risk.

The new restaurant was built on a little knoll overlooking the lake. The grounds were surrounded by a vibrant green hedge with a latched gate. The entry had been landscaped into lots of little rock pools and greenery with a wide wooden boardwalk winding through to get to the restaurant door. There was even a little bridge they had to climb up and over and Tara couldn't keep the smile off her face. 'This is gorgeous. I can't believe it's here and I didn't know.'

'They've only just opened. Mia told me about it when I asked her where I should take you.'

She looked at him. Surprised. 'You told Mia we were going on a date?'

'That's what she said.'

Tara laughed. 'Your family is funny.' And gorgeous, but that was okay. She had settled a lot since her ride that afternoon. Decided that clarity came with enjoying the moment, not worrying about it. She was here with Simon now, and she was going to have a wonderful evening. 'I'm starving.'

'Excellent.'

They started with drinks at the bar, and behind the barman a huge window overlooked the water and showcased the sunset, and to the left a narrow curving terrace gave the diners a water view while they ate.

He watched Tara sigh with pleasure as she took a sip of her pina colada and gazed around. 'This place is amazing.'

You're amazing. He followed her gaze. Took in the colours on the lake. 'It is great.' He saw it through Tara's shining eyes and acknowledged that he hadn't let it soak in. He had been so busy with his thoughts and plans and second-guessing his own emotions he was missing the pleasure. Vowed to stop that right now. Vowed to enjoy the pleasure of company with the woman he wanted to be with—and be like Tara and enjoy things, without worrying about tomorrow. Imagine that!

It was easier than he expected when he tried it. Everything seemed suddenly brighter. Wow.

'How's your drink?'

She pretended to look at him suspiciously. 'Why? You want some?' So then he laughed. Because it was funny.

'No, I don't want some, Miss I'm-Not-Sharing. I have my own drink. Though mine doesn't look as flashy as yours, with its slice of pineapple and pretty pink umbrella.'

She grinned. 'Good. I've never had one before. And I like umbrellas.' She offered him her straw. 'But you can have a sip if you really want.'

I'll sip later, he thought, and suddenly the night was alive with promise and joy, and the conversation took off as he let go of worrying about the past and the future and just experienced Tara's company.

They flowed from the bar to their table, the most private one he could acquire, and the sun went down, as did the glorious seafood and the delightful sparkling wine in the bottle.

By the time he paid the bill they were both pleasantly mellow, and he had no hesitation in capturing her hand in his for the walk home around the lake.

The lake path from the restaurant to the hospital and Louisa's house was lit by yellow globes that matched the moon and it was almost as bright as day as they ambled along.

This time when there was a rustle in the bushes Tara just smiled at the noise and carried on walking.

He glanced back to where the undergrowth still crackled. 'So you're not afraid of snakes in the bushes now?'

'Nope.' She squeezed his hand. 'I'm going to believe it's a lyrebird who can sound like a motorbike. If he wants to, of course.'

'Of course.' And Simon realised he had become decidedly more trusting about other facets of lyrebird lore. He stopped and she stopped too. He pulled her by the hand until she faced him and lifted his fingers to her cheek. 'You look like a lake princess in the moonlight.'

She glanced up at the moon and the angles of her face shone like those of a perfectly carved silver goddess with the reflection of the moonlight shining Tara's truth at him.

She was frowning at him, trying to read him, and goodness knew what was flashing across his face as his mind raced, because she looked a little unsure. 'Thank you for the compliment. I like moonlit nights the best. Never been keen on the dark.'

He just wanted to hold her safe and never let her go. One day he would ask why she preferred to have a moonlit night than a dark one. Hopefully he would have the chance to ask.

He leant in and kissed her gently because if he did

it properly he wouldn't be able to stop and she didn't deserve that, but she lifted her hands up and held his head there.

Tara kissed him back with a warmth and generosity he remembered from the lookout and for a few minutes there he forgot his good intentions. Until they heard some people coming along the path and he put her away from him.

That's right. He had no intention of seducing Tara in a park. 'Let's go home now.'

There was something in the way he said '*home now*' that sent a whisper of promise across Tara's skin. Home. Together. Now. That last kiss had been different, wonderful and absolutely intoxicating. Lucky Simon had heard the people coming because she'd been deaf to the world.

They were walking quite fast now. Seemed he'd decided caution was overrated and that was okay. Seriously okay because, no matter what, she wanted to sleep with this gorgeous, sexy, kind man at least once. She was not going to regret not spending time with Simon for the rest of her life. It might be her last chance.

Louisa and Maeve had gone to Mia's so they would be alone and that removed that last of her resistance, if she'd had any.

Simon held her hand tightly as they walked even more quickly along the lit path. She resisted the urge to run.

CHAPTER TWELVE

SIMON PUSHED OPEN the door and Tara reached up to turn on the lights but he stilled her hand.

'Can you see in the moonlight?'

Her hand fell away from the switch and instinctively they both slowed to draw out the moment. Tara's eyes adjusted and she could see easily as she stared into the strong features above her, cherished the fact that Simon found her very attractive, could almost feel herself unfurling in front of him. The silly, exciting, headlong rush to get here was completed and now it was time to savour their first moments.

Okay. Settle. Slow your breathing. Just soak it in.

He drew her to him, leaned in and brushed her mouth with his. Brushed again. Gently pulling on her lip with his teeth. A mingling of breath and promise and introduction to a Simon she didn't know. One she liked very much.

'You taste so beautiful.'

'Pina colada?'

'The taste of Tara. I like it.' He kissed her again.

'Mmm.' Closed her eyes at his reverence because it made her want to cry and he might think she did so for the wrong reasons. 'I like you tasting me.' Just a little bit gruffly.

He smiled, a brief flash of teeth in the moonlight, and then he was pulling her slowly down the hallway to his room. She wanted to lose herself like she had on the path, but she wanted to savour every moment, store up every stroke of his fingers as his hand trailed down her arm.

They passed her door. Good choice, she thought mistily. 'My room's a mess.'

'Mine's too tidy. I'm sure we'll find something in common.' He bent his body and slid one arm under her shoulder, the other behind her knee, and lifted her easily into his arms and against his chest. 'Something along the lines of I like to hold you in my arms and you like to be carried.'

'Not something I had previously been aware of.' She laid her head back and savoured it. 'It seems you're right.'

He squeezed her to him. Paused at his door. 'Will you spend the night with me, Tara?'

'That sounds very nice, Simon.'

He gave a small deep chuckle as he pushed open his door and closed it behind them. Then he stood her up in front of the bed and reached around behind her to ease the zipper down her back. A long leisurely unzipping that promised much.

He curved the fabric off her shoulders until it slithered into a heap at her feet, a rumpled puddle of material, then helped her step out. She looked back at this gorgeous man, burnished by the gentle light, and decided he looked like a magnificent knight as he stood in front of her. One who deserved something a little more romantic than her serviceable underwear but there wasn't much she could do about it except wish for a second she'd bought the lacy set she'd scorned last week.

Then Simon lifted her hands to his neck and traced them down his chest so that she too could undo fastenings, liking that she could follow his lead and lose the awkwardness of her lack of skill at this slow dance of undressing.

Surprisingly easily, she unfastened buttons until his shirt flapped open and she couldn't help an indulgent exploration of the ridges and hollows and bands of rippled muscles that she'd ached to stroke all evening—and while she was there she undid the silver buckle of his belt—such an unclick of commitment that made her smile a slow, wicked, womanly smile.

She felt his breath draw in as she slipped open the button of his trousers and carefully eased the teeth of his zip over the unmistakable bulge of his erection.

His fingers slid up her back and then around her neck and over her throat so she tilted her head, first a gentle brush of his lips over her throat and then a searing kiss that clouded her vision and had her matching the sudden flurry of movements they both made to remove the last of the clothing between them.

He lifted her again, placed her reverently like a prize across his bed and knelt down beside her, naked in the moonlight, a beautiful gilded warrior to claim his trophy.

The moonlight flooded across them, silvery streams of light with dark stripes where the branches from the tree outside blocked it, so when he lay down beside her the light rippled across his skin from silver to shadow and back to silver again.

She must have been in the stripes too, because he said softly, 'You still look like a mystical creature from the lake.'

'There's no mystery. Just me.'

He gathered her into his arms. Squeezed her to him. 'There's no "just" about you, Tara.'

And then he began to kiss her. Worship her. Inch by inch, kiss by kiss, stroke by stroke, accompanied by whispered murmurs of delight, discoveries that were marvelled over, and sudden indrawn breaths on Tara's side as she too discovered there was another world, a whispering, wonderful, wild world of worship at the hands of Simon Campbell.

As the sun peeped fingers of light towards the tangle of sheets on the bed Simon looked down at the woman he held in his arms. The warmth of sudden knowledge broke through to him like a beam from the dawn. Like

an epiphany. No warning. Just a moment in time between touching and looking—then he realised that, of
course, he loved her! Had done for days. Fool!

Tara was the one. It had been building since the lookout. And he'd denied it, the incredible dance of the lyrebird that had warned him about the truth.

Instead of panic, the relief was overwhelming because his body had been shouting in his ear for the last
torturous days and he'd been talking it down. Saying
they didn't know each other well enough, he couldn't
possibly, but that feeling of delight every time he'd seen
her should have warned him. Well, he knew her now,
in the biblical sense, and that was what it had taken for
him to know, without a doubt, that he'd fallen in love.

Simon tightened his hands around the waist he'd cradled through the night. The satin skin he'd held in his
arms and stroked with wondering hands. Kissed the tiny
intricate rose tattooed on her shoulder. He just knew
there would be a story about that.

Making love with Tara had been everything it had
never been with anyone else.

A revelation, a slow and gentle exploration that had
seen her unfurl like the tail of the lyrebird, he thought
whimsically, into a slow mesmerising dance of magnificent generosity that had enraptured them both. She
gave it all, held nothing back, and knowing her past only
made him more exultant about her generosity.

The trouble was, now he knew he loved her, what he

didn't know was if she loved him. All he could do was pray that Tara would see the same thing.

Prickly, determined, independent little Tara, and he discovered that when he loved, the feeling just grew, shifted, touched the whole world with its glow, irrevocably, from the depths of his soul, and there was no going back. So this was what his father had meant when he'd said it would happen one day and he'd recognise it.

He couldn't believe it. His sisters would be in whoops of laughter. His mother would be thrilled he was thinking of settling down.

Settling down?

That was why everything was so upside down and back to front. So unlike it usually was because he'd never fallen in love before. He was in love with Tara. No wonder he hadn't recognised it.

The last time Tara woke, because there had been several awakenings in more ways than one, Simon wasn't holding her and she felt the loss like a piece of herself was gone. And her heart began to pound. What would happen today?

Nothing or everything? Would he be kind but distant? Would he be loving and different towards her? She hugged herself and assured her newly awakened inner woman that everything would be fine, no matter what. But she didn't believe it.

Thankfully, before she could whip herself into too much of a state Simon poked his head around the door.

The smile on his face wasn't distant at all. Actually, his eyes said he wanted to jump in beside her and she was tempted to crook her finger at him. 'Your breakfast awaits you on the back veranda, my lady.'

She sat up. Realised she was naked. Clutched the sheet and blushed as Simon enjoyed the view with a decidedly proprietorial glint in his eye. 'Maeve and Louisa will be home soon, the girls leave for school in five minutes, and I thought you might like to get dressed before then.'

Absolutely. Crikey. 'Yes. Please.' She waved him away and he pulled his head back but not before he winked at her like a villain in a farce. Well, it didn't seem as though Simon regretted the night.

The tension slid from her shoulders and several unlimbered muscles twinged as she swung her feet out of the bed. Her cheeks heated as she caught a glance of a thoroughly sated woman in the mirror, and she tried one of Simon's winks on herself. She grinned. Felt silly.

But there was a curve to her lips she couldn't seem to move and she slid the same shirt around her shoulders that she'd removed from Simon last night, sniffed the collar, and recognised the faint cologne she would always associate with him, then gathered her own clothes with one hand and clutched the edges of the shirt together with the other hand as she let herself out of the room and into her own.

The fastest gathering on record of clothes for the

day and then she was safely behind the bathroom door before anyone else arrived home.

By the time she was out, dressed and confident, on the outside at least, Louisa and Maeve were home. Maeve was trying desperately to catch her eye but she refused to collide with the knowing looks that kept coming her way and Simon was whistling and avoiding his sister as well.

Diversion was needed. 'How are the girls?'

Louisa seemed oblivious to the undercurrents in the room. Thank goodness somebody was. 'As prettily mannered as you could wish for.' Louisa sighed blissfully. 'I do enjoy their company. And they're so excited about the carols tonight.'

'That's right. The carols by candlelight.' Tara was pretty excited about that too. She'd be with Simon. She wondered if he'd hold her hand in front of his family. The thought was nerve-racking and she stuffed it away to peek at later. 'What time does Mia get home?'

'Angus picks her up from the airport at lunchtime so she'll be back before they finish school.'

It was so weird having a normal conversation. Especially with Simon watching her. She could feel him. And then there were Maeve's eyes nearly bugging out of her head with curiosity. She tried to concentrate on Louisa. 'I've got two home visits this morning but can help any other time if you need me to do something.'

The older lady smiled serenely. 'Thanks, Tara. I'll let you know.'

Tara nodded and followed Simon out to the veranda, where he'd set a place and made her favourite herbal tea and raisin toast. He stood behind her chair and pushed it in when she sat down. Every time she glanced at him she could feel her cheeks heat. And her belly glow. Finally understanding the preoccupation a woman could have with sleeping with her man. Was Simon her man? He leaned across and kissed her and then he sat opposite and calmly sipped his tea.

Maeve arrived, hovered and Tara had a way to go before she reached that skill of composure Simon had. Sipped her tea, ate half a piece of toast and decided to bolt. She rose. 'I've got to go.'

The words sounded abrupt but Simon only smiled at her. Gave her a wink. Maeve looked thwarted and Tara decided exit had been an excellent idea as she walked hurriedly back into the house to get her gear, and knew the rest of the day would require some concentration if she wasn't going to end up staring into space every few minutes with a silly smile on her face.

Carols by candlelight began as the sun set. Angus and Simon had taken the trailer full of chairs and set them up to the left of the stage. It was a warm, sleeveless type of evening and the children were dressed in pretty red dresses and short-legged Santa helper suits, with Santa hats and flashing stars, and dozens of little battery-powered candles to wave in the darkening evening as families from all over the valley began to arrive.

Simon had been to the shops and Tara had never had so many Christmas-themed trinkets in her possession.

Her favourite was a long silver wand with a star on top that glowed silver in the darkening sky. Though the Christmas headband with reindeer made her laugh and the earrings shaped like Christmas trees that flashed on and off and matching bracelet were all very cool. When she'd demurred, Simon had laughed and said she could give them away if she had too much but he hadn't been able to resist buying them because every time he'd seen something new he'd thought she would like it.

Tara liked it. She'd never bought herself anything festive, had thought they were all for little children, but Simon said she looked like a Christmas angel so she hugged them to herself when what she wanted to do was hug Simon.

In the distance the lights from Louisa's house shone merrily and the carols began with a rousing rendition of 'Good King Wenceslas', and Tara turned with amazement as Simon began to sing in a deep, hilarious baritone that, despite his intention to make her smile, was incredibly rich and tuneful.

She had never thought she could ever be this happy, this excited, this included in a family night like tonight, and she shook her head at the gorgeous man beside her as he took her hand in his and hugged her to him.

She saw Louisa smile at them, and even Angus looked across at them warmly. Mia winked and Maeve grinned at her every time she saw them.

Tara was in love!

* * *

The day before Christmas Eve and Tara turned over in bed. Last night had been amazing. Simon had seemed so proud of her, so happy to show everyone that he cared, and just soaking up the night with Simon's arm around her had been one of the most magical evenings she'd ever had.

She was in love but instead of waking in the golden glow she should have, it was the terrified child from the orphanage who woke, and she felt like scooting down the hallway and crawling into Simon's bed for reassurance. She really, really hated that horrible feeling it was all too good to be true.

All those times as a kid when she'd thought maybe she could fall in love with a family, had waited for the call that only other children seemed to get—this was much worse, a thousand times worse.

What if something happened to this precious feeling between her and Simon?

To make it more terrifying, he was a part of the most amazing family of them all. A whole Christmas fairytale and Santa Claus stocking of loving people that she would give anything to be a part of. Could she possibly believe that good things like that could happen to her? She thought of the lyrebird and a little calmness came out of nowhere. Maybe she just needed to learn to believe it?

And then her phone rang, probably a mum with an unsettled baby, just as she was about to get out of bed and dress for work. It took her a moment to recognise the voice from her past. Mick.

That was when she knew it was the end.

She felt shock, and horror, and a queer almost relief from the impending doom she'd worried so much about. Karma-wise she'd probably talked herself into this bad luck. 'How did you find my number?'

'I didn't just find your number.' The smug tone sent icy shivers down her back. Not for herself. She wasn't afraid of Mick, or not much except when he was off his face on some substance, but she was afraid for Louisa getting a nasty shock when she opened the door. Or Maeve. For anyone else who got in his way. More afraid of the look of disgust when the people she cared about in Lyrebird Lake saw that she was the reason he was there.

Mick's gravelly voice recalled her to the present. 'I want my bike, Tara.'

The darned bike. 'The bike is mine. You owed me a lot more than it's worth.'

'It's mine. And I'm coming for it. And that's not all I'm coming for. You and me, Tara. Like old times.'

Like hell. He really was high. She glanced at the clock. 'Where are you?'

'Leaving Sydney soon.'

She didn't know what to do. What to think. Had to stall until she came up with a plan to keep Mick away from Lyrebird Lake and everyone in it until she could sort it.

She was crystal clear in her mind that she'd accepted

the bike wasn't worth it. Thankfully she had grown beyond defining herself because of a possession and was
over her need to have a win over Mick for her self-esteem. If she wasn't so angry with him for risking her
new-found friendships, let alone the precious jewel of
her relationship with Simon, she'd feel sorry for Mick.

Even in her fog of anguish Tara could see he was
missing out in life because of his bitterness about the
past. But feeling sorry for Mick had led her into this
mess of debt and negativity in the first place.

But she was slowly climbing out of that hole. Mentally she already had, and financially she was in the
process, one small payment at a time.

And now, being with Simon had helped her find another stronger and prouder layer of herself. She was
someone a wonderful man admired, and she could leave
here a better person because of that.

The sigh that accompanied the thought seemed to
tear itself loose from her soul. Because she would have
to leave now that Mick had found her. Not with him, but
after him, because he'd just keep coming back every
time he wanted to extort something.

'You could pay me ten thousand dollars' worth of
debts and it's all yours.'

Mick laughed and it wasn't a pleasant sound and Tara
grimaced. He was high on something. 'You'll never get
the money but I will get my bike. I know where you
live. I'm coming to have Christmas with all your little

families. I've seen the house where you live on Google Earth. Bet they don't know about me. But they will.'

'I'm negotiable on the bike, Mick. But there were never *old times* between you and me. Just a short time. I was your friend and you let me down. Nothing else is on the agenda.'

'What's up, Tara? You too good for your orphan buddies now?'

'The blood-sucking ones. Yes. I have a new life. One I've worked hard for. You're not a part of it.'

'That's what you think.'

'Forget it, Mick. I'll give you the bike, and you can get lost. But you can't have it now. I'm working this morning and don't finish until late this afternoon. I'll meet you tonight.'

Blow. That was family night at Mia and Angus's. 'About six.' The whole family was meeting for drinks to be there when the girls went to bed. Apparently they did it every year. She would just have to cry off and meet Mick somewhere out of sight while they all went on and had dinner.

Though how she'd smuggle the bike out of town would be tricky. That was the problem with Harleys. It wasn't like they didn't have a distinctive sound. Even lyrebirds noticed the noise. She'd say she had to go out for one of her women. Early labour. Simon would believe that. Except now she was lying to him. But she couldn't help that.

And then Mick upped the stakes. 'Nope. Think I'll

spend Christmas in Lyrebird Lake. Seems like as fine a place as any. With my good friend Tara.'

Tara felt a clutch of dread. What if she couldn't stop him? If it was too late? The cold wind of the real world was blowing through her life again. She could imagine the children frightened of Mick, Simon sticking up for her and Mick fighting him, Louisa terrified. Nightmare in Lyrebird Lake and she had to stop it all before any of it could happen.

She needed to stall him. Stop him the only way she could think of. 'If you come anywhere near my friends, my work or my home before I say so, I'll douse the bike in petrol and burn it.' Her voice lowered and she put every ounce of conviction she could muster into the threat. 'You know I will.'

A pause and then a bluster. 'You won't have the chance.'

'Try me.' There was a silence. 'Only on my terms and until then…leave me alone. Give me until tonight to figure something out. I'll meet you somewhere away from here and hand it over. Ring me around six some time but I don't want you in this town. Or I will destroy the bike.'

That morning at work Tara found it incredibly difficult to concentrate. She kept imagining Simon's face if he came face to face with wild-eyed Mick, who looked even worse than he was, except when he was high, and he really was a bad man. Why on earth anyone would

tattoo their face was beyond Tara, though she didn't regret the tiny rose on her own shoulder, remembrance
for the tragically short life of Mick's sister.

Maybe if she hadn't gone with Mick for that first tattoo he wouldn't have started painting his body but she
would never know. The past was the past.

She just wished the past and the people from it would
stay there! Especially now she'd glimpsed a future she'd
foolishly thought she had a chance at.

The ward was quiet. They'd had a peaceful birth
earlier in the day, one of Mia's mothers, and Tara spent
the day sitting beside the new mum, gently praising
her early breastfeeding skills. Everything was tidy and
she was thinking she might even get off a little early
when the phone rang to say her last due woman was
coming in.

For the first time in her career she wished a baby
would wait.

Of course, it didn't.

Tara didn't get home at three like she wanted, to
give herself time to get organised. She arrived home
at ten to six and Maeve and Louisa were busy in the
kitchen, making finger food for tonight's family get-
together at Mia's.

Simon had been out all day apparently, shopping,
which was a good thing because every time someone
spoke to her she jumped and he would notice more than
anyone that she was preoccupied and nervous.

When she picked up her phone from her room she

grimaced at all the missed calls. When she tried to return the call on Mick's mobile, his phone was turned off
and she felt unease crawl up her neck. Missing his calls
wouldn't leave Mick in a good frame to negotiate with.

Frustration gnawed at her. She needed to get in contact before he took matters into his own hands.

What if he was already in town? What if he knocked
on the door and frightened Louisa? Or her greatest fear,
picked a quarrel with Simon?

Tara quickly typed in a message. Gave directions to
a place safely away from the town. Tried to imply he
couldn't come to the lake but without him knowing he
had her worried. This was her worst nightmare and she
threw on her jeans and grabbed her helmet.

Behind her eyes a dull throb of tiredness and strain
made her gulp the water beside her bed in the hope it
would help the headache, and she stared through the
curtains to the street as she drank.

Hell. Damn. Blast it. This was so unfair. She didn't
deserve this imploding of her dream town. She felt
like pulling her hair and stomping her feet. But that
had never been her way so she drew a deep breath and
straightened. It didn't matter about her. It was the people at the lake who mattered and she needed to stop
Mick from upsetting them. A sudden vision of Mick
and Simon fighting made nausea rise in her throat.

Just before she left, one last attempt as she paused in
the hallway, she finally managed to get through to Mick.

And as she'd dreaded, he'd borrowed a friend's car and trailer and had stopped for petrol only an hour away.

The dinner started at six-thirty and Tara estimated it would take her an hour to get to Mick, hand over the bike and get home.

Simon had gone to the next big town, shopping with his father, and still wasn't back so at least she could get away.

Tara repeated the directions to the local rubbish dump, on the inbound side of town, she could hand over the bike and walk the four miles home without anyone seeing her.

She had no idea what she'd say when everyone realised the bike was gone but that was the least of her worries. She'd just say she'd had to give it back.

CHAPTER THIRTEEN

SIMON HAD HAD a great day with his dad, had spent most of his time buying quirky gifts for Tara, and couldn't wait to hug her after a day with her filling his mind.

Then he saw Tara standing in the hallway talking on the phone. She hadn't seen him and he stood quietly and soaked in the vision. The light shone on her spiky silver hair, which exposed her gorgeous neck, and he wanted to trace that faint line behind her ear. Kiss that spot where her pulse beat gently against his mouth. He'd done a lot of that the other night. That hadn't been all he'd done and somehow they hadn't been able to recapture a moment when they could be together, alone, since then. He needed to do something about that.

She looked so good he wanted to drag her off to his room and have his wicked way with her right then and there but he guessed he'd have to wait until they could get away.

She'd finished the call so he moved towards her. 'Hi, Tara. Looking forward to tonight?' She jumped, and it wasn't a little one, it was a full-blown knee-jerk fright, and his own heart rate accelerated.

'Sorry.' He frowned, noticed the strain in her face he hadn't seen before, then remembered she'd been at work today. Not a good day? He knew how that felt.

He reached out and touched her shoulder with the idea of maybe sharing a little hug and she jumped again. Looked at him and then away and none of it was encouraging. What was going on? 'You okay?'

He tried to catch her eye but she turned her head. Now he was worried. Maybe she regretted the other night. He hoped not. He glanced at her jeans and boots. 'You going out on the bike?'

'Home visit. Early labour. Probably miss the dinner.'

Bummer. He'd been really looking forward to cuddling up to Tara while they all sat around and toasted the season. He guessed this had happened to all of his previous girlfriends and now the boot was on the other foot. 'Who is it? Want me to come? I could sit outside and reassure the man of the house.'

'You don't know her and, no, I don't want you to come.' A quick hunted glance and he was beginning to wonder if this was bigger than he thought.

Now what did he say? She looked like she was going to cry. 'You sure everything is okay?'

He watched her do that calming thing she did, a big breath, dropping the expression from her face, easing the tension from her shoulders. What had he done to make her that tense?

She shook her head. 'I'll see you later, Simon.'

And that was that. 'Okay.' Not a lot he could do about it except stalk her and that wasn't his style. 'I'll tell Mia you got called out.'

'Just leave it. I'll tell her.' She smiled but it wasn't one that made him feel good. 'Apologise for me. Maybe I'll get there before it all finishes, maybe not. Have a good night.'

'Sure.' He was anything but sure. Watched her go. But the feeling of unease glowed in his gut as he heard the sound of the bike start up. If he didn't know better he'd swear she'd looked panic-stricken for a minute there. Something was going on and he knew Tara well enough to suspect she was unhappy about where she was going. So why would that be? What could possibly make Tara unhappy about going to one of her women in labour? A poor domestic situation? Surely not. If that were the case she'd take someone else because that was the protocol. What if one of her women had a violent partner? Simon wished he'd asked a bit more. The unease grew in his gut and he decided to walk to Mia's and ask her if she knew anything.

Tara blinked back her tears. The wind on her face was achingly familiar and the throb of the engine hummed goodbye. Tara gained little enjoyment from her last ride but she was past lamenting over the loss.

She'd lied to Simon. To his face. But she couldn't see any other way of protecting those she'd come to love.

Yes, she loved Simon, she loved Louisa, she loved every darned person in Lyrebird Lake, it seemed, and all the sighs and shoulder drops in the world weren't going to lighten that load.

She'd let them down. And now she was going to sign away her only possession in the world to stop them finding out about her past, but she couldn't help feeling it wasn't going to stop disaster happening anyway.

She turned off the main road onto the quiet gravel road to the tip. It was good it was quiet because she really didn't want anyone from Lyrebird Lake wondering why she was driving this way at this time of the evening.

And maybe that was why she came round the corner just a little too fast. Hit a patch of gravel just a little bit deep.

And for the first time lost control of the big bike as the front wheel skidded in the gravel and went sideways. Tara fought to stay upright, fought the urge to hit the brake, skidded sideways up the road valiantly upright but at a dangerous angle. As the bike slowed she managed to stay upright and slowed more until she thought she'd manage to correct the angles in the end.

She concentrated, fiercely willing the front wheel to straighten as she pulled it around, but her luck ran out because she'd run out of straight road and didn't make the bend. She hit the grass and flew into the scrub until the bike caught on a strong branch and jerked to a stop, where it fell with lack of forward motion and went down, with Tara frantically shifting her bottom leg so she wouldn't be pinned underneath. Her ankle jerked and caught and she pulled frantically to get it clear and the pain shot up her leg as it twisted.

She could feel her heart racing in her ears. Tara pulled herself backwards on her bottom until she was clear of the bike as its massive weight sank slowly closer and closer to the ground, crushing the undergrowth with a sizzling crackle, until it was lying flat on its side. Tara's back came up against the trunk of a tree she was very glad to have missed. Her ankle throbbed but she wasn't trapped under the bike. Still some good to be found.

But she had no idea how she was going to lift the deadweight of the bike to get it off the ground.

After a minute of gathering her nerves, Tara crawled from her position against the tree and stood gingerly upright to brush herself off. She put a little weight on her ankle; it wobbled but stayed upright with a low-level throbbing. It could have been a lot worse.

At least she'd had jeans on. She'd refused to wear her leathers and walk home in them, but she hadn't escaped unscathed. As well as scratches on her arms as she and the bike had barrelled through the bushes, the areas where the stressed jeans had parted had let in tiny scratches and stings that would be annoying but not kill her. Her biggest dilemma was that she needed to get the bike upright and beat Mick to the rubbish dump before he decided she wasn't coming and head to Lyrebird Lake anyway.

She pulled her phone from her pocket and tried Mick's number but he wasn't answering. Peered at her watch but the screen was broken and she had to pick the plastic out to be able to read the numbers. It must have happened as she'd come through the bushes. She had ten minutes until she was supposed to be there.

She took a big, deep breath as she struggled to stand the bike while putting all of her weight on one leg. Ouch! No luck. Tara tried from the other side.

Pull! No luck, just a twinge of discomfort in her back from the effort and a fiercer ache from her ankle. She walked back again to the lifting side and tried jamming a stick as a lever to get it up. The stick broke.

No luck. She'd known it was going to be an unequal contest. It was all very well to sit astride a big bike. Even pulling it off its stand was fine when she was balanced evenly on her feet. But to lift a heavy motorcycle that was deadweight from lying on its side on the ground was just too much for her to achieve on her own. Even swearing was an effort after the last superhuman effort she'd made to no avail.

It was getting dark. She tried Mick again but he still wasn't answering his phone. The road was deserted, a fact she'd been happy about a few minutes ago and was not so thrilled about now.

It was past the agreed time and he hadn't rung her. Hopefully he had been held up somewhere too, or he'd decided he wouldn't answer the phone when she'd tried to ring him. It was the sort of pathetic thing he would do. There was nothing else she could do but ring for help— and the only person she could ring was Simon. Maybe they could get the bike upright before Mick came.

Simon had walked swiftly around to his father's house and cornered Mia in the kitchen to ask what she knew about Tara's due clients. Still concerned about the idea that one of Tara's birthing women might have a less than salubrious home life, he couldn't settle until he'd been reassured.

But Mia's comment that after her last birth Tara's only due woman was Maeve, had him thrust back into confusion.

So it couldn't be a premature labour because she'd be telling that woman to come for transfer. Which meant only one thing. She'd lied to him. To his face. And he couldn't think of one damn good reason why she'd had to do that.

And then his phone rang. 'Hello?'

'Simon?' It was her.

His hand tightened on the phone as he waved to Mia before he walked back towards the manse. 'Tara? Are you okay?'

Tara's 'Not really…' made his heart rate jump.

'What happened?'

'I came off my bike and I can't stand it up. I need help.'

'Where are you?' He looked up at Mia and pointed towards the manse. Mia nodded and waved him away.

There was a pause. 'I'm sorry about the dinner.'

He brushed that aside. 'Where are you?'

'On the old rubbish dump road.'

He hadn't thought there were any houses down that way. 'And you're all right? You're not hurt?'

'Pride's pretty banged up, my ankle is tender, but physically I'm scratched, that's all.'

He tried to hold them back but the words came out anyway. 'What are you doing out there?'

She sighed. 'It's a long story. I'll tell you when you get here. Turn onto the rubbish tip road and I'm about a kilometre in on the left just as you hit the low part of the road. Watch out for the loose gravel,' she added dryly.

'Twenty minutes!' And it had better be a good reason because he didn't like any of the ones he'd come up with.

CHAPTER FOURTEEN

'SIMON WILL BE here in time. He'll be here.' The words echoed eerily in the encroaching dusk and Tara huddled further into her thin top. It was summer, for pity's sake, and she hadn't had the forethought to bring warmer clothes, but down in the hollow the mist was cool. That's what happened when you forgot the way of the world.

She'd fallen into this trap s-o-o-o many times before you would think she'd have learnt her lesson. Why would Simon Campbell, darling of his two families and, in fact, all of Lyrebird Lake, forgive her for lying to him?

Especially when he didn't understand the reason.

Maybe the fault did lie a little with her. Come on, Tara, a lot with her. She didn't trust him enough to give him the tools to believe her. Hadn't let him into her dilemma because she'd been too afraid he'd turn away from her. So she'd lied instead.

Self-sabotage or what? If she was honest, somewhere in the back of her head the voices had been saying he would let her down. Maybe that was why she'd made this tryst so difficult.

Well, she was in trouble now. It was getting dark, miles from anywhere, and she didn't want to think about the possibility that she'd put her heart on the line again to be broken.

She lifted her chin. She wasn't some twelve-year-old orphan sent on her way. She was a grown woman. A grown professional woman and she would get over this just as soon as she figured a way to get back to civilisation, and she may as well start now because he wasn't going to come.

Then headlights crossed the tops of the trees and in the distance she heard an echo of a car roaring up the hill.

'Simon,' she whispered, and the words floated into the darkness. Now that he was coming, she dreaded seeing the disgust on his face. She'd let him down with her lies but she hadn't been able to think of anything else she could do to prevent her world crumbling. He'd probably think she was leaving with Mick. She may as well. There was nothing here for her now.

But it wasn't Simon. It was Mick. Towing a trailer behind a disreputable old sedan. Tara's heart sank and she considered throwing herself back into the bushes so he wouldn't see her, but it was too late.

He pulled up in a shower of gravel because he'd been driving far too fast as usual. She should have known it wasn't Simon with the car engine screaming up the hill in the dimness.

'Where's the bike?' The words flew out of his mouth

as fast as Mick got out of the car. He looked around suspiciously.

Tara sighed. She'd forgotten how childish he was. 'I lost it in the gravel so it's in the bush behind me.'

'Is it okay?'

'What about me?'

'Oh, yeah. You okay?' But his eyes were scanning the bush and he was on his way before she could answer.

'Fine,' she said to his back, and decided Mick was dumb enough and strong enough not to ask for help to extricate the bike.

She glanced up the road and wished like hell she'd never rung Simon. She considered phoning him back and saying, *Don't come. I'll be home soon.* Except that would involve more explanations and possibly more lies. She'd lied enough. All she could do was hope Mick would load the bike and go as soon as possible.

Mick did manage to get the bike on the trailer before Simon arrived but that was where Tara's luck ran out.

Simon turned off the main road and frowned at the deserted gravel road that stretched ahead in the dimness. He switched on his headlights and slowed right down. She'd said about a kilometre. Something was going on. And he was pretty sure he wasn't going to like it. But he was surprisingly unworried about that. Lots of people did things he didn't like and he got over it. Look at his parents lying to him. Look at Maeve. Though he hadn't got over Rayne's part in that. But this would be okay. Right.

Anyway, he loved Tara and the fact that she'd rung him for help was a big plus.

But he would be much happier when he found her and could see for himself she was unhurt.

And then he saw her. Standing in the gloom at the side of the road beside a dirty sedan and a trailer with her bike on the back. She must have found someone to help her get it home.

Well, that was one problem solved. She was standing, and apart from a limp when she came towards where he parked she looked okay. Thank goodness.

Then he saw the driver of the vehicle and his brows rose. Even in the poor light he could see the heavy tattoos and plaited beard. Noted Tara's guarded stance as he pulled up and climbed out of his vehicle. Thank goodness he'd hurried. The situation was not what he'd expected but as long as Tara was okay...

Mick waved him away. 'We don't need help, mate.'

Simon ignored him. 'You okay, Tara?' He crossed to her side, all the while noting the smudges of blood through the slits in her jeans, the abrasions on her arms and the extreme wariness on her face. He wanted to hug her but she was sending keep-off vibes like a missile launcher, telling him to stay away, and he frowned. 'How's the ankle?'

Mick lifted his head at that and took a step towards Simon. Towered over him. 'Who are you?'

Simon looked him up and down. Remained supremely unconcerned that he was outweighed. He'd faced down bigger men than this guy, and knew how not to antagonise. Usually. 'I'm a friend of Tara's. Who are you?'

'Mick. Me and Tara grew up together. We don't need your help.'

He smiled at Mick. 'Good to meet you, Mick. Then you'll understand if I ask Tara that.' He didn't wait for Mick's answer. 'Tara?'

'Ankle's fine. Sore but I can walk.' Tara was looking worried and he wished he could tell her how skilled he was at managing stroppy people. He was the one they called if a husband lost the plot in his concern for his wife. Though he wasn't feeling his usual detached self as he took in the full magnificence of this quite obnoxious guy, making ownership moves towards Tara.

'It's nice of you to take Tara's bike home for her.'

Mick laughed. 'Yeah. But it's my home. My bike. She gave it back.' He leered. 'I was thinking I might take Tara, too.'

Simon fought down his sudden out-of-character urge to knock the guy's teeth in and looked at Tara.

'And how does Tara feel about that?'

She glared at Mick. 'You've got the bike. Let's go, Simon.'

Simon did a double-take. 'You're giving him the bike?'

Tara straightened. To Simon she ground out, 'It's mine to give.' To Mick, 'I want you out of my life. Merry Christmas.'

Tara walked away from them both, climbed into Simon's car and slammed the door. She stared straight ahead, ignoring them, though her eyes were squinting sideways in the side mirror as she tried to catch a glimpse of what was happening. She'd had the desperate idea if she left they'd both look stupid if they started something, and she didn't think even Mick would drag her out of her chosen car with force. She was right.

Simon opened the car door just as Mick's car started up and drove ahead to find somewhere to turn around.

'What the hell was that all about?'

'Can we just turn the car around and get out of here first? Please!'

Simon reversed the car with very uncharacteristic roughness and speed, and they skidded away from the fateful corner in a shower of gravel, much like Mick's arrival. Tara sighed.

'Don't you sigh at me. What the hell were you thinking? You arranged that. Didn't you? To meet this man in a dark and deserted place, to hand over the bike. By yourself. After lying to me so I wouldn't demand to come with you.'

She looked at him. His face was set. His lips compressed. Those strong shoulders were rigid with disbelief. She'd done that to him. Hurt him. Made him uncharacteristically angry. Knocked herself off the pedestal she'd been trying to balance on. 'You're right. That just about covers it.'

'No, that doesn't just about cover it.' They turned off the road and onto the Lyrebird Lake road and Simon pulled over. Switched the engine off. They sat there for a few seconds and Tara gathered her thoughts. Behind them Mick's lights turned towards Sydney and disappeared. She guessed she did owe Simon an explanation but she wasn't happy with his high-handed tone or the fact that this had all backfired on her. She'd been trying to do the right thing but she'd had nowhere to go. She had lied to Simon.

So she gave it to him straight. No wrapping. It was all a mess now anyway. 'Mick wanted the bike back. He's not pleasant when he's in this mood. I didn't want him to upset anyone in Lyrebird Lake so I'd rather just give it to him.'

'So you arranged to meet him out here? On your own?'

She shrugged. 'I'm not afraid of Mick. He looks worse than he is but I didn't want him being horrible in front of Louisa.' She looked up at him. 'Or Maeve, or Mia.'

She sighed again. Almost defiantly. 'Or you.'

That just inflamed him more. 'And how were you going to get home after you handed this man your only possession?'

'Walk.'

'That's beautiful.' He grimaced in the darkness. 'Walk. On a dark road. What is it, four miles?' His hands tightened on the steering-wheel until his knuckles were white. Despite the quietness of his tone Tara could tell he was furious. 'You put yourself in danger. All the time.'

He shook his head. Flabbergasted as he ran over it in his mind. 'There's the motorbike I was getting used to, the controlled risk of skydiving. I get that, I really do. But then there's being wilfully, personally risky, meeting substance-affected men in deserted places at night. I can't believe you didn't ask me for help.'

'No. I didn't.'

He glared at her. 'Instead of telling me the truth, accepting my help and being safe?'

She shrugged. 'I'm used to looking after myself. I thought I would be safe.'

'See, now I have an issue with that.'

'I rang you in the end.'

'Far too little too late. Maybe we have rushed into this. Or maybe I have. This morning I would have sworn we had a future together but I'm not so sure now. If there's one thing I won't put up with it's being shut out and lied to, especially by someone I l—um…someone I care deeply for!'

Someone he cared deeply for. And she'd spoiled it all.

Tara risked a glance at him and he was staring straight ahead as if the road was going to open up and swallow them at any moment. She almost wished it would.

The silence was loaded with regret on both sides but neither of them seemed to be able to break it. It took for ever to get back to the empty manse.

Then they were home. Everyone else was at Mia's and as Simon helped her in she wondered if he'd go to the family dinner now. But he didn't say anything, just appeared with the cotton wool and disinfectant and bathed her cuts, despite the fact she wanted him to just leave her alone.

Ushered her to bed. But there was a huge distance between them of things that were said and unsaid as he closed her door and left her. On both sides.

CHAPTER FIFTEEN

TARA OPENED HER eyes at six o'clock on Christmas Eve morning and lay in her bed, staring at the ceiling full of ghosts from Christmas past, even though she didn't want to.

Long-gone children's faces, long-gone empty dormitories, less-than-wonderful foster-parent experiences. And all those Christmas Eves full of expectations. Well, she didn't have any of those today after last night.

She'd lost the one man who could have rounded out her world. She sat up and hugged her pillow to her chest.

Simon had been right. She should have faced the music earlier rather than later. Discussed her concerns rationally with the man who cared and had been nothing but supportive. She had a sudden memory of their morning with the breech birth. How safe she'd felt because Simon had been there. How supportive he'd been without being authoritative. How proud he'd been of her ability to understand what had needed to be done and doing it.

She'd thrown away her chance with Simon and

today was going to be a long, long day of tragedy of lost opportunities.

She should have trusted him to understand. She just didn't know how to trust people. Another hard, painful lesson learned. It was too late for her and Simon but she vowed she would try in the future.

But for now she needed to make sure she didn't spoil anyone else's day.

Apart from Simon hating her, today was going to be a good day. She would smile and play cheerful families one last time. She'd let go of the silly pipe dream of happily ever after with Simon that she should never have contemplated. He'd be gone soon and she'd see if she could settle back into the world of Lyrebird Lake. If she couldn't settle then what she'd learnt here would hold her in good stead for the future.

Starting from now, she needed to appreciate the fact that she could hear the cicadas in the tree outside her window. Savour the warmth that was already creeping into the morning. Sniff the air with the enticing fragrance of baking that had hung over the house like an aromatic fog for the last two days. Go outside onto the springy kikuyu grass and watch the nodding reindeer and manger animals gyrate as the sun rose.

Then she'd be ready for what today would bring and what it wouldn't bring.

The feeling of just-out-of-reach simple pleasures drew her out of bed. Today would have to look after itself and she would savour every moment because that was all she had control over.

There was a tinkle of music and she even managed a tiny, crooked smile into her pillow before she put it back on her bed. Louisa had the Christmas music on again. Maeve would be so glad tomorrow when it would be gone. Her eyes stung as she thought about losing Maeve as a friend and then pushed that thought too back into her mind.

She scooted down the hallway with her clothes under her arm. Ten minutes later she let herself out the front door into the misty morning light to start the day on her own. Build her walls of serenity so no one could see the lost little girl inside her.

Except that Simon was there on the seat in front of the manger. She almost turned around and ran back to her room—but instead she lifted her chin. Better to do this when no one else was there.

Simon felt some of his tension ease as Tara came across the grass. At least she was going to talk to him. 'Merry Christmas Eve, Tara.'

Her face said she didn't think so and his own interpretation said that was his fault. He'd done so many things wrong.

'Merry Christmas Eve, Simon.' She sat with a gap he could have driven a car through between them.

When he looked sideways at her a tiny silver tear

slid out of her eye and rolled down her cheek, and he thought his heart would break. 'Don't cry.'

She brushed it away. 'I'm not.' Sat up straighter and rubbed her face.

'Baby Jesus arrives at midnight tonight.'

She looked at him and frowned. And then he could see she imagined a tiny beautifully wrapped doll all tucked up in straw.

'That will be awesome.'

They sat there looking at the space for a physical sign of a new beginning and miraculously he saw the signs of her glimpsing that maybe there was still a chance of a new beginning between them too.

He shifted along the seat and closed the gap between them on the bench, and all the motorised animals nodded.

'You okay?' His hand came across and picked up her fingers. Squeezed them in his. For a few seconds she just let it lie there in his palm and he squeezed her fingers again gently until she returned the pressure.

'I guess you did come to save me.'

'I was later than I wanted to be. You need to learn to trust me.'

She looked down at their hands and then back at his face. 'You need to learn to trust me. I've looked after myself for a lot of years.'

He sighed. She was right. 'I thought I did but then things happened and I lost it again. I'm sorry.'

She smiled at that, a little mistily, and looked away.

He'd better be able to fix this because looking at her face and not kissing her was killing him. 'I'm sorry I was horrible to you last night.'

'You were horrible to me.'

Well, that didn't go as planned, he thought regretfully.

'But I can see why you were.' She straightened her shoulders. 'And I'm sorry I lied to you.'

She was so brave. His Tara. 'You did lie to me. But I can see why you did.'

She nodded in the morning light. 'I didn't want you to meet Mick.'

He smiled ruefully at that. 'I didn't really want to meet Mick either. But I do want you to lose the ridiculous idea that any obnoxious person who comes looking for you is going to affect the way we feel about the Tara we know and care about. You have the whole of Lyrebird Lake behind you. Mick needs to see that. You need to see that.'

He looked at her under her brows. 'And he's not getting your bike.'

'I don't care about the bike.'

'I do. It's yours. I've given his number plate to the police and told them if he gives it back we won't press charges. They checked and it's your name on the paperwork.'

He saw her look of cautious hope but she said again, 'I don't care about the bike. What if he comes back? He can be very aggressive.'

He shook his head. Not the answer. 'Giving him the bike won't stop that. If he comes back we make him welcome. There must have been a reason he was your friend.

'But Mick's really not the bad man here. I am. Can you forgive me? For being angry?' He shook his head. 'I'm having a hard time forgiving myself. I never lose it.'

'You lost it.' She was teasing him now. Typical. 'Pretty controlled kind of guy, eh?' And he deserved it.

'I thrive on it. Usually. Like to have my world lined up and the bases covered.' He glanced at her. It was always good to look at Tara. 'Do you know why I lost it?'

She nodded. 'You were worried about me?'

'That too. But mainly because I've just discovered if I lose you I lose everything.'

He could see she didn't know how to answer that. All he could hope for was that when she did figure it out he'd like the answer.

Finally she did. 'I didn't want you to meet Mick in case I lost you.'

Now, that was good to hear. She did care and she squeezed his hand and turned towards him. A fresh, beautiful, Christmas Eve morning face with far less shadows than it had had a few minutes ago. 'Thank you for understanding, Simon. It's just that he can be very intimidating.'

'So can you.'

She shook her head. 'You're not intimidated by me.'

He had to laugh at that. He who had a burning question he couldn't ask.

'Tara.'

'Yes, Simon?'

'Do you love me?'

She looked away. Then back at him and her face seemed to glow. Even he could see that. His heart leapt. 'I might.'

She was so brave. Braver than him. Thank the stars for that. Time for him to be brave. 'Will you kiss me?' He puckered his lips. She looked at him like he was mad.

'No.'

'Please.'

She leaned over and did a reasonable job considering they were out in the street.

Fearless woman. Yep, there was love in that. He could feel his heart lift and swell and he just wanted to crush her to him. Finally he said it. 'Tara. I absolutely, one hundred percent, irrevocably love you.'

She blinked and chewed those gorgeous lips, and slowly an incredulous and painfully disbelieving smile grew on her beautiful mouth.

He didn't stop while he was ahead. 'And I want to marry you. As quickly as I can because you've spent too much of your life alone and, despite all my dozens of relatives, I've been alone too.'

She nodded. Quite vigorously. Apparently dumbstruck but he could work with that.

'But I need to marry you mostly because I love you, you crazy, adventurous woman.'

She swallowed and it must have helped because finally she said the words he wanted to hear.

'And I love you too, you too-sane, too-careful, too-bossy and will-learn-to-be-adventurous, man.'

She leaned over and kissed him again but this time he took over. Kissed her so thoroughly they forgot where they were until Maeve called from the veranda, 'Hey, you two. Come inside and do that.'

They broke apart and Simon was glad it was still too early for the neighbours to be around.

Tara grinned as Maeve turned and went back into the house. Asked thoughtfully, 'Just how many relatives have you got?'

'We have two sets. Which, now that I come to think of it, is perfectly designed for us.'

She wasn't really taking this in. She was gazing more at the love that was dusting her as it radiated from Simon. The way he looked at her, held her hand as if it was the most precious hand in the world. Hers?

She let the words resonate. 'Perfectly designed? How so?'

His eyes met hers with an exuberance she couldn't help smiling at. 'We have our Lyrebird Lake family, your new mama, Mia...' he grinned at that '...and Angus as dad. He's a very cool dad to come on late in life, let me reassure you there.'

Tara knew that but she loved the way Simon was

painting the picture. His pleasure at this the most precious gift he could share with her, his family, and her heart felt like it was opening like a flower starved of sunlight. One petal at a time.

'You'll have a new grandmother in Louisa, who will be over the moon. And will sew beautiful blankets for our children.' This was said smugly.

Louisa would be her grandmother. A huge lump rose into her throat with that incredible thought.

But Simon had only started as he kept adding depth to the picture. 'And two new little sisters in Layla and Amber, who I hope you will consider as bridesmaids. They look very pretty all dressed up. And Maeve will want to be maid of honour.'

She hadn't even thought about a wedding but suddenly she realised she would have one of those too. And sisters-in-law of her own.

So much to take in, to get used to, to be nervous about even.

But while the joy of a family would be hers, it was nothing compared to the thought of waking up beside Simon in the morning, every morning, and going to bed at night together for the rest of their lives. Spending their lives together. Everything was a wonderful, amazing Christmas tree of bonuses on top of everything. And Simon was her shining, love-filled star.

But he hadn't finished. 'And for your other family, we'll met the sisters and then we'll fly to America. See my dad and mum—it might take a while, but you'll grow to love her. Totally different from Mia, and she has fabulous taste because she thinks the sun shines out of me.'

He looked quite satisfied at that and she laughed. 'Imagine that. I think you're going to be quite a needy husband.'

His eyes darkened. 'I love the thought of being your husband. And I am needy. I need you because I've finally found what's been missing in my life. You're my heart, my love, my future. I look at you and feel the smile shine inside me like Louisa's blue star.'

'I'm your blue star.' He could see she liked that. Good.

'Shining at me as you save me. I love you, Tara.'

Tara could feel tears prickle and swallowed them back. The thought floated across her mind that Simon wouldn't mind her tears, she didn't have to hold back anything, or hide anything, or wait for anything. Simon knew all about her, warts and all, the only person who really did, and he was here and still loved her, and maybe everything that had gone before had been preparing her for this moment.

'I know you said you didn't expect evermore. But I wish you would. Stay with me for ever.'

Yes, please. 'And beyond.' They, she and Simon, were the future. She could see it and it was magic.

'And we are having a wedding cake with candles.'

She blinked and looked back at him. 'What? You can't have candles on a wedding cake.'

He lifted his chin and she recognised the tiny streak of stubbornness that stopped him from being perfect. Thank goodness he wasn't perfect. 'It's our cake. We can have what we want. And on our anniversary every year we'll have a cake with candles, and including your birthday, when you will definitely have candles, in twenty years' time you'll have blown out the same number of candles as everyone else in your life.'

'You're crazy.'

'About you.'

'And I am crazy about you, Simon Campbell.'

'Mrs Campbell.'

'Not yet.'

And suddenly he was serious. Intent. 'I love you, Tara. I'm not blind. I know we'll have our disagreements but I love the woman inside you. The survivor. The nurturer who has never had a chance to share that gift of nurturing. Share it with me, with the children I can't wait to have with you. We're going to have so much fun with our children.'

He was serious again. 'I can't wait to buy the toys you never had.' She could feel her frown but he'd known it was coming. 'Before you fire up, it's not pity, it's love. I can't wait to play the games you never played—with you, when we play with our children. And I know I'm going to love you more every single day. In fact, even thinking about this is driving me crazy. This has to happen as quickly as I can arrange it.'

She laughed. 'We have to finish Christmas first.'

'Yes, we'll have Christmas, our first Christmas together. And Maeve will have her baby. But inside, when all the revelry is around us, I'll know that you are my future. And ahead is a whole life of joy and adventure with you.'

He took her hand and drew her to her feet. 'Thank you, Tara.' He stroked her face and his eyes were solemn as he stared down into her face. 'My Christmas is here because you have given me your love and that is the greatest gift I could ever wish for.'

* * * * *

THE MIDWIFE'S
CHRISTMAS
MIRACLE

JENNIFER TAYLOR

For my granddaughter, Isobel.
My little ray of sunshine.

Jennifer Taylor lives in the north-west of England, in a small village surrounded by some really beautiful countryside. She has written for several different Mills & Boon series in the past, but it wasn't until she read her first Medical Romance that she truly found her niche. She was so captivated by these heart-warming stories that she set out to write them herself! When she's not writing, or doing research for her latest book, Jennifer's hobbies include reading, gardening, travel, and chatting to friends both on and off-line. She is always delighted to hear from readers, so do visit her website at www.jennifer-taylor.com

CHAPTER ONE

'AND last but definitely not least, this is Max Curtis, our acting consultant. Max, this is Lucy Harris, the new midwife who started today.'

'Nice to meet you, Lucy.'

'You too, Dr…er…er…' Lucy flushed when she realised that she hadn't caught his surname. It was hard to disguise her embarrassment when the dark-haired man seated behind the desk laughed.

'It's Curtis, although most people round here call me Max.' He smiled up at her. 'I'm not picky, mind. "Hey *you*" will get my attention fast enough.'

'That's good to know.' Lucy smiled back, relieved by the easy way he had accepted her gaffe. Obviously, Max Curtis wasn't the type of person who took himself too seriously, unlike some of the consultants she had worked with. 'Although I promise that I won't forget your name from now on. I won't dare!'

He chuckled softly, his dark brown eyes creasing at the corners. 'Don't worry about it. The first day in a new job is always a nightmare. There's so much to take in that you don't know if you're on your head or your heels most of the time.'

'That's true,' Lucy agreed. 'I just hope everyone

will be as understanding as you when I get their names muddled up!'

'They will be,' he assured her then reached for the phone when it started to ring. 'Maternity. Max Curtis speaking.'

Lucy sighed as she moved away from the desk, hoping that would be the end of the introductory tour. She honestly didn't think that she could cope with having to remember anyone else. Joanna, the young trainee midwife who had been delegated to show her around, grinned at her.

'That's it. You've met everyone now, apart from the staff who are working tonight and Anna Kearney, our consultant. She's on maternity leave at the moment, so you have that pleasure to come.'

'At least that's one less name to forget,' Lucy declared, rolling her eyes.

'As Max said, nobody will worry about it,' Joanna assured her. She led the way along the corridor, pausing outside the door to one of the delivery suites. There were four suites in total and Lucy knew that every one was currently occupied. Although the maternity unit at Dalverston General was smaller than the one she had worked on in Manchester, she had a feeling that it wasn't going to be any less busy because of that.

'Margaret's going off duty soon and Amanda wants you to take over from her,' Joanna explained, passing on the instructions the senior midwife had given her. 'I've got to help sort out the breakfasts now so I'll have to leave you here. Is that OK?'

'Fine,' Lucy assured her. She smoothed down her brand-new uniform top as Joanna hurried away then tapped on the door and went in, smiling at the middle-aged woman standing beside the bed. 'I believe I'm taking over from you.'

'That's right.' Margaret returned her smile. 'We were hoping that Sophie's baby would arrive while I was still on duty but he's proving to be a tad reluctant to make his appearance in the world.'

'Obviously a determined little chap who knows his own mind,' Lucy said lightly. She went over to the bed and introduced herself to the young mother-to-be. 'Hello, Sophie, my name is Lucy Harris and I've just started working here today. I'll be looking after you when Margaret goes home.'

'You are a proper midwife, though?' Sophie said anxiously. 'You're not just a trainee?'

'No. I've been a midwife for four years and I've delivered lots of babies during that time,' Lucy explained. It wasn't ideal to have to hand over a patient in the middle of a delivery and she was keen to allay the girl's fears. 'I worked at a hospital in Manchester before I came here.'

'Oh, I see. Well, that's all right, I suppose.'

Sophie still sounded a little dubious but Lucy understood. The relationship between a mother and her midwife was a delicate one and needed to be based on trust if it was to be successful. She patted Sophie's hand. 'Everything is going to be fine, Sophie, believe me. Now, if you don't mind, I'd like Margaret to update me as to what progress you've made.'

Sophie closed her eyes as Lucy moved away from the bed. She looked both exhausted and extremely anxious as she settled back against the pillows. Lucy frowned as she studied the girl's strained face.

'When was she admitted?'

'Just before eight p.m. last night,' Margaret replied. 'Her contractions were quite strong, so I was hopeful it would be a fairly speedy delivery even though it's her first baby. Unfortunately, everything started to slow down a couple of hours later and now we've come to a complete standstill.'

'How's the baby doing?' Lucy queried.

'Fine. Heartbeat is strong and there's no signs of distress. It's just going to be one of those stop-go deliveries from the look of it, which is a pity because I was hoping to get it over as quickly as possible.' Margaret must have seen the question in Lucy's eyes and lowered her voice. 'Sophie's not got anyone with her, you see. From what I can gather, the baby's father took off a couple of months ago and she's not seen him since.'

'What about family or friends?' Lucy asked sympathetically.

'She's never mentioned her family so I've no idea what the situation is there. As for friends, well, she hasn't lived in Dalverston all that long. Apparently, the baby's father got a job at the industrial park and that's why they moved here.' Margaret sighed. 'I feel really sorry for her because she's been very much on her own since he disappeared off the scene.'

'What a terrible shame.'

Lucy's heart went out to the girl, although she couldn't help thinking that even if Sophie had had friends and family to support her, it might not have helped. As she knew to her cost, sometimes it was the people you were closest to who let you down most of all.

The thought sent a shaft of pain surging through her but she forced it down. She refused to dwell on the past when she had moved to Dalverston to escape it.

She read through the notes Margaret had made then checked Sophie's pulse and BP, the baby's heartbeat, all the routine tasks that were so essential to the eventual outcome. She had just finished when the door opened and Max Curtis appeared.

'Hi! I thought I'd check to see what progress we're making,' he said as he came over to the bed.

Lucy stepped aside to give him room, somewhat surprised to discover how tall he was. He had been sitting down when they had been introduced so she'd had no idea that he must be at least six feet tall with a leanly muscular physique under a pair of well-cut dark grey trousers and a paler grey shirt. All of a sudden she felt unusually conscious of her own lack of inches. At a mere five feet two, she could best be described as petite, although a lushly feminine figure did make up for what she lacked in height.

'Everything seems to have come to a dead stop, Dr Curtis,' Sophie said forlornly. 'I don't understand why it's happened.'

'It just does sometimes, Sophie,' he assured her. 'It's all systems go and then everything suddenly tails off. Are you still having contractions?'

'No. I've not had one for ages now.'

'Let me take a look and then we'll decide what we're going to do.'

He gently examined her, explaining what he was doing as he checked the position of the baby and how far her cervix had dilated. Lucy appreciated the fact that he didn't rush. He appeared to have all the time in the world and she knew that it would reassure Sophie more than anything else would do. She was pleased to see that the girl looked far less anxious by the time he finished and explained that he was going to give her something to help restart her contractions.

He wrote out an instruction for an intravenous infusion of synthetic oxytocin to be administered. This would augment the naturally occurring oxytocin that caused the muscles in the uterus to contract. He handed it to Lucy after she told him that Margaret was going off duty. 'I'll check back with you later to see what progress we're making. In the meantime, get the switchboard to page me if you have any concerns.'

'I shall,' Lucy concurred.

'Hopefully, this should get things back on track,' he added, slipping his pen back into his pocket. 'We'll give nature a bit of a boost and hope it'll do its stuff.'

'Always the best solution,' she agreed. She had never been an advocate of rushing in unnecessarily and it was good to know that they were in accord in that respect.

'It seems we're in agreement, then.' Max smiled at her then headed towards the door. 'Right, now I'm off to make myself a large cup of black coffee. I need a *serious* injection of caffeine if I'm to get through the rest of the day.'

'That sounds like desperation talking,' Lucy replied lightly.

'Oh, it is, believe me. Given half the chance, I would curl up in this doorway and fall fast asleep!'

He laughed but Lucy could tell that he was only partly joking. She frowned as she took stock of the lines etched either side of his mouth, the weariness in his dark brown eyes, and realised all of a sudden how exhausted he looked.

'Didn't you get much sleep last night?'

'I didn't get any. I was about to get into bed when

I was called back here to see a patient. Eclampsia,' he added succinctly.

'Oh, I see.' Lucy nodded, understanding why he had needed to rush back into work. Eclampsia was a highly dangerous condition for both a mother and her child. It could lead to convulsions and even coma and death if not treated in time. Normally, the condition was picked up as pre-eclampsia during routine antenatal screening. The combination of high blood pressure, protein in the urine and oedema—an accumulation of fluid in the tissues—were all indications of it. She was surprised that alarm bells hadn't started ringing earlier, in fact.

'Was there no sign beforehand that the mother was at risk?' she asked curiously.

'None at all. Mind you, the fact that she missed her last couple of antenatal appointments didn't help.' Max sighed. 'When I asked her why she hadn't been to the clinic, she said that she hadn't had the time. Apparently, she had a hair appointment on the first occasion and needed to get her nails done the next time.'

'Unbelievable!' Lucy exclaimed.

'Yep. I think that just about sums it up. Fortunately, her husband phoned us when she started complaining that she had a headache and that her vision was blurred. He was told to bring her straight in so she was here when she had a convulsion. We administered anti-convulsant drugs and I delivered the baby by Caesarean section. He's in the special care baby unit, but I'm pretty sure he'll be fine. Mum will need monitoring for the next few weeks but she should be all right too.' He shrugged. 'It was worth a sleepless night, all things considered.'

He sketched her a wave and left, his long legs striding along the corridor. Lucy watched him for a moment then closed the door and went to set up the drip. Funnily enough she had enjoyed talking to him. Max Curtis had a relaxed and friendly manner that had put her at her ease, made her feel more positive about the changes she had made to her life recently. Hopefully, moving to Dalverston had been the right thing to do.

She sighed as the doubts suddenly surfaced again. It had been hard to leave her last job when she had been so happy there, harder still to leave all her friends and family behind, but she'd had no choice. Although her parents had tried to persuade her not to go, Lucy knew how difficult it would have been for them if she'd stayed. After all, it wasn't *their* fault that her cousin and her ex-fiancé had had an affair.

Lucy took a deep breath and quelled the moment of panic. She had made her decision and even if it didn't work out as well as she hoped it would, at least it would give her a breathing space, time to put things into perspective. She simply had to remember how much worse it would have been if she'd found out about Richard and Amy *after* the wedding had taken place.

Max made his way to the staffroom then realised that he didn't even have the energy to make himself a cup of coffee. Veering away from the door, he headed for the lift. The cafeteria should be open soon and the thought of a double espresso with his name on it was too tempting to resist.

The staff were just opening up when he arrived, so he gave them his order and sat down, feeling weariness washing over him. The long night had taken its toll, especially as it had been the second night in a row that he'd been called in. With Anna on maternity leave, he had been picking up more than his share of extra hours recently. It wasn't a new occurrence, by any means. Working long and unsocial hours was par for the course in medicine. At one point, he'd been only too glad to work any time he was needed, too. It had been far less stressful dealing with his patients' problems than what had been happening in his marriage.

Max frowned. It was rare that he thought about the past and it surprised him that he should do so now. He had been divorced for three years and he had closed the door on that episode in his life. OK, so he was willing to admit that it had had a knock-on effect, in that he avoided commitment these days, but to his mind that was common sense. Once bitten, twice shy seemed a sensible maxim to live by and he wasn't going to put himself through all that heartache again.

His thoughts moved away from the less than appealing subject of his failed marriage and on to the far more interesting topic of their new midwife. Lucy Harris appeared both highly competent and extremely capable, and he was pleased that their views were in accord. Some of the older midwives were a little entrenched in their ways and it would be good to have a soul-mate on the unit.

The fact that she was also extremely pretty with those huge blue eyes and those shiny auburn curls tumbling around her cheeks was another point in her favour. Although Max shied away from commitment, he had a normal healthy interest in the opposite sex and Lucy Harris was a very attractive member of it. All of sudden his tiredness lifted and he grinned. Working with the lovely Lucy could turn out to be a real tonic.

CHAPTER TWO

SOPHIE JONES's baby finally made his appearance in the middle of the afternoon. Amanda, the senior midwife, helped Lucy deliver him. Lucy guessed that Amanda was keen to put her through her paces, but tried not to let it worry her. By the time Sophie and baby Alfie were transferred to a ward, she was confident that Amanda wouldn't have any more concerns about her, and it was reassuring to know that at least one very important aspect of her life hadn't changed.

Lucy fetched her coat at the end of her shift and left. It had started raining at lunchtime and the gutters were brimming over with water as she made her way to the bus stop. She huddled against the wall when a car sped past, sending a wave of water across the pavement, but by the time she reached the bus stop, her shoes and trousers were soaked through. She joined the queue, hoping that she wouldn't have to wait too long. However, half an hour later she was still there when a car drew up and Max Curtis poked his head out of the window.

'Do you want a lift?' He glanced at her sodden trousers and grimaced. 'You're going to catch your death if you stand there much longer. Hop in.'

Lucy hesitated, not sure that accepting a lift would

be the right thing to do. It didn't seem fair to expect him to drive her home after the long day he'd had. However, the thought of getting out of the rain was too tempting to resist. She slid into the passenger seat and slammed the door.

'Thanks. It's really good of you,' she said gratefully. 'I don't know what happened to the bus. I've been waiting ages and there's been no sign of it.'

'Probably two will turn up together,' he said lightly, putting the car into gear. 'So how was your first day then? Not too scary, I hope.'

'No, it was fine,' Lucy assured him. 'Everyone was really helpful, which makes a huge difference when you're starting a new job.'

'It's a good team,' he assured her, slowing as they came to a set of traffic lights on red. 'Most of them have worked on the unit for a while, so that helps, of course.'

'It must do,' Lucy agreed, turning to look at him. Although he wasn't classically handsome, he was certainly attractive, she decided. The combination of those highly masculine features—a strong jaw, straight nose and perfectly sculpted lips—was very appealing. Rumpled dark brown hair falling across his forehead lent him a rakish air that many women would find pleasing too. She found it strangely engaging which surprised her, given what had happened recently.

'I'm looking forward to being part of a settled team,' she said, hurriedly squashing that thought. She certainly wasn't in the market for another relationship. The fact that her ex-fiancé had betrayed her had destroyed her faith in men. Love, marriage and, most important of all, a family had always been her dream but not any more. She wouldn't give any man that much power over her again. 'The turnover of staff at my last place was a nightmare. You no sooner got used to working with someone before they left.'

'It's always more of a problem in the city. Staff tend to move around more than they do in rural areas. You were at the Royal, weren't you?' he asked, glancing at her.

'That's right. I was there for almost four years. It was really busy, but I enjoyed working there.'

'So what brought you to Dalverston?' he asked, returning his attention to the road as the lights changed. 'Has your family relocated to this part of the world?'

'No, only me.'

'Really?' He shot her a look and she saw the surprise on his face. 'It takes guts to up sticks and leave everything behind like that.'

'I don't know about that. It just felt like the right thing to do,' she hedged, not wanting to go into detail about the reasons for her decision. She sighed softly. Maybe it was silly to feel embarrassed, but what had happened had dented her confidence. She no longer saw herself as the person she had always been, but as a reject, second best. For some reason she hated to think that Max might see her like that too.

'I realised that I was in a bit of a rut and needed a complete change of scene,' she explained, wondering why it mattered what he thought. She barely knew him, so his opinion wasn't going to make much difference to her. 'When I saw the advert for Dalverston, I decided to apply for the post.'

'And got it.' He gave her a quick smile but Lucy could tell that he'd guessed there was more to the story than she'd admitted. 'Well, the Royal's loss is our gain is all I can say.'

He didn't press her and she was glad about that. Maybe it would get easier with time but at the moment it was still too painful to talk about what had happened. They drove into the town centre and she gave him directions to where she lived from there.

Finding somewhere suitable had been harder than she'd expected. Although rent in Dalverston was less expensive than it was in Manchester, it was still a big chunk out of her monthly salary. She and Richard had signed a lease on their flat and there were still several months left to run. Richard had refused to pay his share of the rent after he'd moved out, and unwilling to make the situation even more unpleasant than it already was, Lucy hadn't tried to persuade him. Instead, she'd been paying it all and had needed to trim her costs accordingly. She'd finally settled on a flat in one of the old terraced houses close to the high street. It wasn't the best location but it would do for now. She would find somewhere better when she could afford it.

Max drew up outside. 'Here you are then. Home sweet home.' He glanced up at the building and frowned. 'It looks a bit grim. Couldn't you find anywhere better than this?'

'It's fine, really.' Lucy reached for the door handle, not wanting to explain why her options had been so limited. 'Thanks again for the lift. I only hope I haven't taken you too far out of your way.'

'Not at all. In fact, it isn't all that far from where I live, funnily enough. I just didn't recognise the name of the road. I don't think I've been down here before.'

'You've not missed much,' Lucy assured him wryly, opening the car door. 'I'll see you tomorrow, I expect.'

'You will.'

He waited while she unlocked the front door then drove away, but it was a moment before she went inside. As she watched the car's taillights disappear around a bend, Lucy felt a wave of loneliness wash over her. All of a sudden the evening stretched before her, all those empty hours to fill. She couldn't help thinking about how her life had used to be, when she had come home from work and Richard had been there.

She sighed because she'd honestly believed they'd been happy. Even when Richard had started making excuses and going out at night, she hadn't suspected a thing. It was only when Amy, stricken with guilt, had confessed that Lucy had discovered what had been going on. The fact that she'd felt like such a fool had made it all the more painful.

She took a deep breath and closed the door. It was all in the past now and she had moved on. Even though she didn't feel like the same person, she would survive and build a new life for herself. Just for a moment a picture of Max Curtis appeared in her mind's eye before she dismissed it. Max might play a small role in her life but no man was going to take centre stage ever again.

Max drove home thinking about what Lucy had told him or, rather, what she hadn't said. He'd seen the sadness in her eyes and suspected there was more to her decision to relocate than she had admitted. Had she broken up with her partner, perhaps? If that was the case, then it must have been a very painful split if she'd felt the need to leave everything behind.

He sighed as he turned into the car park of the modern apartment block where he lived. He knew only too well how it felt to want to escape. He'd done that himself, hadn't he? After his marriage had ended, he'd left London and come north, seeking a fresh start. Although he couldn't change the fact that his life was never going to turn out how he'd expected it would, it had helped to meet new people and form new friendships.

Nowadays he was far more philosophical. So what if he could never father a child? It was a blow, yes, but he had come to terms with the idea now and accepted it. At least he knew the truth so there was no danger of him ruining any other woman's life.

Marriage was off the agenda for obvious reasons and any relationships he had were strictly for fun. Maybe it wasn't the life he'd once envisaged for himself, but he couldn't complain. He had a job he loved, good friends and enough money to buy whatever he wanted. In fact, he couldn't understand why he was even thinking about it. Had Lucy Harris been the trigger? But why? What was it about her that made him suddenly wish he could change things?

He had no idea but it was something he needed to bear in mind. Lovely though Lucy was, he didn't intend to get his fingers burned a second time.

Lucy was rostered to work at the antenatal clinic the following morning. She went straight there after she'd signed in and the first person she saw was Max. He was chatting to the receptionist, laughing at something the girl was saying. He looked so relaxed that she felt her spirits immediately lift. It had been a long night and she'd had difficulty sleeping, but there was something about Max that made her feel much more positive about life.

He glanced round when he heard her footsteps and grinned at her. 'Ahah! I see you've drawn the short straw, Lucy. We'll be working together this morning. Is that OK with you?'

'Fine.' She returned his smile, wondering why he had this effect on her. It wasn't anything he said, more a feeling he exuded, and it was very welcome too. 'I've no problem with that.'

'Good.' He gave her a warm smile as he led the way to the consulting room and sat down at the desk while he brought up the list of appointments on the computer. 'It's rather a mixed bag this morning. Normally, we try to split the list so that one of us sees the mums who are here for their first visits while the other deals with the rest. Unfortunately, we're short-staffed today because Diane is off sick. It means you won't have as much time with the new mums as you'd probably like.'

'I'll make up for it at a later date. Most women are a little anxious when they come for their first visit to the clinic and they find it difficult to take everything in. It's usually better to talk to them and discuss their options at their second or third appointment, I find.'

'That's great. I'm glad it isn't going to cause you a problem.' He turned his attention back to the screen, scrolling through the list of names until he came to the one he wanted. 'This is a case I'd like you to be involved in. Mum's name is Helen Roberts. It's her first baby and she had pre-existing diabetes mellitus when she got pregnant.'

'How has she been?' Lucy asked, walking around the desk. She bent down so she could see the screen, feeling her nostrils tingle as she inhaled the citrus-fresh tang of the shampoo he'd used. She couldn't help comparing it to the rather cloying scent of the one Richard had preferred.

'Extremely well so far. We run a pre-pregnancy clinic at Dalverston for women with established diabetes. It's a joint venture between us and the diabetes care team and our main aim is to ensure that blood glucose levels are under control before and at the time of conception.'

'There's a slightly increased risk of the baby being malformed if the blood glucose level isn't right, isn't there?' Lucy questioned, straightening up. She moved back to the other side of the desk, unsure why it troubled her to make the comparison. What difference did it make if she preferred the smell of Max's shampoo?

'There is, which is why a woman with diabetes should seek advice *before* she gets pregnant. As I expect you know, there are increased risks for the mother as well as for the baby. Retinopathy can be a problem for anyone who has diabetes, as can high blood pressure, but there's more chance of them becoming an issue when a woman is pregnant. And of course there's a greater risk of mum suffering from pre-eclampsia, too.'

'It must be daunting for a woman to be faced with all that,' Lucy said quickly, determined to nip such foolishness in the bud by focusing on their patient.

Max shrugged. 'It must be. Thankfully, Helen is a very level-headed sort of person. She's a farmer's wife and has a very practical approach to life. She understood the risks from the outset and has coped extremely well. We've been working closely with the diabetes care team and she's undergone all the recommended tests and assessments.'

'How about the baby?' Lucy asked. 'Is it much larger than normal?'

'Slightly larger than would be expected at this stage but not worryingly so.'

'Controlling the blood glucose level is key, isn't it? If the level isn't strictly controlled, there may be an increase in the amount of glucose that reaches the baby so that it grows faster than normal.'

'Either that or its growth may be stunted,' Max explained. 'I've seen several cases like that and there were complications each time following the births.'

'How many weeks is she?' Lucy asked.

'Thirty-two,' he replied promptly, not needing to refer to his notes.

It was clear from that how interested he was in the case and she couldn't help admiring the fact that it was obviously more than just a job to him. She'd noticed that yesterday, too, when he'd examined Sophie. His patience and refusal to rush were indications of a genuine concern for his patients. She'd worked with a lot of doctors and, sadly, some had treated the mums-to-be in a very cavalier fashion. It was good to know that Max wasn't of that ilk.

'As you know, it's even more important to control blood glucose levels towards the end of the pregnancy.' He picked up a slip of paper and handed it to her. 'Helen has been attending the diabetes clinic on a weekly basis recently. She was there yesterday and the registrar was concerned because her glucose levels have started fluctuating. That's why we're seeing her today. We may need to arrange for her to have another ultrasound to check the amniotic fluid volume as well as the baby's growth.'

Lucy quickly read the note. She sighed as she handed it back to him. 'What a shame that it should happen now after she's been doing so well.'

'Isn't it?' He grimaced. 'Knowing Helen, she will blame herself for this and that's where you can help, Lucy. I want you to make her understand that it isn't anything she's done wrong. The last thing we want is her getting stressed. It won't help her or the baby.'

'Of course. I'll do anything I can,' she assured him.

'Thanks.'

He gave her a quick smile and she felt a trickle of warmth flow through her when she saw the approval it held. Once again, she felt her spirits lift and it was such an odd feeling when her mood had been so downbeat recently. She wasn't sure why Max had this effect on her and didn't have a chance to work it out as he continued.

'Right, now that's sorted out we'd better make a start or we'll still be here at midnight.'

Lucy went to the door and called in their first patient. She'd always enjoyed meeting the mums and being involved in their care and she realised that she was looking forward to it more than ever that day. Knowing that she was part of a team that really cared about these women and their babies made the job so worthwhile.

All of a sudden she was glad that she had made the move to Dalverston, and not just because she'd escaped from a difficult situation either. She would learn a lot from working here, learn a lot from working with Max, too. For the first time in ages, it felt as though she had something to look forward to.

CHAPTER THREE

'LUCY will have a word with you on your next visit, Rachel. You'll be able to decide what you want to do then. Isn't that right, Lucy?'

Max sat back in his seat while Lucy took over. They made a good team, he thought, listening as she explained how they would work out a birth plan the next time Rachel came to the clinic, before she escorted her out to Reception. Although her predecessor had been an excellent midwife, she'd been a little brusque at times. He knew that some of the younger women in particular had found her intimidating, but that definitely wasn't the case with Lucy. She had a gently reassuring manner that put even the most nervous mums at their ease. He couldn't remember when he'd last enjoyed a clinic so much, in fact.

He was in the process of absorbing that thought when she came back into the room. His brows lifted when he saw the frown on her face. 'Is something wrong?'

'I'm not sure. Apparently, Helen Roberts hasn't turned up. From what you told me, it seems rather strange that she would miss an appointment, doesn't it?'

'It's not like Helen,' he agreed. He brought up Helen's file on the computer and checked her phone number. 'I'll give her a call and see what's happened to her.'

He picked up the phone then stopped when his pager suddenly bleeped. It was the code for the maternity unit, so he dialled their number first. 'It's Max. You paged me.' His heart sank when Amanda informed him that Helen Roberts had just been admitted. 'I'll be right there.'

'Problems?' Lucy asked as he hastily stood up.

'Helen Roberts has been rushed in by ambulance. It appears she collapsed on the bus on her way here.'

'That explains why she didn't keep her appointment!' Lucy exclaimed. 'Are you going up to Maternity to see her?'

'Yes.' Max picked up his jacket off the back of the chair and shrugged it on. 'The diabetes care team will need to know what's happened. Can you give them a call for me, please? I've been liaising with Adam Sanders, their registrar, so can you see if he's available? I'd really like his input.'

'Of course.'

Lucy reached for the receiver at the same moment as he went to pass it to her and he felt a ripple of awareness shoot through him when their hands brushed, and quickly drew back. He cleared his throat, unsure why it had happened.

'I'll leave you to sort it out, then. Can you phone Amanda and let her know if Adam can make it? He knows Helen and it will be easier if he reviews the case rather than bring someone else up to speed.'

'Will do.'

'Thanks.' Max turned away, wondering if he'd imagined the faintly breathy note in her voice. Had that brief moment of contact affected her as much as it had affected him?

He sighed as he made his way to the lift because it was stupid to think that Lucy had even noticed what had happened. It had been the briefest touch, after all, and he had no idea why he was making such a big deal of it. It certainly wasn't like him to behave this way.

Although he appreciated the power of sexual attraction, these days sex was merely a means to satisfy a need. There was never an emotional connection between him and the women he slept with. It had never worried him before because that was exactly what he had wanted: to remain detached. However, all of a sudden he found himself wishing for more. How good it must feel to make love to a woman and know that he was the centre of her universe.

Lucy made arrangements for the diabetes registrar to visit the maternity unit then phoned Amanda to let her know he was on his way. She offered to go back and help, but Amanda assured her they could manage and told her to go for lunch. They had a mum booked in to be induced that afternoon and she needed Lucy there.

Lucy tidied up then made her way to the staff canteen. The place was packed when she arrived but she spotted Joanna sitting at a table in the corner with a couple of her friends. Once she had paid for her lunch, she went to join them.

'Do you mind if I sit here?'

'Of course not!' Joanna grinned at her. 'So how did you get on at clinic? I bet it was busy with Diane being off sick.'

'It was.' Lucy sat down and started to peel the plastic film off her tuna mayo sandwich. 'Max was brilliant, though. Even though the list was horrendous he made everyone feel as though he had all the time in the world for them.'

'Uh-oh! It sounds as though we've added another member to the Max Curtis fan club,' Joanna declared, laughing.

'Of course not!' Lucy blushed. She hadn't realised that she'd sounded quite so enthusiastic and hurried to explain. 'It's just nice to work with someone who obviously cares so much about his patients.'

'Ah, so that's it, is it? You admire Max's qualities as a doctor, nothing else?'

'Of course not,' Lucy stated firmly, trying to ignore the niggling little voice that was whispering it wasn't true. Had she imagined that brief moment of awareness that had passed between them? she wondered uneasily. It had been over and done with in a nanosecond so it was hard to believe that it hadn't been her imagination playing tricks.

'I'm not interested in Max, if that's what you think,' she reiterated, as much for her own benefit as anyone else's. She must have sounded convincing because Joanna shrugged.

'Fair enough. It's probably a good thing, too. At least you won't end up disappointed.'

'What do you mean?' Lucy asked in surprise. 'Why should I be disappointed?'

'Oh, just that there's no point setting your sights on Max, is there, girls?' Joanna glanced at the other women who shook their heads. 'You see, Lucy, dishy though Max is, he has one major flaw—he doesn't do commitment. He's quite up-front about it, mind you, makes no bones about the fact that love and marriage aren't on his agenda, so that's something in his favour. A lot of men string a woman along but at least whoever Max goes out with knows the score.'

The conversation moved on to something else but Lucy found it hard to concentrate. What Joanna had told her simply didn't gel with what she had seen. Max didn't seem like the type of man who moved from woman to woman in pursuit of personal pleasure. He cared too much about people to enjoy that kind of life in her opinion, although maybe she wasn't the best person to judge. After what had happened with Richard, she couldn't claim to be an expert on men, could she?

A familiar ache filled her heart but for some reason it didn't seem as painful as it used to be. If she was honest, the thought of Max living the life of an eternal bachelor hurt far more. Maybe it was silly but she felt let down and it was worrying to know that she had made another mistake. From now on she must see Max for what he was: just another man who was out for all he could get.

'Thanks for coming.'

Max shook Adam Sanders's hand then went back into the side room. Helen Roberts had suffered a hypoglycaemic attack after her blood glucose levels had dropped too low. Although she was stable now, it was a blow after she had done so well. He could see the worry in her eyes when he went over to the bed.

'It was just a blip, Helen. You heard what Dr Sanders said, that you've been doing too much and need to rest more. So long as you follow his advice, there's no reason why it should happen again.'

'I was only trying to get everything ready for when the baby arrives,' Helen protested. 'Martin broke his leg last week. One of the bullocks barged into him when he went to feed them, so he's out of action at the moment. I thought I'd finish setting up the nursery—put up the cot and unpack all the baby clothes, things like that. I wasn't doing anything more than any other mum would do.'

'But you aren't just any other mum,' Max reminded her gently. 'All that extra work knocked your glucose levels out of kilter. Add to that the growing demands of the baby, combined with the tendency for insulin resistance to increase during pregnancy and you have a recipe for disaster.'

'I know you're right, Dr Curtis, but it's so hard. I want to do what other women do and get ready for when my baby arrives.' Tears began to trickle down her cheeks and he patted her hand comfortingly.

'I understand that, Helen. But you've got this far and it seems silly to take any risks. Why not let your husband do the unpacking? He's probably sick of being laid up with nothing to do and will enjoy it.'

'Heaven knows what state the place will be in after he's finished!' Helen declared. 'Martin isn't exactly the tidiest of men.'

'I'm sure he'll make a special effort if you ask him.'

'You're right. He will.' Helen wiped her eyes and smiled. 'He's just so thrilled about this baby. We thought we might not be able to have a family because of my diabetes, you see, so it's like a dream come true.'

'It must be.'

Max dredged up a smile but the comment had struck a chord. He had always loved children and had assumed that he would have some of his own one day. Both his brothers had kids and he'd had no reason to think that he would be any different to them. Finding out that the chances of him ever fathering a child were virtually nil had rocked his whole world. Although he'd thought he had accepted it, he suddenly found himself thinking how marvellous it would be if a miracle happened....

He cut off that thought. He wasn't going to put himself through all the heartache of wishing for the impossible to happen. 'I'd like to keep you in overnight, Helen. Dr Sanders wants to monitor your blood glucose levels for the next twenty-four hours and I'd feel happier if you were here while it's done.'

'I understand, Dr Curtis.' Helen sounded resigned. 'Best to be safe rather than sorry.'

'It's just a precaution,' he assured her. 'I'll pop back later to check on you. In the meantime, you're to lie there and rest.'

Max made his way to the desk. Amanda was talking to Lucy when he arrived and he smiled when they both looked up. 'Sorry to interrupt, but I wanted you to know that I'm keeping Helen Roberts in overnight. I know it means tying up the side room but I'd feel happier if she was here while everything settles down. One of the diabetes care team will be popping in at intervals to check her blood glucose levels.'

'That's fine,' Amanda assured him. 'In fact, it will be the perfect opportunity for Lucy to meet her. I know Helen was concerned when Maria left. She was worried in case her replacement didn't have any experience of diabetic pregnancies. You can set her mind at rest, can't you, Lucy?'

'Of course.'

'If there's anything you aren't sure about, I'd be happy

to run through it with you,' Max offered, but Lucy shook her head.

'That won't be necessary, thank you. I've worked with a number of women who had diabetes and I understand the problems they can face during the birth.'

Her tone was so cool that Max frowned. He had the distinct impression that he had upset her, although for the life of him he couldn't think what he'd done. When she excused herself, he went to follow her then stopped when Amanda asked him about the patient they were inducing that afternoon. By the time they had sorted everything out, Lucy had disappeared.

Max was sorely tempted to track her down but in the end he decided not to bother. What could he say to her, anyway? That he was sorry for committing some unknown misdemeanour?

He sighed as he headed to the canteen for a late lunch. Lucy Harris might be a very attractive woman, but that was as far as it went. He had worked out a life-plan for himself and he had no intention of ditching it just because he suddenly found himself harbouring all these crazy ideas.

Maybe Lucy was the type of woman who'd been *born* to have kids, but that had nothing to do with him. The truth was that he was no use to Lucy or any other woman in that respect.

Lucy spent a productive half-hour with Helen Roberts. They discussed Helen's birth plan and Lucy was pleased to see that although Helen hoped for a normal vaginal birth, she was realistic enough to know it might not be possible. By the time Helen's husband, Martin, arrived, she felt they had established a genuine rapport.

'You've been really great,' Helen enthused as she gathered up her notes. 'Maria was very nice but she could be a little intimidating at times, couldn't she, Martin?'

'She certainly put the wind up me,' Martin replied drolly. 'Put it this way, I wouldn't have crossed her!'

'So long as you're happy, that's the main thing,' Lucy said, not wanting to be drawn into a discussion about her predecessor. It would be highly unprofessional for one thing and very unfair when she had never met the woman. 'Now, don't forget that if you're at all worried then you can always phone me. If I'm tied up then leave a message and I'll call you back.'

'Thank you. I really appreciate that. You've been so kind, just like Dr Curtis has,' Helen declared. 'He's really lovely, isn't he? I can't believe that nobody has snapped him up but one of the other mums told me that he isn't married. Is he seeing anyone, do you know?'

'I've no idea.' Lucy summoned a smile, trying to ignore the hollow ache inside her. She wasn't sure why she found the idea of Max's playboy lifestyle so upsetting but she did. 'I've only been here for a couple of days so I haven't had time to get up to speed with the gossip.'

'Well, make sure you do.' Helen grinned at her. 'I don't know what your situation is, Lucy, but you and Dr Curtis would make a lovely couple, if you want my opinion.'

'Which she doesn't.' Martin shook his head when Lucy blushed. 'Now see what you've done, Helen. You've embarrassed her.'

'Rubbish!' Helen said stoutly. 'It was only a bit of fun. You're not embarrassed, are you, Lucy?'

'Of course not,' Lucy lied, wishing the floor would open up and swallow her. She said goodbye and left, but as she made her way to the office she couldn't help thinking about what Helen had said. If the circumstances had been different, would she have seen Max as a potential partner?

Her heart sank because she knew it was true. On the surface, at least, Max was just the kind of man she'd always found attractive. It wasn't just how he looked either. His relaxed and easygoing manner didn't detract from the fact that he was deeply committed to the welfare of his patients, and that was a definite turn-on. That he didn't pull rank and treated the nursing staff as equals was another point in his favour. It was his private life she had an issue with, and that really and truly wasn't any of her business.

Lucy took a deep breath. What Max did in his free time was up to him.

CHAPTER FOUR

THE week rolled to an end and Max had the weekend off for once. He spent it at his brother Simon's house in Leeds. With three boisterous children under the age of ten, it was non-stop chaos from morning till night, but he enjoyed every minute. Being part of a family was a joy, even though it did leave him feeling secretly downhearted about his own life. Although he had a great job and some wonderful friends, it wasn't the same. He couldn't help envying his brother his good fortune.

He drove back to Dalverston early on the Monday morning and went straight to work. When he arrived, everyone was gathered in the staffroom for the monthly team meeting so he poured himself a cup of coffee and went to join them. The meetings had been his idea. Although they were informal affairs, they gave the staff an opportunity to raise any concerns they had. He found it invaluable to be able to discuss any issues before they turned into major problems.

'Morning, everyone.' He took his seat and glanced around the room. Diane was back from sick leave, looking a little peaky, but obviously feeling better. 'Good to have you back,' he said before his gaze moved on. His heart squeezed in an extra beat when he spotted Lucy sitting in the corner. Although he had seen her only briefly in passing since she had refused his offer of help, he had found himself thinking about her frequently, especially over the weekend. As he'd played with his nieces and nephew, he had kept imagining how well she would have fitted in and it was worrying to know that he was thinking along those lines.

Since his divorce, he had kept his personal life in strictly defined compartments: one for his parents and brothers, and another for the women who made brief appearances on the scene. He had never, ever, mixed the two, yet for some reason he had found himself wishing that he could introduce Lucy to his family.

'Good morning,' he said with a smile that would hopefully disguise how alarmed he felt. What was it about her that made him want to break all his rules? He wished he knew because maybe then he would be able to do something about it.

'Good morning,' she replied politely.

Max frowned when he heard the cool note in her voice. Once again he was left with the impression that he was *persona non grata* and it was very strange. What had he done to offend her, he wondered, and how could he make amends? And why in heaven's name did it matter so much?

There was no time to dwell on it right then, however. By necessity the meetings needed to be brief and there was a lot to cover. They discussed various matters but the issue that concerned everyone most of all was the difficulty they were having obtaining supplies. Recent budget cuts meant that they no longer held as large a stock of basic items in the unit and several times they had run out.

Max promised to look into it and the meeting broke up. Although the delivery rooms were empty, a couple of mums were due to be discharged that day so there was a lot to do. He tagged on the end as everyone filed out of the room. Lucy was in front of him and it struck him that it would be the ideal opportunity to have a word with her. If he had upset her, it would be better to get the problem out into the open rather than have it niggling away in the background all the time.

He caught up with her outside the office. 'Can I have a word with you, Lucy?'

'Of course.'

She turned to face him and Max was aware of a definite coolness about the look she gave him. Bearing in mind how well they had got on in the clinic, it seemed very strange, and he didn't waste time beating about the bush.

'Have I done something to upset you?'

'Of course not,' she replied quickly, but he saw the colour that touched her cheeks and knew that she was fibbing.

'Are you sure?' He smiled, hoping she would confide in him if he kept things low key. 'Because I get the distinct impression that I'm in your bad books for some reason.'

'You're imagining it. Now, if that's all, I really do need to get on.'

'Of course. But if I have upset you, Lucy, I apologise. The last thing I want is for us to be falling out.'

'There's nothing to apologise for,' she said tersely, turning away.

Max sighed as he watched her hurry along the corridor. Despite her protestations, he knew there was something wrong and it was frustrating not to be able to do anything about it. Exasperated with himself for letting it bother him, he went into the office and phoned the purchasing manager, not pulling his punches as he told him what he thought about the new system. It was rare he ever spoke so sharply but it paid dividends that day. The man immediately agreed to increase their stock limits and even promised to have extra supplies delivered by lunchtime.

Max hung up, knowing that he should be pleased that the matter had been resolved so speedily. However, it was hard to feel any pleasure when there seemed to be a cloud hanging over him. Maybe it was silly, but he hated to think that Lucy was annoyed with him. For some reason her opinion mattered to him more than anyone else's had done in a very long time.

Lucy went straight to the ward after she left Max. Sophie and baby Alfie were being discharged that morning and she wanted to say goodbye to them. Alfie had developed a mild case of jaundice after his birth and that was why he had been kept in. Extra fluids and phototherapy had soon cleared it up and he was now well enough to go home.

She pushed open the door, doing her best to calm herself down, but she could feel her nerves humming with tension. She hadn't known what to say when Max had asked if he'd upset her. She had never considered herself to be an overly demonstrative sort of person, so the fact that he had picked up on her mood had stunned her. Richard certainly hadn't noticed if she'd been upset. He'd been oblivious to anything that hadn't directly affected him, in fact. She definitely couldn't imagine

Richard worrying in case he'd offended her, let alone apologising for it!

Lucy frowned. It wasn't the first time she had found Richard lacking, yet in the beginning he had appeared so perfect. He'd been handsome, charming, witty, attentive—everything she could have wished for. It was only after they had started living together that she'd discovered he could be incredibly selfish at times too, but she'd been so sure that he was the man she'd wanted to spend her life with that she had made excuses for him.

Was she doing the same thing again? she wondered suddenly. All week long she had struggled to reconcile the impression she had formed of Max as a caring, dedicated doctor with the playboy bachelor Joanna had described. The only explanation she had come up with was that something must have happened in his past to make him behave so differently in his private life. It would be even easier to see that as the explanation after what had happened just now, too. Max had sounded genuinely concerned in case he had upset her, but Lucy realised it would be foolish to take it at face value. It was probably all part of his act, a way to project the right image!

Pain lanced her heart as she made her way to Sophie's bed. Even though she knew how silly it was, she couldn't help feeling disappointed. It was an effort to smile at the girl but the last thing Lucy wanted was anyone guessing how she felt. 'I've just popped in to say goodbye. I bet you're looking forward to going home, aren't you?'

'I suppose so,' Sophie muttered.

Lucy frowned when she heard the despondent note in Sophie's voice. 'What's the matter?'

'I'm just worried in case I can't cope,' Sophie admitted. 'I don't know anything about babies and there's so much to learn.'

'You'll be fine,' Lucy said encouragingly. 'All the staff have said how brilliant you are with Alfie. And they don't say that about all our mums, believe me!'

'I hope they're right,' Sophie said miserably, lifting her son out of the crib.

'They are,' Lucy said firmly, hating to hear the girl sounding so downhearted. 'I'm sure you'll be absolutely fine, but if you do have any concerns then ask your health visitor. She'll be visiting you every day for the next two weeks so you can discuss any problems with her. She'll also be able to tell you when the baby clinic is open. Don't forget that there are people there who can give you advice if you need it.'

'I suppose so.' Sophie still sounded very unsure. She cuddled Alfie for a moment and Lucy could see real fear in her eyes when she looked up. 'It's just a bit…well, *scary* knowing that I'm responsible for looking after him. I'm worried in case I do something wrong.'

'Most new mums feel like that,' Lucy assured her. 'Is there anyone at home who can help you?'

'No, there's nobody.'

'What about your family?' she persisted gently.

'My mum left home when I was a child and I haven't seen her since. My dad brought me up but he died last year.' Sophie's eyes filled with tears. 'I named Alfie after him.'

'I'm sure he would have been thrilled,' Lucy said kindly, passing her a tissue. 'What about Alfie's father? Will he help out?'

'I doubt it. He's left Dalverston and I've no idea where

he's living now.' Sophie blew her nose. 'He never wanted me to have Alfie in the first place. He was furious when I refused to have a termination. I'm glad he's gone because I don't want him anywhere near Alfie.'

'I understand,' Lucy said, feeling very sorry for the girl. She only wished there was something she could do to help her, but once Sophie left the maternity unit she was no longer their concern.

It wasn't an ideal situation by any means and Lucy couldn't help feeling concerned. 'I'll have to get back to work but don't forget that there's help available if you need it, Sophie. You only have to ask.'

'Thank you.'

Sophie dredged up a smile but Lucy could tell that she was still worried. She sighed as she made her way to the desk to see what Amanda wanted her to do. Even with daily visits from the health visitor, Sophie was going to find it hard work looking after Alfie by herself. New babies needed an awful lot of attention and with no family to call on, the girl would be very much on her own.

'Problems?'

She glanced up, feeling a wash of colour run up her cheeks when she realised that she had walked straight past Max without seeing him. Bearing in mind their earlier conversation, she felt obliged to stop. She didn't want him apologising again, not when it might start off all that soul-searching once more. Max might project the image of a caring, committed professional but she had to remember that it was all part of his act.

'I'm worried about Sophie Jones,' she said quickly, not wanting to dwell on that thought.

'Come into the office and tell me about it,' he said

immediately. He opened the office door, his brows rising when she hesitated. 'If you're worried about a patient, Lucy, we need to do something about it.'

'Of course.' She followed him into the room, pausing by the door as he walked over to the desk because it seemed wiser to maintain a little distance between them. When she was close to Max, it seemed to confuse things even more.

'OK, shoot.'

'It's nothing major,' she said quickly, refusing to allow the idea to take root. Max didn't present any danger to her when she knew exactly what he was like. 'I'm just a bit concerned because Sophie doesn't have anyone to help her when she gets home. I know there are lots of young mums living on their own who do a great job of bringing up their children, but most of them have someone they can call on for back-up. Sophie hasn't got anyone and she's admitted that she's worried in case she can't cope.'

'Hmm. It's a difficult situation and I understand why you're concerned,' Max said, frowning. He went over to the filing cabinet and pulled out Sophie's notes, shaking his head as he read through them. 'I wish I'd noticed this before. Look.'

Lucy went to join him, bending down so she could see what he was pointing to. 'There's no contact details, not even a name in the space for next of kin!'

'I know. Worrying, isn't it?'

He straightened up at the same moment as she did and she felt heat flash along her veins when their arms brushed. He'd rolled up his shirtsleeves and the feel of his skin against hers sent a surge of electricity shooting through her. Her eyes rose to his and her breath caught when she saw the awareness they held. Max had felt it too, felt that flash of heat, the tingling jolt of electricity that had sparked between them, and it was hard to hide her dismay as she hurriedly moved away.

What had happened with Richard had hit her hard. Her confidence in herself as an attractive, desirable woman had been rocked and it would be only too easy to use this as a much-needed boost, but at what cost? From what she had heard, Max cut a swathe through women, discarding them once they had outlived their usefulness. Could she accept that, or would she end up wanting more than he was prepared to offer?

Lucy bit her lip. She couldn't answer that question. It all depended on what she wanted from Max and she hadn't worked that out yet.

Max could feel his whole body throbbing. It wasn't a painful feeling but it was definitely worrying. He couldn't remember the last time he had reacted this strongly when he had touched a woman or if, indeed, it had ever happened. Surely it couldn't be a first?

He racked his brain but no matter how hard he tried he couldn't come up with another occasion when the feel of a woman's skin had instantly set him on fire. It hadn't even happened when he'd met his ex-wife, and the thought made him groan under his breath. What was it about Lucy that made him react this way?

Max had no idea what the answer was but he knew that he needed to put a rein on his feelings if he wasn't to make a fool of himself. He glanced at the file, hoping it would help if he focused on the current problem. There was no point torturing himself by recalling how Lucy had looked at him…

'I see that Sophie is registered with Dalverston

Surgery,' he said briskly, cutting off that thought. 'Rachel Thompson's her GP. That's good news.'

'You think it would be an idea to have a word with Dr Thompson about her?' Lucy said quietly.

Max felt a wave of tenderness wash over him when he heard the tremor in her voice. Although she was making a valiant effort, he could tell that she was as shocked by what had happened as he was. His own voice softened because he wanted her to know that there was nothing to worry about. Even if they were attracted to one another they would take things slowly; he definitely wouldn't rush her into his bed.

That was another thought that needed to bite the dust, fast. Max mentally ground it beneath his heel, praying that would be the last he heard of it. Getting hung up on the idea that Lucy would sleep with him was the last thing he needed!

'Yes, I do. Rachel set up an advisory service for teen-age mums in Sophie's position a couple of years ago. Rachel was a teenage mum herself so she understands the problems better than most people do. I've heard a lot of good reports about the work they do.'

'What a brilliant idea!' Lucy exclaimed. 'I know we hold classes for all the new mums but it's impossible to cover everything in the time we can spend with them. The younger mums in particular could do with a lot more help.'

'That's why Rachel decided to set up this advisory service,' Max told her. 'I sat in on a session last year and it was excellent—good, sound advice presented in a way that the girls could understand but not feel as though they were being talked down to.'

'It's exactly what Sophie needs. She's very capable;

all the staff have said how good she is with Alfie. She just needs to gain a bit more confidence in herself.'

'Then the classes would be ideal for her. Another plus is that she'll meet other girls in her situation and hopefully make some friends. She won't feel quite so alone if she has someone her own age to talk to.'

'It's the perfect solution. Thanks, Max. I'll give Dr Thompson a call and see what she has to say.'

Lucy smiled at him, her whole face lighting up with delight, and Max felt another surge of heat flow through him and wash away every sensible thought he'd had. Maybe he didn't want to rush her, but he had to start somewhere.

'Look, Lucy,' he began, then stopped when the phone rang. He tried to curb his impatience as he reached for the receiver, but it was frustrating to be interrupted at such a crucial moment. 'Maternity. Max Curtis speaking.'

It was A and E requesting his assistance with a patient who'd been involved in an RTA. She was twenty weeks pregnant and bleeding heavily, and they needed him there, stat.

Max promised them he'd be straight there and hung up. He explained to Lucy that he had to go and left, sighing as he made his way to the lift. Another couple of seconds and he would have asked her out, but would that really have been the wise thing to do? Lucy wasn't the sort of woman he usually went out with. She would expect more from a relationship than a few casual dates, invest more of herself into it too. Was he prepared for that when it went against all his rules?

For the past three years, he had avoided commitment yet he knew in his heart that he wouldn't be able to do that with Lucy. Lucy made him dream about home and family, made him long for happily-ever-after, and they were all the things he could never have.

What he needed was a distraction to take his mind off her. It had been months since he'd been out on a date, now that he thought about it. He'd been too busy with work to worry about socialising and it was time he rectified that. There was a new nurse in A and E, who'd made it clear that she was interested in him; he would invite her out for dinner at the weekend.

As for Lucy, well, he would get over this crush or whatever it was in time. He had to. He certainly didn't intend to have his life disrupted all over again.

CHAPTER FIVE

THE day flew past. They had no sooner admitted Fiona Walker, the patient involved in the RTA, when two other mums phoned to say they were in labour. It meant they were really stretched to keep up but Lucy was glad because it gave her less time to brood about what had happened with Max. Maybe he did see her as an attractive and desirable woman, and maybe it was a boost to her confidence, but in her heart she knew it would be a mistake to get involved with him.

She had just escaped from one disastrous relationship and she needed to concentrate on putting her life back together. Perhaps a time would come when she felt able to trust a man again but not yet. And definitely not someone like Max. No matter how good he made her feel, Max was strictly off limits.

Lucy felt a little better after she had made her decision. By the time her shift ended, she felt much calmer about what had happened. Amanda was in the office when Lucy went to sign out; she looked up and grimaced.

'What a day! I couldn't believe it when those two mums turned up one after the other like that.'

'It has been hectic,' Lucy agreed. She filled in the

time next to her name then glanced at Amanda and frowned. 'Aren't you supposed to be off duty now as well?'

'I wish! I'm still trying to sort out the Christmas timetable,' Amanda explained. 'Every time I make a start on it, something happens, but I need to get it done soon.'

'Are you having problems finding people to work?' Lucy asked sympathetically.

'Yes. Normally, we use a rota system so that anyone who works nights over Christmas is off at New Year. Unfortunately, there aren't enough staff to do that this year.' Amanda sighed. 'Folk aren't going to be too pleased when they find out they're having to work both holidays.'

'I don't mind working,' Lucy offered. She shrugged when Amanda looked at her in surprise. 'I wasn't planning on doing anything so I may as well work.'

'Are you sure?' Amanda said uncertainly. 'I thought you'd want to go home and see your family.'

'No, it's fine. Really.' She smiled at the other woman, not wanting to explain why she preferred to remain in Dalverston. She had been dreading Christmas and the New Year, if she was honest. Her parents would expect her to go home and she couldn't face the thought of seeing everyone again. Working over the holidays would give her the perfect excuse to avoid it. 'You can put me down for Christmas and New Year if it helps.'

'Oh, it does!' Amanda assured her. She added Lucy's name to the timetable then printed out a copy and held it aloft. 'All done! Am I glad we hired you. I can't imagine anyone else volunteering to do a double stint of nights!'

'It isn't a problem,' Lucy said quickly, feeling a little uncomfortable when she would benefit from her offer far more than Amanda would. She picked up her bag and turned to leave. 'I'll be off, then. See you tomorrow.'

'Rightio… Oh, before I forget, what are you doing on Saturday night?'

Lucy paused. 'Nothing. Why?'

'A few of us have decided to go out for a pre-Christmas meal,' Amanda explained. 'It's just me, Joanna, Cathy and Margaret so far, although I'm hoping a couple of the community midwives will be able to join us. We're going to that Indian restaurant in the town centre so how do you fancy it?'

'I'd love to come,' Lucy agreed immediately. It was just what she needed, in fact, the first step towards building a social life. The first step towards taking her mind off Max, too. She hurriedly dismissed that thought. 'What time are you meeting up?'

'Seven o'clock outside the restaurant,' Amanda informed her, then looked up and smiled. 'Oh, good. I was hoping to catch you before you left. How do you fancy coming out for a curry on Saturday night?'

Lucy glanced round to see who Amanda was talking to and felt her heart jolt when she saw Max standing in the doorway. It was hard to maintain an outward show of calm as he came into the room. It wasn't just the fact that Max had seemed attracted to her that had shocked her, of course, but that she had reciprocated. Bearing in mind what had happened recently, she should have been immune to his appeal, but there was no point pretending. Even though she knew that Max was the last man she should get involved with, there was something about him that drew her.

Max could feel his body humming with tension as he walked into the office. He nodded to Lucy, hoping she couldn't tell how on edge he felt. Maybe he did intend to get over this...*crush* he seemed to have developed on her but it could take a little time. 'Sorry. I'm afraid I can't make it on Saturday. I've made other plans.'

'Oh, I see!' Amanda grinned at him. 'So who's the lucky lady, then? Don't tell me it's still that nurse from Paeds? She must be well past her sell-by date by now!'

Amanda laughed but Max was hard pressed to raise a smile. Even though he knew she hadn't meant any harm, he couldn't help feeling uncomfortable about Lucy hearing the comment. Although he was the first to admit that he'd been out with a lot of women, it wasn't nearly as many as people seemed to believe.

There was little he could do to redress the situation, unfortunately, so he changed the subject. 'I just came to see how Fiona Walker's been doing since she was transferred from A& and E. Has the bleeding stopped yet?'

'I'm not sure. Lucy has been monitoring her,' Amanda informed him.

'How is she?' Max repeated, turning to Lucy. He felt his heart give another unsteady lurch and had to batten it down, wondering exactly how long it would take to get things back onto a more even keel. The problem was that he had never experienced this kind of reaction before so he had no way of knowing if it would take days or even weeks. He sighed under his breath. Knowing that he could be in for a rough ride every time he spoke to her wasn't the most comforting prospect.

'The bleeding has eased off, although it hasn't

stopped. Diane did another ultrasound and the baby is still moving about so that's a good sign. And there's been no cramping either,' she added quietly.

'Good. All we can do is hope that everything settles down.' He turned to Amanda, determined to get a grip on himself. No matter how long it took, he knew what he needed to do. 'I'll be here for another hour at least so call me if there's a problem.'

'Will do, although it won't be me you hear from.' Amanda stood up. 'Thanks to Lucy, *I* am going home.'

'Lucy?' Max queried, wondering what she meant.

'Yes. Lucy has only gone and volunteered to work nights over Christmas *and* New Year.' Amanda picked up the timetable and showed it to him. 'I've been struggling to get this finished for days and now it's all sorted, thanks to her. She's a real star, wouldn't you agree, Max?'

'I...um...yes, of course.' Max summoned a smile, wondering why it bothered him so much to learn that Lucy had offered to work over the holidays. Surely she would want to be with her family at this time of the year, he thought. It was what he planned to do, spend time with his parents and brothers, and he couldn't understand why she didn't want to do that too...unless she preferred to remain in Dalverston rather than to go home and face whatever situation she had run away from.

His heart ached at the thought of what she must have been through but there was nothing he could do about it. He left the office and went to check on the two mums who'd been admitted that afternoon. One had just delivered a baby girl and there was nothing he needed to do except congratulate the parents. The other was well advanced with her labour and once again his services weren't needed. Diane was on call that night so technically he was free to leave. However, there was paperwork that needed doing first.

He went to the desk and entered Fiona Walker's notes into the computer. It was a job that Diane would normally have done but he'd never been one to worry unduly about protocol. He sighed as he printed out a copy for the patient's file, aware that it was merely an excuse. The truth was that he was filling in time because he didn't want to go home and spend the evening thinking about what had happened that day.

It was pointless going over it, time and time again. The fact was that Lucy wasn't right for him and he most definitely wasn't right for her. He had already taken the first step towards addressing the problem by asking someone else out and, hopefully, that should be the end of it. Once he got back into the swing of dating, he would forget about Lucy and the danger she presented to his peace of mind.

Lucy took her time getting ready on Saturday night. She had a long soak in the bath then washed and dried her hair, brushing the chestnut curls until they gleamed. It had taken her ages to decide what to wear but she'd finally decided on a jade-green top teamed with a pair of black trousers. High-heeled black patent shoes added a touch of elegance to the outfit as well as adding a welcome couple of inches to her height. When she stepped in front of the mirror, she couldn't help thinking that she looked more like herself than she had done in ages. The past six months had taken their toll but it felt as though she had turned a corner now. Moving to Dalverston had been the right thing to do, even if it had posed a few problems she had never anticipated.

Lucy clamped down on that thought as she fetched her coat and left the flat. There was no way that she was going to start thinking about Max again tonight. The restaurant was in the high street and she was able to walk there. Margaret and Joanna had already arrived and they decided to go inside to wait for the others rather than stand in the street. Amanda was the last to arrive, full of apologies for keeping them waiting.

'Sorry, sorry! My taxi didn't turn up and I had to phone for another one.' She draped her coat over a chair and sat down. 'Anyway, guess who I saw on my way here?'

'No idea,' Cathy piped up, handing her a menu. 'So come on, tell us—who did you see?'

'Only Max with that new nurse from A and E.' Amanda grinned when everyone gasped. 'That's not the best bit either. I saw them going into Franco's.'

'Franco's?' Margaret's brows shot up. 'It costs an arm and a leg in there. I should know because Jim took me there on my birthday and he's never stopped moaning about how much it cost him ever since!'

'It's the most expensive restaurant in town,' Amanda agreed. 'Max must have high hopes for the evening if he's coughing up that sort of money!'

Everyone laughed but Lucy found it impossible to join in. The thought of Max wining and dining the other woman as a prelude to spending the night with her was almost more than she could bear.

The thought seemed to cast a shadow over the evening. Far too often, she found herself wondering what Max was doing. Was he turning on the charm, steering the evening in the direction he wanted it to end? She sighed because it had nothing to do with her what he did. Max was a free agent and if he chose to sleep with every single nurse in the hospital that was up to him. She had no right to feel hurt when he was simply living up to his reputation, no rights at all where he was concerned. For some reason that thought made her feel even worse.

The evening proved to be less of a success than Max had hoped it would be. Normally, he enjoyed getting to know the women he dated. He genuinely liked women and was interested in finding out what made them tick. However, he found it hard to summon up any real enthusiasm that night.

He did his best, of course, but he was very aware that he was merely going through the motions. It was a relief when he could bring the evening to an end and drive his date home. He could tell that she was disappointed when he refused her offer of coffee but there was nothing he could do about it. The truth was that he wasn't interested in coffee or anything else that was on offer. Although sex may have been enough of an inducement at one time, it held little appeal for him now, and it was worrying to admit it.

He drove home and let himself into his apartment. Tossing his keys onto the sideboard, he took a long look around the place he'd called home for the past three years. Everywhere was perfect from the gleaming, pale wooden floors to the stark, white-painted walls. He'd bought the furniture as part of the package when he'd moved in: chunky black leather sofas; chrome and glass side tables; a state-of-the-art entertainment system. It was the archetypal bachelor pad and all of a sudden he loathed everything it represented.

This wasn't him, not the person he really was inside. He had been hiding behind this façade for the last three years and he couldn't hide behind it any longer. Discovering that he could never father a child had been a devastating blow. It had left him feeling as though he was less than a man and he had tried to compensate for that by having all those affairs. However, in his heart he knew that sex was no longer the answer.

He sank down onto the sofa as he forced himself to face the truth. He could sleep with a million women but it wouldn't change the way he felt about himself, certainly wouldn't change the facts. He would never be a father, never experience the joy of holding his own child in his arms. There would always be this huge gap in his life and nothing he did could make up for that.

It might have been different if he could have shared his sorrow with someone who loved him enough to bear the burden with him, but it wouldn't be fair to expect any woman to give up her dreams of motherhood for him. It was why his marriage had failed. Becky's feelings for him hadn't been strong enough to compensate for them not having a child. While Max didn't blame her for feeling that way, it hurt to know that he hadn't been enough for her, that she'd needed more. It made him see that it would take a very special woman to love him purely for himself.

Just for a second an image of Lucy appeared in his mind's eye before he dismissed it. There was no point going there. What he needed to do was to focus on the positive aspects of his life. He loved his job and couldn't wish for a more fulfilling career, but maybe it was time to set himself a new challenge. Once Anna was back from maternity leave, he would start applying for a permanent consultant's post, he decided. It would be a wrench to leave Dalverston, but a change of scene would do him good. He would make a fresh start somewhere else, maybe even think about moving abroad. His skills were in demand all over the world and he wouldn't have a problem finding a job. He would concentrate on his career and on making sure that the women who came to him delivered healthy babies.

It would be some compensation for what he could never have.

CHAPTER SIX

LUCY was on lates the following week, so she went into work at lunchtime on the Monday to find the maternity unit a hive of activity. With just two weeks left before Christmas, the staff had decided to put up some decorations and everywhere looked very festive. She smiled as she stopped to admire the nativity scene that had been arranged on the end of the reception desk.

'This is gorgeous. Where did you get it?'

'The husband of one of our mums made it for us,' Margaret told her. 'He's a carpenter by trade and he makes these in his spare time.'

'It's beautiful,' Lucy said, picking up one of the figures so she could admire the intricate carving.

'Apparently, he has a stall at the Christmas market,' Margaret explained, unravelling a shiny foil paper chain. 'I think I'll see if he has any left when I go into town tomorrow night. My grandchildren would love one.'

'I'm sure they would,' Lucy agreed, placing the figure back in its place. 'I'll just put my coat away and give you a hand if you like. I'm supposed to be showing some new mums around the unit today but they aren't due to arrive until two, which gives me plenty of time.'

'That would be great,' Margaret said gratefully.

'There's another box of decorations in the storeroom if you could fetch it on your way back.'

'Will do.'

Lucy put her coat in her locker then went to the storeroom and switched on the light. The box was on the top shelf and she had to stand on tiptoe to reach it. Hooking her finger under the edge of the carton, she eased it forward then gasped when it suddenly tumbled off the shelf.

'Careful!' All of a sudden Max was there. He deftly caught the box and placed it on the floor, shaking his head as he straightened up. 'Good job it didn't fall on top of you. It's really heavy.'

'I didn't realise that,' Lucy said shakily. She cleared her throat when she heard how strained she sounded but seeing Max so unexpectedly had thrown her. Even though she knew it hadn't anything to do with her, she couldn't help wondering if he had spent the weekend with that nurse he'd taken out on Saturday night.

'It's only supposed to be full of Christmas decorations,' she said hastily, not wanting to go down that route again. Far too often over the weekend she'd found herself thinking about what Max might be doing and she had to stop. 'I didn't think it would weigh so much.'

Max grimaced. 'It's heavy enough to give you a nasty bruise if it landed on you. I wonder what's in it.' Crouching down, he peeled off the sticky tape and opened the box. 'Ahah, there he is. I was wondering where good old Freddie had got to.'

He held up a garishly-coloured plastic reindeer. It had an eye missing and one antler was bent at a very odd angle. Lucy frowned when she saw it.

'Why on earth have the staff kept that thing? It's hideous!'

'Shh, mind what you say. You'll hurt poor Freddie's feelings,' Max admonished her. 'I'll have you know that Freddie is the unit's lucky mascot. So long as he's on duty then it's guaranteed that a baby will be born here over Christmas.'

Lucy burst out laughing. 'Bearing in mind how many of our mums are due to give birth in the next couple of weeks, I doubt if Freddie's services will be needed!'

'Take no notice of her, Freddie,' Max said firmly. He held up the reindeer and looked straight into its one good eye. 'She doesn't *mean* to be rude. She just doesn't understand your magical powers.'

'No, I don't,' Lucy agreed, smiling. The fact that Max was happy to play the fool showed her yet another side to his character and one that she found very appealing too. Richard had tended to stand very much on his dignity, but obviously Max didn't care a jot about that.

It was worrying to know that once again she had found things to admire about him and she hurried on. 'So how did Freddie acquire these magical powers?'

'I'm not sure how it happened. Maybe Santa had something to do with it,' he replied, completely deadpan. 'But ever since Freddie appeared on the scene, we've had a baby born in the unit on Christmas Day.'

'That's some record. I mean, from the look of him he must have been around for a very long time. I certainly can't remember seeing anything like him in the shops,' she added wryly.

'I don't expect you have,' Max agreed, grinning at her. 'Freddie is definitely a one-off.'

'You're not kidding! Why is he called Freddie,

though? I thought Rudolph was the only name for a reindeer.'

'Apparently, the staff named him after the head of the obstetrics department at the time.' He turned the reindeer around and pointed to its nose. 'Plus he doesn't have the requisite red nose to be called Rudolph.'

'Oh, I see.' Lucy chuckled. 'Right, so now that I know all about our illustrious Freddie, I'd better take him to Margaret. No doubt she has a special place all lined up for him,' she said, bending down to pick up the box.

'I'll carry that.'

Max gently moved her aside and Lucy sucked in her breath when she felt his hands gripping her arms. It was only the lightest of touches yet she was deeply aware of his fingers pressing into her flesh.

'I can manage,' she said, quickly straightening up.

'I'm sure you can but why struggle when you don't need to?'

Max lifted the box off the floor and she felt her heart give a tiny jolt when she saw the awareness in his eyes. Had he felt it too, she wondered giddily, felt that immediate heightening of the senses that always seemed to happen whenever they touched?

She knew it was true and it was scary to know that once again Max felt exactly the same as she did. As she followed him out of the storeroom she couldn't help wondering why it kept happening. What was it about him that made her feel this way? What was it about her that made him respond?

She had no idea what the answer was but she knew that she needed to be extra-vigilant. It would be only too easy to give in to this attraction they felt but it would be a mistake to do so. She'd had her heart broken once and she didn't intend to have it broken a second time.

Max may be attracted to her but she had to remember that was all it was. He wasn't interested in having a real relationship with her or any other woman.

Max carried the carton to the desk then made his apologies and left. He was meeting Diane later to go over her assessment and he wanted to run through a couple of points he needed to cover. He sighed as he let himself into the consultants' lounge because he knew it was just an excuse. He already knew what he wanted to say, but it had seemed wiser to put some distance between himself and Lucy.

He poured himself a cup of coffee and sat down, determined that he was going to master these feelings that kept running riot inside him whenever he was near her. He had enjoyed that brief conversation they'd had more than he had enjoyed the whole of Saturday night and it was worrying to realise the hold she was gaining over him. If it had been anyone except Lucy, he would have suggested they have an affair because it was obvious that she was attracted to him too. However, he was wary of doing that when he knew there could be repercussions.

Although he had no idea what had happened in her past, it was obvious that she had been hurt and he wouldn't risk it happening again. He also didn't intend to make the mistake of getting hurt himself. It made him see that the tentative plans he'd made about finding a consultant's post would need to be put into operation as soon as possible. If he had another job lined up when Anna returned from maternity leave, it would make life much simpler. He could move away from Dalverston and right away from temptation.

* * *

'We'll start with the delivery rooms first.'

Lucy opened the door to one of the suites and ushered her charges inside. Five mums had turned up for the tour and she smiled when she heard them gasp in surprise.

'It's much nicer than I thought it would be!' Rachel Green exclaimed. 'I was born at Dalverston General and my mum said the delivery room she was in was really horrible—all dark and dingy.'

'The maternity unit was rebuilt a few years ago,' Lucy explained. 'I wasn't here then, but I've seen photos of the old unit and this is much nicer.' She led the way to the en suite bathroom and switched on the light. 'Apparently, the facilities in the old unit had to be shared, but the new rooms are all en suite, so you have your own bath and a separate shower, plus loo.'

'I wish we had an en suite at home,' one of the other mums declared. 'I'm fed up with having to trail along the landing every time I need to go to the loo during the night. I must have got up at least a dozen times last night and I'm worn out!'

Everyone laughed at that. Lucy smiled when she heard them swapping stories about their own experiences. It was good for them to know that they weren't alone in suffering these minor discomforts.

'Is there a separate suite for water births?' Rachel Green asked once everyone had settled down. 'I've been wondering about a water birth but I wasn't sure if it was possible to have one here at Dalverston.'

'It is,' Lucy assured her. She crossed the room and pulled back a folding screen so they could see the birthing pool. 'Two of the suites are equipped with birthing pools, so it isn't a problem.'

'Oh, I'm not sure if I fancy a water birth,' one of the others said, grimacing.

'It's not for everyone,' Lucy agreed. 'Some women don't like the idea and others do. It's a matter of personal choice.'

'My mother-in-law is really against it,' Rachel told her, sighing. 'She keeps trying to persuade me to change my mind but I've read so many good reports about water births that I really fancy giving it a try.'

'A lot of women find that giving birth in water is less stressful. The buoyancy of the water helps to support them and makes it easier for them to relax. And that can make the whole process of giving birth far less painful.'

'What about the baby, though?' another mum asked. 'Isn't there a risk that it could drown?'

Lucy shook her head. 'No. The baby is still receiving oxygen via the umbilical cord when it's born, so being submerged under the water for a short time won't harm it. Once it's lifted out of the water then it will start to use its lungs to breathe.'

'What if there's a problem during the birth?' someone else piped up.

'Then we would ask the mum to get out of the pool,' Lucy explained. 'We carry out all the usual checks during the birth, so we would pick up on any problems if they occurred. And it goes without saying that if there was any indication beforehand that a water birth wasn't the right choice then we would advise against it.'

Everyone seemed happy with her answers, she was pleased to see. She was a firm believer in the benefits of a water birth and could only hope that it might encourage some of the other women to consider the idea. It obviously hadn't put Rachel off because she smiled happily.

'I'm going to tell David's mum all that the next time she starts going on about me having a *proper* birth. It might stop her nagging me to death!'

'But remember, Rachel, it's your choice, and you need to make that clear to her,' Lucy said firmly. 'Actually, I think we've got some leaflets about water births in the office. I'll give you one to take home. Maybe that will help to convince her.'

She made a note to fetch the leaflets after they'd finished their tour and carried on. They visited one of the wards next and once again everyone was impressed by the bright and airy facilities. After that, they went to the nursery and then the special care baby unit, where any sick babies were treated. Although they could have missed it out, Lucy knew that a lot of mums found it reassuring to learn that such facilities were available if necessary.

The women were a little subdued as they made their way back to the meeting room afterwards, but they soon brightened up after they'd had a cup of tea. Lucy left them to chat while she went to the office for the leaflets. Max was there, talking to Amanda, but he merely nodded when she went in and she didn't know whether to feel pleased or sorry.

She sighed as she headed back to the meeting room, wishing that she didn't feel so ambivalent. One minute she had decided to avoid him and the next she was disappointed because he hadn't spoken to her, and it was all very confusing. She knew that she needed to sort out her feelings, although what that would achieve was anyone's guess. It certainly wouldn't change the fact that Max's attitude to life was very different from her own.

Once the tour was over, it was time for Lucy to go for

her break. There were just her and Cathy on duty that evening and she was hoping it wouldn't be too busy. She had just got back when Anita Walsh, one of the community midwives, phoned to say that she was sending a patient in to them. Anita was on her way back from visiting another of her mums and was stuck in traffic. She promised to get there as soon as she could, but in the meantime she would be grateful if someone would look after her patient for her.

Lucy assured her that she would sort everything out. She made her way to Reception and a few minutes later Emma Baker and her husband arrived. She booked Emma in then showed the couple to the delivery suite they'd be using. It was Emma's third child and she was very matter-of-fact about the birth. She was only due to stay in the unit for six hours following the birth and would be sent home after that so long as everything went smoothly.

Lucy did Emma's obs then set up the foetal monitor to check the baby's progress. She was a little concerned when she discovered that its heartbeat was much slower than it should have been. It was a sign that the baby could be in distress due to a lack of oxygen and needed monitoring.

She decided to wait a couple of minutes and do another foetal heart tracing as it could turn out to be a temporary blip. Emma's contractions were strong and the tightening of her uterus could have reduced the supply of oxygen reaching the baby via the placenta. She got everything ready then did another tracing of the baby's heartbeat, along with a recording of the uterine contractions. Checking it back, she was in no doubt that the baby was becoming increasingly distressed.

'Is something wrong?' Emma asked after she'd finished.

'I'm not happy about the baby's heart rate,' Lucy explained gently. 'It's slower than it should be, which means your baby is starting to show signs of distress.'

'But this didn't happen with the other two,' Emma protested. She turned to her husband. 'Did it, Peter?'

'No, it didn't,' he stated emphatically. 'Are you sure that machine is working properly?'

'There's nothing wrong with the equipment,' Lucy assured him. She could tell they weren't happy with her findings but there was little she could do about it. The baby was her first concern and she knew that she needed a doctor to take a look at it.

Lucy explained all this to Emma, then went to the phone and asked the switchboard to page Diane. The registrar phoned her back almost immediately to say that she was with a patient who was threatening to miscarry and didn't know how long she would be. She suggested that Lucy page Max if it was urgent.

Lucy sighed as she contacted the switchboard again. Although she would have liked a little more breathing space before she saw Max again, obviously it wasn't to be. She would just have to play it cool and not allow herself to get carried away. Max may be an extremely attractive man but she wasn't about to embark on another disastrous relationship. She had learned her lesson the hard way and she wasn't going to repeat her mistakes.

Max was on his way out of the hospital when his pager beeped. He groaned as he turned round and headed back inside. So much for hoping he might get an early finish for once, he thought ruefully as he made his way to the lift. Lucy met him in the corridor and he had to make a determined effort not to react when he saw her standing there. However, he couldn't deny that his heart seemed to be kicking up a storm and it was annoying after he had resolved to behave sensibly from now on.

'Did you want me?' he asked, adopting a deliberately neutral tone.

'Yes. I need you to take a look at a patient for me, please.' She led the way to the delivery room and paused outside the door to hand him the printout from the foetal monitor. 'As you can see from this, the baby is showing signs of distress. It's the mother's third child and she's roughly six centimetres dilated, but I wasn't happy about waiting.'

'It could be a while yet before the baby is born,' Max agreed, glancing at the tracing. He reached past her to open the door, feeling his senses spin when he realised all of a sudden just how petite she was. Her head barely came up to his shoulder yet for some reason he had never noticed it before. It was difficult to concentrate as he followed her into the room when at every turn he seemed to discover something new and fascinating about her.

'Dr Curtis would like to take a look at you, Emma,' Lucy explained as she led him over to the bed.

Max dredged up a smile, determined that he was going to get a grip on himself. 'Lucy tells me that your baby appears to be a little distressed, Emma. I'd just like to examine you and see what's happening, if you don't mind.'

Emma didn't look too happy as he gently examined her, feeling her tummy first so that he could check the position of the baby in case that was the cause of the problem. Everything was exactly as it should be; the baby was lying with its head well down, in a perfect position to be born.

'That's fine,' Max said moving to the bottom of the bed. 'Baby's in a good position so that isn't the problem.'

'We never had anything like this happen with the other two,' Emma's husband said curtly. 'Are you sure there really is a problem?'

'I'm afraid so. I know it must be hard to accept after you've had two trouble-free births, but trust me when I say that we all want the same thing. We want to make sure that your baby is safe and well.'

He carried on with his examination when the couple didn't raise any further objections, frowning when he spotted a loop of the umbilical cord protruding down through the mother's cervix. 'Take a look at this,' he said softly to Lucy.

She bent down to look and nodded. 'I see what you mean, although it wasn't there before.'

'It's probably slipped further down as the baby's moved down the birth canal.'

Max straightened up, knowing that there was no time to delay. 'A loop of the umbilical cord is protruding down through your cervix, Emma. It means there's a very real danger that your baby could be deprived of oxygen. The safest way to avoid that happening is to perform a section.'

'A section!' Emma exclaimed in dismay. 'You mean you want to operate?'

'Yes. If you were fully dilated, I might have recommended a forceps delivery but we can't afford to wait. A section will be quicker and safer.'

'I don't know... I mean, I never imagined anything would go wrong.' Emma bit her lip. It was obvious that she was upset at the thought of having her baby delivered by Caesarean section when she'd expected to have a normal birth.

'Dr Curtis wouldn't suggest a section unless he was absolutely sure it was the best thing to do,' Lucy said quietly.

Max felt his heart lift when he heard the conviction in her voice. There wasn't a doubt in his mind that she meant what she said and the fact that she so obviously trusted his judgement filled him with joy. He cleared his throat, not wanting her to suspect how moved he felt by her vote of confidence.

'Lucy's right. I am not an advocate for stepping in unnecessarily, believe me. However, there are occasions when it would be foolish not to do so. Your baby could suffer permanent brain damage if he's deprived of oxygen and that is a risk I'm sure none of us wishes to take.'

'No, of course not,' Emma agreed shakily. 'I'd never forgive myself if that happened. If you think a section is necessary then that's what we'll do. Isn't that right, Peter?'

'I…um…yes, of course,' her husband muttered, looking a little shocked.

Max wasted no more time as he went to the phone and informed Theatre that he would be operating. In a very short time, Emma was on her way. He followed the convoy out of the room, pausing briefly to have a last word with Lucy. 'The baby should be fine and so will Emma. She'll be back with you in no time at all.'

'Thank you. I know they're in safe hands.'

Max felt that little tug on his emotions again. Why did her opinion matter so much? he wondered. He knew he was good at his job and didn't need anyone to tell him that, yet it meant something really special to know that she believed in him.

He shrugged, trying not to get too hung up on the idea. 'As I've said before, we make a good team, Lucy. I doubt if Emma would have agreed to this op so readily without your input. She was obviously swayed by the reference you gave me.'

She gave a little grimace but he saw the colour that tinted her cheeks. 'I only told her the truth.'

'Then thank you.' His voice dropped and he could hear the emotion it held even if she couldn't. 'It's good to know that you have such faith in me, Lucy.'

He turned away, knowing that he was in danger of saying too much. It would be a mistake to do that, a huge mistake to let himself get carried away. He sighed as he headed for the lift. A few kind words and he was like putty in her hands!

CHAPTER SEVEN

LUCY popped into the special care baby unit to see Emma's baby before she went home. Although little Ruby Rose Baker didn't appear to have suffered any ill-effects from what had happened, it was normal practice to keep any babies born by Caesarean section in the unit for the first couple of days. Anita Walsh, the community midwife, was there when she arrived.

'I can't believe this has happened!' Anita exclaimed. 'It was a textbook pregnancy from the start, just like Emma's previous two were. She didn't even suffer from morning sickness!'

'No wonder she was so stunned when she was told that she needed a section,' Lucy said sympathetically. 'It must have been a real shock for her.'

'It was. She was only expecting to stay in for a few hours and now she'll be here for a week.' Anita sighed. 'I know how stubborn Emma can be when she sets her mind on something, so I expect she kicked up a bit of a fuss. I'm really sorry that you got landed with this, Lucy.'

'It wasn't your fault,' she assured her. 'Anyway, Emma seemed to accept what needed to be done once Max had explained how dangerous it could be for the baby.'

'Now, that I can believe,' Anita said with a laugh.

'Not many women can resist when Max turns on the charm!'

Lucy smiled dutifully but it was painful to have Max's reputation as a silver-tongued charmer confirmed once more. She tried to shake off the feeling of disappointment that filled her as they left the unit, but it was hard to shift it. Although she knew how foolish it was, she didn't want to have to see Max in anything other than a positive light.

'So how are you settling in?' Anita asked as they headed along the corridor. 'It must be a big change for you living here after the city. I'm not sure if I could make the move the other way.'

'I really like it here,' Lucy replied truthfully, glad to have something other than Max to occupy her thoughts. 'I certainly don't feel as though I'm missing out by not being surrounded by all the hustle and bustle of city life.'

'What about your friends and family, though? You must miss them,' Anita suggested.

'I do, but it's easier for everyone if I'm living here,' she said without thinking.

'What do you mean by that?' Anita asked in surprise.

Lucy sighed when she saw the curiosity on the older woman's face. Although she didn't want to go into detail about what had led her to leave Manchester, she could hardly refuse to answer. 'Oh, just that I split up with my fiancé a few months ago and it caused a bit of a stir. That was the reason why I decided to move to Dalverston, in fact. I wanted to make a completely fresh start.'

'Oh, dear, I am sorry.' Anita patted her hand. 'It can't have been easy for you, Lucy, but I'm sure you did the right thing.'

'I'm sure I did too.' Lucy summoned a smile, although she couldn't help wondering if she was right to say that.

She sighed as she said goodbye to Anita and went to fetch her coat because she knew what was behind her doubts. It was this situation with Max that troubled her and until she had worked out what to do about it, it would continue to do so. It was worrying to think that she had escaped from one difficult situation only to jump straight into another.

It was almost eight p.m. before Max was ready to leave. After he'd finished in Theatre, Diana had paged him about her patient. By the time they had discussed possible courses of treatment, he'd needed to check on Emma Baker again. Still, the upside was that he'd been far too busy to think about Lucy.

He groaned as he made his way across the car park. Every thought he had these days was followed by another one about Lucy and it was scary to know how hung up he was on her. Maybe he had made plans to address the situation, but it was the here and now that worried him, what would happen in the next few weeks. Although he'd had no problem avoiding commitment in the last three years, it was different with Lucy, very different indeed, and that's what worried him. He simply couldn't trust himself to do the sensible thing.

It was a disquieting thought and he found it impossible to shrug it off as he got into his car. There was a Christmas market being held in the town that week and there was a lot of traffic about when he left the hospital so it took him twice as long as normal to reach the town centre. The market was being held in the main square and the traffic was even worse there because of the numerous diversions that had been set up to avoid it. Max followed the signs, wishing that he had stayed in work until the market closed. At this rate he'd still be driving around at midnight!

He had just reached the junction with the main road when he spotted a commotion on the pavement. A young woman had collapsed and a crowd was starting to gather around her. Pulling into the kerb, he jumped out of his car and hurried over to see if he could help.

'I'm a doctor,' he explained as he pushed his way through the bystanders. He crouched down next to a young man who was obviously with the woman and introduced himself. 'My name's Max Curtis and I'm a doctor at Dalverston General. Is there anything I can do to help?'

'It's my wife. She…she's having a baby!'

The man looked as though he was ready to keel over at any second so Max moved him aside. He smiled at the young woman. 'My name is Max Curtis and I'm a doctor. As luck would have it, I work in the maternity unit at Dalverston General.'

'Thank heavens for that!' she exclaimed.

'Can you tell me your name and when your baby's due?' he asked, checking her pulse.

'Alison Cooper and my baby *was* due on New Year's Day, although I don't think he's going to wait that long,' she added ruefully.

'So how long have you been having contractions?' he continued, wanting to build up a clearer picture of what was happening.

'I'm not sure. I've been having pains on and off for a couple of days but I assumed they were Braxton Hicks' contractions. I wanted to visit the Christmas market tonight, so we drove over here from Ulverston, but as we were walking back to the car, my waters broke.'

'And how long ago did that happen?'

'About ten minutes,' she began, then groaned as another contraction started.

Max checked his watch, needing to know how frequent her contractions were. He also needed to examine her, although he was loath to do so with all these people watching. He was just trying to work out how to afford her some privacy when he heard someone calling his name and glancing round he saw Lucy pushing her way through the crowd.

'What are you doing here?' he demanded, feeling his heart squeeze in an extra beat as she crouched down beside him.

'I just got off the bus and saw the crowd. Somebody said that a woman had gone into labour, so I came to see if I could help. I take it that someone has phoned for an ambulance?'

'I did,' Alison's husband told them anxiously. 'It's taking ages to get here, though.'

Max bit back a sigh. With the amount of traffic on the roads that night it could be a while before an ambulance arrived. In the meantime, he and Lucy would have to deal with the situation. He turned to her, trying not to notice how pretty she looked in the light from the streetlamp, but that was like trying not to notice if the sun was shining. Every cell in his body seemed attuned to her as they crouched side by side on the pavement and his racing heart seemed to race that little bit faster. It was hard to appear the calm professional when his emotions seemed intent on doing their own thing.

'We need to examine her but not here with everyone watching. Can you find somewhere close by which would give us some privacy?'

'Of course.' She looked around then pointed towards a row of shops across the road. 'I'll see if anyone has a room they will let us use.'

'Great. Thanks, Lucy.'

'No problem.'

She gave him a quick smile as she stood up. Max let himself bask in its glow for a second before he turned his attention back to Alison. There was a time and a place for everything, he reminded himself sternly, although maybe that wasn't the best advice. He was trying to *avoid* getting involved with her, not staving off the moment until a later date!

Lucy could feel her heart racing as she hurried across the road and sighed. It wasn't just the adrenalin rush from dealing with this situation that was causing it to happen. It was being with Max that made her feel so keyed up. Maybe she didn't intend to get involved with him but it was proving harder than it should have been to stick to that.

She pushed the thought to the back of her mind as she hurried into the first shop she came to, which happened to be a sweet shop. The shop keeper, an elderly woman, had been watching what was happening through the window and came hurrying to meet her.

'Is that young woman all right? I'm on my own in here, otherwise I'd have gone out to see if I could help.'

'She's fine, or she will be if we can get her somewhere a little more private,' Lucy explained. 'She's having a baby and the pavement isn't the best place for that.'

'Good heavens!' the old lady exclaimed. 'A baby? Really?'

'Yes. I know it's a lot to ask but do you have a room we could use? An ambulance is on its way but it could take some time to get here with all the traffic. It would be better if she could wait somewhere a little less public.'

'Of course, dear. You can use the storeroom.'

The old lady opened a door and showed her the storeroom. Although it was full of boxes, it was warm and clean and would be perfect for their needs. Lucy thanked her and hurried back to tell Max the good news.

'We can use the storeroom in the sweet shop. It's ideal for what we need.'

'Good.' He lowered his voice. 'I don't think this baby is going to wait for the ambulance to arrive so let's get her inside as quickly as we can.'

They helped Alison to her feet and then with Max supporting her on one side and her husband on the other, they led her over to the shop. They had to stop halfway when another contraction began and Lucy could understand Max's eagerness to get her inside. The old lady had found some clean towels and laid them on the floor to form a makeshift bed and they quickly got Alison settled. Lucy helped Alison out of her underclothes and waited while Max examined her. The baby's head was already crowning and she knew it wouldn't be long before it was born.

'It's not going to be long now,' Max confirmed, smiling at Alison. 'It must be every child's dream to be born in a sweet shop, I imagine.'

Alison laughed. 'It's not what I had planned, believe me.'

She broke off when another contraction began. Lucy

beckoned to her husband and told him to sit down beside her and hold her hand. He still looked very shaky and the last thing they needed was him fainting. As soon as the contraction ended, she turned to Alison.

'I want you to wait until you feel another contraction begin before you try to push this time.'

'But I want to push now!' Alison exclaimed.

'I know you do, but you'll only tire yourself out if you try to push too soon. You need to work with your contractions and use them to help you deliver your baby.'

Alison did her best to follow their instructions and in a very short time the baby's head emerged. Lucy gently supported the head as it turned until it was once more in line with the baby's body. After another couple of contractions first one shoulder and then the other were delivered before the rest of the baby slid out into her hands. Lucy laughed when the child let out an angry wail.

'Congratulations! You have a beautiful little boy. And he obviously has a fine pair of lungs from the sound of it.'

She gently cleaned the baby's face with one of the towels then placed him on Alison's tummy, smiling when she saw the awe on the parents' faces as they saw their son for the first time. She glanced at Max, wanting to share the moment with him, and was shocked by the emotion she saw in his eyes. He was staring at the child with such longing that she felt her heart ache, even though she had no idea what was going on.

There was no time to ask him either as the sound of a siren announced the arrival of the ambulance. The crew carried a birthing kit on board so once the cord had been clamped and cut, and the placenta expelled,

Alison was placed on a stretcher and loaded on board. Lucy wrapped the baby in a blanket and placed him in his mother's arms.

'You did brilliantly, Alison. Not many women would have coped so well in the circumstances. You should be proud of yourself.'

'Thank you. Although I wouldn't have managed half so well if you and Max hadn't been there,' Alison told her sincerely.

'It was our pleasure.' Lucy ran her finger down the baby's soft little cheek then climbed out of the ambulance. The crew closed the doors and that was that. She sighed as she watched the vehicle making its way along the road. 'Talk about being in the right place at the right time.'

'It was fortunate,' Max agreed, but she could hear the grating note in his voice and once again found herself wondering about what she had witnessed.

Bearing in mind Max's reputation as a womaniser, she would never have imagined that he would be keen to have a child of his own. However, there was no doubt about what she had seen and she had to admit that she was intrigued. She longed to ask him what was going on, yet at the same time she knew it could be a mistake to do so. Her emotions had been all over the place recently, so could she risk getting drawn into a situation she might not be able to handle?

It was the uncertainty that scared her most of all, the fact that she couldn't answer that question with any degree of assurance. She sighed softly. In her heart she knew that it would be better if she left things alone rather than delve any deeper, yet it was hard to do that.

The truth was that she hated to think that Max might be suffering and not be able to do anything to help him.

Max could feel the flood of emotions that had hit him as he had watched Alison's baby being born swirling around inside him. He had honestly believed that he had come to terms with the fact that he would never have a family of his own, but he couldn't deny the yearning he'd felt just now and it filled him with sadness. There was no point wishing for the impossible, no point at all hoping that a miracle would happen. He would never father a child and that was the end of the matter.

He turned to Lucy, trying to ignore the nagging ache in his heart. 'I'll give you a lift home.'

'There's no need. Really.' She glanced along the road and shrugged. 'There doesn't seem much point in you trying to find a way through all this traffic when it'll only take me a couple of minutes to walk home from here.'

Max appreciated the sense of what she was saying, but all of a sudden he was loath to let the evening end there. Maybe it was foolish, but he knew that spending some time with her would help him deal with this sorrow he felt. 'In that case, how do you fancy having a look around the market? It's open until ten so there's plenty of time left. I don't know about you, but I could do with chilling out after everything that's happened tonight.'

'I'm not sure,' she began, but he didn't let her finish. The thought of sitting on his own in the flat with all these thoughts whizzing around his head was more than he could bear.

'Please say you'll come. We can wander around for a

while and soak up the atmosphere. It will be the perfect stress-buster after such a hectic day.'

She sighed softly. 'Anita was right. You can be very persuasive when you choose.'

Max laughed although he wasn't sure if the comment had been meant as a compliment. 'I won't ask you why she said that. All I can say is that I'd really enjoy your company, Lucy.'

She hesitated a moment longer then shrugged. 'All right, then, I'll come. But what about your car? You can't leave it here in case it gets towed away.'

'Good point.' Max frowned, hating to think that his plans might be scuppered by the lack of a parking space. His expression cleared as his gaze alighted on the sweet shop. 'I know, I'll ask the lady in the sweet shop if I can park it at the side of her shop. Hang on a moment while I see what she says.'

It took just a couple of minutes to arrange to leave his car in the alley next to the shop. Despite the lateness of the hour, there were still crowds of people milling about as he and Lucy made their way to the town square. The market stalls looked very festive with strings of brightly coloured lights hanging from their awnings. Max stopped when they came to a stall that was selling roasted chestnuts and sniffed appreciatively.

'Now, this is what Christmas smells like to me. Mum always used to buy us hot chestnuts when we were kids and it really takes me back to my childhood whenever I smell them.'

'I've never had chestnuts,' Lucy admitted, grinning when he gasped in feigned horror. 'Obviously, I was a deprived child, although don't tell my mum I said that or she'll have a fit!'

'Your secret is safe with me. Cross my heart and hope to die,' he promised with due solemnity, drawing a cross on his chest with his finger.

Lucy chuckled. 'I don't expect you to go to such extremes to guard my secret, Max.'

'That's a relief,' he declared, grinning at her. He dug in his pocket for some change and bought two bags of chestnuts, handing her one of them. 'Careful, they're hot.'

Lucy grimaced as she juggled the bag from hand to hand. 'You're not joking. My fingers are already singed!'

'Here.' Max took the bag from her and popped it in his pocket. 'We'll share this bag first,' he told her, lifting out a plump chestnut. He quickly peeled it and handed it to her, then peeled another for himself.

'Mmm, this is delicious.' She licked her fingers then held out her hand. 'Can I have another one, please?'

Max laughed. 'You made short work of that for someone who's never tasted chestnuts before.'

'There's a first time for everything,' she assured him cheekily, waggling her fingers under his nose.

Max chuckled as he peeled her another chestnut. They wandered around the market while they ate them, looking at the various stalls. Lucy stopped to admire some delicate glass ornaments, shaking her head when he suggested she buy one.

'There's no point,' she explained, putting the ornament back in its box. 'I'm not having a tree this year, and as I'm not going home, there's no point buying one for my parents either.'

Max frowned when he heard the sadness in her voice. Even though it had been her decision to work over the holiday, he could tell that she was upset about not spending time with her family. It made him wonder once again what had happened to make her decide not to go home. It must have been an extremely painful experience if she preferred to cut herself off from the people she loved.

The thought lingered at the back of his mind as they carried on. When they came to a stall that was selling mulled wine, Lucy stopped.

'Now, this is what reminds *me* of Christmas. Mum makes mulled wine every year on Christmas Eve. My sister and I always used to leave a glass for Santa to go with his mince pie.'

'And did he drink it?' Max asked, loving the way her eyes had lit up at the memory.

'Of course—or at least somebody did.' She grinned at him. 'Dad reckons that Christmas isn't the same since Laura and I stopped believing in Father Christmas, so let's just say that I have my suspicions.'

Max laughed. 'Well, I think you and your sister should reinstate the tradition. After all, you can't *prove* that Father Christmas doesn't exist, can you? Maybe he still pops in but doesn't leave you any presents these days because you're all grown up.'

'That's exactly what my dad said,' she told him, rolling her eyes. 'You men certainly stick together!'

'Can I help it if we take a more logical view of matters?' he said, spreading his hands wide open in a gesture of innocence.

'Logical? You class hedging your bets in case Father Christmas actually does exist as an example of superior male logic? Oh, *please*!'

'Until someone comes up with proof that Santa is a

myth then I intend to keep a completely open mind on the subject,' he declared loftily.

'I suppose you feel the same about the Tooth Fairy and the Easter Bunny?' she retorted and he grinned.

'But of course.'

She shook her head. 'You are completely mad, do you know that?'

'Not mad, just reluctant to let all the magic disappear from my life.' He smiled at her. 'There are worse sins than clinging onto the things that make childhood such a wonderful time.'

'You're right, there are,' she conceded.

Max felt his breath catch when she smiled up at him. When she looked at him that way it was hard to remember that he was supposed to be acting sensibly and the temptation proved just too great. Bending, he placed his mouth over hers. Her lips were cool from the night air yet he could sense the heat beneath the chill and groaned. Kissing Lucy was like nothing he had ever experienced before!

His lips clung to hers, demanding a response, and a surge of delight rushed through him when he felt her kiss him back. He had no idea how long they would have stood there if the sound of laughter hadn't reminded him that they were standing in the middle of the square with people milling about all around them. He drew back reluctantly, seeing the shock in her eyes, and knew that she was as stunned by what had happened as he was.

'I suppose I should apologise, although I'm not sorry that I kissed you,' he said truthfully. 'I've been wanting to do it for ages.'

'Have you?' she whispered, her voice catching.

'Yes.' Reaching out he brushed his knuckles over her

mouth and felt her shudder. There was a definite tremor in his voice when he continued. 'There's just something about you, Lucy, that draws me, even though I know how crazy it is.'

'Because you don't do commitment?'

'No, I don't.' He sighed, wishing he could explain why he lived his life the way he did. He just couldn't bear to think that she might view him differently if he told her the truth about himself. Would she consider him to be less of a man if she found out that he couldn't father a child, he wondered, or, worse still, *pity* him? He had no idea and he wasn't about to risk finding out.

'I'm far too busy with my career to devote the time it needs to a long-term relationship,' he explained, aware that he was taking the coward's way out. Although his career was important to him, it wasn't the real reason why he had avoided getting involved these past three years.

'I understand, Max, and it isn't a problem.' She shrugged when he looked at her. 'I'm not interested in having a long-term relationship either.'

'You're not?' he queried, unable to hide his surprise.

'No. I won't bore you with the details. Suffice to say that I don't plan on getting involved with anyone again for a very long time, if ever. So don't worry, Max. I'm certainly not holding out for the happily-ever-after, if that's what worries you!'

CHAPTER EIGHT

LUCY couldn't believe she'd said that. Panic gripped her as she ran the words through her head again. They sounded less like a statement than an invitation to have an affair, and that wasn't what she wanted...

Was it?

Desire rushed through her as she recalled the heat of Max's mouth when it had closed over hers. His lips had drawn a response from her that she'd been powerless to refuse and that had never happened before. Not once in all her life had she been swept away by passion, never had she felt such hunger or such need. Max's kiss had aroused her in ways that no man's kisses had ever done, not even Richard's.

The shock of that discovery made her gasp and she saw Max look at her in concern. 'Lucy? Are you all right?'

Lucy struggled to get a grip on herself. She had truly believed that she had been in love with Richard but how could she have been if his love-making had left her unmoved? 'I'm fine. Just a bit tired after everything that's happened tonight.'

'We both know that isn't true! At least be honest with me if nothing else. You're upset because I kissed you, aren't you?'

'Yes, but not in the way you mean.' She looked him straight in the eyes. Maybe she would regret this later but she wouldn't lie to him. As he had said, the very least they could do was to be honest with each other. 'I'm not upset because you kissed me, Max, but because of how it made me feel.'

'And how did it make you feel?' he asked, his voice grating in a way that made a shiver dance down her spine.

'More alive than I've ever felt before.'

'That's how I felt, too.'

'Is it?'

'Yes. So where do we go from here, Lucy?'

Lucy bit her lip because she had no idea what to say. If she told him the truth, that she wanted him to kiss her again and not only kiss her either but make love to her, she didn't know where it would lead. Max had made it clear that he wasn't interested in commitment, but could she have a purely physical relationship with him while remaining emotionally detached? Although she had sworn that she wouldn't get involved with a man again, she was no longer sure if she could stick to that. Not with Max.

'I don't know,' she said candidly. 'I really don't know where we go from here, do you?'

'No.' He sighed. 'It would be only too easy to make the wrong decision, wouldn't it? Maybe it would be best if we called a halt right now rather than find ourselves in a situation we both live to regret.'

'It seems the most sensible thing to do,' she agreed softly, hoping he couldn't hear the hurt in her voice. Maybe it did make sense, but she couldn't pretend that it didn't upset her to know that he could dismiss what had happened with such ease.

'I think it's time I went home,' she said quickly before she ended up saying something that would embarrass him. Max may have enjoyed kissing her but it certainly hadn't been enough to make him change his whole outlook on life. 'Thank you for the chestnuts. I really enjoyed them.'

'I'm glad.' He smiled at her, his brown eyes filled with a warmth that made her heart ache. It would be only too easy to see it as a sign that he really cared about her but it would be a mistake. 'Thank you for spending the evening with me, Lucy. I wouldn't have missed it for the world.'

'Me too,' she admitted huskily. She felt her breath catch when he bent towards her, but he merely kissed her on the cheek before he stepped back.

'Are you sure you'll be all right walking home on your own?'

'I'll be fine,' she assured him, quelling the feeling of disappointment that filled her. 'The one advantage of living so close to the town centre is that it only takes me a couple of minutes to walk home.'

'That's good, I suppose, although I have to confess that I wouldn't fancy living where you do.'

She shrugged. 'Needs must, I'm afraid. I have to watch every penny I spend at the moment.'

Max frowned. 'So that's why you opted to live there?'

'Yes.' She summoned a smile when she saw the concern on his face. The last thing she wanted was him thinking that she was looking for sympathy. 'Anyway, it's not nearly as bad as it looks.'

'If you say so.'

Lucy could tell he wasn't convinced but there was nothing she could do about it, so she said goodbye and left. Most of the stalls were closing up for the night and people were drifting away. As she made her way home, she couldn't help wondering what might have happened if Max hadn't decided they should call a halt. Would he have wanted to come back to her flat and spend the night with her? Would she have let him?

She sighed because there was no point going down that route. From now on she had to think of Max simply as a colleague, no matter how difficult it was going to be.

The next few days passed in a whirl of activity. Max knew that he was deliberately keeping himself busy so that he didn't have time to think about what had happened. Although he was sure that he had made the right decision, it didn't make it any easier. Having experienced the wonder of that kiss he and Lucy had shared, his body continually craved more.

In an effort to break the cycle, he finished early on Friday and went to visit his parents. He was hoping that the change of scene would do him good, but far too often during the weekend he found himself thinking about Lucy and it was worrying to realise the hold she had over him.

He knew that he had to do something about it, so as soon as he got home on the Sunday he went through all the recent copies of the medical journals he subscribed to. There were a couple of consultants' posts that sounded promising so he ringed them in red then sat down to update his CV. Once that was done, he wrote covering letters, popped everything into envelopes and took them to the post box. He felt much better afterwards, more settled. He was doing something positive about the situation, giving himself a reason to keep away from Lucy, and that had to be a good thing.

He went into work the following day, feeling a lot more upbeat. Amanda was on duty and she grimaced when she spotted him walking towards the desk.

'You certainly know when to take time off! If I didn't know better, I'd think you possessed second sight or something.'

'Why? What's happened?'

'Where do you want me to begin? First of all Margaret slipped on a patch of ice on Friday night and sprained her ankle, and then Joanna phoned yesterday to say that she had a rash all over her face and didn't know if she should come into work.' Amanda rolled her eyes. 'I told her to see her GP this morning and she's just rung up to say that he thinks it's German measles.'

'I see.' Max frowned. Although German measles, or rubella to give it its proper name, was a relatively mild viral infection, it could cause serious repercussions for a baby if the mother caught it in the early stages of pregnancy. He couldn't help feeling concerned. 'When was the last time that Joanna worked in the antenatal clinic?'

'The end of November. I checked on that as soon as she told me what her GP had said,' Amanda informed him.

'She wouldn't have been infectious then,' he said in relief. 'The virus can only be transmitted from a few days before any symptoms appear until one day after they've disappeared.'

'Thank heavens for that!' Amanda exclaimed.

'Definitely,' he agreed, then frowned. 'I'm surprised that Joanna hasn't been vaccinated against rubella, though. Isn't that one of the things they usually check on before people start their midwifery training?'

'You're right, it is, and to be fair to Joanna, she thought she had been vaccinated. However, it turns out that her parents decided not to have it done.'

'Really!' Max exclaimed. 'Why ever not?'

Amanda sighed. 'Joanna was just a baby when the combined measles, mumps and rubella vaccine was introduced. There was a lot of adverse publicity at the time and many parents were wary about letting their children have it. It seems that Joanna's parents decided not to go ahead with it too.'

'I see.' Max frowned thoughtfully. 'I wonder how many other members of staff are in the same position. It might be worth checking to make sure that everyone is immune. I can arrange for blood tests to be done after Christmas for those willing to be tested.'

'That sounds like a good idea to me,' Amanda agreed, then looked up and smiled. 'What do you think, Lucy?'

Max felt his stomach lurch when he turned and saw Lucy standing behind him. Although it was only a few days since he'd seen her, it felt as though a whole lifetime had passed. He longed to take her in his arms and feel the softness of her body nestled against him. It was only the fact that Amanda was there that stopped him, and the realisation scared him. Even though he knew how foolish it would be to get involved with her, it didn't stop him wanting her!

'I'm sorry. What did you say?' Lucy could feel her

heart hammering. She dragged her gaze away from Max, but she could feel his eyes boring into her and shivered. The past few days had been the longest of her entire life. Knowing that she wouldn't see Max over the weekend should have provided a welcome breathing space, but it hadn't turned out that way. She had missed him so much that it was hard not to show him just how pleased she was to see him.

'Max has suggested that everyone is tested to make sure they're immune to rubella,' Amanda explained. 'I think it's a good idea, don't you?'

'Yes, I do.' Lucy took a deep breath. Getting involved with Max would be a mistake. She needed time to get over what had happened with Richard and she couldn't afford to be drawn into another difficult situation. 'I'm more than happy to be tested and I'm sure everyone will feel the same.'

'Good. I'll make all the necessary arrangements, then.'

Max was all business as he turned to Amanda and asked her for an update about what else had happened while he'd been off. Lucy collected the file she needed and left them to it. With two members of staff off sick, it promised to be another busy day. Thankfully, she was working the early shift and shouldn't see very much of Max. Unless there was a crisis, then, she'd be able to avoid him.

She sighed as she made her way back to the delivery room. Although her head told her that it was a good thing, her heart definitely didn't seem to agree.

Lucy stayed on after her shift should have ended. Although Amanda had managed to find someone to cover the evening shift, she hated to leave them in the lurch, so it was gone three by the time she felt able to leave. She went to the staffroom for her coat, smiling when she found Cathy in there, nursing a mug of tea.

'You look as though you needed that.'

'Tell me about it.' Cathy took a swallow of her tea then groaned appreciatively. 'You can forget about sex. I'd rather have a mug of tea any day of the week!'

'I'm sure your boyfriend would be thrilled to hear you say that,' Lucy replied, laughing.

'Oh, Neil knows exactly how I feel,' Cathy assured her. 'We wouldn't have lasted this long if he hadn't been so understanding, believe me.'

'How long have you been together?' Lucy asked, slipping on her coat.

'Almost two years, although I've known him since we were at school together. Don't tell him I said this but I wouldn't swap him for the world, although I might just consider it if George Clooney came knocking on my door!' she added, grinning.

Lucy laughed. 'You and a million other women.'

'Hmm, good point. I don't think I'd fancy going out with a guy who dozens of other women lusted after, would you?'

'No, I wouldn't.' She didn't realise how sharp she'd sounded until she saw Cathy look at her in surprise.

'That came from the heart. Do I take it that you've had a bad experience?'

'You could say that.' Lucy shrugged. 'My ex was considered to be heart-throb material. The problem was that he knew it too.'

'Is that why you split up?' Cathy asked sympathetically.

'No. I could have coped with the female adulation. What I couldn't handle was him seeing other women while still professing his love for me.'

'Ouch!' Cathy grimaced. 'It sounds as though you had a lucky escape, if you ask me.'

'I suppose so.'

'There's no suppose about it,' Cathy said firmly, standing up. She went to her locker and took out her bag. 'What you need is to have some fun and forget about him, and I know the perfect way to do it.' She handed Lucy a ticket. 'It's the staff Christmas party tonight. I was supposed to be going with Joanna but obviously she won't be able to make it now, so you can have her ticket.'

'Oh, I don't know if I should,' Lucy began.

'Rubbish! Of course you should! It'll be fun, trust me. And you never know, you might meet someone who'll take your mind right off your ex!'

Lucy laughed as she took the ticket. However, as she left the staffroom she couldn't help thinking that it wasn't Richard who had occupied her thoughts recently. She sighed. She had a feeling that it was going to take more than a few hours of fun to stop her thinking about Max all the time.

CHAPTER NINE

MAX wasn't planning on going to the Christmas party, even though he had bought a ticket months ago. After his last disastrous date, he had given up on the idea of socialising for the moment. However, as the day wore on, the prospect of spending the evening on his own held even less appeal. He knew what would happen. He would spend the time thinking about Lucy and it wouldn't help one little bit. The Christmas party could turn out to be the better option.

He went home to shower and change then drove back to the hospital. The party was being held in the staff canteen and there was quite a crowd in there when he arrived. He got himself a drink from the makeshift bar and went to find the others, stopping en route to speak to various people he knew. Everyone was in high spirits and he only wished he felt as cheerful as they did. However, he was suddenly very conscious of the fact that this would be the last Christmas he spent in Dalverston and the thought weighed heavily on him. It was hard to appear his usual happy-go-lucky self when he joined the staff from the maternity unit.

'We didn't know you were coming, Max!' Anita Walsh exclaimed. 'You should have said and then we could have picked you up in the minibus to save you driving.'

'I wasn't sure if I could make it,' he hedged, not wanting to explain why it had been a last-minute decision. He held up his glass, wanting to deflect any more awkward questions. 'OK, guys, I'd like to propose a toast. To everyone who works on the maternity unit. May we all enjoy the fruits of other people's labours!'

Everyone laughed as they clinked glasses. Max was relieved that he had managed to divert attention away from himself. There were several former members of staff there that night and he decided to have word with them. If he kept circulating, hopefully no one would notice that he wasn't his usual ebullient self.

He was just heading over to speak to Maria, who had retired recently, when he saw Lucy crossing the canteen and his heart seemed to leap right up into his throat. He'd had no idea that she would be there that night. Tickets had sold out months ago, long before she had moved to Dalverston. Now the shock of seeing her so unexpectedly turned his limbs to stone. He could only stand and stare as she drew closer.

Lucy felt shock scud through her when she spotted Max. She'd never dreamt that he would be there that night and wasn't sure what she should do. She paused, wondering if she should beat a hasty retreat, but just at that moment Cathy spotted her.

'There you are!' Cathy exclaimed as she came hurrying over to her. 'I thought you must have changed your mind and decided not to come after all.'

'I…um…I'm sorry I'm late but the bus didn't turn up so I had to find a taxi.'

'I should have asked you if you wanted to come in

the minibus,' Cathy said apologetically. 'I never gave it a thought. Sorry.'

'It doesn't matter,' Lucy said quickly. She shot a glance at Max and felt herself colour when she realised that he was watching her. Her heart seemed to be beating at double its normal speed when she turned to Cathy again. 'I'm here now and that's the main thing.'

'Of course it is.' Cathy grinned as she led her over to the rest of their group and raised her glass aloft. 'OK, folks, now it's my turn to propose a toast. Here's to a fun-filled night!'

Everyone cheered as they raised their glasses. Lucy joined in but she was so conscious of Max that it was hard to act naturally. She shot another glance in his direction and was relieved to see that he was talking to a glamorous older woman and no longer looking at her. She made her way to the far side of the group, wondering how soon she could leave without it causing comment. Being around Max was the last thing she needed at the present time.

Someone put some music on and people started to dance. When Cathy urged everyone to join in, Lucy went willingly. With a bit of luck she'd be able to slip away while they were occupied. Max was dancing with the other woman now, laughing as he guided her around the floor in a stately waltz. They passed Lucy and she blushed when he caught her staring and winked at her.

The first track ended and another one began. It was a popular tune and more people came onto the floor. Lucy doubted if anyone would notice her leaving in all the crush so started to edge towards the door, only to stop when Adam Sanders came over and asked her to dance.

There was no way she could refuse without it appearing rude, so she followed him back to the floor. Max was dancing with Cathy now. Lucy could hear her laughing at something he was saying but looked the other way in case he thought she was watching him again. One dance led to a second before she was able to excuse herself, ignoring Adam's obvious disappointment. She sighed as she made her way towards the exit. Adam was very nice but she just wasn't interested in him.

'Will you dance with me, Lucy?'

All of a sudden Max appeared at her side and she stopped dead. 'Dance with you,' she repeated numbly.

'Uhuh.' He placed his hand on his heart and grinned at her. 'I promise on my honour that I'll do my very best not to trample all over your toes.'

Lucy's mouth quirked before she could stop it. 'That doesn't sound very encouraging. Just how bad a dancer are you?'

'You'll have to judge for yourself.' He smiled as he held out his hand. 'Come on, Lucy. Take pity on me. If you won't dance with me then I'll be left standing here like a wallflower!'

'I don't think so. I imagine you could find yourself another partner easily enough.'

'Maybe. But it's you I want to dance with, so won't you say yes? Please?'

Lucy felt her stomach muscles clench when she saw the expression in his eyes. She knew she should refuse but it was impossible when he looked at her so beseechingly. She placed her hand in his and let him lead her back to the floor. There was a fast number playing this time and everyone was having a wonderful time. Max laughed as he swung her round to face him.

'I hope you're ready for this.'

'Bring it on,' she assured him, and he chuckled.

'Well, you only have yourself to blame.'

He spun her round, twisting her this way and that until she was breathless. Despite what he had said, he was an excellent dancer and she glowered at him when the music came to an end.

'There's absolutely nothing wrong with the way you dance!'

'That's all down to you.' He smiled at her. 'I've raised my game to keep up with my partner.'

'I don't think so!' she scoffed. 'If you ask me, insinuating that you're a rubbish dancer is just a line. I expect a lot of women fall for it, don't they, Max?'

'If it helped to persuade you to dance with me, that's all that matters,' he said quietly.

Lucy felt heat flash through her veins when he pulled her into his arms. The music had changed to a slow tune now and when the lights were dimmed, she closed her eyes, giving herself up to the seductive rhythm. She could feel his lips nuzzling her hair and sighed, enjoying the feeling of closeness and the fact that it made her feel special to be held like this, desired.

'I could dance with you like this for ever, Lucy.'

Lucy frowned when she heard the grating note in his voice. Bearing in mind what he had said about not wanting a long-term relationship, it seemed very strange. Opening her eyes, she tipped back her head and looked at him. 'I thought you avoided commitment?'

'I do. But it doesn't mean that I don't have feelings.'

He drew her to him so that she could feel his arousal pressing against her. Lucy swallowed when she felt her nipples immediately peak in response. She was wearing a black silk dress that night and she knew that Max could tell she was aroused too.

He drew her even closer, his fingers splaying across the base of her spine as they swayed together in time to the music. Lucy could feel the tension growing with each second that passed and shivered. It was obvious that Max wanted her and it made her wonder why he'd been so keen to call a halt when he had. Surely it would have made more sense if he'd tried to persuade her to have an affair with him?

She was still trying to puzzle it out when the music stopped and the lights came up. She stepped out of his arms, feeling light-headed and giddy as the thoughts whizzed around her head. Leaving aside Max's motives, what would *she* have said if he had tried to talk her into having an affair? It was easy to claim that she would have refused but was that really true? Although she knew that Max was the last person she should get involved with, there was no point pretending that she didn't want him. But was it purely lust she felt, or something more? She wished she knew because maybe then she would know what to do about it.

Max could barely think thanks to the flood of emotions that filled his mind as well as his body. He had never felt this strongly about any woman and the thought scared him half to death. He knew that he needed to get a grip on himself but it was proving harder than he'd expected to do that.

'Come on, you two, get a move on. The buffet's being served and all the food will be gone if we don't get there pronto.'

Max jumped when Cathy tapped him on the shoulder.

He summoned a smile, but it was hard to disguise how worried he felt. 'I'm not hungry, thanks. I think I'll pass.'

'All the more for the rest of us,' Cathy quipped. 'What about you, Lucy?'

'I'll get something in a minute, thanks.'

Lucy smiled at the other woman but Max could tell the effort it cost her and his heart seemed to scrunch up inside him. Lucy was obviously finding it as difficult as he was to deal with this situation, and that was even more worrying. He turned to her as Cathy moved away to badger someone else.

'Are you all right?'

'I'm fine, thank you.'

When he heard the wobble in her voice, Max was hard pressed not to haul her back into his arms and to hell with the consequences, only he knew that he couldn't do that. It wouldn't be fair to her or to himself to let this situation develop any further. Lucy deserved so much more than he could ever give her. She deserved a man who could give her children, and he wasn't that man. He couldn't bear to think that one day she could come to hate him, couldn't stand the thought that his shortcomings as a man would come back to haunt him once again.

The pain he felt was so sharp, so intense, that he could barely stand it. He knew that he had to leave before he ended up making a fool of himself. When Amanda came over to speak to them, he quietly excused himself. Most people were queuing up for the buffet and nobody noticed him leaving, so he was able to make his escape without it causing a fuss.

He sighed as he left the hospital and headed over to

his car. So much for hoping the party would take his mind off Lucy! All it had done was to make him see how impossible the situation was. The sooner he left Dalverston the better. Lucy could get on with her life and he could get on with his.

Lucy had the following two days off and spent them catching up with any jobs that needed doing. Although her flat was tiny, she spent a long time making sure everywhere was clean and tidy. She knew that she was keeping busy for the sake of it but it was the only way she could cope with what had happened between her and Max.

The fact that he had left the party without saying goodbye to her had hurt. There had seemed to be a real connection between them that night, yet he had walked away without a word. She couldn't help feeling let down even though she knew it was foolish. Max didn't do commitment and she didn't want him to, so why did she feel so upset?

By the time she went into work on Christmas Eve, Lucy felt more confused than ever. It didn't help that the unit was almost deserted when she arrived. With no new admissions that day, most of the staff had been sent home early. Even the wards were eerily quiet as the majority of patients had been discharged.

'It's like the *Marie Celeste* in here,' she observed when she went into the office for the handover.

'Don't knock it!' Tina Marshall, one of their part-time staff who was working that night, admonished her. 'I, for one, will be perfectly happy if it stays like this. I've got three children who are bouncing off the walls with excitement, waiting for Father Christmas to arrive.

I doubt if I'll get any sleep when I get home in the morning, so the quieter it is tonight, the happier I'll be.'

'Thank heavens my lot are past that stage,' Amanda declared. She quickly updated them about the remaining patients in the wards and then stood up. 'That's it, then. Diane's gone to the canteen for her break, but she should be back soon. Oh, and the staff choir will be doing their rounds at some point, singing Christmas carols. You'll never guess who's playing Father Christmas this year.'

'Why? Who is it?' Lucy demanded, but Amanda just grinned.

'Wait and see!'

No amount of pleading would make her tell them so in the end they gave up. Lucy went to the desk after Amanda had left. There was a stack of notes belonging to the patients who had been discharged that day that needed filing so she took them into the office and set to work. It didn't take her very long to finish the job and she was just wondering what she should do next when she heard voices in the corridor.

She hurried to the door and gasped when she saw a group of people gathered around the desk. They were dressed in an assortment of costumes ranging from elves and fairies to sheep. Father Christmas cut a fine figure in his flowing red robes, although she had no idea who was beneath the bushy white beard until he spoke.

'Ho, ho, ho. A merry Christmas to you, young lady,' Max said in an exaggeratedly deep voice that made her want to giggle.

'And a merry Christmas to you, too, Santa,' she replied, almost choking on her laughter.

'We've come to spread a little Christmas cheer,' he

informed her. He handed her a song sheet. 'Everyone's welcome to join in, elves, fairies, staff and patients.'

'Thank you.'

Lucy smiled as she took the sheet from him and he smiled back. Just for a second his eyes held hers and she felt her heart leap when she saw the awareness they held. She was immediately transported back to when he had held her in his arms at the Christmas party. There *had* been a connection between them that night, just as there was a connection between them now. Maybe it wasn't what either of them wanted but there was no point trying to deny it.

It was all very unsettling. When the choir began to sing the first carol, Lucy found it hard to concentrate. However, the familiar strains of 'Away in a Manger' soon had her singing along. They went into the wards where Max handed out fluffy white teddy bears to all the babies. He had a word with each of the mums and she couldn't help noticing how they all responded to him. It wasn't just the fact that Max was a very attractive man but that he obviously cared about people, and they responded to that. Once again she found herself thinking how at odds his attitude was to the way he lived his life.

They left the wards and made their way to the special care baby unit where Max placed a teddy on every incubator. When the choir began to sing 'Silent Night', Lucy wasn't the only one with tears in her eyes. There was something incredibly moving about hearing the beautiful old carol sung in a place where the most vulnerable babies were cared for.

'That was really lovely,' she said sincerely as they left SCBU.

'It always leaves a lump in my throat,' Max admitted as he followed her along the corridor.

'Me too. So where are you off to next?' she asked, pausing when they came to the stairs.

'There's just Women's Surgical left to do and that's it. I can hang up my robe and beard. I must say that I won't be sorry to part with the latter. It's incredibly hot and itchy!'

Lucy laughed when he began to scratch his chin. 'Good job you won't have to wear it for very much longer. Do you usually play Father Christmas?'

'No, this is a first for me. Sam Kearney was supposed to be doing it this year but he got held up in Resus. He phoned me to ask if I'd take over for him and I couldn't think of a way to refuse.'

'Well, I'm sure everyone appreciated your efforts.'

'Let's hope so.' He gave her a quick smile then went to catch up with the rest of the party.

Lucy went back to the office, wishing that she could have thought of something to keep him there a bit longer. She sighed because it was dangerous to think like that. She needed to stay away from Max instead of concocting reasons to be with him. She found the laundry list and went to put away the fresh supplies that had been delivered. Tina helped her and they had just finished when the phone rang.

'I'll get it,' Lucy said, hurrying to the desk. 'Maternity. Lucy Harris speaking.'

It was Helen Roberts's husband, phoning to tell them that Helen had gone into labour. He sounded frantic with worry and Lucy understood why when he explained that he had phoned for an ambulance only to be told that it could be some time before one reached them.

Apparently, there'd been a serious accident on the motorway and every available ambulance had been deployed there. With his leg still in a cast, Martin was unable to drive Helen to the hospital himself.

'Is there anyone else who could drive her here?' Lucy asked.

'No, nobody. Mum and Dad are away on a cruise and they won't be back for another week,' Martin told her anxiously.

'How about a neighbour, perhaps?'

'Jack Walsh is our nearest neighbour—he lives about ten miles away,' Martin informed her. 'I know it doesn't sound very far, but we've had a lot of snow in the past few days and the roads are virtually impassable in places. It could take an hour or more for Jack to get here.'

'That's probably as long as it would take an ambulance to get to you,' Lucy said, trying not to show how concerned she felt. She knew how dangerous it would be for Helen to give birth without the necessary precautions being taken. Poor glycaemic control during labour and birth could affect the baby, causing respiratory distress and hypoglycaemia amongst other things. Helen would need either insulin injections or intravenous dextrose plus insulin to keep her stable. She realised that she needed to discuss the situation with someone else.

'I need to speak to one of the doctors about this, Martin, so I'm going to have to phone you back.'

'You won't be long, will you? We really need help here asap.'

'I'll be as quick as I can,' she assured him. She hung up then contacted the switchboard and asked them to page Diane, quickly explaining what had happened as soon as the registrar phoned her back.

'I don't know what to suggest,' Diane admitted worriedly. 'Obviously, the situation is extremely urgent but without an ambulance to ferry Helen here, I don't know what we can do. I'll give Max a call and see what he says.'

Lucy hung up, checking her watch to see how much time had elapsed. Although the conversation had taken only a few minutes, every second counted. When the phone rang, she snatched up the receiver. 'What did Max say?'

There was a tiny pause before Max's voice came down the line. 'Diane just told me what's happened. I've spoken to Ambulance Control and they're trying to organise an ambulance, but it could take some time to get one out to the farm.'

'What about the neighbouring authorities?' she suggested, trying to still the thunderous beating of her heart, but hearing his voice so unexpectedly had thrown her off balance. 'Can they help?'

'Apparently they've already deployed any spare ambulances to the RTA. Ambulance Control will have to try further afield, possibly Lancaster or Penrith.'

'But they're miles away from here!'

'I know. I'm not happy about it either, but it's the best they can do in the circumstances. In the meantime, I'm going to drive up to the farm myself. I was on my way home when Diane phoned me but it won't take me long to get back to the unit and collect what I need.'

He paused and Lucy realised that she was holding her breath as she waited for him to continue. 'The thing is that I need someone to go with me. I've had a word with

Carol Jackson, the nursing manager, and she's agreed to find cover. A couple of the community midwives are on standby and I'm sure one of them will come in if it's necessary. So will you come with me, Lucy? Please.'

CHAPTER TEN

'How much further is it now?'

Max changed down a gear, keeping his gaze locked on the increasingly treacherous surface of the road. Thick snow blanketed the surrounding countryside, with drifts several feet deep in places. He couldn't imagine how an ambulance would manage to negotiate these roads in such appalling conditions, which made it all the more imperative that they get through.

'A couple of miles.' Lucy angled the light from the torch so that she could see the map. 'There should be a turning down here on the left any second now... There it is!'

Max slowed the car to a crawl before he turned into the lane. Even so, he felt the rear end slide sideways and held his breath as he steered into the skid. The last thing they needed was to end up in a ditch!

'I'm glad I'm not driving.' Lucy grimaced as the car righted itself and they set off down the lane. 'It's horrendously slippy.'

'It is. I can't see an ambulance making it up here, can you?' Max observed, resisting the urge to look at her. He needed to keep his attention on the road, he reminded himself, then sighed. Just sitting next to Lucy was distracting enough.

'No, I can't. So what are we going to do if we can't get Helen to the hospital before the baby arrives?'

She sounded worried and he hurried to reassure her. 'Exactly what we would do if Helen was in the unit. We have everything we need, Lucy—insulin, dextrose, pain relief, the lot.'

'And what if she needs a section? I mean, it could happen, Max. I know the recent scans of the baby seemed fine but....'

'But nothing. We'll deal with that if and when it happens.' He reached over and squeezed her hand. 'Don't go borrowing trouble, as my granny used to say.'

She gave a shaky laugh as she withdrew her hand. 'Your granny sounds like a very wise woman.'

She busied herself with the map, making it clear that she didn't want any more reassurances. Max gripped the steering-wheel, feeling his fingers tingling from the brief contact they'd made with hers. Could Lucy feel it too, he wondered, feel those frissons of awareness flickering under her skin? He thought she did, and it only made him feel even more conscious of her sitting beside him. To know that Lucy shared these feelings he had was both a torment and a joy.

It was another ten minutes before they finally reached the farmhouse. Max heaved a sigh of relief as he switched off the engine. 'I didn't think we were going to make it down that last stretch. The snow was so thick that the tyres couldn't get a grip.'

'I'm glad it's over,' Lucy said thankfully, opening the car door. She hurried round to the back and opened the tailgate, reaching for the box of supplies they'd brought with them.

'I'll take that if you'll carry my case,' Max told her,

lifting the box out of the Land Rover. They headed to the house and Lucy knocked on the door. Martin opened it and it was obvious how relieved he was to see them.

'Thanks heavens you made it!' He ushered them into the kitchen, using one of his crutches to direct them along the hall. 'Through there on your left. Helen's in the sitting room. We've been sleeping downstairs—it's easier than negotiating the stairs with these things.'

'We'll find her,' Max assured him. He led the way to the sitting room and found Helen lying on the sofa. 'How are you doing?'

'Not too bad.' She summoned a smile but Max could see the worry in her eyes. 'It's the baby I'm more concerned about. If my glucose levels aren't right then it could cause problems when it's born, couldn't it?'

'Yes, it could, but that isn't going to happen, Helen. We're going to keep a close watch on your blood glucose levels, aren't we, Lucy?' He turned to Lucy, trying to ignore the flood of emotions that filled him. He didn't have time to worry about how he felt when he needed to concentrate on Helen and her baby.

'We are. In fact, we shall do everything exactly the same as we would have done if you'd been in hospital,' she confirmed, using his own words to reassure Helen. They obviously worked because Helen's smile was less forced this time.

'Thank you. That's good to hear.'

The next half-hour flew past. After he had checked Helen's blood glucose levels, Lucy helped him set up the drip. The mixture of dextrose and insulin would help to maintain Helen's glucose levels during the birth, although they would need to monitor the situation very closely. The sofa pulled out into a double bed, so once

Martin had told them where to find clean sheets and blankets, they got that ready as well.

Max had brought a portable foetal monitor with him and as soon as Helen was comfortably settled, he checked the baby's heart rate and was relieved to find that it appeared perfectly normal. Although he knew they were doing everything possible to ensure both the mother's and the child's safety, he would feel a lot happier once they got Helen to hospital.

He excused himself and went into the hall to phone the ambulance control centre for an update. It wasn't good news and it was hard to hide his concern when he went back to the sitting room. Lucy obviously realised something was amiss because she came hurrying over to him.

'What's happened?' she said quietly so Helen and Martin couldn't hear her.

'Apparently, an ambulance was dispatched half an hour ago. Ambulance Control has just received a message to say that it's stuck in the snow and the crew don't think they'll be able to go any further. They've been told to return to base once they've dug themselves out.'

'So what's going to happen now?'

'I've asked them to get onto the air ambulance service and see if they can help. If we can get a helicopter out here, that will solve our problems.'

'Will it be able to fly in these conditions, though?'

'I really don't know. All we can do is cross our fingers and hope we get a break. Anyway, how's Helen doing?' he asked, refusing to dwell on what they would do if the helicopter failed to reach them.

'Her contractions are speeding up.' Lucy took her cue from him. Her voice held no trace of the anxiety he knew she must be feeling. Max couldn't help feeling proud of the way she was responding to the challenge but deemed it wiser not to say anything. He couldn't afford to let his emotions get in the way of him doing his job.

'Is she fully dilated?'

'Not yet. She's about eight centimetres so we've a bit of time yet. Is there anything in particular that I need to look out for when the baby is born?'

'We'll start with the usual assessment and carry on from there. There's been no indication that Helen's baby is suffering from congenital heart problems, but obviously we need to be aware of that,' Max explained. 'Hypoglycaemia can be an issue, so a blood glucose test will need to be done two to four hours after the birth, which is another reason why we need to get the baby to hospital as soon as possible. Other tests will be carried out if there are any clinical signs to indicate that there's a problem.'

'It's better if the baby feeds as soon as possible, isn't it?' Lucy clarified.

'Yes. Within thirty minutes of the birth is recommended, then every two to three hours after that until feeding maintains pre-feed blood glucose levels at a minimum of 2.0 mmol/litre.'

'And if it drops below that level?'

'If it happens on two consecutive readings, the baby will need to be fed by tube or given intravenous dextrose. However, I'm hoping neither of those will be necessary and definitely not while we're here.'

'Amen to that,' Lucy agreed fervently.

'It's going to be fine,' Max assured her. 'All we

have to do is hold the fort until the air ambulance gets here.'

'As simple as that, eh?' she said, rolling her eyes. 'We sit tight until the cavalry arrives.'

Max laughed. 'That's it. Easy-peasy, as my niece Emily would say.'

Lucy looked at him curiously. 'I didn't have you down as a doting uncle.'

'No?' He shrugged. 'My brothers have five children between them, so I've well earned my stripes.'

'You like children, then?'

'Of course I do. Why wouldn't I?'

'Oh, no reason.'

She gave him a quick smile and moved away. Max sighed as he watched her go over to Helen. Lucy obviously thought that his bachelor status was a sign that he wasn't keen on children and that couldn't be further from the truth. Just for a second he longed to explain the situation to her before he realised how pointless it was. Lucy wasn't going to play any part in his future, so it wouldn't make a scrap of difference to her if he couldn't have kids.

Lucy made a note of Helen's blood pressure then glanced at the clock. Twenty minutes had passed since Max had spoken to the ambulance control centre. Was the helicopter on its way, or had the crew decided that the weather conditions were too bad for them to risk flying? She had no idea what they were going to do if it failed to arrive. All they could do was sit tight and hope that help would arrive eventually.

She frowned as she unfastened the cuff from around Helen's arm because that thought had reminded her of what Max had told her. In her experience, men like him, who enjoyed such a hedonistic lifestyle, weren't usually interested in other people's children. However, there'd been genuine affection in his voice when he had spoken about his niece and it was yet another factor that didn't add up.

'I'll get onto Ambulance Control again and see what's happening.'

Lucy glanced round when Max suddenly appeared at her side. 'Good idea. We need to know if that helicopter is on its way,' she agreed, hoping he couldn't hear the uncertainty in her voice. She'd made one massive error of judgement with Richard and she would be a fool to make another one now. She should accept the situation for what it was and stop trying to justify Max's behaviour all the time.

'Fingers crossed,' he murmured, heading for the door.

Lucy put the sphygmomanometer back in its case then checked the drip. Although Helen's contractions were strong, she still wasn't fully dilated. It would be a while yet before the baby was born, which meant there was still time to get her to hospital if the helicopter arrived soon.

'No sign of that helicopter yet?' Martin asked anxiously.

'Max is phoning ambulance control for an update,' Lucy explained as calmly as she could because it wouldn't help if she appeared worried as well.

'I should have insisted that you went to stay at your mother's,' Martin said, turning to glare at his wife. 'There wouldn't have been a problem if you'd been in town.'

'And how would you have managed here on your own, with your leg in plaster?' Helen retorted.

'I'd have coped well enough,' Martin said gruffly. 'Anyway, Bert would have given me a hand if I'd needed it.'

Helen rolled her eyes as she turned to Lucy. 'Bert's our stockman and the most curmudgeonly old devil you can imagine. I don't think he's said more than a dozen words to either of us since Martin took over the farm after his father retired. Somehow, I can't picture Bert playing nursemaid!'

She broke off when another contraction began. Lucy smiled to herself when she saw Martin lean over and rub Helen's back. Despite their disagreement, it was obvious how they felt about each other. They had the kind of close and loving relationship she had always dreamed about, a relationship that grew stronger with time. With a sudden flash of insight she realised that her relationship with Richard would never have been like that, even if it had survived. It took selflessness to put the other person first, to find happiness by making them happy, and Richard wasn't capable of that. He always put his needs before everyone else's and was only truly happy if he was getting what *he* wanted.

In her heart, Lucy had known that but she had chosen to ignore her doubts. She had been as much at fault as Richard had in a way because she had deliberately deceived herself, and that was something she must never do again. She looked up when the door opened as Max came back, and felt her pulse begin to race. If she was to be truthful about her feelings from now on then she couldn't lie about the way she felt about Max. It would be only too easy to fall in love with him, even if it would be a mistake.

'The helicopter's on its way. It was ferrying another

casualty to Penrith, which is why there's been a delay, but it should be here in roughly ten minutes' time.' Max frowned when the information was met with silence. 'Did you hear what I said, Lucy? The helicopter's on its way.'

'I…um…yes. That's brilliant news.'

She gave him a bright smile but he could tell how forced it was. If he hadn't needed to prepare for the helicopter's arrival, he would have demanded to know what was wrong, but he simply didn't have the time to spare.

'We need to find a place where it can land,' he explained, turning to Martin. 'Obviously, it has to be flat and well away from any trees or overhead cables that could snag the rotors.'

'The field behind the house is the best place,' Martin said immediately.

'Great. Can you show me where it is…? Oh, and have you got any torches or anything similar which we can use to guide them in?'

'Sure. I've a stack of lanterns in the barn, we can use them.'

Martin grabbed his crutches and hurriedly left the room. Max followed him, leaving it to Lucy to get Helen ready for the transfer. He sighed as he followed Martin across the farmyard. Maybe it was a good thing that he hadn't tried to find out what was troubling her. He was already in far deeper than he should have been and he needed to keep his distance, even if it was proving extremely difficult to do so. He just had to remember that he was doing this for her sake as well as his and hope that it would help.

* * *

The flight to the hospital was extremely bumpy. A strong wind had sprung up, threatening to blow them off course at one point. Lucy heaved a sigh of relief when the helicopter touched down safely on the landing pad on the hospital's roof. As soon as the blades stopped spinning, Helen was lifted onto a trolley and rushed inside. Lucy hurried along beside her. Max had stopped to thank the crew but he soon caught up with them.

'I want you to check her blood glucose levels as soon as we get her into the delivery room. The stress could have had an adverse effect.'

'Right.' Lucy hurried on ahead, automatically checking the board behind the desk to see which rooms were vacant. She was surprised to discover that two suites were occupied.

'It looks as though it's been busier than we expected,' she said, elbowing open the door to suite number three. 'Tina must have been run off her feet.'

'I'll check everything's OK once we've got Helen settled,' Max told her. He helped the porters line up the trolley beside the bed so that Helen could slide across, then attached her to the foetal monitor. He smiled when the baby's heartbeat echoed around the room. 'Well, this little fellow seems happy enough. He obviously enjoyed his first ride in a helicopter.'

'I just wish Martin had been able to come with us,' Helen said, her voice catching. There'd been no room for Martin in the helicopter so they'd had to leave him behind. 'He desperately wanted to be at the birth and now he's going to miss it.'

'There's still time for him to get here,' Lucy assured her, mentally crossing her fingers. 'It could be a while yet before your baby is born, so if he can get someone to drive him here he might make it in time.'

She knew it was a long shot, but if it stopped Helen fretting that was the main thing. Max gave her a quick smile as she set about checking Helen's glucose levels and her heart lifted. Even though she knew how dangerous it was, it felt good to know that she had earned his approval.

CHAPTER ELEVEN

HELEN's baby was born at four fifty-five on Christmas morning. True to his word, Martin was there for the birth. A neighbour had driven him to the hospital on his quad bike and he was covered in snow when he arrived. Lucy laughed when Trish ushered him into the room.

'You look like the abominable snowman!'

'I feel like it,' Martin declared, stripping off his jacket. He dumped it on the floor in the corner then hobbled over to the bed and smiled at his wife. 'I told you I'd be here, didn't I?'

'You did.' Helen smiled as she took hold of his hand and held it tightly. 'Although if you'd left it any later you'd have missed the main event!'

Everyone laughed before they concentrated on what needed doing. The baby's head had crowned and a few seconds later it emerged. After another few contractions, first one shoulder and then the other were delivered before the rest of the body slid out. Lucy quickly wiped away the mucus from the baby's mouth and held him so that his head was lower than his body. He hadn't breathed yet so she blew hard on his chest then tapped the soles of his feet when he still didn't respond. Max was tying and cutting the cord and as soon as he'd finished, she carried the baby over to the table, using a length of narrow tubing to clear any remaining mucus from his airway then massaged his chest and back with a towel. However, he still didn't make any attempt to breathe.

'What's wrong?' Helen demanded. 'Why isn't he crying?'

Lucy was too busy to answer and left it to Max to explain that they needed to start artificial respiration. Using a small-sized bag, she puffed air into the baby's lungs, watching as the tiny chest rose. Max came to join her and she saw the worry on his face when he checked for a pulse.

'Heart's stopped beating.'

Lucy nodded, not needing him to explain what they had to do next. She puffed some more air into the baby's lungs then watched as Max used the tip of his index finger to gently press on the baby's chest and massage his heart. The method for resuscitating a baby was basically the same as that used to resuscitate an adult. The difference was that one needed to be extremely gentle.

They repeated the process several times before Max held up his hand. 'Wait a moment... Yes! His heart's beating. Come on, little fellow, how about a nice big breath for your uncle Max?'

As though he had understood, the baby suddenly took his first breath. Lucy smiled in delight when he let out a loud wail. 'That's it. Have a good scream and let everyone know that you're not happy about being poked and prodded.'

Max chuckled as he watched the baby's face change from a waxy white to an angry red colour. 'I think he's taking you at your word. There's definitely nothing wrong with his lungs, from the sound of it.'

'There certainly isn't,' Lucy agreed. She wrapped the baby in a warm blanket and carried him over to his anxious parents. 'Here you go. One very grumpy little boy who needs some TLC from his mum and dad.'

'Thank you so much.' Tears were streaming down Helen's cheeks as she cradled her son in her arms. 'I was so scared when he didn't cry...'

She broke off, overcome with emotion. Lucy patted her hand, understanding how terrifying it must have been for her. 'He's fine now and that's the main thing.'

'Was it because of Helen's diabetes?' Martin asked in a choked voice. 'Was that why he couldn't breathe on his own at first?'

'Not at all. Some babies just need a little encouragement before they take their first breath,' Max assured him, playing down the drama of what had happened.

'But his heart wasn't beating either,' Helen put in. She bit her lip. 'Does it mean there's something wrong with him—with his heart, I mean?'

'Obviously, we can't rule it out until we've done some tests. All I can say is that none of the scans you had indicated that there's a problem.' His tone was gentle. 'I know it's difficult, Helen, but try not to worry. You won't do yourself any good if you get worked up.'

'I'll try,' Helen assured him. She dropped a kiss on her son's head then smiled at her husband. 'He's beautiful, isn't he?'

Lucy moved away from the bed as the couple set about the age-old ritual of counting their child's fingers and toes. They were such lovely people and she only hoped that nothing would show up in the tests to spoil their delight at becoming parents. She gave them a few minutes on their own then went back and explained that the baby needed to be fed. She knew that Helen was keen to breastfeed so she helped her get comfortable and showed her how to hold her son so that he was in the best position. They all laughed when he immediately began suckling greedily.

By the time she went off duty, Lucy was much more hopeful that everything would be fine. Max had arranged for an echocardiograph to be done as well as a range of other tests, but with a bit of luck nothing untoward would show up. As she went to fetch her coat, she couldn't help thinking how well everything had turned out after such a traumatic start. Diane was in the staff-room when Lucy went in and she grinned at her.

'I bet you're ready for home after the night you've had.'

'It was a bit hairy at times,' she agreed. 'How did you get on? I was surprised when I saw that there'd been two more admissions.'

'One of them has gone home,' Diane told her. 'Turned out it was a false alarm so she decided not to stay. The other is still in the delivery room. It could be a while yet before the baby arrives so it looks as though you've won this year's competition.'

'What competition?' Lucy asked in surprise.

'The midwife who delivers the first Christmas Day baby wins a bottle of champagne,' Diane explained.

'Really?'

'Yes. I don't know who started it but it's become a bit of a tradition around here. The consultant pays for it so it looks as though Max will have to cough up this year. Make sure you remind him.'

'Oh, right. Yes, of course,' Lucy agreed, knowing full well that she had no intention of doing so. Although it was a nice gesture, she would feel extremely uncomfortable about demanding that Max should buy her a bottle of champagne and even more uneasy at the thought of them sharing it!

Heat rose to her face and she hurriedly closed her locker. She didn't intend to go down that route, certainly didn't want to picture them clinking glasses and staring into one another's eyes. 'I'll get off, then. Are you working tonight?'

'Yes, unfortunately.' Diane grimaced as she wound her scarf around her neck. 'My boyfriend's not at all happy about it either. He's done nothing but grumble ever since I told him I had to work over Christmas. I wouldn't mind, but it's not as though we actually do anything. Christmas is usually spent vegging out in front of the television!'

'You're not alone,' Lucy laughed. 'That's what most folk do.'

'I suppose so.' Diane laughed. 'I know I shouldn't complain. At least it proves that he misses me when I'm at work...or I *think* it does.'

Lucy was still laughing as they left the staffroom. They waved goodbye to the day staff and headed to the lifts. The night shift was going off duty and they had to wait a couple of minutes for the lift to arrive. Lucy felt her heart jolt when the doors opened and Max stepped out. He smiled when he saw her.

'I'm glad I caught you. I just wanted to let you know that everything is looking very positive for Helen's baby. The echocardiograph is clear and his blood glucose levels are stable.'

'That's wonderful news. Have you told Helen and Martin yet?'

'No. I'm on way to do it now. Anyway, I won't keep you. I'm sure you're looking forward to getting home.'

He started to turn away but just then Diane piped up. 'Don't forget that you owe Lucy a bottle of champagne, Max.'

'Do I?' He glanced back, a frown drawing his brows together. Lucy could feel the colour rushing to her cheeks again as the images she had tried to dispel earlier came flooding back. Max's eyes would be so deep and intent as they stared into hers...

She took a quick breath to chase away the pictures, wishing with all her heart that Diane hadn't said anything. However, it seemed the registrar was determined that Lucy should receive her prize.

'Yes. The midwife who delivers the first baby born on Christmas Day wins a bottle of champagne, Max. You must know that.'

'Of course. Sorry, I'd forgotten all about it.' He turned to Lucy and shrugged. 'I'll sort it out as soon as I can if that's OK with you.'

'It's fine. Really. Don't worry about it,' she said, quickly stepping into the lift. The doors glided shut and she breathed a sigh of relief. With a bit of luck Max would forget all about it.

It was almost eight a.m. by the time Max arrived home that morning. Having left his car at the farm, he'd had to beg a lift and that had delayed him. As he let himself into his flat, he could feel weariness washing over him. He had been on the go for almost twenty-four hours and what he needed now was a long, hot shower followed by several hours of uninterrupted sleep.

The shower was soon accomplished; however, by the time he got into bed, he discovered that he no longer felt sleepy. He closed his eyes and tried to relax, but sleep eluded him. He kept thinking about what had happened the night before. It was as though everything he and Lucy had done was imprinted in his mind and he kept going over and over it, remembering what she'd said and how she'd looked until he thought he would go crazy. He knew that he couldn't allow himself to get so hung up on her, yet he couldn't seem to stop it.

In the end he got up and dressed rather than lie there any longer, torturing himself. He made himself a pot of coffee then phoned his brother Simon and told him that he wouldn't be able to make it for Christmas dinner seeing as he didn't have any transport. Simon immediately offered to drive over to collect him but Max refused. Apart from not wanting to ruin his brother's day, he didn't feel like socialising.

He finished his coffee then wandered around the flat, wondering what to do with himself. What he needed was a distraction, something to take his mind off Lucy and this situation he was in. In the end, he decided to go for a walk. Although it was bitterly cold outside, at least the icy air should help to clear his head.

Max followed the roads without any particular destination in mind. It wasn't until he found himself outside Lucy's flat that he realised he'd been heading in that direction all along. Even though he knew it was madness he needed to see her, talk to her, just *be* with her. It was like an addiction and he couldn't fight it any longer.

Taking a deep breath, he rang the bell.

* * *

Lucy had just stepped out of the shower when the door-bell rang. She frowned as she fastened the belt on her robe, because she certainly wasn't expecting any visitors. She was tempted to ignore it until it occurred to her that maybe the caller was here to see one of the other tenants and had rung her bell by mistake.

She ran downstairs and opened the front door, feeling the blood drain from her head when she found Max standing on the step. He gave her a crooked grin as he took stock of what she was wearing.

'Happy Christmas. I hope I didn't wake you up.'

'No. I'd just got out of the shower when you rang the bell.' She took a quick breath, struggling to contain the rush of emotions that were flooding through her. Although she had no idea what he wanted, she couldn't pretend that she wasn't pleased to see him.

'Has something happened?' she said, hurriedly clamping down on that thought. 'It's not Helen, is it? Nothing's happened to her or the baby?'

'No, they're both fine.' He shrugged. 'I couldn't sleep so I went for a walk. I was just passing and thought I'd check that you were all right after last night's escapade.'

'Oh, I see.' Lucy nodded, although she had no idea why he'd felt it necessary to check on her. 'I'm fine, as you can see, so there's no need to worry about me.'

'Good.' He gave another shrug and she felt a ripple of surprise run through her when she realised how on edge he looked. It was obvious that there was something troubling him and she knew she wouldn't rest until she found out what it was.

'I was about to make some coffee. Would you like a cup?' she offered.

'I don't want to intrude...' he began, but she didn't let him finish. If something was worrying him then she wanted to help, if she could.

'You aren't.'

'In that case, then, thank you. A cup of coffee would be great.'

He stepped into the hall, closing the door behind him. Lucy led the way up the stairs, wondering if she was mad to have suggested it. Getting involved with Max would be a mistake and she knew it, so why was she deliberately courting trouble? She bit her lip as she led him into the flat because ever since she'd met Max she'd been behaving strangely.

'This is...er...cosy.'

Lucy looked round when he spoke, an unwilling smile curling her mouth when she saw him glance around the room. 'That's how the letting agent described it, funnily enough. If you ask me, I think poky sums it up far better.'

Max laughed out loud. 'Now I'm in a real quandary. I don't know whether to agree with you, or be polite and deny it!'

'There's no need to be polite. This place is the pits and anyone can see that. Anyone who's not an estate agent, that is.'

'If it's any consolation it would be classed as spacious in London. Even a broom cupboard down there sends the average estate agent into paroxysms of delight.'

'You lived in London before you moved here?' Lucy asked, making her way to the alcove that served as her kitchen.

'Yes. I went to university in London and ended up staying after I qualified. I lived there for over twelve years, in fact.'

'So why did you decide to leave?' she asked, filling the kettle with water.

'I decided that I wanted a complete change of scene after my divorce.'

'Divorce?' Water slopped onto the work top as she put the kettle down with a thud. 'I had no idea that you'd been married!'

'It's not something I talk about.'

'I understand.' She frowned. 'Although I do find it strange to learn that you were married when you told me quite emphatically that you aren't interested in commitment.'

'I'm not. Let's just say that what happened had a huge bearing on how I view life these days.'

Lucy had no idea what to say to that. However, her heart was heavy as she mopped up the water and plugged in the kettle. Max must have been dreadfully hurt by the failure of his marriage if it had changed his whole outlook on life. The thought of him having loved another woman to such an extent was so painful that she felt tears spring to her eyes and quickly blinked them away. She had no right to feel hurt, no rights at all where he was concerned.

'I imagine we're all influenced by past experiences,' she said quietly, refusing to dwell on that thought.

'We are.' He paused and she heard the question in his voice when he continued. 'I get the feeling that whatever happened in your past has had a big impact on you, too, Lucy.'

Lucy bit her lip as she debated what to say. Should she tell him about Richard and the whole sorry mess? It seemed such a huge step to take and yet she realised all of a sudden that she wanted him to know what had turned her into the person she was today.

'It did. For one thing it led me to move here, and that's something I certainly wouldn't have done.'

'Do you want to talk about it?'

His tone was so gentle that any doubts she had disappeared in a trice. Max obviously cared what had happened to her and the thought made it that much easier to open up.

'There's not a lot to say really. I was engaged to this guy when I discovered that he'd been cheating on me.' She shrugged. 'I'm not the first woman to find herself in that position and I doubt I'll be the last, either.'

'But that doesn't make it any less painful.'

Tears prickled her eyes again when she heard the compassion in his voice. 'No, you're right. It doesn't. I was devastated when I found out what had been going on. It completely knocked my confidence. I thought Richard loved me, you see, but it turned out that he'd been out with a string of women during the time we were together. That would have been bad enough, but what hurt even more was finding out that he'd been seeing my cousin, Amy.'

'That must have been a terrible shock.'

'It was. Our mothers are twins, you see, so Amy and I grew up together. We were always very close but when this came to light, it caused a huge rift not only between us but both our families as well. Mum naturally took my side while my aunt felt she had to defend Amy. It got to the point where they were no longer speaking to each other.'

'It must have been very difficult for you.'

'It was horrible. I felt so stupid too, because it had

never crossed my mind that Richard might be with another woman when he was supposed to be working late!'

Tears began to stream down her cheeks and she heard Max utter a low oath as he pulled her into his arms. 'Don't cry, sweetheart. He isn't worth a single one of your tears after what he did.'

He nestled her head against his shoulder, murmuring softly as all the pent-up emotions came pouring out. Lucy cried until she had no more tears left, but it was the release she'd needed and once it was over, she felt calmer, able to see the situation for what it was. She wasn't responsible for Richard's actions. It had been his choice to cheat on her and she wasn't to blame.

'Are you OK?'

Max's voice was so gentle that she shivered. She felt her breath catch when she looked up and saw the way he was looking at her with such tenderness in his eyes. It seemed like the most natural thing in the world to reach up and press her lips to his...

He uttered something rough deep in his throat as he claimed her mouth in a searing kiss. Lucy clung to him as the room started to spin. When he raised his head and looked into her eyes, she knew that he could see how she felt and didn't care. Maybe it was madness, but at that moment she wanted him to make love to her more than she had wanted anything in her whole life.

CHAPTER TWELVE

MAX could feel his heart pounding. There wasn't a doubt in his mind about what he could see in Lucy's eyes, yet how could he respond to it? It wouldn't be right to make love to her when she was so vulnerable.

He gently eased her out of his arms, feeling his heart ache as he was deprived of the warmth and softness of her body. It was a long time since he had denied himself the pleasure of making love to a woman but this wasn't just any woman. This was Lucy and he would do anything to protect her.

'I shouldn't have kissed you like that,' he said gruffly, struggling to come to terms with that idea. What was it about her that made him want to shelter her from harm? He had no idea but he couldn't deny that it was how he felt.

'It wasn't your fault, Max. After all, it was me who started it.'

Max had to steel himself when he heard the plea in her voice. It would take very little to push him over the edge and make him do something he would regret. He had to remember that he needed to protect himself as well as her, and hope that it would help to keep him strong.

'You were upset and I took advantage of that. I'm sorry.' His tone was brusque and he saw her recoil.

'There's no need to apologise,' she replied in a taut little voice that cut him to the quick. 'These things happen so forget it. I'll make us that coffee, or would you prefer tea?'

'Neither, thank you. I think it would be better if I left.' He turned towards the door, pausing when she gave a harsh laugh.

'Don't worry, Max, I'm not trying to trap you, if that's what you're afraid of.'

'Trap me?' he repeated uncertainly, glancing round.

'Hmm. First I lured you up here with the promise of coffee and then I tried to coerce you into my bed with tears.' She stared back at him and his heart ached when he saw the hurt in her eyes. 'You're probably wondering what comes next, so let me make it perfectly clear that I don't expect anything from you. I know you're a free agent and very keen to remain that way.'

'It isn't that.'

'No?'

'No,' he said firmly. He took her hands and held them tightly, wishing he could explain why it would be a mistake for them to get involved. It was only the thought of what she would think of him after he'd told her that stopped him. 'I don't want to hurt you, Lucy. You've had a really rough time recently and you're extremely vulnerable at the moment. It would be only too easy to do something that you'll regret.'

'And you think I'll regret it if we make love?' she said softly, her eyes holding his.

'Yes.' Max had to swallow because his mouth was so dry all of a sudden that it was difficult to speak. 'You aren't the kind of woman who sleeps around,

Lucy. You're the kind who needs commitment and that's something I can't give you.'

He bent and brushed her cheek with his lips, realising his mistake the moment he felt the softness of her skin beneath his mouth. He knew he should pull back but it was impossible to do so when every cell in his body was screaming that it needed this contact, that it needed more...

He turned his head until her mouth was suddenly under his, so soft and sweet, so warm and tempting that he knew he was lost. Hauling her into his arms, he kissed her with all the hunger that had been building up inside him for weeks. That first kiss may have been wonderful but it had barely taken the edge off his desire. He wanted her so much, wanted to kiss her and caress her, wanted to feel her body under his as they reached undreamed-of heights together.

The thought tipped him over the edge. All thoughts of behaving sensibly fled as he trailed kisses along her jaw and down her neck. Her skin was so warm and silky that he groaned as his lips glided over it. When he reached the collar of her robe, he pushed it aside so that his mouth could continue its journey, trailing kisses along her collar bone to the tip of her shoulder before working his way back to the tiny hollow at the base of her throat where a pulse was beating wildly. He paused, feeling the rapid throb against his lips. He had never wanted any woman as much as he wanted her!

'Don't stop.'

Her voice was husky with desire and Max felt every cell in his body react to it. He drew back and looked at her, knowing what he would see in her eyes, yet even then he wasn't prepared for how it made him feel. To know that she wanted him this much was like being offered a slice of heaven.

'I won't stop unless you ask me to,' he told her, his own voice grating with the force of his desire. He knew she understood what he meant when he saw her eyelids lower and tensed. It was one thing to invite his kisses but was she sure that she wanted him to make love to her, one hundred per cent certain that she wouldn't regret it?

Tension thrummed through his body as he waited for her to speak, made him feel so light-headed that it was a moment before he realised that she was looking at him.

'I won't want you to stop, Max. I'm absolutely certain of that.'

It was all he'd needed to hear and his heart leapt with joy as he pulled her back into his arms and held her so that she could feel the power of his arousal pressing against her. When his hands went to the belt on her robe, she trembled, not with fear or uncertainty, he knew, but with a passion equal to his own.

His hands were shaking as he parted the front of her robe because he knew this was a moment he would remember for the rest of his life. He closed his eyes for a second while he savoured the thought then looked at her, letting his gaze travel over the lushly feminine curves of her body. Her breasts were full and beautifully shaped, her waist incredibly narrow, her hips generously curved, and his pounding heart raced out of control.

'You're so beautiful,' he murmured. Reaching out, he let his fingers graze over one taut nipple and heard her gasp, so did it again only it was his turn to gasp this time. Everything about her was perfect, alluring, and he wanted nothing more than to enjoy the delights of her body.

He went to pull her back into his arms but she shook her head. 'No. Not yet. We need to even things up a bit first.'

Max had no idea what she meant and before he could ask, her hands went to the zip down the front of his leather jacket. He hadn't even realised that he was still wearing it until that moment and his head spun when it struck him how completely under her spell he was.

She drew the zipper down and his breath locked in his throat when she slowly parted the edges of his jacket and slid it off his shoulders. It was incredibly erotic to stand there and let her undress him. When her hands went to the hem of his sweater and started to lift it, he felt the blood pound through his veins.

Max stood rigidly still while she drew the sweater over his head and tossed it over the back of the sofa. He could feel the coolness of the air on his bare skin, such a stark contrast to the heat that was building inside him that his desire seemed to double in intensity.

'You're beautiful too,' she whispered huskily. Lifting her hands, she let her palms glide across his chest, a tiny frown creasing her brow as she followed the contours of muscle and bone as though committing them to memory.

Max's stomach muscles clenched when he felt her fingers caressing his skin. Everywhere she touched, nerve endings were firing out signals, alerting him to what was happening. When her palms glided over his nipples, he shuddered as a raft of sensations were unleashed inside him. She must have felt the tremor that passed through him because she paused, her hands resting lightly on his sensitised flesh.

'Did I hurt you?'

'No.' He pulled her back into his arms, feeling his mind explode with desire when her naked body came to rest against his. 'It wasn't pain I was feeling, my sweet. Far from it.'

'Oh!'

Max smiled when he saw her colour. The fact that she could still blush like that when they were on the verge of making love touched him deeply. Bending, he dropped a kiss on her lips then another on the tip of her nose. Her eyelids came next; he kissed her eyes closed, breathing in when he felt her lashes tickle his lips. Kissing had always been a pleasant enough experience in the past, but he had never felt this tenderness before, this desire to protect and cherish. It made him see that making love with Lucy would be unlike anything that had gone before. This would be a first for him in so many different ways.

The thought was just too much. Max kissed her again, on the mouth, with a passion that made them both tremble. He could feel the ripples running under his skin when he took hold of her hand and led her into the bedroom, tiny shock waves of sensation that made his nerves tingle and his flesh feel as though it was on fire. The room was small and cramped even with the bed pushed up against one wall, but he didn't care about their surroundings. He only cared about Lucy and what they were doing.

Sitting down on the bed, he pulled her down beside him and kissed her again, a slow, drugging kiss that soon had them clinging to each other. When she lay back against the pillows and held out her arms, he lay down beside her, smoothing his hand down her body, feeling her skin glide beneath his fingers like warm silk as he followed the curves and dips. They were both breathless when his hand made its way back up and came to rest on her breast, both of them filled with excitement and expectation, and it was the most wonderful feeling to know they were so perfectly in tune.

Max felt joy fill him as he stripped off the rest of his clothes and took her in his arms. This wasn't just sex; it could never be simply that. This was love-making in its purest form, the moment when two people became one single being. As he entered her, he knew that he had been given something so special that he would be forever in her debt. He would never regret this night and he would do everything in his power to make sure that Lucy never regretted it either.

The room was cold when Lucy awoke a short time later. She pulled the covers over her, feeling her heart fill with a host of emotions when her arm brushed against Max's shoulder. She didn't regret what had happened; how could she when it had been so marvellous. However, she knew that it could cause problems in the future. Max had made it clear that this wasn't the start of something more and she mustn't make the mistake of thinking that it was.

'Regrets already?'

She turned when he spoke, seeing the concern in his eyes. 'No. I'm not sorry it happened, Max.'

'But?'

'There isn't a but,' she said firmly, closing her mind to the insidious little voice that was whispering in her ear. She was a grown woman and if they were merely destined to have an affair then she could handle it. She didn't need promises of undying love to make it right! 'I went into this with my eyes open and I don't regret it.'

'Are you sure?'

'Quite sure. How about you, though? Are you sorry it happened?'

'No, I'm not.'

He pulled her to him, his mouth seeking out the hollow at the base of her throat. Lucy shivered when she felt the tip of his tongue tasting her skin. Their love-making had been a revelation. She had never imagined that she could feel such passion. It wasn't just that Max was a skilled lover either; it was the fact that there'd seemed to be a real connection between them. Their minds had been in tune as well as their bodies and it was that which had made it so amazing. If she'd been on the brink of falling in love with him before this had happened, how did she feel now?

Lucy closed her mind to that question because she didn't want to have to deal with the answer. They made love again and it was every bit as wonderful as the first time. As she lay in his arms afterwards, she knew that if there'd been any way to change his mind about the future then she would have leapt at it, but there wasn't. He was determined to stay single and after his previous, unhappy experiences, could she blame him?

The thought that Max must still care for his ex-wife if their divorce continued to affect him nagged away at her as they got up and took a shower. Naturally, they got sidetracked so that it was gone two o'clock by the time they went back into the bedroom. Lucy groaned when she realised how late it was.

'Is that the time already? I'm due in work in a couple of hours.'

'Do you want me to go?' Max offered immediately.

'No!' Lucy flushed when she realised how insistent she sounded. She mustn't make the mistake of appearing needy or she would scare him away. Although she had no idea how long this would last, she wanted to store away enough memories to see her through the coming years.

She gave a light laugh, determined not to look too far into the future. 'You're not leaving until you've had that cup of coffee I promised you. And how about something to eat? My mum would have a fit if she found out that I'd let a visitor leave without offering him sustenance.'

'Mine too,' he agreed, smiling as he fastened the belt on his trousers. 'Sounds as though they'd get on like a house on fire.'

'It does.' Lucy picked up her hairdryer. It was a figure of speech, she told herself sternly. Max certainly hadn't meant to imply that he wanted their parents to meet!

'Shall I make us something while you finish getting dressed?'

Lucy glanced up, feeling her heart turn over when her gaze landed on him. He hadn't put on his sweater yet and the sight of his naked torso made her pulse leap. He looked so wonderfully, gloriously male that it was difficult to concentrate on the question. 'I've not got anything very exciting in the fridge, I'm afraid. It didn't seem worth stocking up on Christmas goodies just for me, so I only bought basics.'

'Leave it to me—I'll see what I can rustle up.'

'Well, if you're sure you don't mind....'

'Of course I don't mind.' He dropped a kiss on her lips. 'You just concentrate on making yourself look beautiful, not that it will take much effort.'

He dropped another kiss on her lips and left. Lucy smiled as she switched on the hairdryer. She hadn't been looking forward to Christmas, but it was turning out to be a lot better than she had expected!

She finished drying her hair then hunted through the wardrobe for something to wear. She finally decided on a pair of black cord jeans teamed with a red velvet top, which looked suitably festive. She could hear Max whistling in the other room and smiled. She definitely hadn't expected to spend Christmas Day with Max either!

As soon as she was ready she made her way into the sitting room, only to come to an abrupt halt at the sight that met her. Max was standing by the stove and he turned when he heard her coming in.

'I hope you don't mind me raiding your cupboards.'

'Of course I don't mind,' she whispered, staring around in amazement.

He had drawn the curtains to block out the daylight and placed lighted candles around the room instead. The soft glow they gave out lent the shabby room an almost magical charm. More candles had been placed in the centre of the table, the flickering light from their flames reflecting off the glasses and cutlery. Lucy was so touched that he had gone to so much trouble that it was several seconds before she could speak.

'I never expected anything like this, Max. It looks absolutely beautiful. Thank you so much for doing all this.'

'So long as you like it, that's all that matters,' he

said softly. He picked up a couple of glasses and came towards her. 'I hope you like Bucks Fizz, although I'm afraid the fizz part is lemonade not champagne!'

Lucy laughed as she accepted one of the glasses. 'I shall make a note to always keep a bottle of champagne in the fridge from now on!'

'Starting with the bottle I owe you.' He gave her a warm smile as he touched his glass to hers. 'Happy Christmas, Lucy.'

'Happy Christmas,' she repeated, feeling a shiver run through her when she saw the way he was looking at her. Maybe it wasn't champagne, but it was every bit as potent as she had imagined it would be to share this drink with him, and the thought made her heart race.

They finished their drinks and Max took the empty glasses over to the sink. He came back and pulled out a chair then bowed. 'If Madame would care to take her seat, luncheon will be served very shortly.'

Lucy giggled as she sat down, loving the fact that he was as happy to play the fool as the ardent lover. 'Thank you, waiter. May I ask what's on the menu?'

'Omelettes *aux herbes fines*. Not exactly Christmas fare, but the chef does make the most amazing omelettes.' He kissed the tips of his fingers and she laughed.

'They had better be good after the build-up you're giving them!'

'Manna from heaven,' he assured her, grinning wickedly as he headed to the stove.

Lucy sighed as she watched him set to work, beating the eggs. It would be only too easy to see this rapport between them as a sign that their relationship would last, but it would be a mistake to do that. She had to remember that Max wasn't interested in her long-term.

It was a sobering thought and one that she couldn't ignore. It was a relief when Max brought in the plates. He set them down with a flourish.

'Luncheon is served.'

Lucy nodded regally, doing her best to play her part. She was going to enjoy this magical Christmas day, every single second of it, and not ruin it by worrying about what might happen in the future. 'Thank you, waiter.'

'My pleasure, Madame.' Tearing off a length of kitchen roll, he draped it across her lap with huge aplomb. *'Bon appétit.'*

'You've obviously done this before,' she said, laughing.

'I have indeed. I waited tables while I was medical school. The extra cash helped to top up my grant. In fact, at one point I was working evenings in a fast food outlet during the week *and* doing silver service in an up-market restaurant at the weekend.'

'Is that where you learned how to make an omelette?' she asked, cutting into her omelette, and he nodded.

'Yep. The chef was a nightmare to work for. He used to throw a tantrum if things weren't done the way he wanted them. Needless to say, the turnover of kitchen staff was horrendous and several times I ended up acting as his sous chef.'

'Really? So how did you get on with him?'

'All right, funnily enough. Oh, he still used to storm around the place but I learned to ignore him. It was good practice for when I did my rotations. Some of the consultants I worked for made him look like a real pussy cat!'

He rolled his eyes as Lucy laughed. She cut another sliver of omelette, sighing appreciatively as she popped it into her mouth. 'This is delicious. How did you manage to make it so light?'

'You add a splash of water to the eggs,' he informed her. 'I've no idea why but it seems to work. And you mustn't beat them too hard either.'

'I'll remember that,' she assured him.

They finished their meal and Lucy made a pot of coffee for them. Max was sitting on the couch when she took the tray in; he looked up and grimaced.

'I'll have dents in my bottom if I sit on this thing for very long. The springs are poking right through the cushions.'

'Tell me about it.' Lucy sighed as she gingerly perched on the edge of the couch and poured coffee into two mugs. 'It should be sent to the tip along with the rest of the furniture.'

'I take it that you rent the place fully furnished?'

'Yes. I couldn't afford to buy furniture when I moved here so I went for the easy option.'

Max frowned. 'I'd have thought it was cheaper living here than in the city. It's definitely less expensive to rent a place, I've found.'

'It is, and once the lease has expired on the flat in Manchester then I'll be much better off. I won't be paying rent on that as well.'

'You're still paying rent on your old flat!' he exclaimed.

'Yes.' Lucy grimaced. 'We'd only just signed the lease when I found out what my ex had been up to. He refused to pay his share of the rent after we split up, so it was down to me.'

'He sounds like a real piece of work,' he said in disgust, then shrugged. 'Sorry. It's not my place to say that.'

Because he didn't want to get involved? Lucy summoned a smile, but it hurt to know that Max was keeping his distance after what they had shared. 'Don't apologise, it's true. I only wish I'd realised sooner what he was like. It would have stopped a lot of people getting hurt.'

'You mean your family? Is that why you decided not to go home for Christmas and New Year, because of the upset it had caused?'

'Yes. I was afraid that if I went home everything would get raked up again and that's the last thing I want.'

'I imagine it would have been difficult to see your cousin after what has happened?'

'It would, although I don't blame Amy. She'd just split up with her boyfriend when Richard came onto her and I think that's why she ended up falling for him. He caught her at a weak moment, not that she was the first by any means.'

Max didn't say anything else. He let the subject drop, not that she was sorry. What had happened suddenly seemed of very little consequence if she was honest. It made her see that her feelings for Richard hadn't been nearly as deep as she'd thought, nowhere near as deep as the feelings she realised she had developed for Max. She knew that when she and Max went their separate ways, it would be far more painful.

CHAPTER THIRTEEN

MAX couldn't settle after he left Lucy. He went back home, intending to spend the evening watching the Christmas Day film, but it failed to hold his attention. In the end, he switched off the set while he sat and thought about everything that had happened that day.

Making love to Lucy had been everything he had dreamed it would be and more. He had never expected to feel such a connection to another person as he had felt to her, and the thought filled him with despair because at some point soon he would have to let her go. All he could have were a few short weeks and he really shouldn't allow himself even that much.

He sighed. He had done the one thing he had sworn he wouldn't do and now he had to ensure that he didn't make matters worse. That comment Lucy had made about her fiancé catching her cousin at a particularly vulnerable moment could apply equally to her. It brought it home to him that he needed to be extra-careful about how he handled the situation. Although he wished with all his heart that things could be different, it would be wrong to allow her to fall in love with him. The fact was, she would be much better off without him messing up her life.

* * *

Christmas Day had turned out to be quite busy, Lucy discovered when she arrived for work that night. Cathy was doing the handover and she lost no time updating her.

'There are two mums still in delivery. One's had her baby and she'll be moving onto a ward as soon as Anita has finished tidying her up. The other mum will be a while yet from the look of things. Helen Roberts is in the side room. The diabetes care team have asked us to monitor her blood glucose levels as they've nobody on duty tonight. She's on between-meals testing as well, so the last check will be due around midnight, if you could make a note of that.'

'Of course. What about the baby? How's he doing?'

'Fine. He's feeding well and all the tests are clear.'

'That's good to hear.'

They completed the handover and Cathy stood up to leave. 'That's it, then. Let's hope you have a quiet night, unlike last night.'

'It was quite an experience,' Lucy agreed.

'I'll bet it was.'

There was a strange note in Cathy's voice and Lucy looked at her in surprise. 'Sorry, am I missing something?'

'I heard all about you careering around the country-side with Max. The whole hospital's been buzzing with it, in fact.' Cathy grimaced. 'Tell me to mind my own business, but I think you should know that a lot of folk are wondering if you're the latest candidate to fall under Max's spell.'

'But it was work!' she protested, trying to control the blush that rose to her cheeks. Maybe last night had been to do with work but this afternoon certainly hadn't been.

'That's what I keep telling everyone but you know how people love to gossip, especially about Max. Just be careful, though. I think the world of Max—we all do—but he's an inveterate womaniser. I'd hate you to get hurt, Lucy.'

Cathy said her goodbyes and left before Lucy could say anything. She sighed as she left the office. Whilst she didn't regret what had happened, Cathy's advice was a timely reminder that she needed to take care. Just because she and Max had slept together, it didn't mean they had a future.

The evening flew past. Thankfully, Lucy had no time to brood because she was far too busy. The second baby, a girl, finally made her appearance just before nine p.m. Although it had been a long and tiring labour for the mother, everything was fine. Once mum and babe had been moved onto a ward, Tina went for her break. She'd only just left when the front doorbell rang to warn them there was someone waiting outside. Diane was in the office so Lucy popped her head round the door.

'Someone's just rung the bell. Can you hold the fort while I see who it is?'

Leaving Diane in charge, she hurried downstairs. Security was extremely tight on the maternity unit. All the external doors were kept locked during the night and anyone who wanted to be admitted had to ring the bell. Most mums phoned ahead to warn them they were coming in but there were always a few who just turned up. Opening the door, she peered out but there was nobody about. She frowned, wondering if it had been children playing a trick by ringing the bell. It had happened a couple of times, although it seemed unlikely on Christmas Day. Stepping outside, she scanned the car park but still couldn't see anyone.

Lucy went to go back inside when she heard a noise. She stopped dead, trying to work out where it was coming from. There was a bench seat against the wall close to the door and she realised that the sound was coming from that direction. She hurried over to the bench and gasped when she saw a Moses basket tucked on the end of it. There was a baby in it, wrapped in blankets and with a pale blue knitted hat on its head.

Lucy hurriedly picked up the basket and carried it inside. Although she would have liked to have gone and looked for whoever had left it there, her main concern was to make sure the baby was unharmed. She quickly made her way back to the maternity unit, seeing the shock on Diane's face when she saw what Lucy was carrying.

'Someone left this on the bench by the front door,' she explained as she carried the basket into the office. Placing it on the desk, she stared down at the baby. 'I've no idea who left it there because there was nobody about by the time I got to the door.'

'We'll have to inform the police,' Diane said immediately. 'I'll do it while you make sure he's all right. We'll use one of the delivery rooms for now. There's always a few mums in the nursery at this time of night, doing feeds, and it would be better if we kept this to ourselves for now.'

'Of course.'

Lucy carried the basket into one of the delivery rooms and placed it on the bed. Although the baby was well wrapped up, it was bitterly cold outside and she wanted to make sure that he wasn't suffering from hypothermia.

Babies rapidly lost body heat and even a relatively short period of being exposed to the elements could cause a drop in their temperature. She fetched a thermometer and took his temperature, relieved to find that it was within normal limits. She had just finished when Tina appeared.

'I can't believe this has happened!' Tina exclaimed as she came over to the bed. 'How could any mother abandon her child like that? And on Christmas Day too!'

'Whoever did it must have been desperate,' Lucy said sadly. She lifted the baby out of the basket when he started to grizzle and stroked his cheek. 'He's obviously been well cared for—you can tell that just by looking at him. Both his clothes and the blankets he was wrapped in are spotless.'

'I suppose so,' Tina conceded. 'Anyway, the police are on their way. Diane said to tell you that they want to interview you, apparently. She's going to phone Max and let him know what's happened. I expect he'll be here shortly, too.'

'Oh. Right.' Lucy felt her heart lurch at the thought of seeing Max again so soon. She had to make a conscious effort not to let Tina see how on edge she felt. 'I think this little fellow might be hungry. Will you stay with him while I go and rustle up a bottle?'

Lucy popped the baby back into the basket and made her way to the nursery. There were a few mums in there so she had a quiet word with the sister and explained what had happened. Once she had made up a bottle of milk, she went back to the delivery room. The police had arrived and they were keen to interview her, so she handed the bottle to Tina while she made a statement.

She had just finished when Max arrived and she felt her pulse start to race when he came straight over her.

'Are you all right, Lucy? This must have been a real shock.'

'I'm fine.' She smiled up at him, loving the way his eyes had darkened when he looked at her. Max might be reluctant to commit himself, but he couldn't hide the fact that he cared about her. The thought made her heart overflow with happiness. 'I'm more concerned about finding the baby's mother. She obviously needs help.'

'We'll find her,' he said softly, giving her shoulder a gentle squeeze.

The police wanted to ask him some questions next so Lucy excused herself. Tina had finished giving the baby his bottle so she volunteered to change his nappy. She undid the poppers down the front of his pale blue sleep suit, smiling when he started gurgling and kicking his legs.

'So you think this is a game, do you?' she said, tickling his tummy. He wriggled even harder, his chubby little legs flailing up and down with excitement, and she laughed. 'You're a lively little fellow, I must say.'

She changed his nappy and was about to pop him back into his clothes when Max came over to her. 'The police need his clothes and the basket in case they contain any clues as to who he belongs to.'

'Of course. I'll undress him now.'

Lucy quickly slipped off the baby's sleep suit and vest and handed them to one of the officers who placed them in a plastic bag. Although the mums were asked to bring in clothes for their babies, there was a selection of baby clothes in each delivery room in case someone forgot. She found a fresh vest and a sleep suit and took them over to the bed.

'Can you tell us roughly how old he is, Doctor?' the older police officer asked as Lucy started to dress the baby.

Max frowned. 'Well, he's not a newborn.' He pointed to the baby's tummy. 'The stump of his umbilical cord has fallen off and that usually happens in the first couple of weeks. If I had to make a guess I'd say he's about four to five weeks old and that he's been well looked after too. He's definitely not undernourished.'

'I see. And is there any way of checking if he was born here?' the officer continued, making a note on his pad.

'You think that's why the mother left him here?' Max said in surprise.

'It's possible. Most women who abandon their babies choose a place where they know the child will be looked after. It's possible that this little chap's mum gave birth to him here and that's why she chose to leave him outside your door.'

'It makes sense, I suppose.' Max sighed. 'We keep a record of all the babies who are born in the unit, but I'll need to speak to the hospital's manager before I can give out information like that. It's a question of patient confidentiality, you understand.'

'I understand, Dr Curtis. Rules are rules. But the sooner we find the mother, the better. In my experience, the longer this goes on, the less chance we have of tracing her.'

Lucy could tell that Max was torn between the desire to help all he could and the need to protect their patients' privacy. She hurriedly intervened, wanting to take some of the pressure off him. 'What happens now? To the baby, I mean.'

'He'll be taken into care and placed with foster-parents,' the officer explained. 'I'll get onto the child protection team as soon as we get back to the station and arrange for them to collect him.'

'Actually, I'd feel happier if he remained here tonight,' Max said firmly. 'Although he appears to be perfectly fit and healthy, I'd like to keep him under observation. We can find a place for him in the nursery, can't we, Lucy?'

'Of course,' she said immediately.

The policemen agreed that it was probably the best option and left shortly afterwards to check the CCTV footage. There were cameras covering all the outside doors and they were hoping that the incident had been captured on film. Lucy sighed as she fitted a plastic identification tag around the baby's wrist before she took him to the nursery.

'I hope they find his mother. I hate just putting the date and the time he was found on this tag instead of his name.'

'Hopefully, his mum will come forward soon and claim him,' Max said quietly.

'Is that why you were so keen to keep him here?'

'How did you guess?' He smiled at her. 'I know it's a long shot, but the fact that she left him outside our door suggests that she trusts us. I think it's far more likely that she will get in touch with us if she thinks the baby is here rather than with the police.'

'You could be right. So what do we do if she does contact us?'

'Try to reassure her that she isn't in any kind of

trouble. She must be in a pretty bad state to have abandoned her child like that and the last thing we want is for her to think that she'll be in trouble with the authorities.'

'I feel so sorry for her,' Lucy said sadly, looking down at the baby. 'I can't imagine what she must be going through at the moment, can you?'

'We'll do everything we can to help her, Lucy. I promise you that.'

His tone was so gentle that her heart ached. Max was such a good person, kind, caring, considerate of other people's needs. Maybe he did portray the image of a carefree bachelor, but she was more convinced than ever that it was all a front. It didn't seem right that he should continue to deny himself the kind of life he deserved because his first marriage had failed and she needed to make him understand that.

'Look, Max,' she began, then stopped when the door opened and Diane appeared.

'Sorry, Max, but you're wanted on the phone. It's Alan Harper, the hospital's manager. Apparently, the press have found out about the baby being abandoned and phoned him at home.' Diane grimaced. 'He's none too pleased, either, seeing as he knew nothing about it.'

'How on earth did they get hold of the story so soon?' Max exclaimed, hurrying to the door. He paused to glance back. 'Can you book him into the nursery and make sure all the staff know that any phone calls concerning him are to be directed to me. There'll probably be a lot of crank calls once the news gets out, but if the mother does phone, I want to speak to her.'

'I'll make sure everyone knows what to do,' she assured him, and he smiled.

'Thanks, Lucy.'

Lucy sighed as she took a blanket off the rack and wrapped the baby in it. Maybe it was a good thing that she'd been interrupted when she had. It wasn't her place to give Max advice and he would probably have resented her interfering. After all, if he'd wanted to change the way he lived, he would have done so. The fact that he hadn't pointed to just one thing: he must still be in love with his ex-wife if their divorce continued to exert such an influence over him.

She knew she should accept that, but it was hard to accept that Max loved another woman after what they had shared that afternoon. She had felt closer to him that day than she'd felt to anyone else and knew that if she continued to see him, her feelings would grow stronger. She knew that she should call a halt but she couldn't face the thought. The truth was that she had fallen in love with Max and didn't want to lose him.

By the time Max returned to the maternity unit, over an hour had passed. Alan Harper had decided to consult a member of the trust's legal team to ask his advice about handing over the information the police had requested. He'd insisted that Max should be included in the discussion so a conference call was set up. However, in the end nothing definite was decided. It seemed that everyone was reluctant to take any steps that could result in the trust being sued, so more lawyers would need to be consulted before a final decision was made.

Max was seething when he stepped out of the lift. Although he understood the need to protect their patients' privacy, nobody seemed to appreciate how urgent the situation was. Lucy was working at the desk and she frowned when she saw his grim expression.

'What's wrong?'

'Bureaucracy gone mad is what's wrong. Instead of doing all we can to help the police find the mother, we've been banned from handing over any information.' He shook his head. 'Everyone's more concerned about the trust being sued than anything else.'

'It's a sign of the times,' she said softly. 'Court cases are rife these days. Nobody's immune, not even hospitals.'

Max sighed. 'You're right, of course. It's just so frustrating not to be able to do anything to help.'

'I know.' She picked up a printed sheet and handed it to him. 'I checked back through our files and this is a list of all the babies born here during the past six weeks. If we discount all the girls it leaves fifteen in total.'

Max glanced at the paper and shook his head. 'Nothing leaps out at me. How about you?'

'I feel the same. I recognised some of the names, the babies I delivered, but that's as far as it goes. He could be any one of them.'

'Or he might not be on this list at all. After all, there's no guarantee the baby you found was born here.'

'That's what's so worrying. The police have so little to go on.'

'Did they find anything on the CCTV footage?'

'Yes, but it's not much help, I'm afraid.'

She handed him half a dozen grainy photographs. Max grimaced as he squinted at the blurred image of a hooded figure carrying the Moses basket. 'You can't even tell if it's a man or a woman from these!'

'I know. The police have taken the tape back to the station to see if they can clean it up, but they didn't sound too hopeful. In the meantime, they want us to show these pictures to everyone who works here in case someone knows who it is.'

'I doubt they'll recognise her from these.' He handed back the photographs. 'There's been no phone call?'

'Not yet, but everyone knows what to do if she rings,' she assured him.

'There's not much more we can do, then, is there?' He glanced at his watch and groaned. 'It's gone midnight already!'

'I didn't realise it was so late. I need to check Helen Roberts's blood glucose levels again.'

She got up and came around the desk. Max stepped aside to let her pass, feeling his body stir when she accidentally brushed against him. He took a deep breath to control the surge of desire that flooded through him, but he could tell that she'd realised what was happening when he saw her face colour. It took every scrap of willpower he possessed not to haul her into his arms and kiss her until they were both senseless.

'I'll be in the office if you need me,' he told her, his voice grating from the strain of keeping a rein on his feelings.

'You're not going home?' she asked, and he could hear the tension in her voice too. His heart started to race when he realised that she felt exactly the same as he did.

'No. I'd rather stay here in case the mother phones.'

'She might not phone tonight, though. It could be to-morrow before she plucks up enough courage, or the day after that. You can't work twenty-four hours a day, Max, until she gets in touch. You'll wear yourself out!'

Max smiled when he heard the concern in her voice. It felt good to know that she cared about him, very good indeed. 'I understand that, but if she does call tonight then I'd like to be here so I can talk to her.'

'It's up to you, of course. But promise me that you'll be sensible and go home in the morning.'

'I promise, on one condition.'

'And that is?'

'That you'll come home with me, Lucy.'

CHAPTER FOURTEEN

PALE winter sunshine was filtering into the room when Lucy awoke. Just for a second she had no idea where she was before it all came rushing back. She was in Max's flat. In his bed.

Rolling onto her side, she studied his sleeping face as she recalled what had happened when they had arrived at his apartment earlier that morning. Their hunger for each other had been so great that they hadn't made it further than the living room. Max had made love to her right there on the sofa, his powerful body pressing her down into the smooth leather cushions. It had been an explosion of raw passion, the release they had both needed so desperately. Max had wanted her as much as she had wanted him; surely that had to mean something?

Lucy sighed as she tossed back the quilt. Maybe he *did* want her but it wasn't proof that he was looking for more than a physical relationship, was it? She had to accept that this was probably all she could have and enjoy it while it lasted.

She made her way into the en suite bathroom and stepped into the shower. Like the rest of the apartment, it was state of the art and she spent several minutes trying to work out how to turn on the water. She was so engrossed that when the glass door slid back and Max appeared, she jumped.

'I wondered where you'd got to.'

'I…um…I was attempting to take a shower,' she explained, feeling her breath catch when he stepped into the stall. Even though it was only hours since they'd made love, she could feel the hunger building inside her again as she took stock of his naked body.

'It can be a bit tricky to work out all these switches,' he agreed, reaching past her to turn one of the dials. Water suddenly began to flow from the shower head and she gasped when she felt its coolness on her bare skin.

'It's freezing!' she protested, trying to move out of the way.

He caught her hand and stopped her. 'You won't feel cold in a moment,' he said softly, his eyes holding hers as he raised her hand to his lips.

Lucy's pulse leapt when she felt his tongue glide across her palm. When he reached her wrist he didn't stop but carried on up the inside of her arm, licking the droplets of moisture off her skin. Although the water was still beating down on her, she no longer felt cold but boiling hot, burning up inside. When his mouth moved from her arm to her breast, she cried out, shuddering as his lips closed over her nipple. Her legs felt so weak all of a sudden that she could barely stand but he eased her back against the tiles and held her there while his lips and tongue continued to work their magic, licking, stroking and caressing every inch of her until she was mindless with passion.

He drew back and looked into her eyes. 'Do you still feel cold?'

'No,' she murmured, feeling herself trembling with desire.

'Good.'

He smiled as he lifted her until she was straddling his hips. His mouth found hers at the very moment that he entered her and she closed her eyes as a wave of intense pleasure swept through her. She didn't need to look at Max to know that he felt the same. They were so completely in tune that she could tell exactly how he was feeling. She clung to him as they climaxed together, and in the final second, just before the world dissolved, she couldn't hold back any longer.

'I love you,' she whispered. 'I love you.'

Max could feel the words echoing inside his head, growing louder and louder with every beat of his heart. Lucy loved him—could it be true?

He wanted to leap up and punch the air in delight, but how could he? How could he celebrate when it was the one thing he should never have allowed to happen?

He set her back on her feet, reaching around her to turn off the water, feeling the pain bite deep into his gut when he saw her eyes open because he knew he would have to hurt her.

'Max? What is it? What's wrong?'

He had to steel himself when he heard the alarm in her voice. It would be so easy to accept what she was offering him, but it wouldn't be right when he had nothing to offer her in return. 'We need to talk, Lucy.' Opening the glass screen, he took a towel off the rack and handed it to her. 'Why don't you get dressed while I make us some coffee?'

'I don't want coffee! I want to know what's wrong.'

'Let's leave it until we're dressed,' he said flatly, deliberately removing any trace of emotion from his voice.

She didn't say another word as he stepped out of the stall, but she didn't need to. Max could feel her pain as he strode into the bedroom and dragged on his clothes. He didn't think he had ever felt as bad as he did at that moment, knowing that he had to hurt her even more. It was only the thought that he was doing it for her sake as well as his that gave him the strength to continue.

The coffee was ready by the time she appeared at the kitchen door. Max filled a couple of mugs and placed them on the table then pulled out a chair for her, but she made no attempt to sit down. She just stood and watched him, her face looking unnaturally pale in the glare from the overhead spotlights.

'So this is it, Max? You've had enough of me already?'

Her tone was bitter and he flinched. Sitting down at the table, he took a sip of his coffee, hoping it would steady him. He needed to make her understand that this was the right decision, the *only* decision that made any sense.

'I told you that I wasn't looking for commitment,' he said quietly.

'Yes, you did. No one could ever accuse you of being untruthful.' She laughed, and his heart ached when he heard the pain in her voice. 'I suppose it's my own fault. I committed the ultimate sin, didn't I? I should never have told you that I loved you.'

'Look, Lucy...'

'No. Please don't say anything. I feel foolish enough without you trying to reassure me that it doesn't matter. All I can say is that I'm sorry if I embarrassed you, Max. I never intended to do that.'

She spun round on her heel and he realised that she was going to leave. Was that what he really wanted? Did he want her to walk out of his life, thinking that she'd been at fault in some way? He shot to his feet and hurried after her. She already had her coat on by the time he reached the sitting room and his hands clenched when he saw her fumble with the buttons. He couldn't bear to know that she was upset and that it was all his doing.

'Lucy, I'm sorry! If anyone's to blame then it's me. I should never have got involved with you in the first place. I knew how dangerous it was but I kept telling myself that I could handle it.'

'Dangerous,' she repeated, turning to look at him. 'What do you mean by that?'

'That I knew from the first moment we met that I could very easily fall in love you.'

'And would that have been such a bad thing?' she asked, her voice catching.

'Yes.' Max could feel the blood pounding through his veins. He knew there was only one way to make her understand why they couldn't have a future and that was to tell her the truth. The thought of how she would react was almost more than he could bear but he had to do it.

'I'm no use to you, Lucy. ' He held up his hand when she went to interrupt. 'No, let me finish. The fact is, I'm no use to any woman because I can never father a child.

That's why you're better off without me messing up your life.'

Lucy felt the room start to spin. She grabbed hold of a chair and clung to it while everything whirled out of control. She heard Max say something but she had no idea what it was. When he took her arm and sat her down on the sofa, she didn't protest. She couldn't. Every single word seemed to have disappeared from her mind apart from the words he had uttered: he could never father a child.

'Here, drink this.'

He placed his mug of coffee in her hand and helped her raise it to her mouth. Lucy shuddered when she felt the hot liquid trickle down her throat. She took another sip then set the mug down on the coffee table, afraid that she might drop it. Max was sitting beside her now and she could tell that he was waiting for her to speak, but what could she say? She was so shocked by what he had told her that she had no idea how to respond.

'Wh-when did you find out? That you couldn't have children, I mean?' she managed at last.

'Three years ago. Becky and I had been trying for a baby for a while. When nothing happened, we decided to have some tests done.' He shrugged. 'It turned out that I was to blame.'

'It must have been a terrible shock for you,' she said softly.

'It was.' He gave her a tight smile and her heart wept when she saw the anguish in his eyes. 'I've always loved kids and just assumed I'd have some of my own one day. Finding out that the chances of it happening were virtually nil was a lot to take in.'

'But there is still a chance that you could father a child,' she said quickly.

'A very *slim* one. Apparently, I produce enough sperm but they have poor motility.'

'Surely there are steps you could have taken? I don't know much about fertility treatment but they can do wonderful things these days. Did you and your wife never think of trying it?'

'No. To be honest, I don't think we could have coped with the strain, let alone the disappointment if it had failed. We'd been going through a rocky patch even before we decided to try for a baby and that was the final straw. It was simpler to call it a day.'

'I'm so sorry, Max. It must have been a horribly difficult time for you.' She squeezed his hand, wishing there was something she could say to make him feel better.

'It's all over and done with now.'

He moved his hand away, making it clear that he didn't want her sympathy, and she sighed. Although she understood how painful it must have been for him to discover that he was unlikely to father a child, he couldn't let it affect his life for ever.

'Are you sure about that?'

'What do you mean?'

'You already admitted that your divorce is the reason why you steer clear of long-term relationships. It doesn't sound to me as though it's all over and done with from that.'

'Obviously, it has a bearing on how I lead my life these days. It wouldn't be right for me to expect any woman to forgo having children because of me.' He looked steadily back at her. 'I certainly wouldn't put you in that position, Lucy. It wouldn't be fair.'

'But surely it should be my choice,' she protested.

'Some choice.' His tone was grim. 'Stick with me and give up your dreams of becoming a mother. Or find some other guy who can give you all the children you want. I know which option I'd choose.'

'You make it sound so...so *clinical*! But you can't just turn your feelings on and off like a tap, Max.'

'You can when it's the sensible thing to do.' He stood up abruptly. 'Maybe you think you could live with the situation right now, but a few years down the line, you'll change your mind.'

'How do you know that?'

'Because I've seen how you are with the babies on the ward, how much you love them. Be honest, Lucy. Do you really think that you'll be happy if you never became a mother? Because I don't.'

Lucy hesitated. Although she longed to deny what he said, it wouldn't be right to do so without thinking about it first. She had always assumed that she would have a family one day, so could she really imagine being childless?

'I thought not.' Max obviously took her hesitation as a sign that she agreed with him. His face was set when he looked at her. 'I don't think there's any point letting this affair continue, is there?'

'If it's not what you want, Max, then, no, there isn't any point.' She stood up, trying not to let him see how much it hurt to hear him speak to her in that distant tone. Tears stung her eyes as she picked up her bag. It had never been just an affair to her. It had been so much more!

'You may as well know that I'm planning on leaving Dalverston in the near future. That should make life simpler for you.'

Lucy couldn't hide her surprise as she turned to him. 'Leaving?'

'Yes.' He shrugged. 'I decided that it was time I applied for a permanent consultant's post. Anna is due back from maternity leave at the end of January so it's the perfect time to make the move. I have a couple of interviews lined up in the next few weeks, so hopefully it won't take too long to find a suitable position.'

'Then all I can do is wish you luck,' she said hollowly, her head reeling when it struck her that he must have been planning his departure for some time if he already had interviews scheduled. The thought that she had only ever been a fleeting distraction to him was more than she could bear and she knew that she had to leave before she did the unforgivable and broke down.

She hurried to the door and let herself out, bitterly aware that Max didn't try to stop her. Why would he when he was probably relieved to see the back of her? All that talk about him being afraid of falling in love with her had been so much hot air. There'd never been any chance of that happening!

Tears ran unchecked down her face as she hurried down the drive. She'd thought she knew how it felt to have her heart broken but she'd been wrong. This was far worse than anything she had experienced before. She had lost the man she loved with all her heart and she couldn't imagine how she would ever get over it.

Max stood at the window, watching as Lucy ran down the drive. The urge to go after her and beg her to forgive him was so strong that he almost gave into it. His hands clenched as he fought for control but it was hard to stand there and watch her walking away from him. Maybe he had done the right thing, the *only* thing, yet he couldn't help feeling as though he had thrown away something really precious. There was going to be a huge gap in his life now that Lucy would no longer be a part of it.

The days passed in a blur. Lucy was aware that she was functioning on autopilot most of the time but it was the only way she could cope. If she allowed herself to think about what had happened then she would break down.

Thankfully, she saw nothing of Max. Although she knew he was in work during the day, he was never around when she arrived in the evening for the night shift. She suspected that he was avoiding her and was relieved. The less she saw of him the better, she told herself, but it was hard to pretend that everything would be fine when it was such a long way from being that.

Fortunately, they continued to be extremely busy and that helped. The baby she had found had been placed with foster-parents now. The mother still hadn't contacted either them or the police. Although permission had been granted to hand over the details of all the babies born in the unit during the period in question, nothing had turned up during the police's enquiries. Lucy knew that any hopes of tracing the mother were fading fast.

Her second stint of nights came to an end on New Year's Day and she had the rest of the week off. She was planning to go home and visit her parents. What had happened in the past had paled into insignificance compared to recent events and it was time her family knew that she had put it behind her. She was planning to catch the ten o'clock train because as she knew from experience, it was pointless trying to sleep when she got in. As soon as she closed her eyes, her mind started racing, going over everything Max had said to her. She had to accept that whatever they'd had was over.

Lucy made herself a cup of tea when she got home then took a shower. It was barely eight o'clock by the time she got dressed again, way too early to set off to the station. She decided to go to the newsagent's and buy a magazine to read on the journey, so fetched her coat. It was still very cold outside but the snow had disappeared at last. After she'd bought her magazine, there was still plenty of time left before she needed to leave so she decided to go for a walk. The canal was close by and a walk along the towpath would help to blow away some of the cobwebs.

There were a couple of people walking their dogs along the path when she set off but apart from them there was nobody about. She decided to walk as far as the lock and then make her way back. She could see the old lock-keeper's cottage in the distance and guessed it would take her about ten minutes to get there. She rounded the final bend and stopped when she saw a familiar figure standing on the edge of the lock basin. It was Sophie Jones, the young mum whose baby she had delivered on her first day at Dalverston General. She couldn't imagine what Sophie was doing there at that hour of the day and hurried towards her.

'Sophie? Are you all right?'

Sophie spun round and Lucy tried to hide her dismay when she saw the state the girl was in. Her clothes were filthy and it looked as though she hadn't washed in days.

There was no sign of Alfie and Lucy's heart turned over as she wondered what had happened to him.

'What are you doing here, Sophie?'

'Nothing. I...I just felt like a walk, that's all,' Sophie muttered.

'Me too. It's a lovely morning, isn't it?' She gave the girl a reassuring smile. 'Where's Alfie? Have you left him with someone, a friend or a neighbour perhaps?'

'I don't know where he is, but he's better off without me!'

Tears suddenly began to pour down Sophie's face, and Lucy felt more alarmed than ever. 'What do you mean that you don't know where Alfie is? What have you done with him?'

'I left him outside the hospital,' Sophie whispered. 'I knew he'd be safe there.'

'Alfie was the baby I found on Christmas Day!' Lucy exclaimed in shock.

'Yes.' Sophie gulped. 'I didn't know what else to do. I tried phoning everyone I could think of—the clinic, the doctor, the health visitor—but all I kept getting were messages to say that I should call back after Christmas. I couldn't wait that long. Not with the flat in that state!'

'Tell me what happened,' she said firmly. 'Why was your flat in such a state?'

'It was some boys. They broke into the flat above mine and ripped out all the pipes. There was water pouring through my ceiling, so I got in touch with the landlord, but he wasn't interested when I told him what had happened. He's planning to sell the building to a property developer and he couldn't care less what goes on there. Most of the other tenants have moved out because they couldn't put up with the conditions any longer.'

'It sounds dreadful.'

'It is. I put out pans and bowls to catch the water, but on Christmas Day the whole ceiling fell in. Everything was ruined—the furniture, Alfie's pram, every single thing I own.'

'I am so sorry, Sophie. I can't imagine how you must have felt. Is that why you left Alfie at the hospital?'

'Yes.' Sophie dashed her hand across her eyes. 'I didn't want to do it, but how could I keep him when we had nowhere to live? I thought he'd be better off with someone else, someone who could look after him properly.'

She gave a choked little sob as she turned away. Lucy wasn't sure what happened next, whether she lost her footing or deliberately stepped off the lock wall, but one minute Sophie was standing in front of her and the next second, she had disappeared.

'Sophie!'

Horrified, Lucy ran to the lock and peered into the water, but there was no sign of the girl. Instinct kicked in at that point, cutting through her panic. Shrugging off her coat, she leapt into the lock, gasping when the icy water closed over her head. Kicking her feet, she propelled herself back to the surface and looked frantically around. Sophie was floating, face down, on the water a couple of yards away so she swam over to her. She managed to roll her over and was relieved when the girl started to cough.

'You'll have to help me,' she panted, struggling to keep them both afloat. The water was so cold that her legs were already going numb and she knew that she wouldn't be able to support them for very long. 'Try to kick your feet while I tow you over to the side.'

Sophie did as she'd instructed but it was obvious the cold was affecting her too. It seemed to take for ever to reach the side of the lock where metal rungs had been embedded in the wall to form a ladder. Taking hold of the girl's hand, Lucy closed her fingers around one of the rungs.

'Do you think you can climb up?' she panted, her breath coming in laboured spurts.

'I…don't…know,' Sophie replied, her teeth chattering with cold.

'You have to try. Come on. I'll help you.'

She managed to guide Sophie's foot onto a rung then used her shoulder to boost her up the ladder. It was painfully slow and Lucy could feel her hands as well as her legs going numb with the cold. Sophie was halfway up the ladder now and she knew it was time that she got out as well.

She grabbed hold of a rung and tried to haul herself out of the water, but the weight of her clothing was dragging her down. It didn't help either that her hands were so cold that it was hard to maintain her grip on the metal rung.

Lucy gasped as she fell back into the water. She could hear Sophie shouting and did her best to reach the ladder, but she was too far away from it now. The water closed over her head as she sank beneath the surface and her last thought before the blackness descended was about Max and how much she loved him. It didn't matter if they could never have a family; she just wanted to be with him.

CHAPTER FIFTEEN

IT WAS the worst week of Max's entire life. Worse even than when he'd found out that he would never be a father. He missed Lucy so much, missed seeing her smile, hearing her laugh, just missed being with her. In the short time he had known her, she had come to mean the world to him and he couldn't imagine what his life would be like without her. It was only the thought of the harm it could cause that stopped him seeking her out and telling her how he felt.

He spent New Year's Eve at home on his own, having turned down several invitations. He didn't feel like celebrating and would have been very poor company if he'd gone out. He went into work on New Year's Day and did his best to appear upbeat when everyone wished him a happy new year but his heart was heavy. He wasn't looking forward to the coming year when he would be leaving Dalverston, and leaving Lucy.

He tried to shrug off the feeling of hopelessness and concentrated on work. There'd been two admissions during the night and both mums were hoping that their baby would be the first to be born in the unit that year. One of the women had suffered from high blood pressure throughout her pregnancy and when her BP started to rise to dangerous levels, Max decided that a section would be the safest option.

The procedure went smoothly and he was back on the unit within the hour. Amanda was on the phone when he returned and he could tell that she was upset. 'What's happened?' he asked as soon as she'd hung up.

'That was A and E on the phone. Apparently, they've got Lucy down there. I'm not sure what's happened exactly, but they said something about her being pulled out of the canal.'

'The canal!' Max exclaimed in horror. 'Did they say anything else, has she been badly injured?'

'No. They just asked if we had a contact number for her family. I said I'd have a look and phone them back.'

'I see.' Max spun round, his heart hammering with fear. The situation must be serious if A and E needed to get in touch with her family. 'I'm going down there right now. Page me but only if it's urgent, OK?'

'I…um…yes, of course,' Amanda agreed, looking a little startled by his hasty departure.

Quite frankly, Max didn't care what anyone thought. His only concern at that moment was Lucy and what had happened to her. He ran along the corridor, taking the stairs two at a time rather than waiting for the lift. A and E was heaving with people but he pushed his way through the crowd gathered around the Reception desk.

'You've got Lucy Harris here. Where is she?' he demanded when the receptionist looked up.

'I'm not sure. Just let me check.' The woman started to scroll through a list of names on her computer while

Max tried to curb his impatience. 'Ah, yes, here it is. She's in Resus, Dr Curtis.'

'Thanks.'

Max hurriedly made his way along the corridor, feeling his stomach churning as he stopped outside the door to Resus. This was where the most seriously injured patients were treated and he couldn't bear to think that Lucy was in need of this kind of specialist care. His hand was shaking as he pushed open the door because he didn't know what he would do if anything happened to her.

'Max! This is a surprise. What are you doing here?'

Max looked round when he recognised Sam Kearney's voice. 'I believe you've got Lucy Harris in here. How is she?'

'A lot better than she was, I'm happy to say.'

Sam led him over to the corner and pushed aside a screen. Max felt his heart bunch up inside him when he saw Lucy lying on the bed. She was covered from toes to chin with insulated blankets and there was another blanket wrapped around her head. Although her eyes were closed he could hear her breathing and some of his panic subsided. She was alive and that was the most important thing.

He turned to Sam. 'Do you know what happened? Someone said that she'd been pulled out of the canal.'

'That's right. From what I can gather, she jumped in to rescue a girl who'd fallen into the lock. Lucy managed to help her out but couldn't get out herself. It was pure luck that a chap walking his dog heard the girl screaming for help. He managed to haul Lucy out.'

'Thank heavens for that!' Max declared in relief. 'So how badly injured is she?'

'She's suffering from hypothermia. Core body temperature was a shade below thirty-five degrees when she was admitted but, as you can see, it's risen since then.' Sam directed his attention to the monitor and Max nodded.

'That's a positive sign, isn't it?'

'It is, although she's not out of the woods just yet,' Sam warned him. 'As the body's temperature drops, there is increasing dysfunction of all the major organs, so we'll need to monitor her for the next twenty-four hours or so. On the plus side, however, her heart rate is steady and her sats are improving.'

'I see.' Max went over to the bed, feeling his heart swell with relief when Lucy's eyes slowly opened. 'How do you feel?' he asked, his voice thickened with emotion.

'I'm not sure. Cold, I suppose. And scared...'

She tailed off as though it was too much effort to continue. Max reached for her hand and held it tightly in his. 'There's nothing to be scared about, sweetheart. I'm here now and I'm going to take care of you, if you'll let me.'

Bending, he pressed a gentle kiss to her lips, feeling his pulse leap when he felt her kiss him back. In that moment everything became crystal clear. He loved her and that was why he'd been so scared when he'd found out she'd been injured. He had been fighting his feelings for weeks but he could no longer hide from the truth. He loved her. It was as simple and as complicated as that. He was still reeling from the discovery when he heard Sam laugh.

'Ever had the feeling that you're surplus to requirements? I'll be back in a few minutes, not that I think you're going to miss me.' Sam looked pointedly at the ceiling. 'Whoever put that there has a lot to answer for.'

Max grinned when he saw the bunch of mistletoe hanging from the ceiling. 'Remind me to thank them!'

Lucy smiled as Sam sketched them a wave and left. 'If you're not careful, people will start talking. You don't want to ruin your reputation, do you, Max?'

'For being the eternal bachelor, you mean?' He raised her hand to his lips. 'Those days are well and truly over.'

'Are they?' she whispered, searching his face.

'Yes.' He took a deep breath. It was such a huge step and he wasn't sure even now if it was the right thing to do.

'Just tell me, Max.'

Her voice was soft, the look she gave him so filled with love that all his doubts disappeared. Bending, he looked into her eyes, wanting there to be no mistake about what he was saying. 'I love you, Lucy. I love you with all my heart and my soul and I want to spend the rest of my life with you, if you'll let me.'

She closed her eyes for a moment and when she looked at him again he could see tears sparkling on her lashes. 'I love you too, Max. With my heart and my soul and every tiny bit of me.'

'Oh, my darling!' He swept her into his arms and kissed her with all the love he felt. He had never dreamt this moment would happen so it made it all the sweeter, all the more precious. They were both breathless when he let her go and he laughed wryly as he checked the monitoring equipment.

'Hmm, your pulse rate shows a definite increase and your temperature has risen too. This could be an alternative method for treating cases of hypothermia. What do you think?'

'Fine, so long as it's only me you're planning on treating, Dr Curtis.'

Max chuckled. 'Oh, it is. Most definitely.' He kissed her lingeringly then smiled into her eyes. 'I'm not interested in anyone else. I haven't been interested since I met you.'

'No?' She arched a brow. 'What about that date you had a couple of weeks ago?'

'A complete and total failure. I spent the evening wishing I was with you,' he confessed.

'So it didn't lead to a night of unbridled passion?' she asked lightly, but he heard the question in her voice.

'No, it didn't. You stole my heart the moment I met you, Lucy. It just took me a while to admit it. But you're the only woman I want, now and for evermore.'

'I'm so glad,' she said simply. 'It's how I feel too. You are the only man I shall ever want.'

'You do understand what it means, though, about us not having a family,' he said quietly, because he needed to be sure that she had thought it through properly.

'Yes. I wish things could be different, Max, but I know that I'll be happy so long as I have you.'

'Are you sure? It's such a big decision and I don't want you to regret it at some point.'

'I won't regret it. I promise you that.' She smiled up at him with her heart in her eyes. 'I love you, Max, and whatever the future brings, we shall face it together.'

Max was so choked with emotion that he couldn't say anything. He kissed her on the mouth, letting his lips say everything he couldn't. There were tears in his eyes this time when he drew back. 'I love you, Lucy. I want to spend my life with you so will you marry me? Please.'

'If you're sure it's what you want then yes. Yes, I'll marry you, Max!'

Max gave a great whoop of joy. He was about to take her back in his arms when he suddenly became aware that people were clapping. He pushed back the screen, grinning when he discovered that they had attracted an audience. 'I take it that you lot were listening?'

'Too right we were.' Sam clapped him on the shoulder. 'It's not every day that you get to hear the hospital's most die-hard bachelor being brought to heel!'

Everyone laughed at that, Max included. He turned to Lucy and smiled. 'I hope you weren't planning on keeping this a secret.'

'No. I don't care who knows.'

'Let's hope you still feel that way after the hospital grapevine gets to work.'

He pointedly closed the screen then kissed her again. One kiss led to another and probably would have led to many more if his pager hadn't bleeped. He groaned as he unhooked it off his belt and checked the display. 'Maternity. I hate leaving you here like this, but I have to go. I'll come back as soon as I can—that's a promise.'

'I understand, Max, and I'll be fine, honestly.' She kissed him on the mouth then sighed. 'Odd how something so wonderful has come out of what could have been a tragedy.'

'It is. Sam told me that you saved someone's life,' Max said soberly. 'You were very brave, Lucy.'

'I only did what anyone else would have done.' She

frowned. 'Did you know that it was Sophie Jones who fell into the lock?'

'No, I had no idea! What was she doing by the canal in the first place?'

'I'm not sure, but she was in a terrible state. It will take too long to explain it all to you now, but that baby I found was hers. It was Alfie.'

'Really?'

'Yes. I'll tell you the whole story later when you've got time to listen. All I will say is that I can understand why she left him outside our door. That poor girl has been through an awful lot and she desperately needs help.'

'Then we'll make sure she gets it.'

He gave her a last kiss then made his way back to the maternity unit. It was obvious from the expressions on people's faces that the hospital grapevine had already been working overtime but Max didn't care who knew about him and Lucy. In fact, he was sorely tempted to take out an advert in the paper and announce the news to the world at large. The woman he loved had agreed to marry him. Now, that really was a cause for celebration!

Christmas Day, one year later...

Lucy smiled as she walked into the sitting room and knelt down in front of the Christmas tree. Although it was ridiculously early, she hadn't been able to stay in bed any longer. Excitement coursed through as she placed a small package under the tree. It might not look very much but she knew that Max would love this gift more than any other.

'So this is where you've got to.'

She looked round when Max suddenly appeared, feeling her heart fill with love. The past year had been so wonderful that several times she'd had to pinch herself to prove she wasn't dreaming. They had been married in the spring in a simple civil ceremony held in the grounds of a hotel on the banks of Lake Windermere. Her cousin Amy had been one of her bridesmaids, along with her sister and Max's three small nieces. Family was important to them both and it was good to know that any rifts had been healed.

They had stayed in Dalverston after both agreeing that they wanted to start their married life there. Max had been appointed to the post of consultant on a permanent basis when Anna Kearney had decided not to return to work following her maternity leave. Although they both lived and worked together, Lucy knew that she would never grow tired of being with Max. He was her whole world.

'I couldn't sleep,' she told him as he came and crouched down beside her.

'Too excited about what Santa has brought you, I expect,' he said, dropping a kiss on her lips.

Lucy sighed as she snuggled against him. She had never realised how much she could love someone until she had met him. 'I love you,' she murmured.

'And I love you too.' He kissed her again then picked up one of the gaily wrapped parcels. 'Happy Christmas, my darling.'

Lucy took it from him and ripped open the paper. There was a velvet-covered box inside and she gasped when she opened the lid and saw a silver charm bracelet nestled against the satin lining. 'It's beautiful, Max! I love it.'

'Good.' He took the bracelet out of its box and fastened it around her wrist. 'The woman in the jeweller's shop told me that it holds about twenty charms, so that's the next twenty Christmases covered. I thought I'd start you off with this.'

He showed her the first charm, a tiny silver elephant, and she laughed. 'A reminder of our honeymoon in Thailand? We had such fun that day when we rode those elephants, didn't we?'

'We did, but then every day I spend with you is fun, Lucy.' His eyes were tender as they traced her face and she sighed.

'We're so lucky, Max. We have everything anyone could want.'

'Yes, we do,' he agreed, but she saw the cloud that crossed his face and knew what he was thinking. Happiness bubbled up inside her as she thought about the gift she had placed under the tree. She was going to save it till last because she knew that Max was going to love it more than any other.

They took it in turn to open their presents, eagerly exclaiming at what the other had bought for them. By the time they finished there were just a few gifts left under the tree. Max picked up a large box covered in red paper with tiny reindeer printed all over it.

'Alfie is going to love this. I can't wait to see his face when he sees this toy tractor.'

'I think you like it almost as much as Alfie will,' Lucy teased, laughing at him.

True to his word, Max had done everything in his power to help Sophie. He had contacted the local council and insisted that she should be placed on their priority housing list. Sophie had moved into her new flat in the summer and was thrilled to have a place of her own. He had also liaised with the child protection team and it was thanks to Max that Alfie was now back home with his mother and obviously thriving. The fact that Sophie was planning to train as a nursery nurse was yet more proof of how the girl had turned her life around with a bit of help.

'What's this?' Max frowned as he held up the parcel she had placed under the tree that morning. 'I don't remember seeing this before. Who's it for?'

'You,' Lucy said simply.

'Me?' He ripped off the paper and Lucy saw the colour drain from his face as he stared down at the plastic wand it had contained. 'Is this what I think it is?' he said, his deep voice grating.

'Yes.' Reaching over she pointed to a small window in the plastic stick. 'See those two blue lines? They mean I'm pregnant. Happy Christmas, Max. You're going to be a daddy.'

'But how…? When…?'

Words failed him and she laughed because she knew exactly how he felt. She felt that way too, stunned and gloriously, wonderfully happy.

'I think *how* it happened is pretty easy to explain. We just did what any couple does when they love each other. As for when—well, by my reckoning it must have been that weekend we spent in Paris. The dates certainly fit. According to this, I'm eight weeks pregnant.'

'I can't believe it.' There were tears in his eyes as he reached out and pulled her into his arms. 'I know that doctor I saw didn't completely rule out the chance of it happening, but I thought he was trying to let me down gently.'

'Apparently not.' She kissed him on the mouth, then drew back and looked at him. 'I know it must be a shock for you...'

'It is! But it's the most wonderful shock I've ever had. Thank you, Lucy. Thank you so much. Sharing my life with you has been like a dream come true and to know that we're having a baby as well is just the icing on the cake. I didn't know it was possible to feel this happy!'

He kissed her hungrily, telling her through actions as well as words how thrilled he was. Lucy kissed him back, feeling her heart swell with joy when she realised that this time next year they'd be parents. They would be celebrating Christmas as a family and she couldn't wait!

COUNTRY MIDWIFE, CHRISTMAS BRIDE

ABIGAIL GORDON

Abigail Gordon loves to write about the fascinating combination of medicine and romance from her home in a Cheshire village. She is active in local affairs, and is even called upon to write the script for the annual village pantomime! Her eldest son is a hospital manager, and helps with all her medical research. As part of a close-knit family, she treasures having two of her sons living close by, and the third one not too far away. This also gives her the added pleasure of being able to watch her delightful grandchildren growing up.

CHAPTER ONE

THE first thing Lizzie Carmichael did when she arrived back at the cottage after the wedding was to ease her feet out of the elegant but not very comfortable shoes she'd worn as part of her outfit.

The second was to put the kettle on, and while it was coming to the boil there was something else she needed to do—take stock of the rented property that she'd moved into late the night before.

There'd been no time during the morning as the marriage of her friend Dr David Trelawney to Laurel Maddox, a practice nurse, had been arranged for eleven o'clock and by the time she'd sorted out some breakfast in a strange kitchen and dressed carefully for the special occasion it had been time to present herself at the church in the Cheshire village of Willowmere where the wedding was to take place.

The cottage she was renting had been David's temporary home while he'd been having an old house beside a beautiful lake renovated for Laurel and himself. He'd only moved into his new home the day before, which had made her arrival a last-minute thing.

The wedding had been a delightful occasion and a

pleasant introduction to the surrounding countryside, but Lizzie was in Willowmere to work. She'd transferred from St Gabriel's, the big hospital in the nearest town where she'd been employed ever since she'd qualified as a midwife, and where she'd got to know David, to take up a position in local health care that she just hadn't been able to refuse.

She'd been offered the chance to take charge of a new maternity centre that would be functioning in just one week's time in an annexe adjoining the medical practice on the main street of the village.

It would be a place where local mothers who wanted to have their babies at home would not have to rely on the services of a community midwife from the hospital some miles away, but would receive care before the birth, during the birth and in the sometimes traumatic days afterwards on a more personal level and from a much nearer source, under the supervision of a senior midwife.

The project was being funded by Lord Derringham, a local landowner who was on the board of governors at St Gabriel's, and it was due to be officially opened on the coming Friday by his wife.

Before then Lizzie would be taking a keen interest in the final arrangements that were being put in place and if necessary introducing ideas of her own, while at the same time getting to know the rest of the staff in the village practice.

The person she was going to be involved with the most was the senior partner at the practice, James Bartlett. She would be answerable to him with regard to any emergencies that occurred either before a birth or during it, and would take his advice as to whether the mother-to-be should be transferred to St Gabriel's with all speed, or just as a necessary precaution.

He'd been best man at the wedding in the old stone church and before the ceremony had begun she'd introduced herself to him. He'd seemed pleasant enough, but there hadn't been time to say much under the circumstances and she was hoping that come Monday it would be different.

She'd brought some ideas of her own with her and would be eager to discuss them with him, and at the same time be ready to take note of what he had to say from his point of view. Until then she was going to spend what was left of the weekend getting to know the place that was going to be her home for the foreseeable future.

When she'd been asked if she would take on the responsibility of the new venture she'd agreed without hesitation. Since she'd lost Richard, her husband, in a pile-up on the motorway three years ago and in the horrendous aftermath of the accident had also lost the baby that would have been their firstborn, her job had become the only thing she had left to hold on to and she gave it everything she'd got.

David had also worked at St Gabriel's, then as a registrar, before deciding to move into rural health care, and she was going to be doing the same.

When he'd mentioned that he would soon be vacating the cottage he was renting in Willowmere to start married life in the house by the lake, she'd got in touch with the letting agents and now here she was. Just across the way was one of the special attractions of the place: a flower-filled peace garden that she'd been told was the pride of the local folk who had paid to have it put there and contributed to its upkeep.

She'd sold their house after Richard and the baby had been taken from her, unable to bear seeing the nursery he'd been working on half-finished, and conscious all the time of the empty half of the bed that would always be there to remind her.

The leafy suburb where they'd lived had been left behind and she'd moved into an apartment near the hospital...*and at the same time had bought a single bed.*

It had been a modern, impersonal sort of place where she'd eaten and slept, and she would probably have stayed there for ever if the Willowmere position hadn't come up. Now she'd gone to the other extreme and was renting a small limestone cottage in an idyllic Cheshire village that she hadn't seen until the night before.

When she'd made the tea and sipped it slowly in her new surroundings, off came the suit she'd worn for the wedding, on went jeans and a sweater, and back went the long fair swathe of her hair into a ponytail as she began to unpack the boxes that held her belongings.

Once that had been accomplished it was time to find a shop as the only food in the place was a loaf she'd brought with her and a packet of cereal, which would have made rather dry eating if she hadn't noticed a farmer delivering milk to nearby properties and been able to obtain a supply from him. He'd asked if she wanted a regular delivery and she'd been quick to say yes. It would be one less thing to shop for when she was busy at the clinic.

On her way to seek out the shop, or hopefully shops, Lizzie was promising herself that if she should come across a café of some sort she was going to eat there as it was beginning to feel a long time since she'd had food at the wedding reception.

There *was* something along those lines, she discovered. The atmosphere in the Hollyhocks Tea Rooms was welcoming and the food was excellent. She would be dining there again, she decided as she left the place. As she looked around her, taking in her surroundings, she saw the doctor who'd been best man at the wedding coming towards her with a young child on either side of him. She recognised the twins, a boy and a girl that she'd already seen once that morning in the company of a dark-haired, youngish woman and an elderly lady.

James Bartlett was smiling as they drew level and as she observed the bright-eyed little girl and solemn small boy he said, 'Hello, Lizzie. You won't have met my children.' He placed the palm of his hand on top of each of their small golden heads. 'Pollyanna and Jolyon.'

'I saw them at the wedding,' she told him with an answering smile, 'but didn't realise they were yours. I suppose that having your best man's duties to perform they were with their mother.'

'We haven't got a mummy,' the boy called Jolyon said matter-of-factly. He pulled at the neck of the smart little shirt he'd worn for the wedding. 'I'm too hot, Daddy.'

'We'll be home soon,' his father told him, 'and then you can change into your play clothes.'

His sister was looking down at Lizzie's feet, now encased in comfortable casual shoes, and into the silence that followed his father's reply she said, 'Where are your blue shoes?'

James's smile was fading fast. This is just too embarrassing, he was thinking. He'd only stopped to say a brief hello to Lizzie Carmichael and within seconds Jolyon had told her about the great gap in their lives, and as Pollyanna had a thing about clomping around in Julie's shoes, no doubt she would ask Lizzie if she could try her shoes on some time.

'The shoes are at the cottage where I'm living,' Lizzie told her easily. 'They were hurting my feet.'

'I wear my mummy's shoes and pretend I'm grown up,' Pollyanna explained.

'Yes, well,' her father interrupted gently, 'perhaps we can talk about that another time, eh, Polly?' He smiled apologetically at Lizzie. 'The person you saw with the children was Jess, their nanny, and somewhere nearby would be Helen, my housekeeper. You'll no doubt get to meet them soon. Willowmere is a very friendly village.' And with his son tugging to be off and his daughter wanting to linger, he wished Lizzie a brisk goodbye and the trio went on their way.

Lizzie felt embarrassed that she'd been so presumptuous as to take for granted that the slender dark-haired woman she'd seen with the children was their mother. She wondered what had happened, and hoped she hadn't upset them. It had been an easy enough mistake to make as they'd seemed so content in the woman's company.

It was out of character, though, as after losing Richard and the baby she never presumed anything, took nothing for granted. If something good happened in her private life it was a bonus, and there hadn't been many of those over the last few years.

Meeting David and subsequently the lovely Laurel, who'd had her own bridges to build, had been one, and she hoped that one day she might have the pleasure of seeing the young bride at her maternity clinic. But there would be plenty of time for that, and she, Lizzie, would

be around for all of it as she intended to settle permanently in Willowmere, circumstances permitting.

She'd been going to ask James about the shops in the
village but had been sidetracked by the children, and now
as she looked around her Lizzie saw that there was no need
to have enquired. They were all there on the main street,
one after the other, starting with the post office at one end,
an attractive delicatessen next to it, then the usual
butcher's, bakery, greengrocer's and the rest, all of them
with a quaint individuality of their own that set them apart
from the usual shopping facilities of the modern age.

As James walked up the drive of Bracken House, his
detached property next to the surgery, with the children
skipping along in front, he was wishing that his introduction to the latest member of health care in the village
had been more dignified.

Theirs was going to be essentially a working relationship and already Polly and Jolly in their innocence had
turned it into something less official, and *he'd* ended up
reciting his domestic arrangements as if by some remote
chance Lizzie might want to hear them.

She was an unknown quantity and that was how he
would like it to stay until Monday morning. Time then
to see if the bright star of the maternity unit at St
Gabriel's was going to be the right one for Willowmere
and the nearby rural communities.

He was well pleased that home births were being
highlighted through the generosity of Lord Derringham,
and knew that his lordship would have insisted that his
project be properly staffed, and he supposed that what
little he'd seen of the newcomer so far was reassuring.

She was in her early thirties, according to the information he'd been given, which made her five or so years younger than himself, and was unattached which he supposed could mean anything. But her having moved into the tiny cottage that David had been renting seemed to indicate that as well as being unattached Lizzie Carmichael lived alone…though he was presuming, of course.

At the opposite side of the surgery there was an annexe built from sturdy local stone, as were most of the buildings in the village, and the new maternity unit was taking shape inside.

The annexe had served various purposes over the years. At one time it had housed James's sister, Anna, who was now working out in Africa with her husband, Glenn.

After years of separation, they had married in January and were finally living their dream, and James was delighted for them.

The inside of the annexe had now been gutted and the whole structure altered to accommodate the needs of the expectant mothers who would be attending the centre, and now the woman whose calling brought her in touch with other women's babies all the time had arrived in Willowmere.

When Lizzie went upstairs to bed that night the shoes she'd worn for the wedding were where she'd taken them off. She remembered the interest that James's little girl had shown in them, which she supposed wasn't surprising. They had high heels, open, strappy fronts, and were made out of pale blue leather to match the suit she'd been wearing. They'd been an extravagance of the kind that she rarely allowed herself and hadn't been all that comfortable when it came to wearing them, but to the small Pollyanna they must have seemed quite exciting if she was into putting her small feet into her mother's old shoes.

It was the evening of what had been a mellow Sunday in September. James had read the children a bedtime story and as their eyelids were beginning to droop he was about to go downstairs for a quiet hour with a new medical journal that he'd been trying to find time to read when through the window on the landing he saw the midwife walking alongside the river that ran behind the house and the practice.

Lizzie was alone and there was a solitariness about her that was so unmistakable that he forgot how he hadn't wanted to be involved with her out of working hours and he opened the back door of Bracken House and called, 'Hi, there, it's a beautiful night. Are you getting used to your new surroundings?'

She halted beside the fast-flowing river as he walked down to his garden gate.

'Yes,' she replied. 'So far I'm acquainted with Willow Lake because of David and Laurel, have dined in the excellent tea rooms, shopped on the main street, and now I'm exploring the river bank, but not for long as I intend to have an early night. It's been hectic moving here at the last minute and I want to be on top form for tomorrow.'

'So you haven't had anyone to help you with the move?'

'Er, no,' she said, seeming mildly surprised at the question. 'It was no problem, though. I'm used to sorting out my own affairs.'

'Would you like to come in for a cold drink or a coffee?'

She hesitated for a moment, then said politely, 'Yes, thank you. It is rather warm. A cold drink would be nice.'

He nodded and opened the gate that gave him access to the river bank, and as he led the way into the house Lizzie was still wishing she could act naturally with this man who was going to be a close colleague in the days and weeks to come.

Maybe it was because he was so impressive to look at, or perhaps she wasn't as confident as she'd thought she was over her new appointment. Whatever it was, he was giving her the opportunity to get to know him better and she supposed she may as well accept the offer of some light refreshment.

The house, when she went inside, was impressive by anyone's standards, pleasant, roomy, with children's clutter in a couple of the rooms. Pointing to doors down a side passage, James said, 'That is my housekeeper's domain during the week, a sitting room and bedroom where she can do her own thing. At weekends Helen usually goes home. She has one of the new apartments further along the river bank.'

Lizzie nodded. She was looking around her and thinking that the cottage she was renting would fit into a corner of Bracken House, yet it was big enough for her needs in the solitary life she'd chosen.

He'd gone into the kitchen to get the drinks and while he was there her glance was fixed on a photograph of a smiling raven-haired woman holding a tiny baby in each arm. It had to be the mother, she thought, and the infants had to be the children who had both captivated her and aroused her curiosity the day before.

When James brought a jug of home-made lemonade in, he saw the direction of her gaze but made no comment, and after her wrong assumption when she'd had the nanny down for the mother, Lizzie was not going to risk a repeat of that kind of thing.

'You will have seen the new centre from the outside, no doubt,' James said, steering the conversation towards less personal channels. 'What do you think of it?'

She smiled and he thought she should do it more often. 'What I've seen so far is impressive. I haven't met Lord Derringham, but from what I've heard he isn't sparing any expense.

'I've also been told that as well as it being a thank-you gesture to the practice for the care that David and Laurel gave to his son when he had an accident up on the moors, his lordship has a young family of his own and is keen to see first-class maternity care in Willowmere and the surrounding villages.'

'That is correct *and* the reason why you are here.'

'Mmm. I'm known as workaholic and I suppose it's true. Midwifery is the most rewarding of occupations and comes with the responsibility of bringing new life into the world carefully and safely for the sake of the newborn and its mother.'

She finished her drink and was getting up to go, feeling that she'd flown the flag enough for her love of the job. James could have invited her in solely to be hospitable and she'd been going on like someone with a one-track mind, yet wasn't that what she was? There was nothing else in her life to wrap around with loving care, just the mothers and babies that came and went.

'Thanks for the drink,' she said as she stepped into the dusk. 'Until tomorrow, then?'

He nodded. 'Yes, until tomorrow.'

As he put out the empty bottles for Bryan Timmins, the farmer who delivered the milk each morning, and then locked up for the night, James was glad that he'd invited Lizzie in for a drink.

He'd been wrong to think that Monday would have been early enough to get to know the newcomer. He'd got a new slant on her in the short time they'd been together and was going to feel more relaxed in her company when they met up again in the morning.

Her devotion to the job was clear to see and would be most welcome, but he was just a bit concerned that it seemed to have such a hold on her, as if there was nothing else that mattered. Yet he could be wrong about that. She could have lots of other interests that she hadn't mentioned, as during their first conversation of any length Lizzie was hardly going to recite chapter and verse all the things that made up her life. They were her affair and hers alone.

He hadn't told her he was a widower, had he, though he wasn't sure why. He made no secret of it in his dealings with either of the sexes, yet with her the words had stuck in his throat, and even if she was the least curious of women, he would expect her to wonder why his children had no mother.

No doubt Lizzie would find out soon enough that he

was the most sought-after catch in Willowmere, with lots of experience in dodging the net.

Monday morning came and at Bracken House it was time to get ready for the children's first day of a new school year. Jess had arrived with her usual promptness and as she gave the children their breakfast and sorted out the new uniforms that went with the new term, Helen was busy in the kitchen, putting together a packed lunch for Jolyon, who didn't like school dinners.

It was as James came down the stairs, showered and dressed in one of the smart suits that he wore at the practice, that the phone rang. When he picked it up a voice that was beginning to sound familiar spoke in his ear.

'James, forgive me for bothering you, but you're the only person I know in this place,' Lizzie cried frantically. 'There's a bull at my kitchen window. I'd left it open and it's staring at me while it's munching one of the plants on the window sill. I've never been so near one before and I'm scared. I don't know what to do.'

'It will belong to Bryan Timmins, who delivers your milk,' he said as he watched Helen put his breakfast on the table. 'I'll be right over. Keep the door shut, Lizzie, and I'll phone Bryan to come and get it while I'm on my way.'

'Please don't be long,' she begged. 'It's nearly finished eating the plant and I'm scared what it's going to do next.'

'I'm coming,' he promised, and before the children got wind of it and wanted to come he was striding swiftly down the main street to where the cottage stood beside the peace garden, which he was relieved to see had so far escaped the wanderer's appetite.

When Lizzie opened the door to him, wrapped in a tightly belted robe with hair hanging limp from the shower, she said anxiously, 'It's still there! I don't know what to do, James!'

'All right,' he soothed as he went through to the kitchen. 'Bryan is on his way. We'll soon have it back where it belongs.' He smiled when he saw the unwelcome visitor. 'It isn't a bull, Lizzie. She's just a harmless cow from his dairy herd that has wandered through the broken fence at the bottom of your garden. I'll point her in the right direction while we're waiting for Bryan to show up.'

He opened the back door of the cottage, went outside and herded the obedient cow towards the gap in the fence.

As Lizzie watched in complete mortification he stopped and looked down at his feet and she saw that Daisy had left a calling card. James had stepped in a cow pat.

With his expression giving nothing away, he continued herding the intruder towards the field from where it had come, and Lizzie didn't know whether to laugh or cry.

What a ghastly beginning to her first day at the village practice, she was thinking. It was almost time to put in an appearance and she was only half-dressed, hadn't had any breakfast, and her knight in shining armour was going to have to change his trousers, which were spattered around the bottoms, and clean up what looked like a pair of hand-made shoes.

At that moment the farmer appeared and apologised for his animal's wanderings. 'Daisy wouldn't harm you,' he said. 'Will you forgive her for the intrusion on to your property if I mend your fence?'

'Yes,' she agreed weakly.

On receiving her agreement, he went to take charge of the cow and when James returned to the cottage she said awkwardly, 'I'll pay for the dry cleaning and any damage to your shoes.'

'Forget it,' he said easily. 'That's what country life is all about. I'm going to go and get changed and will be hoping that my breakfast hasn't dried up in the oven. What about you? Have you eaten?'

'Not yet, no,' she said uncomfortably. 'I'm so sorry for making such a fuss. The thought of being late on my first day at the clinic doesn't bear thinking about, so I'm going to grab a slice of toast and then get dressed...and thank you for coming to my aid. I don't usually freak out like that, I can assure you.'

'I'm sure you don't,' he told her, 'but even a harmless cow can seem menacing when close to. Bye for now, Lizzie,' he said. He paused with his hand on the latch of the garden gate. 'Make sure you have a proper breakfast, not just a piece of toast. There's no rush. The mothers-to-be aren't queuing up for your services yet, so no need for further panic.'

He'd been smiling as he'd said it, but as she went back inside Lizzie wondered just how much James had meant it. Had he seen the episode with the cow as a confidence crisis on her part? If he had, she would have to remind him that she was here to see babies safely into the world. The animal kingdom was someone else's responsibility.

Lizzie ignored James's advice not to skip breakfast and had just a glass of milk before quickly drying her hair and then putting it in a long plait that swung smoothly against her shoulders. It was hardly the height of fashion but was soon done and time was something she hadn't got if she wasn't going to be late at the clinic.

Uniform, tights and shoes were soon on, followed by a swift application of make-up, and she was on her way, carrying the case that went everywhere with her when on duty.

She would be hungry before the morning was over, she thought as she hurried along the main street, but it was an important day in her life and she was not going to be late for it.

Every time she thought about the cow at her window her face burned. The animal hadn't got horns, she should have known it wasn't a bull, but she would still have felt most uneasy at finding it there.

There were children on the street, all heading for the village school and the first day of term. Ahead of her she could see James's twins skipping along beside the nanny and she wondered what she did for the rest of the day during term time once she'd seen them safely inside.

When James stepped out of the front door of Bracken House he saw her coming up the street with the brisk grace of a woman who was in charge of her life, and thought whimsically that there was no resemblance to the dishevelled person who'd begged him to come quickly and get rid of her unwelcome visitor earlier that morning.

This was the real Lizzie Carmichael, he thought, dressed in the standard blue uniform of her calling, with hair swept back into a plait of all things and sensible flat shoes on her feet that bore no resemblance to the ones that Polly had admired.

His daughter hadn't been the only one who had noticed the wedding guest in pale blue elegance.

Though his interest had been only mild curiosity until she'd introduced herself as the person appointed by St Gabriel's to be in charge of the new maternity clinic. Since then it seemed as if she was everywhere he turned.

'Well done,' he said in a low voice when she was near enough to hear him, 'but you haven't eaten, have you? You can't have, there hasn't been time.'

'No. I've had a glass of milk, though.'

'I see. So shall we go inside? I'm sure you must be eager to see where you're going to be working. Once you've had a good look round and I've introduced you to the surgery staff I suggest you pop across to my place and Helen will make you a pot of tea and a bacon sandwich, or whatever you're used to at this time of day. I think we can manage without you for half an hour or so.'

Lizzie could feel her colour rising. She wasn't used to being looked after. He'd already done her one favour with regard to the cow. She was uncomfortably aware that he'd changed his suit, and that his shoes had got back their shine, both chores he could have done without on a Monday morning before he'd had his breakfast. And hadn't there been just a hint of patronage in his last comment?

But she could hardly refuse the offer in the circumstances and so she said in the same polite tone as on the night before when she'd been invited into his home for a drink, 'That is very kind. An offer I can't refuse.'

He nodded. 'That's good, then. So shall we start the day? I told the receptionists last week not to make me any appointments for the first hour this morning so that I can be available to show you around, and once that's done I'll leave you to get acquainted with the new maternity clinic.

'You will have your own receptionist. We have four at present, and one of those will be transferred so that your patients can go straight to maternity care without visiting the surgery, unless you decide they need to.

'Although yours will be a separate unit, a communicating door has been made between the two places to save time and energy, but the only person you will be answerable to in the surgery will be me.'

Lizzie nodded, trying to force the morning's embarrassing events from her mind. She was determined that from now on James would only see the calm, collected, professional Lizzie Carmichael, and nothing more.

CHAPTER TWO

WHEN the door swung open and James stepped back to let her precede him into the building Lizzie knew immediately that she was going to be happy there, not just in the pristine, well-appointed rooms with every facility for antenatal and postnatal care, but in Willowmere itself.

She had found the perfect combination in this pretty Cheshire village where outside late summer was starting to turn the colour of the leaves on the trees and inside was the place where she was going to revel in the role that she'd been asked to play.

There was a waiting room painted in cream, beige and gold, with a honey wool carpet to match. Plenty of comfortable chairs that were not too low for heavily pregnant mothers to rise up from were arranged in rows, and in a corner was a reception desk.

Through a door at the end was a consulting room where she would interview new patients and listen to the problems of those already registered with the clinic.

Next to it there was a room divided into cubicles where she, and James if necessary, would check on the progress of the babies and the general health of the mothers-to-be. It was equipped with scales, a medicine cupboard for on-the-spot medication if needed, and various other items that her practised eye had noted, such as comfy cotton gowns for examination time and disposable sheets, plus a pile of glossy magazines to leaf through while waiting. Through another door were hand washbasins and toilets.

'So what's the verdict?' James asked when she'd observed everything without comment.

'Wonderful!' she exclaimed, eyes bright with enthusiasm. 'It's so relaxing and clean looking. Who were the brains behind all this?'

'The hospital hired a firm to do the make-over, but Lady Derringham had the last word on the décor and positioning of the facilities. You will be meeting her on Friday at the official opening.

'You might have noticed that there hasn't been room to put in any kitchen space for your needs, but we have that kind of thing in the surgery and you will be welcome to use it whenever you want.'

He was smiling. 'And now do you think you can drag yourself away while I introduce you to the people on the other side of the communicating door?'

'Yes, of course,' she replied, and went to meet Ben Allardyce, a well-known paediatric surgeon, who was standing in for his wife, Georgina, the only female GP in the practice, while she was on maternity leave.

And then there was Gillian, one of the two practice nurses, holding the fort while Laurel was on her honeymoon, and Sarah Martin, a pretty, curvy girl and the youngest of the receptionists, who would be transferring to the new maternity centre.

Elaine Ferguson, the practice manager, came and

shook hands and the good feeling that Lizzie had felt when she stepped into the place was still there.

Life without Richard and the child she'd been carrying would have been an empty thing if it hadn't been for her job, she thought. Maybe here in Willowmere she might find a different kind of solace in friendly folk and delightful surroundings as everyone was making her most welcome.

The one who stood out amongst them the most, however, was the man who was now speaking in a low voice for her ears only. 'It's half past nine, my first patient is due any moment. I'm going to take you to Helen for a belated breakfast.'

Lizzie nodded with head averted, afraid to speak in case the tears that were threatening began to roll down her cheeks. She just wasn't used to this, she thought unevenly. It would be easy to get to like it, and then what?

Loneliness had become a way of life and it was partly her own fault, but it had its advantages. By not ever getting close to anyone again she'd avoided any more pain. So was this beautiful Cheshire village going to make her see life differently? Did she want to be side-tracked into a kind of lifestyle she hadn't bargained for?

As James's middle-aged housekeeper plied her with eggs, bacon, hot buttered toast and a pot of tea Helen said chattily, 'So, my dear, you're the midwife who is coming to work in the new maternity clinic at the practice.'

'Yes, that's me,' she said, smiling across at her.

'James is highly delighted at the new arrangement,' Helen informed her. 'His life revolves around health care in the village. It comes second only to his love for his children and his sister. I kept house for his parents when he and Anna were young until I went to live in Canada to be with my daughter while her children were small, but now they're grown up I've come back. I was homesick and James needed some help in the house, so here we all are.

'Jess, their nanny, is also a classroom assistant during term time, which works well as she's at school the same hours as the children and is available all the time during the holidays.

'We leave James to it at the weekends to give him some quality time with Polly and Jolly. All those who love him would like to see him married again but he shows no inclination to put anyone in their mother's place and seems happy enough. But I mustn't go rambling on, though you'll find out soon enough that he lost his wife in a car crash when the children were just a few weeks old.'

That was how she'd lost Richard, Lizzie thought. How weird that they should have both lost their partners in similar circumstances. Obviously all Willowmere would know what happened to James's wife. It was that kind of place.

Not so with her situation. Most of the staff who'd been at St Gabriel's when her own life had been torn apart had moved on. Any that remained had their own lives to lead, their own peaks and valleys to cope with, and that was how she'd wanted it to stay.

As she made her way back to the practice building, having thanked Helen most sincerely for taking away her hunger pangs, she avoided the surgery and went straight to the clinic. She was still trying to come to terms with what Helen had told her about James. How he was bringing up his children as a single father, and providing a high standard of health care for Willowmere at the same time.

That being so, it was to be expected that there wouldn't be much opportunity for a life of his own and it could be one of the reasons why he'd never remarried. Though for most people who found themselves alone the need for someone to fill the gap outweighed every other consideration, but not in his case, it would seem, and neither was it so for her.

Her face was warming again at the memory of how she'd dragged him away from his breakfast that morning because of the placid Daisy's appearance at her kitchen window.

Presumably he'd eaten when he'd got back, but she wouldn't have been the only one who'd had to put a spurt on timewise, and then after all that he'd taken the trouble to arrange for Helen to cook breakfast for her.

Their lives were similar in some ways, she thought as she let herself into the clinic once more, but vastly different in others. Whatever his problems, James's life sounded as if it was full and rewarding, except for the one big gap of a loving wife and mother, and if what his housekeeper had said was correct, those who cared about him would like to see the blank space filled.

But the length of time it remained empty was often an indication of the depth of the loss. It brought with it a steadfast loving faithfulness that was a barrier to any other relationships.

Memories of Richard were so clear and tender there was no way she wanted any other man to hold her close in the night or sit across the table from her at mealtimes. As for the baby she'd lost, there were moments when she envied a radiant mother as she placed her child in her arms, but it was also like balm to her soul every time she brought a newborn safely into the world.

Unlike the man in the surgery next door, her life was only half-full, but she'd learned to live with that, she always told herself when she was feeling low. Though was half a life better than none, she sometimes wondered.

It seemed that James lived by a different set of rules from hers. In the middle of his busy life he had found time to show her an impersonal sort of kindness that was heart-warming, and she was going to repay him by making his dream of a maternity clinic in the village an efficient reality.

She spent the rest of the morning unpacking deliveries of stationery and medical supplies, and at lunchtime went across to the Hollyhocks Tea Rooms for a quick bite. It was a luxury she knew she would probably have to forego when things got busy at the unit, but she had the next few days to settle in at her own pace before the grand opening on Friday, when as well as the Derringhams some of the bigwigs from St Gabriel's would be there.

James appeared again just before his afternoon surgery was about to commence and said, 'How's it going? I thought we might have seen you at lunchtime. If you remember, I said that you're welcome to join us whenever you feel the need.'

'Yes, I know,' she told him, 'but I thought you might be feeling you've seen enough of me for one day.'

'I'm not with you,' he said, and then laughed. 'Ah, you mean Daisy. Don't give it another thought. My mother was born and bred in the countryside but she was nervous if they came too near, and she would never go within a mile of a pig sty.'

He was making it up as he went along because he didn't want this newcomer with hair in a long golden plait and a clear violet gaze to have any reason to regret having moved to the beautiful village where he'd been born.

She'd positively sparkled when she'd seen the new clinic for the first time, but for the rest of it she seemed rather subdued and he wondered what went on in her life.

Yet did that matter? If Lizzie was as good as she was said to be, he couldn't ask for more and with that in mind he said, 'Would you be prepared to come back this evening for a couple of hours while I put you in the picture regarding our present antenatal arrangements and pass on to you the medical notes of the expectant mothers at presently under our care, who will be transferred from the surgery to the new clinic?

'As you know, we are a doctor and nurse short at the moment, with David and Laurel on honeymoon, which means that I have no spare time during the day,' he explained, 'otherwise I wouldn't break into your evening. We could have met at my place or yours, I suppose, but as a matter of protocol I wouldn't want patients' records to leave the surgery.'

'I don't mind in the least,' she said immediately. 'I have plenty of time on my hands. I've been going for a stroll and then having an early night, so I'm not going to be missing anything.'

It was there again, he thought. A solitariness that

was so different from his own life. He was surrounded by people he cared for, and who cared for him.

If time for himself was hard to come by, so what? The children were happy and healthy, and the pain of losing Julie was lessening as the years went by, yet it would never go away completely because she wasn't going to see her children grow up, and that was always what hurt the most.

Lizzie was waiting for him to finish what he'd started and bringing his mind back to the present he said, 'Would eight o'clock suit you? The children will be asleep by then. I don't think they'll need much persuasion as the first day of a new school year is always exhausting for everyone concerned, and Helen is there to keep an eye on them.'

He was checking the time. The waiting room was filling up.

'Yes, eight o'clock will be fine,' she told him.

'Right, I'll see you, then,' he said briskly, and off he went, hoping that the pride of St Gabriel's maternity services wasn't thinking that he was overdoing the getting-to-know-you routine.

As Lizzie walked home in the late afternoon she was wishing that she hadn't been quite so eager to fall in with James's suggestion that they meet again that evening. Anything to do with the new clinic was of paramount importance to her, but she felt as if she needed to get her breath back after such an eventful day of ups and downs, the downs issuing from her continuing mortification over the cow episode, and the ups a deep satisfaction with the arrangements of the clinic.

Not to mention what had happened when she'd gone to the Hollyhocks Tea Rooms for her lunch.

Emma, the usually rosy-cheeked wife of the partnership who owned the place, had said hesitantly, 'Is it you that's going to be in charge of the new baby clinic that's opening on Friday?'

'Yes, it's me,' Lizzie replied, wondering what was coming next.

'I think I'm pregnant,' Emma had said. 'I've done a test that I bought from the chemist and it was positive. So can I come to see you?'

'Of course,' she'd said, smiling at her across the counter. 'That's what I'm going to be there for. Is it your first baby?'

'Yes, and we just can't believe it. We've been married a long time and had almost given up hope.'

'So how about coming in on Friday after the opening and being my first patient?'

'I'd love to be that! Simon is over the moon. He's been getting all the recipes mixed up this morning, so watch out for salt instead of sugar in your apple crumble,' she'd warned laughingly.

On the whole the ups had far outweighed the downs and she wanted it to stay that way, but there had been a slight lift of the eyebrow when she'd impulsively told James that she had plenty of time on her hands, as if he found it hard to believe that anyone could be in that position, and the last thing she wanted was to arouse his curiosity.

She was getting on with her life the best way she knew how, and providing a useful service to the community took away some of the loneliness that rightly or wrongly she didn't confide to anyone.

But she'd committed herself to returning to the clinic that evening and when she gave her word about anything, she kept it.

The children were full of their first day at school when James came in from the surgery that evening, or rather Pollyanna was. Jolyon was his usual self and his contribution to the discussion was that their new teacher had said he had a funny name.

'She said unusual, not funny,' Pollyanna corrected him, 'and that she thought it was very nice.'

'It means the same,' he protested, ignoring the last bit, 'and why isn't any other kid called the same as me, Daddy? Why am I not called Sam or Tom?'

Jess had given them their evening meal and was standing in the doorway of the dining room ready to leave, but she paused and said in a low voice, 'The teacher was just trying to be nice, but as we know Jolly has a mind of his own.'

James nodded and, taking Jolyon to one side, said to him, 'There was a boy in my class at school who didn't like his name because he was the only one who had it, but as he grew older he began to change his mind because everyone was envious that he had such a super name and wished that theirs wasn't Sam or Tom.'

'What was he called?' Polly chipped in.

'His name sounded very much like yours, Jolyon, but not quite. He was called Joel.'

Apparently satisfied with the explanation, Jolyon nodded his small blond head and ran off to play, and as he ate his solitary meal James was smiling at the difference in his children. Polly accepted everything as it came her way, but not so her brother—he had to know the whys and wherefores before he was happy.

When he arrived at the new clinic there was no sign of Lizzie and he thought that maybe she wasn't the eager beaver that she'd seemed to be earlier, but when he glanced across the road in the dusk to where the ancient village church stood he saw a flash of colour amongst the gravestones that surrounded it and seconds later she was coming towards him through the lychgate.

'There are some really old graves in the churchyard, aren't there?' she commented, and wondered why a shadow passed over his face. But, of course, maybe his wife's was one of the newer ones, she thought, although she hadn't seen it if it was. So less said about that the better. Changing the subject, she asked politely, 'Have the children enjoyed their first day back at school?'

'Er…up to a point in Jolyon's case,' he said wryly. 'Pollyanna was her usual happy self, but her brother is not so easily pleased. They had a new teacher who apparently commented on his name in what appears to have been the nicest possible way, but he took it to mean that she didn't like it. He and I had a little chat and it was sorted.'

She was smiling. 'It is a fact that young children want to be the same as their friends and don't want to be different, but if they have an unusual name, they often come to like it as they get older. My name isn't unusual but I have had to answer to many forms of it over the years, such as Beth, Liz, Bet and Lizzie, which is the one that has stuck, though in truth the one I like best is Elizabeth, my given name.'

'What do your family call you?'

'I have no family, but when I did have they called me Lizzie.'

'You have no family at all?' he questioned in amazed disbelief, so much aware of his own blessings he felt guilty.

'No,' she said steadily, and her tone told him that was the end of the discussion, as did the fact that she was observing the pile of patients records on the reception desk in the waiting room and settling herself on one of the chairs that were placed in neat rows across the room.

As he came to sit beside her Lizzie said, 'I think the seating arrangements in here have too much uniformity. I want it to be that while the mothers-to-be are waiting their turn they can chat to each other easily, with the chairs scattered around the room. So if it's all right with you, I'm going to rearrange them. It is very important for women to be able to share their fears and excitement, *and* their problems, with each other, especially if they are first-time patients taking what can be a scary step into the unknown.'

'It's fine by me,' he told her. 'You are the one who is going to be in charge of this place. My function will be to be there if you need me. I would only interfere if I thought it absolutely necessary, and with your record of excellence at St Gabriel's having preceded you, I can't see that ever happening.

'But, Lizzie, don't let this place take over your life completely,' he continued, and couldn't believe what he was saying when the fates had sent to Willowmere someone as dedicated to health care as the woman sitting beside him. 'There are lots of things to do in the village, people to get to know, beautiful places to explore, as well as looking after the pregnant women in our midst.

'So why don't I take you to Willowmere's only pub, The Pheasant, when we've finished here? It will give you the opportunity to socialise a little.'

It was there again, Lizzie was thinking. He was picking up on the emptiness of her life and she didn't want him to be concerned about her. For one thing, she hardly knew the man, and for another, apart from during working hours when they would have to be in contact, she wanted to be left to get on with her life, such as it was.

But James was putting himself out to make her feel welcome when he must have plenty of other things to do in his busy life, and it would seem ungrateful to refuse his suggestion, so she said, 'Yes, if you're sure that you have the time.'

'Yes, I'm sure,' he said calmly, and, passing her the first lot of patients' notes, began to explain who they were and what they would be expecting from her.

When they'd finished going through them Lizzie said, 'It would seem that there will shortly be another name to add to these.'

'I'm not with you,' he commented.

'I went to the café across the road at lunchtime and Emma asked for an appointment as she's done the pregnancy test from the chemist and it showed positive. So we've arranged for her to be the first patient at the clinic after the opening on Friday.'

'Emma pregnant!' he exclaimed. 'Wonderful! She and Simon have wanted to start a family for a long time. She had a miscarriage when they were first married and there has been nothing since.'

'So I will have to take great care of her, won't I?'

'Yes, you will,' he agreed, 'and now am I going to take you for that drink?'

'Er…won't your housekeeper wonder where you've got to?' she said with an unmistakable lack of enthusiasm, and he wanted to laugh. He could think of two or three unattached female members of the community, and one who was already in a relationship, who would have jumped at the idea, but not so this one, it seemed.

'No, not at all,' he assured her perversely. 'But to put your mind at rest, I'll call at the house before we go and let her know where I will be if she needs me.' And Lizzie had to go along with that.

The Pheasant was crowded and when they walked in various people greeted James and observed his companion with curiosity, which was satisfied somewhat as he introduced her as the new community midwife who was joining him for a drink to celebrate the opening of the new clinic.

By the time they'd found a couple of seats and James had fought his way to the bar and back, Lizzie was feeling more relaxed, grateful for the way he had introduced her into the socialising throng without causing her embarrassment.

At the same time she was telling herself if she was going to fit into the life of the village she was going to have to start living again, and after three years of shutting herself away from everything but her job, it was not going to be easy.

James was observing her expression and almost as if he'd read her mind he said, 'That wasn't so bad after all, was it? Everyone was listening when I introduced you, so now they all know who you are.'

'If you say so,' she agreed. 'You know the people here better than I do. Have you always lived in Willowmere?'

'Yes. My father was in charge of the practice before me, but after my mother died he began to fail and my sister, Anna, gave up all her plans for the future and came home from university to help me during a very difficult time. Thankfully her life is now back on course again.'

He was speaking about his family in the hope that she would mention the absence of hers, but the ploy wasn't working. Lizzie wore a wedding ring, he'd noticed, but there was no husband around.

Maybe she was divorced and that was the reason for her reticence, yet a marriage break-up seemed as nothing to some people, but it had to be a daunting experience in many ways.

He had his children and his sister in his life, and if what she'd said was true, the woman sitting opposite had no one. Small wonder that she wasn't the life and soul of the party, but he needed to bear in mind that she'd only arrived in Willowmere a few days ago.

It was dark when they left The Pheasant with no moon above and James said, 'I'm going to walk you home, Lizzie, and will want to see you safely inside before I leave you.'

'I'll be fine,' she protested.

'Yes, I'm sure you will, but nevertheless that is what I'm going to do.'

'All right, then...and thanks,' she said awkwardly without any social grace.

They walked in silence, past the shops all shuttered for the night, then skirted the single-storey village school built from the familiar limestone, and then the peace garden came in to sight, with the cottage across the way.

He watched in silence as she unlocked the door and stepped over the threshold and when she turned to face him, said, 'Goodnight, Lizzie. Make sure you lock up when I've gone.'

She nodded mutely and watched until he disappeared from sight, then did as he'd said, and when that was done she sat on the bottom step of the stairs and wept because a stranger's concern was breaking down her defences.

From what she'd seen of James so far he seemed to be that kind of person, considerate and caring towards everyone, herself included as the latest addition to the health care of his beloved village, and she didn't want it to be like that. She didn't want to have feelings in the half of her life that was empty, because with feelings came weakness and she needed to be strong to face each day.

As he walked home, James was telling himself that he had enough responsibilities in his life without attempting to take on the emotional burden that Lizzie obviously wanted to keep private. She was going to be the right one for the job and that was all that mattered.

It was Friday afternoon and Lady Derringham was about to cut the tape that had been placed across the entrance to the new maternity clinic in front of those assembled for the occasion, which included her husband, the chairman of the primary care trust for the area, dignitaries from St Gabriel's, and Lizzie and James.

Lizzie could see Emma from the tea rooms at the front of the crowd that had gathered to watch the opening ceremony, and she smiled. Emma had been to see James and her booking-in appointment was arranged for that day.

Shortly she would have her photograph taken as the first patient to attend the clinic. It would be open for business and Lizzie's feeling of being on the edge of things would disappear.

James was observing her and noting that today she was well and truly in her midwife mode, immaculate in the blue uniform of her calling, hair in the golden plait and eyes bright with the significance of the moment.

As his glance met hers he decided that the other side of her personality that had seemed so solitary and with-drawn must have been a figment of his imagination. She was calm, confident, unfazed by the ceremonial aspect of the gathering…and content.

The scissors had snipped, the tape was cut, and her ladyship was saying, 'I now declare the Derringham Maternity Clinic well and truly open.' And as she stepped inside they all trooped in after her.

As James came to stand beside Lizzie he said, 'You are happy today, aren't you?'

'Yes,' she replied. 'More than I've been in a long time.'

He nodded. 'That's good.'

CHAPTER THREE

THE crowd had gone, the officials from St Gabriel's had driven off in their cars. Only Lord and Lady Derringham remained and Lizzie was discovering that Olivia Derringham's interest in the clinic was not going to be a passing thing.

As the person who was going to be in charge she had been expressing her appreciation of the facilities that had been provided and the uplifting design of the place and Olivia said, 'If you think it would be all right, I'd like to volunteer to come in for a couple of mornings each week to give what assistance I can, even if it is only to make tea, help out the receptionist and perhaps settle the patients in the cubicles as they wait to be seen.'

'That's a very kind offer,' Lizzie told her, slightly taken aback. 'I'll speak with James, but I'm sure it would be fine. Most of the time I will be on my own, except for the receptionist who is being transferred from the surgery, and I'm presuming that it will be quite busy, with expectant mothers from surrounding villages transferring to this clinic as well as those from Willowmere. I've been told that extra staff will be brought in if needed, but the hospital trust is waiting to see what the workload turns out to be first. So I would much appreciate help from someone like yourself.'

Olivia Derringham nodded and went on to say, 'I suppose you know that we have donated the clinic as our way of thanking two members of the village practice who I believe are on honeymoon at the moment. I would have liked them to be here, as what they did for our son—you know he had a nasty fall while on a sponsored walk that they were also taking part in—was something that my husband and I won't forget. But when they made their wedding plans they had no idea that the clinic would be finished so soon and urged us to go ahead with the opening rather than there be any delay, so here we are, and you'll let me know about helping out then?'

'Certainly. Thank you for your kind offer of support, Lady Derringham.'

'Lizzie, the name is Olivia. I was working in a burger bar when I met His Lordship, and now I need to remind my husband, who is deep in conversation with Dr Bartlett, that we need to be home in time for nursery tea.'

'You look somewhat stunned,' James commented when they'd gone. 'What gives?'

'I don't know if you would agree to this, James, but Her Ladyship has offered to help in the clinic for a couple of mornings each week.'

He frowned. 'But she isn't trained!'

'Not doing midwifery. She's volunteered her time to help out in Reception where needed, make tea and coffee, and make sure the patients are comfortable. In other words, she's offering to be a general dogsbody.'

'Amazing!'

She laughed. 'She has no airs and graces. They met

in a burger bar, of all places. She worked there. Don't you think it's rather romantic? She is a very nice woman. I'm sure we'd get on well.'

'Yes, I'm sure you would,' he agreed. 'Well, let me look into this and I'll let you know shortly.' Lizzie smiled and he thought how she looked bright-eyed and happy now, but he knew that no matter how he tried to tell himself otherwise, somewhere not too far away was the other Lizzie, subdued and wanting to be left alone. But as he'd told himself several times since they'd met, that was her affair.

'Until their son's accident and David and Laurel's involvement in it, we only saw the Derringhams rarely,' he explained. 'This is a new dimension her wanting to help in the clinic, and it is very commendable.'

'Where do they live?'

'At Kestrel Court, a large place on the way to the moors. His Lordship owns an estate up there, with grouse shooting and the like. Dennis Quarmby, one of my patients, is his gamekeeper, and the husband of Gillian, the practice nurse, is his estate manager.' He checked his watch. 'And now I need to be going. I've left Ben Allardyce coping with the late surgery on his own, which is a bit much, but fortunately he doesn't seem to mind. What are *you* going to do now the ceremony is over? Wait for Emma to appear?'

'Yes, I'm expecting her at any moment. She was with those watching and then the photographer approached her. She will know that I'm free now, and then after I've tidied up I think I'll call it a day.'

He was on the point of departure. 'Yes, do that. Have a nice weekend, Lizzie.' Hoping that she might pleasantly surprise him, he added, 'What do you usually do?'

'A big shop on Saturdays and maybe take in a film. On Sundays I do my laundry and tidy up wherever I'm living at the time.'

He wondered what she meant by 'living at the time', but didn't comment. Had she come from a series of bedsits? But he'd asked enough questions. Any more could be seen as intrusive and as it appeared that she wasn't interested in how *he* spent *his* weekends or, if she was, she clearly wasn't going to ask, he said goodbye and returned to his patients.

With Emma sitting opposite her, Lizzie was discovering that she was thirty-two years old and, according to the date of her last period, was now eight weeks pregnant.

'Your blood pressure is fine,' she told her when she'd checked it, 'but I see from your notes that you're on medication for it, so we'll keep a close eye on that.' She gave her a reassuring smile. 'How are you feeling?'

'I've got morning sickness and sore breasts so far,' Emma told her.

'Both to be expected, I'm afraid. For the morning sickness try smaller meals more frequently, and ginger biscuits or ginger tea will help lessen the nausea. What about tiredness and exhaustion?'

'Oh, I'm tired all right, and it's partly due to the tea rooms being so busy, as well as my being pregnant. Simon wants me to take a back seat and employ someone to take my place, but I don't know that I want to sit around all day.'

'Perhaps a bit of both is the answer,' Lizzie suggested. She gave Emma a pregnancy pack full of information, took bloods and a urine sample, and arranged the twelve- and twenty-week scan dates. 'I'll see you in a month's time, Emma, unless you have any concerns before then.'

About to lock up, she looked around her and thought that it was just a week since she'd arrived in Willowmere and it had been a strange one. Since meeting James Bartlett at the wedding and then again with his children outside the Hollyhocks Tea Rooms, he'd seemed to be everywhere she'd turned, though she'd been the one who'd kick-started the cow episode that she would so much like to forget.

He had asked how she usually spent her weekends and she'd told him without embellishments, as she didn't see it being any different here in Willowmere, except that she might get out more on foot than she'd done in the town as the countryside was breathtaking.

She went to bed early but sleep was a long time coming because her mind was full of the day's events: the exciting opening of the clinic; the unexpected offer of help from Olivia Derringham; Emma's pregnancy after a long time of waiting; and in the midst of it all was the amazing James with his busy, well-organised life, which included the enormous task of bringing up his children on his own.

No matter how much help he had from outside, the responsibility for their health and happiness was his, and having met the delightful pair briefly it would seem that he was to be congratulated.

She would have done the same if she'd been given the chance, she thought as she twisted and turned under the covers, but it hadn't worked out like that, and ever since she'd been living in a cold zone with regard to family life.

As the hours ticked by, sleep was coming at last. Soon she would slide into oblivion's comforting respite, she thought drowsily, but it was not to be. The bedside phone was trilling and when she picked it up James's voice came over the line.

'Lizzie,' he said, 'I'm sorry about this.'

'It's all right,' she told him, unable to disguise her surprise. 'What is it, James?'

'We have a pregnant patient who has got a bleed. They've been in touch with the emergency services but there is going to be some delay as there has been a serious accident on the motorway and there are huge hold-ups, so I'm going up there to check her out. She lives in a remote farm on the edge of the moors and the thing is, she's asking for you.'

'Is she one of those whose notes you've passed on to me?' she asked, now fully awake.

'No, she's from your St Gabriel's clinic and was about to transfer to Willowmere when she heard you were going to be based here, but this has cropped up. Can I ask you to come with me? I know that it's barely seven o'clock, but her mother says she's frightened and very weepy.'

'Of course I'll come. Who is she, James?'

'Kirsten Williams. Do you recall her?'

'Yes. She's seventeen years old and due to give birth in a couple of months. I've been seeing her regularly at the hospital. Kirsten didn't want to have the baby at home and has had no problems so far. This is something out of the blue.'

'It would seem so,' he agreed. 'Is it too soon to say I'll pick you up in ten minutes?'

'No. I'll see you then.'

She was at the gate waiting for him, dressed in her uniform, devoid of make-up and with hair tied back loosely. There had been no time for the long fair plait that he was getting used to seeing.

As she settled herself in the passenger seat he said, 'Having to forego your breakfast is getting to be a habit, isn't it? I really am sorry to be having you back on the job so soon.'

She smiled across at him. 'Today it is for a much more worthy cause, and what about *your* breakfast? I presume Helen will be giving the children theirs?'

'I've already seen to that,' he said with a wry smile, 'and, yes, she's with them now. I asked her if she could pop round to keep an eye on them as she doesn't usually come to us at the weekend. Their day starts quite soon, I'm afraid. Children who go to bed early get up early.'

'Yes, I would imagine so,' she said, and there was something in her tone that told him to drop the subject.

As he drove up the hill road she said, 'I'm going to have to get to know the area and have bought a couple of maps but they're in my car, and even so, if I'd been on my own I would have been floundering a bit.'

He was pulling up outside a rambling farmhouse and almost before they'd got out of the car Kirsten's mother was framed in the doorway and in a nearby field a man waved in their direction and carried on baling hay.

There was no sign of an ambulance so it seemed that the motorway was still blocked and James said in a low voice, 'If she needs to go to hospital we might have to take her, Lizzie, and we'll have to use the side roads instead.' She nodded. The thought had already occurred to her and she smiled reassuringly at the anxious mother, who had led the way upstairs the moment they'd set foot in the house.

'Lizzie!' the girl on the bed wailed when they entered a bedroom so much that of a teenager it made what they were there for seem bizarre, but it wasn't the first time they'd been in that sort of situation and it wouldn't be the last.

As James examined Kirsten she sobbed. 'If I lose the baby it will be my fault because I've said all along that I didn't want it, that I was going to have it adopted, but I didn't really mean it. I want my baby, Lizzie!'

'It's OK, Kirsten,' she said gently, taking hold of her hand. 'We're here and if Dr Bartlett decides you need to go to St Gabriel's and the ambulance still hasn't arrived, we'll take you. Are you hurting anywhere?' she asked with the thought of a slow labour in mind, or even a faster one.

Kirsten shook her head. 'No. It's just the blood.'

'When did it start?'

'It was there when I got up to go to the bathroom early this morning.'

'How much?'

'More than spotting, and it was bright red.'

James had finished examining her and, observing Kirsten's mother, white-faced and anxious, said, 'Kirsten will be better off in hospital, Mrs Williams, and we can check the baby there.' He turned to the girl on the bed. 'You haven't had any falls or accidents in the last few days?'

'No, nothing.'

'Pregnant women do sometimes experience blood loss during pregnancy,' he explained, 'so we're going to take you to hospital and place you in their care.'

'I've got a case packed,' her mother said, 'and I'm coming with you. I would have taken Kirsten myself but I don't drive, and the farmhand is too busy to leave what he's doing.'

Was there no husband and father in this household? Lizzie wondered. There'd been no mention of one. Perhaps Mrs. Williams ran the farm single-handed except for the man they'd seen baling the hay.

Having taken note of her mother's comments, James was turning to Kirsten and saying, 'Just slip on a robe of some sort, Kirsten, and once we've got you and your mother settled in the back seat of the car with a blanket round you, Lizzie and I will take you to St Gabriel's by a different route from the one that's blocked.'

While he'd been speaking Lizzie had cancelled the call to the emergency services and within minutes they were off, driving through the still sleeping village in the quiet morning.

As the buildings of the big hospital in the nearest town came into sight Lizzie was thinking that this was unreal. She'd been gone from St Gabriel's for just one week and she was on her way back to the wards that she knew like the back of her hand, and driving them there was the man that she'd thought would be just a figurehead at the surgery, someone that she saw briefly during working hours.

Instead, it was as if he was taking over her life with his brisk concern for his patients and her own well-being, and though it was very pleasant in one sense, there was the risk that she could get to like it, which just wouldn't do. The last thing she would ever want would be to make a fool of herself over James Bartlett.

In everything except her innermost feelings she was cool and capable but relationships of a personal kind were taboo. So why would she be there like a shot if James invited her out again? He was someone dedicated to looking after others, she thought, even putting up with an outsider who didn't know her own mind.

'Lizzie! What are you doing here? Dare I hope that you've come back to us?' Giles Meredith, the top gynaecologist at St Gabriel's, said in greeting when he came to see Kirsten in the emergency admissions section of the maternity wing.

He shook hands with James and said, 'It must be some service you are giving your pregnant patients if both their GP and midwife are bringing them here in person.'

Lizzie smiled, the two of them went back a long way. Giles was the nearest thing to a father figure she'd ever known as she'd lost her parents when quite young and been brought up by her mother's unmarried sister, who had endured the responsibility for just as long as was necessary and then been eager to take a back seat.

'Maybe you haven't heard that the motorway is blocked, Giles,' she explained. 'The emergency services couldn't get through to us and we needed to bring Kirsten here as quickly as we could.'

James sensed an easiness in Lizzie's manner towards the well-respected Giles Meredith that he hadn't witnessed before, and again he wondered which was the real her, the restrained loner, or the bright, career-minded midwife. Or maybe there was yet another side to Lizzie that he had yet to see.

'Ah, I see,' the gynaecologist commented, and he turned to where Kirsten was lying hunched on the bed in a small cubicle with her mother seated beside her. 'It says on your admission notes that you've had some bleeding, Kirsten. Is that right?'

She nodded mutely.

'In that case, an ultrasound scan is called for.' She observed him in alarm and he was quick to reassure her. 'We just need to see how baby is doing. We will be keeping you in for the time being until we are confident all is well, but before you have the scan I want to examine you. Again, it won't hurt. Then we'll see what your blood pressure has to tell us.'

'We are going to leave you with Dr Meredith now, Kirsten,' Lizzie told her. Turning to her mother, she said, 'He is the best, Mrs Williams. Kirsten will be in safe hands.'

'So you're not coming back to St Gabriel's, then, Lizzie?' Giles teased as they prepared to leave.

'No,' she replied, 'and if you saw Willowmere and the new clinic you would understand why.'

And what about the handsome widower by your side, doesn't he have anything to do with it? he thought, but Lizzie was Lizzie and since she'd lost her husband she'd never shown interest in anyone else.

As they were about to pull out of the hospital car park a few minutes later James said, 'What is your guess about the bleeding?'

'Placenta praevia? The placenta is too low and blocking the uterus?'

'Hmm, great minds think alike. We'll have to see what Meredith comes up with, though.'

'Yes, of course. I've just told Kirsten's mother that he is the best. Giles is a friend as well as a colleague. He was there for me at a very bad time in my life.'

There was silence as James waited for her to continue satisfying his curiosity, but it seemed as if that was to be his crumb for today and he didn't pursue it.

Yet it seemed that there was another little snippet of information coming his way from the woman who had appeared in his life and was making the road he was used to travelling seem rigid and unexciting.

Lizzie was pointing to a block of apartments opposite the hospital. 'You see the one with the 'For Sale' sign? It's mine. That's why I'm renting the cottage near the peace garden. I can't buy a place in Willowmere until it's sold.'

'I see,' he said slowly. 'So you were even nearer the job here than you are now. Did you never find it rather suffocating?'

'Occasionally maybe, but I needed somewhere to live and it was convenient.'

'Do you want to go across to check that everything is secure? There might be some mail.'

'I rarely get mail,' she told him evenly, 'but, yes, I suppose I could while I'm here, though I've only been gone a week. Do you want to come with me, or wait in the car?'

There was only one answer to that, James thought. His curiosity wasn't going to let him stay where he was, though he couldn't see an empty apartment providing any clues about Lizzie's life before Willowmere.

'I'll come with you,' he replied.

As he stepped over the threshold he saw immediately that it was a modern, soulless sort of place, the kind where one could go weeks without seeing another resident. But maybe after a long hectic day on the maternity wards it was what Lizzie had felt she needed.

Everything was intact, and as she'd thought there was no mail. As if reading his mind, she said, 'It's a far cry from where I'm living now, isn't it?'

He could hardly disagree with that. 'Yes, I suppose it is, and if it is solitude you want you won't get much of that in Willowmere where we all look out for each other.' Unable to resist the opportunity, he asked, 'But why, Lizzie? What has life done to you to make you feel like that?'

It was a beautiful day but her smile was wintry as she told him, 'I'll tell you some time, and hope that you of all people will understand, but at the moment I'm starving. Can I treat you to breakfast somewhere?'

I'm all for stopping to eat,' he agreed, taking the hint, 'but if you want to be independent, how about fifty-fifty?'

'No. You had Helen feed me the other day if you remember, so now it's my turn.'

Her manner was more relaxed now and he thought that Lizzie would be even more beautiful with the long fair plait, expressive eyes and fine-boned slenderness if she was cherished and content instead of the solitary woman that she seemed to be. But maybe she preferred her completely independent life.

'Is there a Mr Williams?' she asked as they drove

around, looking for somewhere to eat. 'I got the impression without anyone actually saying so that there wasn't.'

He nodded. 'You could be right. I've not been called out to the farm often over the years, and when I have been I've only ever seen Loretta Williams and Kirsten there, as if the mother runs the place herself. There's no Mr Williams registered with us. But it's isolated up there. If that is the case one would expect Loretta to be able to drive, unless the fellow who waved to us has a car and lives in.'

Unaware that just a few moments ago James had been taking stock of her, while they'd been discussing the absent husband Lizzie had been thinking that his eyes were so amazingly blue the tiny creases round them were barely visible, and though he had a strong jaw line, his mouth was kind, and when she saw that he was observing her questioningly she said to change the subject, 'Were the children still asleep when you phoned me about Kirsten?'

'No, as I left Helen was giving them their breakfast. When they heard me say I would pick you up they wanted to come with me, which they couldn't, of course, so to take their minds off it I promised to let them stay up late tonight.

'They're a handful sometimes, but they're good kids. Polly is the easy one to cope with, what you see is what you get with my small daughter, but Jolly is a different matter and doesn't always live up to his name. Yet they get on well together in spite of the difference in their personalities.'

He found a parking space and pulled in. 'They have no mother as Jolly was quick to inform you when we met outside the Hollyhocks on the day of Laurel and David's wedding, but as well as having me there all the time they have Jess and Helen, and my sister, Anna, who will shortly be coming home from Africa, adores them, and that being so we do the best we can. Right, this isn't appeasing our hunger, is it? Shall we go and find the nearest eating place that is serving breakfast?'

As they ate together in a café in the town centre Lizzie was experiencing a feeling of unreality. It was as if the clinic was something in the background and the man seated opposite was the reason why she'd come to Willowmere, which was crazy.

She needed Monday morning to come quickly, she thought, so that the job she loved would fill her thoughts instead of the village doctor that she was seeing so much more of than she'd expected. Her career had been her lifeline over the last three years and she wanted it to stay that way.

James was just part of the package, she told herself, but when she looked up from the cooked breakfast she'd ordered to find him observing her thoughtfully she could feel her face warming.

'What?' she asked uneasily.

He smiled. 'I was thinking that you might be feeling that I'm crowding you a bit, that you haven't come up for air since you came to the village. Lizzie, did you have any regrets while we were at St Gabriel's with the chance to compare the two? It registered that Giles Meredith would like to have you back.'

'That was just Giles,' she said, regaining her composure, 'and you heard what I said to him, didn't you? That if he saw the village and the clinic he would know there was no chance.'

She wasn't to know that Giles would have put the man sitting opposite at the top of her list of reasons for liking the place if he'd been asked.

Her response to James's first question was slower and she sensed he guessed what was going through her mind. 'No, I don't feel overwhelmed by you, certainly not with regard to the job,' she told him, 'but I've been out of circulation in every other way for quite some time, my own choice by the way, and am not sure how much I want to have to polish up my social graces to get back into it.'

It was only half the story, she thought sombrely, but she wasn't going to open up her heart to a man she'd only just met, even if he was as kind and charismatic as this one.

His brow was clearing. 'That's all right, then. Just as long as I'm not crowding your space. By the way, when the children heard me on the phone to you this morning Polly said, "Is it the lady with the blue shoes?" I can see that you will have to keep your eye on them or she'll be asking if she can add them to her collection.'

'I'd already decided to give them to her as they aren't very comfortable,' she told him. 'Yet I can't do that without finding something for Jolyon too. As soon as I do, she can have them.'

'I can't let you do that!' he exclaimed. 'If I remember rightly, they looked expensive and I don't want Polly to think she can coax them off you.'

Lizzie felt her cheeks start to warm again. There must be those of her sex who would like to take the reluctant widower to the altar and saw his children as a means of getting him there.

She shuddered to think that he might suspect that the newcomer to Willowmere came into that category, and her calling him out to the bull that had been a cow came to mind.

James had already finished eating and when she pushed her plate to one side, having suddenly lost her appetite, he said, 'Are we ready to go, then? Helen said there was no need for me to rush back, but I don't want to be too long as she looks forward to her weekends.'

'Yes,' she said, getting to her feet, and went to pay for the food before he could intervene.

There was silence between them on the journey back to Willowmere, with Lizzie feeling that the least said the soonest mended, and James wondering why what he'd said about Pollyanna and the shoes should create coolness between them. The last thing he wanted was for Lizzie to feel that she had to bring gifts for his children.

CHAPTER FOUR

WHEN they arrived back in Willowmere James stopped the car in front of Bracken House and said, 'I'll let Helen know I'm back before I drop you off at your place.'

At the same second that he got out of the car the front door opened and Pollyanna and Jolyon came running down the path, crying excitedly, 'Daddy! Are we going to the park?'

Lizzie felt envy rise in her throat like bile. If only her baby had been spared, she thought, holding back tears. It would have given some sort of purpose to her life.

When James went to greet them he held out his arms, and as they ran into the circle of them she turned away, surprised at the wave of emotion that such a simple gesture had caused.

When she turned back the three of them were approaching, and she swung her legs out of the car and stood waiting for them to draw level, ashamed at being envious of the life James had made for himself and his children. She dredged up a smile.

He was some man, this country doctor, she thought. He had to be for him to be making such an impression on someone like herself, who had jaundiced views on almost everything except maternity care.

It couldn't be easy with a busy practice to run, as well as bringing his children up on his own in a stable family home, and with no one to turn to for comfort in the dark hours of the night. But it seemed as if that was the life he had chosen for himself and he seemed content enough.

The children were observing her curiously, Pollyanna smiling and bright-eyed and Jolyon with a youthful gravity that made her want to sweep him up into her arms and kiss away his frowns.

'We always go to the country park by the river on Saturday mornings,' James explained into the silence that had fallen upon them. 'There is a safe children's play area, a pond covered in waterlilies, where the heron rules the roost, and lots of wildlife all over the place that are attracted by the river.'

'We take bread for the ducks as well,' Pollyanna explained.

'Mmm! It sounds like great fun,' Lizzie told her, suitably impressed. 'I'll have to go and see the park for myself one day.' She looked at James. 'So why don't you go now? There is no need to drop me off at the cottage—it's only minutes away.'

'If you come with us you can see the ducks and the swings and everything now,' Pollyanna said, her quick-silver mind leaping ahead.

'Lizzie might have other things to do, Polly,' James said in mild reproof.

'If I have, they can wait,' Lizzie said, smiling down onto the little girl's upturned face, unable to resist. 'That would be lovely, as long as *you* don't mind me tagging along, James.'

'Of course not,' he said easily. 'It will be someone to chat to while the children feed the ducks and play on the swings. I'll just pop inside to thank Helen for holding the fort and wish her a pleasant rest of the weekend, and then we'll be off.'

As soon as she'd agreed to join them Lizzie wished she hadn't, but she couldn't resist Pollyanna's suggestion and when it seemed as if James had no problem with her joining them the idea had taken hold of her. But now as they approached the park beneath a mellow sun she wasn't so sure. She was going to be butting in on one of the children's weekend treats and James would have invited her along out of politeness.

Yet those doubts were soon laid to rest when they arrived at the play area of the park. Pollyanna was up the steps to the top of the slide within seconds, but Jolyon stood watching, instead of following his sister.

James had gone to catch her at the other end and the cautious member of the twosome asked, 'Will *you* come down the slide with me, please?'

'Oh…yes, of course I will,' Lizzie told him, the urge to hold him close coming over her again. 'If you get on first, I'll sit behind you and hold you tight.'

When James looked up after catching Pollyanna at the bottom and saw them coming down, his eyes widened, and before he could say anything Jolyon was pulling on Lizzie's hand the moment they were back on their feet and crying, 'Again!'

'Incredible!' his father in a low voice as his son raced back up the steps. 'I can't count the number of times I've tried to get Jolly to come down the slide with me when he didn't want to come down on his own, but he's such a cautious child.' His glance took in Lizzie's slenderness. 'He was always afraid I would get stuck between the two sides.'

'Lady!' Jolyon was shouting from the platform up above, and James frowned.

'You'll have to excuse him, but he doesn't know your name, does he? What do you suggest the children call you?'

'Just Lizzie. I don't mind.'

'Are you sure?' he called as she began to climb the steps.

'Yes, I'm sure,' she replied, smiling down at him.

The two of them had been down the slide at least a dozen times and now Jolyon was sliding down on his own, and as James came striding across from where he'd been pushing Pollyanna on the swings he said laughingly, 'There's an ice-cream van over there. Can I buy you a cornet as a token of my appreciation for the way you've helped Jolly to conquer his fears?'

Her eyes were sparkling, her mouth tender, and he thought that she was beautiful when she was happy, and happy Lizzie had been while they'd played with the children. She would make some child a lovely mother, but was there a man in her life?

There was no sign so far, despite the wedding ring. He supposed he could sound Giles Meredith out about it, but he wouldn't do that. It would be an invasion of her privacy and there was nothing to say that Giles would be willing to satisfy his curiosity if he did.

They'd fed the ducks that had been out of the water

and on the river bank in a flash when the children began to throw the bread. Had watched the heron bend its long neck before dipping its beak in the lily pond and coming up with a flapping fish, and now it was time to go.

The children were hot and hungry, ready for their lunch, and Lizzie was starting to feel as if she'd been around long enough as a result of Pollyanna's impulsive invitation. For all she knew, James might be putting up with her company on sufferance just to please the children.

As she was about to say goodbye Jolyon's solemn blue gaze fixed on her and he said, 'Will you come and play with us again?'

Before she could reply Pollyanna enquired, 'Have *you* got any boys and girls?' And now it was James who seemed to be watching her intently.

'No. I haven't got any children,' she told her, 'and, yes, I'd love to play with you both again, Jolyon, but it will depend on what your daddy says. My name is Lizzie, by the way, and I'm a nurse, the kind that helps babies to be born.'

She sent James a smile. 'I don't want to intrude in your lives. I'm going, James. I'll see you on Monday with flags flying and doors open at the new centre. All I need now are some patients.'

'They'll be there,' he promised, 'enough to keep you fully occupied. You might be glad of some help from Lady D. Enjoy what's left of the weekend, Lizzie.'

'We'd like a baby to love, wouldn't we, Jolly?' Pollyanna said, halting Lizzie in her tracks. 'Could you get *us* one? But you need a mummy for a baby, don't you, and we haven't got one.'

'That might be a bit difficult, then. I think that you'd

better talk to your daddy about it,' she told her gently, and she glanced at James, who was observing his daughter with raised brows. 'Over to you, Dr Bartlett.'

As she let herself into the cottage Lizzie was smiling, even though she knew she was doing the very thing she'd always vowed not to, but how could she resist those children? They were so different, so enchanting, but she had a feeling that the pleasure of spending time with them would be short-lived.

There must have been lots of willing members of her own sex eager to be a second mother to them and a new wife to their father, but it was clear that like herself James had no inclinations of that sort. So she couldn't see an invitation to go to the park with them being repeated, and in any case it had been Pollyanna's idea, not his. He'd gone along with it because his small daughter had put him on the spot.

She spent the rest of the weekend washing, ironing and unpacking her belongings, and on Sunday morning rang St Gabriel's to check on Kirsten. They confirmed that it was placenta praevia that was causing the bleeding. That was the bad news. The good news was that it had stopped and the placenta was almost back where it should be, but they had no intention of sending her home until they were satisfied there was no danger to mother or baby.

Lizzie wasn't going to disagree with that. For one thing Kirsten had been her patient previously and might soon be again if she transferred to the new clinic, and she had all the sympathy in the world for young girls who were left to cope alone with the results of teenage hormones.

Every time she thought about Pollyanna asking her to get them a baby James's expression came to mind, and she had to smile. She was bright, didn't miss a thing, and at almost six years old was just as aware as Jolyon in his deeper-thinking way that the usual procedure for having a baby required a mother.

When it had come to Pollyanna explaining that they would have a problem regarding that, it ceased to be amusing and Lizzie felt more like weeping. But the only person who could grant them that wish was James and she wondered what he'd said to them after she'd left.

Whatever it might be it was not her business, and as she went up to bed on Sunday night the only thoughts in her mind were about the days ahead in the maternity centre and the challenge that it was going to be.

As she made her way there on a crisp Monday morning, carrying the bag that always went with her when on the job, Lizzie could feel her heart beating faster, and it wasn't just with anticipation.

Her relationship with James had moved on over the weekend with the unexpected invitation to join him and his children in the park, and she wasn't as cool as she would like to be about meeting up with him again.

She wasn't used to being in that sort of situation and if it hadn't been for his children it wouldn't have occurred, yet she wouldn't have missed it for the world. But from now on she was going to have to adopt a more distant approach to everything that concerned them both, with the exception of the clinic, which came top of her priorities.

As she walked along the main street towards the

surgery there were lots of people about, residents on their way to work, deliveries being made to some of the shops before they opened for the day, and children on their way to the village school with whoever was in charge of them.

When she looked across the street Pollyanna and Jolyon were amongst them again, trotting along with Jess. James's small daughter was chattering away to her, but his son, who was gazing around him, saw her and she heard him say, 'There's Lizzie!' Polly and Jess glanced across and the three of them waved enthusiastically.

It was just a small gesture but as she waved back there was a warm feeling inside her, a feeling of belonging, being accepted into the community, a fitting start to her first day as the village midwife.

At the same moment that she was letting herself into the clinic James came through the door that connected it to the surgery, and she was relieved to see by his manner that this morning he was purely the doctor. The easy-to-get-on-with, doting father of before had been put on hold.

Sarah Martin, the young blonde receptionist, was with him and when he'd formally introduced them he said briskly, 'All good wishes for your first full day, Lizzie. You know where I am if you need me. The staff have a coffee break round about eleven. Sarah will sort out yours and hers, and remember there's the kitchen next door if you want to use it at lunchtime.'

She nodded without meeting his glance, focusing on the demands of the day ahead to take her mind off the degree of pleasure she was experiencing in being near him again. Heaven forbid that she should join the list of those who would like to be the second Mrs Bartlett.

James was observing her keenly and wondering what had happened to the delightful woman who had sat on the grass in the park with the children on either side of her, waiting for him to appear with the ice-cream cornets.

But, of course, Lizzie had her midwife's hat on this morning. If he read her mind correctly she would have only one thought in it, the purpose for which she'd come to Willowmere. And that was just how it should be, but it didn't stop him from experiencing a niggling feeling of disappointment.

When she'd left them on the Saturday morning he'd told the children, 'The babies that Lizzie looks after have already got a mummy to love them, Polly. So I'm afraid she can't give one to us, but one day you might have a baby of your own, and won't that be lovely?'

Thankfully that had sent her thoughts off in another direction and all the way home she'd been thinking of names for it.

There were four mothers with appointments that first morning, each at different stages of their pregnancies and with different questions and concerns. She had seen two of them before when they'd been under her care in Antenatal at St Gabriel's and now because they lived in Willowmere they were taking advantage of the new facilities.

Colette Carter, the first one to be seen, was forty-two years old and the owner of a beauty salon in the village. Previously childless, she and her husband, who had a car sales outlet across the way from the post office, had been less than enthusiastic when she'd found she was pregnant.

They were Willowmere's leading socialites and

wanted to stay that way, but today when Colette put in an appearance Lizzie discovered that everything had changed. They'd felt the first flutters of the baby's movements and the realisation had transformed the couple's thinking.

Because of her age and the pregnancy being sixteen weeks along, she was due to go to St Gabriel's soon for an amniocentesis to check for any abnormalities in the foetus she was carrying. After Lizzie had checked her blood pressure and listened to the baby's heartbeat, Colette was anxious to know what was involved in the process.

'Ultrasound scanning is used to show the position of the baby and the placenta,' Lizzie explained, 'and then a needle with a syringe on the end is inserted through the wall of the uterus so that a small amount of the amniotic fluid that surrounds the baby can be drawn off to check for any abnormalities.'

'And suppose there are some?' Colette questioned nervously. 'What then?'

'You will be told about them and the risks involved to the baby and yourself, and you would need to decide whether to continue with the pregnancy or not.'

Referring to the patient's records, Lizzie said, 'There's no known history of Down's syndrome or other genetic disorders in either of your families, but the test is important for your age group as there is an increased risk in women over thirty-five. It's just a precaution, Colette, so go home and try not to worry.'

Of the other three patients with appointments, two were local women who already had young families so they'd been through it before and knew the routine. One of them was in the early stages of pregnancy so it was just a matter of blood tests, a urine sample and checking her general health and lifestyle. The other one, whose pregnancy was further advanced, was due for a blood test to assess the functioning of the placenta.

The last patient due to be seen hadn't arrived and Lizzie went to ask James if he could shed some light on the absence of Eugenie Cottrell.

He had just finished morning surgery and was about to set off on his home visits when she appeared, framed in the doorway of his consulting room.

'Hi,' he said, smiling across at her. 'How has it gone?'

'Fine, so far,' she told him. 'Except that my last appointment hasn't turned up and I wondered if you'd heard anything from her that might explain it. Does the name Eugenie Cottrell ring a bell?'

He groaned. 'She rang just five minutes ago asking for a home visit. I wasn't aware that she's pregnant and was booked in to see you, or I would have come across to let you know that she's got some sort of severe stomach bug. I have her notes here. As one of Willowmere's more colourful characters Eugenie leads a very full life, with lots of partying and suchlike. She's an artist and lives in a cottage called The Hovel in woods near Willow Lake. There was a drink problem at one time. It's to be hoped that it's sorted if she's pregnant. Do you want to come with me, or wait until she makes another appointment?'

'I'll tag along. From the sound of it this woman might need a watchful eye kept on her. Does the name of her property indicate the state of the place?'

'No, not really, it's just her sense of humour. Eugenie attended the same school as me and was a loose cannon back then.'

He was picking up his car keys and heading for the forecourt of the practice, and when she'd been next door to get her bag and told Sarah where she was off to Lizzie joined him with a feeling that it might have been wiser to have made her own way to this patient's home. But considering that it was in woodland and she didn't yet know the area very well, it had to be the most sensible thing to do.

As they passed the lake, sparkling in the midday sun beneath the graceful willow trees, the house that David had renovated with loving care for Laurel and himself came into view and Lizzie said, 'When are David and Laurel due back from their honeymoon?'

'This coming weekend,' he replied. 'They will both be back on the job next week, which will give Ben Allardyce a chance to spend more time with Georgina and baby Arran. He and she had a rough time for a few years after their little boy was drowned. The pain and grief of it separated them, instead of bringing them closer together, and they divorced. But that is all behind them now and they are blissfully happy.'

'So that is another tragic instance of losing someone who was loved a lot,' she said tonelessly.

He gave her a quick sideways glance. 'You mean, like me?'

'Er…yes.'

In truth she'd been thinking of both of them, but *her* sorrow was tucked away in a corner of her heart and she didn't want to bring it out for an airing while she was with James.

It was clear that in the Willowmere Health Centre of which her project was part, there were two families who had faced up to loss and were getting on with their lives. So why wasn't she doing the same?

Maybe meeting James and the Allardyces was what she needed to jolt her out of the half-life that she'd been living for the last three years.

He was observing her expression and wished he knew what she was thinking. There had to be a reason for Lizzie's changes of mood. He sensed that something deep within her was the cause of them and wished he knew what it was, but one thing was for sure, he hadn't known her long enough to ask those kinds of questions.

They were driving through the woods now along the rough track that led to the cottage called The Hovel, and she said, 'Aren't the trees beautiful as the leaves start to turn, James? I just love the colours of autumn.'

'Mmm, me too,' he agreed, and as a red roof appeared with a smoking chimney perched on it he wished they could spend the afternoon getting to know each other better, instead of fulfilling the function that was part of his life's blood.

An unshaven guy with a pleasant face opened the door to them when they arrived and after they'd introduced themselves, said, 'Eugenie's upstairs and she has got *some* bellyache.'

'Lead the way, then,' James suggested, and the two of them followed him up a narrow winding stairway into a colourful bedroom with purple satin sheets.

The woman they'd come to see was huddled beneath them, moaning softly, and when she saw them she said, 'I've got the most awful stomach pains, James.'

'Have you been vomiting?' he asked, as he and Lizzie stationed themselves on either side of the bed.

'No, it's not that kind of thing, I don't feel sick, but I've got dreadful pains in my stomach.'

'Are you losing blood?'

'Um…a bit,' she said evasively.

'I've Lizzie Carmichael with me,' he told her. 'She is the midwife you would have seen if you'd been well enough to keep your appointment this morning. So how long have you been pregnant, Eugenie?'

'I've missed four or five times.'

'And so far you've had no antenatal care?'

'I was feeling OK. It was Zac downstairs who made me make the appointment at the new place in the village.'

'Is he the father?' Lizzie asked.

'Yes.'

'We need to get you to hospital,' James told her after he'd examined her. 'You could be on the point of miscarrying, and that is the cause of the pains. How long have you been losing blood?'

'Since the middle of the night.'

'I've called an ambulance,' Lizzie said decisively. 'The sooner we get you to St Gabriel's the better, Eugenie. I just wish you'd come to us when you knew you were pregnant rather than putting yourself and the baby at risk this way.'

'I know I've been stupid,' the woman lying amongst the satin sheets said, 'but I get so engrossed in my painting everything else comes second. Will *you* tell Zac that I might be going to miscarry?' she begged James.

He sighed. 'Yes, if you want me to, but wouldn't you rather tell him yourself?'

'No. He'll be upset. I don't like to see him like that.'

She fixed her gaze on Lizzie. 'If they can save my baby, will I still be able to come to the centre in the village?'

'Yes, of course,' she said reassuringly, 'but first we have to get you into hospital care.'

The ambulance had been and gone with Eugenie's devastated partner beside her, and as Lizzie and James drove back the way they had come through the woods she sighed. 'I hope I wasn't too hard on her.'

He glanced over at her. 'You certainly weren't happy about our patient not having taken advantage of the care provided for pregnant women. Did I detect a personal note creeping in?'

'Are you just asking or telling me off?' she enquired.

'I'm not just asking and neither am I telling you off,' he replied equably. 'Would you like to tell me about it? You don't have to.'

His quiet, nonjudgmental tone crept under Lizzie's defences. 'Yes, I was once pregnant and lost my baby. Not because of any lack of care on my part, or that of the NHS, or because of the tricks that nature plays, but it was due to someone's carelessness, and I've had to live with that ever since.'

'And the baby's father?'

'He isn't around any more.'

'I see.'

'How can you when you don't know anything about me?' she said stiffly.

'I know this much. You are top notch at the job, you like my children and they like you, but at this moment you don't like me much because you think I'm prying into matters that you don't want to discuss.'

He was wrong there, she thought. She liked him a lot.

Too much for her own good. But it would pass and so would the edgy moment that had come from her sharpness with the woman back there in the woods.

It was nothing new. She was never envious when she placed a newborn into a loving mother's arms, but she had to admit Eugenie's lack of care and attention had hit a raw spot.

'You're wrong about that,' she said steadily. 'How can I not like you when you've been so kind to me? Remember the cow episode, and you asking Helen to make breakfast for me, *and*, top of the list, inviting me to join you in the park.'

'But you don't like me enough to tell me what it is that drags you down sometimes,' he said dryly.

'I've just told you part of it. As for the rest, I've learnt from experience that loving too much, giving one's heart to someone completely, leaves no defences in times of grief and despair. So I steer clear of that sort of thing and find life a lot easier by doing so.'

'I take it this is about the baby you lost?'

'Some of it, yes.' There was no way she could tell him that she too had lost a partner in similar circumstances to him, and that instead of facing up to her loss, as he had done, had secreted it away in her heart where it lay like a stone.

'And now can we talk about something else?' she urged. 'Eugenie's paintings, for instance. They were all over the place, weren't they, and most unusual, like the woman herself. She's very talented.'

'Mmm, she is,' he agreed. 'I have one in my bedroom that she painted of Julie, my wife. Eugenie did it from memory but it's an incredible likeness.'

There was nothing she could reply to that. All her photographs of Richard were shut away in a drawer because it hurt too much to look at them. That was the difference between them. James was living in the present, and where was she? Somewhere halfway to limbo?

They were back in the village and as he pulled up in front of the practice he said, 'It's lunchtime, Lizzie. Have you anything planned?'

'I've brought a sandwich and am going to make tea to go with it in the surgery kitchen.'

He nodded. 'Good. I'm going to pop back home. I want to phone my sister in Africa and can sometimes get her about this time, so I'll have a bite while I'm there and will see you shortly.'

As they went their separate ways Lizzie thought that her first full morning at the centre had been memorable, to put it mildly. The last thing she'd expected was to be out in the district with James again for a similar reason to the previous occasion, a pregnant patient who might lose her baby.

When she'd brought Eugenie Cottrell's records up to date she phoned St Gabriel's for a second time to ask what was happening with Kirsten.

She was told that the bleeding had stopped and that the placenta, as it sometimes did, had gone back into place, but that they were keeping the pregnant teenager in for a while longer to make sure that there would be no immediate recurrence of the problem, and after those reassurances she went for her lunch.

CHAPTER FIVE

As THE week progressed, the new centre was functioning smoothly. Lizzie was delighted when James
accepted Olivia Derringham's offer of assistance for
two half-days per week, and was grateful for her input.

Olivia was pleasant and helpful and thrilled that her
husband's gift to the village was now established and
working. She told Lizzie that when she'd been expecting their last child, Georgina Allardyce, who at that
time had been Dr Adams, had come out to her several
times for various problems associated with the pregnancy, even though the actual birth was to take place in
a private hospital.

'The village practice is dear to our hearts,' she explained. 'And I've been thinking, what about if some
time in the future we could offer the mothers who want
to have their babies at home a birthing pool, so that they
could have the use of it in their own home when the time
came, if they so wished? What do you think? Though
we are talking about more funding on quite a large scale,
so it might have to wait a little while.'

'That would be fantastic!' Lizzie told her. 'Maybe we
could start a fund for it. I'm sure that James would be

all for it and so would the more forward thinking of our expectant mothers.'

Olivia smiled at her enthusiasm. 'You could try twisting the arm of the primary care trust, and I'll do the same to my husband.'

When Lizzie met James in the kitchen in the lunch-hour he said, 'You look very perky today. What gives?'

Ever since Monday's visit to the house in the woods and the revealing conversation he'd had with her on the way back, they had met only briefly, usually in connection with those who came for antenatal care and were also involved with the surgery.

On one of those occasions he'd told her that Eugenie had been kept in St Gabriel's for bed rest and to get her blood pressure down, which had been sky high, as he'd discovered when he'd examined her at the cottage.

'According to the father-to-be she hasn't miscarried yet, but as we know only too well it doesn't say that she isn't going to,' he'd said with businesslike brevity. 'He seems a really decent guy and if she does carry to full term I can see him in the role of house-husband, caring for the child while she paints.'

It had been a sombre moment, so it was good to see Lizzie now lit up like a light bulb. She'd made clear her attitude on relationships and he'd been asking himself if it had been a warning, a keep-your-distance sort of statement. The only thing that was clear regarding what she'd said was that *she* had no yearnings towards him.

She liked him for his good deeds, he thought wryly, which made him sound a bore, but that was as far as it went, and for someone who was supposed to be the catch of the village it was black comedy at its best.

'Lady Derringham has suggested that we try for a birthing pool some time in the future,' she said. 'What do you think?'

'I think that we are a long way off that sort of thing. We are talking about thousands of pounds. I read of a similar venture at a birth centre somewhere and it cost in the region of thirty-five thousand pounds. We have to learn to walk before we can run, Lizzie. A thousand coffee mornings and bring-and-buy sales wouldn't fetch in that sort of money, though I do understand your enthusiasm. If I don't understand anything else about you, I understand that.' He was being perverse and knew it. The thought of a birthing pool was as dear to his heart as it was to hers and if the opportunity arose, he would welcome it with open arms.

'It was more the primary care trust we were thinking of and Lord Derringham's fondness for the practice,' she said, deflated by his downbeat reaction. 'But I suppose you're right. Olivia and I were letting ourselves get carried away with the idea.' And picking up the mug of tea that she'd just made, she went back to her own domain.

On Friday afternoon Sarah said, 'Did you know that it's the harvest festival on Sunday morning, Lizzie?'

'I've seen a notice about it,' she replied, 'but hadn't really absorbed it as I've been so busy here. What does it involve?'

'It starts with a parade of the farmers driving hay carts and trucks around the village, displaying their produce, followed by farm machinery such as tractors and combine harvesters, and ends up outside the church.

'At the start of the service the farming families walk

down the aisle with offerings from their harvests and place them in front of the altar, and when it is over the foodstuffs are taken to a centre that feeds the homeless.'

'I see,' Lizzie said thoughtfully as two things occurred to her. The first was that it was a lovely idea, and the second that James and the children might be there. Contrary to the comments she'd made to him on the way back from Eugenie's cottage, it would bring light into her weekend if they were.

Saturday had dragged by as Saturdays often did, and on Sunday morning Lizzie joined the village folk waiting for the farming community to appear with their various offerings in an assortment of vehicles.

As the procession came trundling along, led by the village's brass band, a small hand was placed in hers and Jolyon said, 'When are you coming to play with us again, Lizzie?'

She turned. James and Pollyanna were behind her, smiling at the surprise on her face, and contentment settled on her like a blessing when James said, 'They haven't forgotten the time you came to the park with us, Lizzie. You're top of the pops.'

'I don't know why,' she said laughingly. 'Your children are irresistible.'

And so are you, he thought in slow wonder, in spite of you being so much on the defensive sometimes. But that wasn't so today. Lizzie was smiling widely as she bent to hear what the children were saying above the noise of the band, and as the long fair plait of her hair swung loosely with the movement he felt the urge to press his lips against the soft skin on the back of her neck.

She straightened up at that moment and caught him off guard as she turned to face him, and a tide of colour rose in her cheeks as their glances met.

'Are you going in to the service when the procession is over?' she asked quickly to cover confusion. 'The children are deciding who is going to sit where.'

'Yes. Of course,' he replied. 'We never miss the harvest. This is a farming community mostly and I think that the children need to know where a lot of the food they eat comes from, don't you?'

'Er…yes,' she replied absently, still thrown by what she'd seen in his eyes.

'So let's go in and get settled, then,' he suggested, 'and am I right in thinking that I'm going to be on the end with you in the middle of your fan club?'

'It would seem so,' she said laughingly, and taking the children each by the hand she led the way into the old Norman church that stood only yards from the surgery complex.

As the four of them made their way to the front so that Pollyanna and Jolyon could see what was going on, there were a few surprised glances coming their way as the church was already half-full, and James thought wryly there was no cause for excitement amongst the locals. It wasn't what it looked like.

He was breaking the routine of almost six years by allowing himself to be attracted to the one woman who wasn't interested in him. The only things that made Lizzie sparkle were the job and his children, and he was damned if he was going to use Polly and Jolly as a means of getting through to her.

When the service was over and the church was filled

with sacks of grain, vegetables from the fields and fruit from the orchards, he discovered keeping to that vow wasn't going to be easy.

He always took the children to the Hollyhocks for Sunday lunch. He had a regular table booked and today would be no different except for one thing. They wanted Lizzie to join them, wanted her with them. And so did he, but not in the way it was happening, with the impetus coming from Polly and Jolly. He wanted it to have come from her, but knew that wasn't likely.

She was observing him questioningly and said, 'I don't want to intrude, James.'

'You won't,' he said smoothly. 'I have a table booked, so we won't have to queue.'

He was watching her expression and thought she was going to refuse. Even though she was enchanted by the children Lizzie wasn't going to join them. But he was wrong.

After a moment's silence she said, 'Then that would be lovely, James, if you're sure.'

He was sure. Sure she was only coming for the children's sake, and would accept that for the moment if it was what made them happy. It was strange how they'd taken to her just like that, they all had, and as far as Polly and Jolly were concerned it wasn't because they'd been starved of female company after losing their mother.

There had been Anna, his sister, who'd put her life on hold for them, and now they had Jess, who was great, though she did have a life of her own too and was now engaged to a young farmer from the next village.

And then there was his housekeeper, Helen, who was amazing and very fond of them, but he thought that the children must see something in Lizzie that they hadn't already got.

As they walked the short distance to the tea rooms he gave a quick sideways glance to where she was walking along with one child on either side. The children were chatting to her happily and he thought that maybe Lizzie found something in them that *she* needed, too.

His needs didn't seem to come into it, he thought wryly, but he'd put up with that sort of a situation long enough to be able to cope with it. The vacant space in the bed was likely to be there for some time to come.

He wasn't the only one who'd been badly hurt in the past. From what he could gather, Lizzie too had known sorrow. She'd lost a child, which was enough agony for any woman in a lifetime, *and* the father of it was no longer with her to offer comfort, for what reason she hadn't been prepared to say. But she'd made it clear that she wasn't going to risk getting hurt again.

Yet surely she could talk about it to him, of all people. He'd had to travel along a painful road himself, though for him there'd been Anna and loving friends to support him, but it didn't sound as if it had been like that for Lizzie.

There was a fresh face behind the counter when they went into the Hollyhocks Tea Rooms and Simon introduced her as his sister. When they'd asked about Emma, and James had introduced Lizzie as the new midwife, he said, 'She's resting and is only going to do a couple of hours each day while she's pregnant.'

'You'll look after her, won't you?' he asked Lizzie anxiously. 'We've waited a long time for this. When she was pregnant before, she was unwell all the time and in the end she had a miscarriage.'

'We will be taking great care regarding that and every other problem that might arise,' Lizzie assured him. 'Do feel free to come to the clinic with Emma when she has an appointment. That way you can keep a check on the progress of the pregnancy first hand.'

'Yes, I'll do that,' he promised, his expression lightening, and as they turned away to go to their table she said, 'It's such a shame that everyone can't look forward to the birth with an easy mind.'

'Yes,' he agreed, 'but it would be just too good to be true if such an amazing and complicated thing was always worry free.' He smiled. 'That's what you and I are here for, isn't it, to iron out the creases if we can?'

With his glance on the children, who were already wriggling onto chairs placed around a table for four, he said, 'And in the meantime, shall we satisfy our hunger?'

Pollyanna and Jolyon were each holding a menu and he said laughingly, 'That isn't necessary. They have the same thing every time we come here.'

'And what's that?' she asked, sharing his amusement.

'Chicken and chips, with ice cream for afters.'

'Sounds good. I'll have the same.'

'Are you sure? There's lots to choose from.'

'Yes. That will be fine. What about you?'

'Salad, I'm trying to keep trim.'

Lizzie looked away. She could have told him that to her he *was* trim, with a few other attractions added on for good measure. He was tall, athletic and attractive in a casual sort of way, with the kind of good looks many women would look twice at.

But obviously he hadn't responded or someone would have stepped into his dead wife's shoes before now. Her expression softened at the thought of Pollyanna's love of wearing her mother's shoes. One day she would give her the blue ones that she'd coveted if James had no objections.

She could have stayed with them for ever, but when they'd finished the meal Lizzie rose reluctantly to her feet and with a smile that embraced them all but was mainly directed at James, said, 'I think it is time I gave you some space. It was lovely to share the harvest with you and be invited to lunch, but there are only so many hours in a weekend, James, and I don't want to intrude in too many of them, so I'll say goodbye until Monday morning.'

She saw the children's downcast expressions and putting to one side her intention of keeping it light between them, said, 'Maybe you could come to have lunch with me at my cottage one day. It would be nice to cook for more than one.'

'Ye-es!' Pollyanna and Jolyon chorused, but James merely nodded, which made Lizzie wish she hadn't been so premature with the invitation. That being so, she didn't linger. She made her way quickly out on to the street and headed for home.

When she'd taken off her jacket and kicked off her shoes she sank down onto the sofa and stared into space, reliving every pleasurable moment that she'd spent with James and his children and trying to ignore the voice of common sense that was whispering in her ear, You're not ready for this.

It was true, she wasn't, but if she looked at it from that angle she never would be. Being with them was chipping away at the ice around her heart and if it began to melt, what then?

Apart from the moment when she'd caught something in his expression as she'd raised her head from listening to what the children had been saying when the band had been playing, James wasn't giving out any signals and neither was she. But it didn't stop him and the children being the first thing she thought of on awakening and the last thing in her mind at night.

For the rest of Sunday she did the few chores needing to be done, and once that was accomplished she wandered restlessly around the cottage's small rooms until the streetlamps began to come on and a yellow harvest moon appeared in the sky.

Slipping on a jacket and picking up her purse, she went out into the night and looked around her, undecided which way to go. She could see the lights of The Pheasant beaming out across the main street and there were a few people strolling in that direction, off to share the company of friends or just simply to relax for a while, and the extent of her loneliness was starkly clear at that moment.

She would stick out as a woman on her own if she went in there, and the last thing she wanted was to be conspicuous. What would James be doing at this moment? she wondered as just a short distance away the lights of Bracken House were lighting up the surgery forecourt. Tucking the children up for the night maybe, or going over the surgery accounts with the practice manager as he sometimes did out of hours.

He wasn't doing either of those things. Pollyanna and Jolyon had been asleep for a while, and his intention of going next door to the surgery to bring back some paperwork that he wanted to look over regarding the practice hadn't materialised because he couldn't concentrate on anything except the effect that Lizzie was having on him.

The way she smiled, the way she would bring herself down to the children's level when they wanted to play, was bewitching, but he couldn't help wishing that sometimes she would elevate herself to the plane that he moved on.

Yet did he want to disrupt the life he'd made for himself and set sail on uncharted seas? He'd put thoughts of Lizzie to the back of his mind when they'd separated after lunch, but Pollyanna hadn't let that last long.

As he'd been brushing her hair before she went to bed she'd asked unexpectedly if she could have it like Lizzie's, and he hadn't been able think of a reason why not, unless it was that for the first time ever he was going to have to make a plait of his daughter's long golden tresses.

He opened the front door with sudden determination. He *would* do some practice work, he decided as he stepped out into another mellow night. No use yearning for what could threaten his ordered life.

As he looked down the street he saw her, standing irresolute not far from The Pheasant, and his intentions to do something useful went by the board.

In a matter of a few strides he was beside her and saying, 'Hello again. Is everything all right?'

It is now, Lizzie thought, but didn't voice it. The pleasure of being near him again was washing over her in a warm tide. 'Yes. I came out for a change of scene and was debating whether I wanted to walk into The Pheasant on my own.'

His smile was wry. 'Can't do anything about that, I'm afraid. I have two sleeping children upstairs, but I can offer you a drink at home if you want to come inside.'

Lizzie hesitated. She couldn't think of anything she would like more but…

'You would prefer it if the children were there, wouldn't you?' he said levelly. 'I'm just a means to you being with them, aren't I? I'm only asking you in for a drink, Lizzie.'

'I know you are,' she replied uncomfortably, 'and I don't need Pollyanna and Jolyon to chaperone us. Yes, I'd like to have a drink with you, James.'

'So come this way, then,' he said calmly, and as they walked the few steps to Bracken House he went on, 'You weren't the only one at a loose end. I couldn't settle and was about to go next door for some paperwork to keep me occupied. You arriving on the scene has given me the excuse I was looking for.'

He led her into the sitting room and when he'd opened a bottle of wine and was pouring it, said, 'You'll never guess what Pollyanna has asked me to do. She wants her hair in a plait like yours.'

'Really!' she exclaimed laughingly. 'I can imagine how much you'll be looking forward to that. I'll bet you wished me far away.'

'Not at all,' he protested. 'With Polly and Jolly having no mother, I'm always ready for them to have the benefit of pleasant and trustworthy female company to help fill the gap.'

'But you've never done anything about filling it yourself…on a permanent basis?'

'I might have done if the right woman had come

along, but she hasn't so far and the gap remains. Better no one than make a mistake, don't you think?' With a quizzical smile he added, 'You may be surprised to know that I rarely discuss my private life with anyone. In fact, this is a first.'

Lizzie placed her wineglass carefully on the small table beside her and rose to her feet. She had a feeling like she was drowning. They were discussing the fact that James had no wife. It was a good moment to explain that she had no husband, but the words were sticking in her throat in case he thought that she was using the opportunity to inform him that *she* was available on the marriage market.

'What's wrong?' he wanted to know. 'Why are you about to rush off? Is it something I've said?'

She shook her head. 'No. It is something that *I* have left *unsaid*. You might be surprised to know that my life has not been unlike yours, James, and I can't see it altering in the near future. I was married to someone I loved dearly and lost *him*, as well as the baby I was carrying, in a ghastly accident on the motorway. It was three years ago and I've never found anyone since to equal Richard.'

There was amazed concern on his face and she thought guiltily that the last sentence wasn't true. *She had found someone*. He was standing next to her. And she shuddered to think what he would say if he knew.

'Don't go,' he said gently, his blue gaze full of compassion. She sank back down onto the chair. 'You've had to cope with that all alone? No relatives or friends?'

'There was an aunt way back who brought me up when I lost my parents quite young. But she saw it as a chore more than anything else and was only too willing to let me spread my wings when I was old enough. She hasn't been in contact since, but I do have friends. Giles Meredith at St Gabriel's and his wife were there for me at the time and a few others, but I think they've wearied of my desire for solitude and have drifted away.

'But don't feel sorry for me, James. I have mid-wifery, the job that I was cut out for, to keep me sane, and I count myself fortunate because now I'm working in this lovely village with you and lots of other kind people around me.'

She was smiling now. 'And if you would like to refill my glass, why don't we drink to Willowmere, the new maternity clinic *and the village practice*?'

As they clinked their glasses together on that he said softly, 'You are welcome here at Bracken House any time, Lizzie. I get weary of my own company sometimes.'

She didn't take him up on that, but as her glance held his over the top of the glass she offered, 'If you have any trouble with the plait I'll be only too pleased to oblige.'

'What? Every morning?'

'Yes, if need be.'

That would suit him just fine, he thought, starting each day with them all together, him, her and the children. But he wasn't going to risk having Lizzie shy away from him by telling her so. Not after them begin-ning to understand each other better after the revealing conversation they'd just had. So he said with a change of direction but still with the same thought in mind, 'Do you want to go up and have a peep at them?'

'Mmm, yes, please,' she said immediately.

James preceded her up the stairs and led her into a large airy bedroom where Pollyanna and Jolyon's beds were side by side, and as she looked down at them, sweet and defenceless in sleep, Lizzie thought that his children had lots of love in their lives, they didn't need hers.

Unaware of the direction of her thoughts, James said unwittingly, 'Anna will be home soon, as I told you, and they are both really excited as they're very fond of her. For a long time she helped look after them like the mother they'd never known, and I had to be careful who I employed to fill the gap when she married Glenn and went to work in Africa.'

'Fortunately Jess has been great and Helen looks after them like a doting grandma, so the separation hasn't upset them too much. Polly lives every moment as it comes, but Jolly is a different matter. There is a depth to his thinking that amazes me and at the same time worries me. He needs stability even more than Polly.

'I sometimes feel that I'm the only thing in his life that he's sure of and I should have done something about it long ago, but as you've just so rightly said some people are hard to replace, impossible in fact.'

She was one step ahead of him on that, Lizzie thought, by already being in the process of discovering that it wasn't quite so impossible as *she'd* previously thought. She wanted to reach out and hold him close for comfort, but she lacked that sort of confidence and so instead said in a low voice, 'From what I can see, you're doing a wonderful job of bringing up your children, James. Don't ever feel guilty about that.'

At that second Pollyanna stirred in her sleep and he

whispered, 'If Polly wakes up and finds you here, she'll be out of bed in a flash, so maybe we'd better go back down.'

She nodded reluctantly and he thought surely Lizzie could see that he was aware of the attraction she had for the children and that she was equally drawn to them. But he wasn't going along a road that led to a mother for his children who wouldn't love him too, and there were no signs of *that* so far.

It was almost midnight and James wasn't happy when Lizzie got up to go. 'They'll be coming out of the pub about now,' he said. 'It can be a bit rowdy sometimes and I can't leave the children to see you safely home.'

They'd chatted about various things after he'd taken her up to see them, none of them personal after their previous discussion. Then James had insisted that she stay for supper and the time had flown, with Lizzie wistfully thinking that this was what she was short of, some congenial male company. But she reminded herself that the solitary life had been her own choice in those days of pain and grief and she'd never felt the need to regret it…until she'd met James.

'I'll be fine,' she assured him. 'It's only a few minutes' walk away.'

He shook his head. 'That may be. But the fact remains that I invited you here and it's up to me to see that you're safe.'

A lump came up in her throat at his concern and as tears pricked she fought them back lest she make a spectacle of herself. The next moment she was observing him in amazement as he said, 'Helen always keeps the spare room ready in case of visitors. I would be happier if you stayed the night.'

Lizzie could actually feel her jaw dropping. 'And what would I do for nightwear?' she croaked.

'I can find you a pair of my pyjamas. They'll be a bit voluminous on you.' Laughter was in the eyes looking into hers as he added, 'Better too big than too small, don't you think?'

'Err, yes, I suppose so,' she agreed, 'and, yes, I will stay if it puts your mind at rest.' Now it was her turn to be amused. 'But what about your reputation if Helen finds me on the premises when she turns up in the morning, or Jess when she comes to get the children ready for school?'

'Their amazement will only be equalled by their relief.'

'What do you mean by that?'

'At finding me with a member of the opposite sex. I don't know whether you are aware of the fact but the whole village is trying to marry me off.'

'Is that so? Well, I can assure you that I will be long gone before they arrive.'

'OK. Whatever,' he said easily. 'But I will sleep more soundly knowing that you're tucked up in the spare room instead of walking home on your own.'

It was only half-true. He *would* feel happier, but he would also be very much aware that the only woman he'd looked at twice for a long time was sleeping under his roof in a pair of his pyjamas.

When they were about to separate on the landing he said, 'How long is it since you slept with someone else in the house?'

She gave a rueful smile. 'A long time. It will be a

pleasant feeling knowing that I'm not alone, yet I can't complain as it has been my own choice.'

He nodded. 'Sleep well, Lizzie.' Turning, he went into his own room and closed the door firmly behind him as if to say that was the last she would see of him until morning.

CHAPTER SIX

LIZZIE awoke the next morning to the sound of whispering, and when she opened her eyes Pollyanna and Jolyon were beside the bed in their nightwear, eyes full of solemn curiosity.

As she smiled at them Jolyon asked, 'Lizzie, why are you wearing Daddy's pyjamas?'

'They're too big,' Pollyanna pointed out.

'Er, yes, they are a bit,' she agreed. 'Your daddy invited me to supper last night and it was late when we'd finished, so he asked me to stay.'

'And didn't you have a nightie?' Pollyanna questioned.

'Not with me, no.'

'You could have had one of Mummy's.'

'I don't think your daddy would have liked that.'

While they'd been speaking Jolyon had wriggled under the bedclothes and was now snuggled contentedly beside her. Patting the bed at the other side, Lizzie held out her arms to Pollyanna and she didn't hesitate.

At that moment James called, 'Children, you are not to disturb Lizzie. It's Monday morning and Jess will soon be here. Breakfast is ready so, chop, chop, let's be seeing you at the table.'

Having no response, he was coming up the stairs and as they heard him go into their room the children snuggled out of sight under the bedclothes.

Seconds later he knocked on the door and Lizzie called, 'Come in, James.' When he appeared she asked innocently, 'Can't you find them?'

She watched his mouth curve with amusement as he observed the small mounds on either side of her, and wondered what it would be like to be kissed by him. For his part James was taking in the vision of his unexpected guest with hair splaying across the pillow minus the plait and the rest of her submerged in his pyjamas.

At that moment the children came whooping out from under the bedclothes with excited cries and he thought that his wish was being granted. The four of them were going to start the day together, but it seemed that the thought was premature as Lizzie was checking the time and saying, 'I need to get mobile or I'll be late for the clinic.'

'Surely you've time to have breakfast with us?'

She shook her head. It was a tempting offer, but she didn't want to be there when Helen and Jess arrived. She needed time to recover her sanity before her working day began, and to do that she needed to be away from James for a while.

Other requirements were that she needed a shower and to get dressed in her uniform when she got back to the cottage. If there was any time left after that she would have some breakfast.

James took the children downstairs and when she was ready to leave, Lizzie stopped in the doorway of the kitchen where they were eating and said, 'Thanks for your hospitality, James, which I would like to return. Will you and the children have lunch with me at my place next Saturday, if you haven't got anything arranged?'

'We don't have anything arranged, do we, children?' he asked the twins.

'No!' they cried enthusiastically.

Just as he'd known she would, Pollyanna asked, 'Can I try your blue shoes on, Lizzie?'

'Yes, of course you can,' she replied, 'and what would *you* like to do when you come to lunch, Jolyon?'

'I want to see Daisy the cow that you thought was a bull.'

'I'm not so sure that Lizzie wants to be reminded of that,' his father said reprovingly.

'I can see that I'm not going to be allowed to forget it,' she said good-humouredly, 'but you can certainly see Daisy if she's anywhere around, Jolyon. For all we know it might be from her that we get our milk.' Her glance switched to James. 'I really must go. I'll see you later at the practice.'

He was at the worktop, pouring that same milk on to the children's cereal, and when he looked up there was regret in his eyes.

'What?' she asked.

'Maybe we'll have breakfast together another time.'

'Er…yes, maybe we will,' she said uncertainly, and wondered what the how, why and where of it would be.

As she left Bracken House, Bryan Timmins was coming up the path with the daily delivery of milk that he made to most of the houses in the village, and if he was surprised to see the new community midwife leaving James Bartlett's house at that time of day, he concealed it well and wished her a civil good morning.

As Lizzie hurried homeward she thought that she should be thankful that it hadn't been Helen or Jess that she'd met back there. That really would have caused raised eyebrows, yet would it have mattered? There wasn't going to be anything between James and herself except mutual respect, and on her part a growing affection for his children that he didn't appear to have any problems with.

He frequently made it clear that he was a one-woman man and until she'd met him she'd felt the same about Richard, but now she was starting to feel that it would be no betrayal of her love for her husband if ever James looked *her* way.

They'd both known sorrow and had kept faith, but suddenly the ice around her heart was melting because she'd met a country doctor who stood out like a star in a dark sky.

He'd said jokingly that the villagers would like to see him take a new wife, but it had been clear that he had no serious intent on that score, and if he ever did have she couldn't see him looking in the direction of someone like herself.

From what she knew of him so far, James would want a wife who would love his children like a mother. But first and foremost he needed someone who would love *him* as a wife, and when it came to passion she'd only ever made love with Richard and that had been so long ago she'd almost forgotten what sleeping with a man was like. Would her blood ever warm again with the heat that came from desire? she wondered.

They arrived at the practice at the same time, not late but with no time to spare, greeted each other briefly, then went their separate ways. And as Lizzie's day got under way the steady arrival of expectant mothers from Willowmere and the surrounding villages kept her too busy to think about her own concerns.

'Doesn't this kind of job make you feel broody?' Sarah asked when they stopped for lunch.

Lizzie's expression was serene enough, but she admitted, 'Yes, it does sometimes, but it also gives me a great feeling of fulfilment when I've been there for the mother all through the pregnancy and at the end am there to bring the child safely into the world.'

She knew that Sarah was engaged to be married quite soon and said, 'I'll be delighted to do the same for you whenever the time comes.'

It had been said jokingly and Lizzie was surprised to see a warm tide of colour stain Sarah's cheeks. When she spoke the reason for it was there. 'I think it might have come already,' she confessed. 'I've missed two months on the run.'

'And have you done a pregnancy test?'

'No. I don't want to be pregnant before the wedding,' she wailed. 'Sam is in the army and when he came on leave before being posted abroad for three months we got carried away on the night before he left.'

'So why not go to see Ben? He's a famous paediatric surgeon. Not a gynaecologist, of course, but would be a good guy to see if you feel embarrassed about consulting James.'

'I've told James that I think I could be pregnant and he said if I want to consult him to pop into the surgery, though I think I'd rather go to the chemist,' Sarah said. 'But the staff there have known me since I was small and I don't want it all over the village before I've told Sam.'

'So better to see one of the doctors, then, as they are bound by patient confidentiality,' Lizzie soothed. 'They'll be on their rounds now, but pop into the surgery as soon as Ben or James, if you'd prefer to see him, are back. It's a pity that Georgina isn't around. She would be the ideal one to consult, but she's occupied with her own baby at the moment and it could be a long time before she wants to return to the life of the GP.'

The lunch-break was over, there were a couple of women in the waiting room so it was time to get back. Sarah had to put her possible pregnancy out of her mind until one of the doctors came back from his house calls.

When Sarah came back in the middle of the afternoon after going next door, her expression said it all. There was a mixture of dismay and apprehension in it, but there was also a kind of dawning wonder as she said, 'I've seen Dr Allardyce. James had been called out to an emergency and wasn't there. *Oh, Lizzie, I'm pregnant!*'

'So what do you think your fiancé and your parents will say when you tell them?' Lizzie asked.

'Sam will be thrilled. We'd planned the wedding for as soon as he comes on leave once his three months out there are up, and by then I'll be three and a half months pregnant. As for my mum and dad, they'll be a bit stunned at first but as long as I'm happy about it they won't mind. They understand how hard it is for Sam and I to be apart for so long.'

'And are you?'

'Happy? I will be when I've got used to the idea.'

Lizzie was smiling. 'So shall I book you into the clinic?'

'Yes, please,' was the reply, and Sarah went back to her duties with a dazed expression on her face.

'I haven't experienced any morning sickness so far,' she announced when there was a lull between patients in the late afternoon. 'Do you think I will, Lizzie?'

'You might not,' she replied. 'Though you'll be lucky if you don't, but not all pregnant women have to endure it.'

Sarah had gone dashing off home to phone Sam and to tell her parents her news, and Lizzie was on the point of locking up the clinic for the night when James appeared. It was the first time they'd seen each other since arriving that morning, and her spirits lifted.

When she'd gone to the surgery kitchen in the lunch-hour to make a snack he'd been out on his house calls and must have been busy since then as she'd seen nothing of him until now.

She wasn't to know that after the time they'd spent together over the weekend he was feeling the need to be near her again, to see her, speak to her, but not to touch as that could trigger off events that might be regretted in the cold light of common sense.

'So how has *your* day been?' Lizzie asked, taking in every detail of the tall figure in the smart suit, with the direct blue gaze and kissable mouth. Their glances met, his questioning, hers warm, and she hoped he didn't think she only wanted to know him because of his children. In other words, that she saw him as a means to an end. The idea was almost laughable. Wasn't the usual ploy getting to know the children to get to the father?

In truth she was just allowing her starved heart a little ease in the company of all three of them, father, son and daughter, that was all. Yet in that moment in the deserted clinic it was only the two of them that mattered, and Lizzie knew that no matter what she said to herself she was on the point of falling for a man who had kept faith for nearly six years since losing his wife. But was he likely to turn to *her* if he was ready for a new beginning? As her doubts resurfaced, she thought not.

'My day has been a busy one as always,' he said easily in reply to the question. 'Otherwise I might have come across sooner.'

'Did you want me for something?' she asked awkwardly, and he wondered what she would say if he told her that he'd come because he hadn't seen her since the start of their working day and he'd needed to get another glimpse of her before she left for home.

He couldn't believe what was happening to him. The honey-haired midwife with eyes the colour of violets had originally impressed him with her expertise and devotion to the job, but now she was getting to him in a different way and the last thing he wanted was to be out of control of his feelings.

He was sorry for her, deeply so. To lose a husband and an unborn child at the same time was a ghastly thing to have to live with, and from what he'd seen of Lizzie so far it seemed as if it had turned her spirit inwards because *she'd* had no one to turn to.

He had been fortunate in that respect as friends and family, in the form of Anna, had rallied around him unstintingly and now here he was, nearly six years on and becoming alive again.

She was waiting for a reply to the question and on the spur of the moment he said, 'Helen lives at Bracken House during the week so once Polly and Jolly are asleep I'm free to go out if I want to, and I wondered if you would like to go for a stroll by the lake later this evening, and maybe when the light has gone we could have a drink in The Pheasant or a coffee at the Hollyhocks?'

'Oh, well, yes, that would be nice,' she replied, trying to conceal her surprise. 'What time would you want me to be ready?'

'I'll call for you at half past seven if that's all right. It should give us an hour or so of daylight before night falls.' Turning towards the connecting door that separated the clinic from the surgery, he said with sudden brevity, 'Bye for now, Lizzie,' and returned to his own part of the premises.

James was already regretting the idea, she thought when he'd gone, and she wasn't so sure it was a good thought either, yet she knew she would be ready and waiting for his ring on the doorbell when half past seven came.

He was late and when she opened the door to him his first words were in the form of an explanation. 'I never leave the house until the children are asleep and they were ages in settling down tonight,' he said apologetically. 'Since learning to read they do the bedtime-story bit and I listen, and the one that Jolly had chosen went on for ever, but they caved in at last and are now in dreamland.'

'You don't have to explain,' she told him gently, her doubts about the wisdom of them being alone together forgotten. 'In any loving family the children must come first by the very fact of them being young and defenceless. Don't ever feel you have to apologise for loving your children, James.'

There was wistfulness in her voice and it made him want to take hold of her and soothe away the pain, but he wasn't going to. He could tell that Lizzie wasn't sure about them spending the evening together, let alone cuddling up to each other, be it innocent or otherwise.

An autumn sun was getting ready to set by the time they reached the lake and as the house that David had renovated to its former splendour came into view James broke the silence that had fallen between them by saying, 'The newlyweds will be back with us on Monday so we'll be fully staffed at the surgery once more, which will leave Ben free to pursue his own interests if he wishes.'

Lizzie was only half listening. On the day of the wedding she'd been too wrapped up in the bride and bridegroom to take too much note of the house, but now she was gazing entranced at the elegant dwelling that David had resurrected from local stone and carried the name of Water Meetings House.

James was following her glance and said, 'The reason David rebuilt this place was because it had been the childhood home of his mother who had died when he was very young. He had never seen it until he came to live in Willowmere. Just a little further along the road is the place where the two rivers that flow through the village meet, hence the name Water Meetings House.'

'I think I might buy a property when I've adjusted to the new job and new surroundings,' she told him. 'I've been like a piece of flotsam with no fixed abode for the last few years and I'm beginning to feel it is time I put down some roots. I'm committed to renting the cottage for at least six months, but it can take that long for a house sale to go through, so that would be no problem.'

'No, indeed,' he agreed absently.

She observed him questioningly, but it seemed as if he had no further comment to make so she concluded that her future plans were of no interest to him, and that she was being a little too hasty in thinking that his suggestion they spend the evening together was for any reason other than his desire to be hospitable.

She might have thought differently if she'd known that the reason for his reticence was because he'd been imagining her making Bracken House her permanent home and had been staggered at the way his thought processes were working.

But as she didn't, she turned the conversation into safer channels by asking if he knew that Sarah had seen Ben that afternoon and he'd confirmed that she was pregnant.

'Yes,' he said. 'I saw her as she was leaving and she told me about the baby.' He was smiling. 'Young Sarah couldn't be in a better place to be pregnant. I'm told that there will soon be a wedding coming from that direction which will please Edwina Crabtree and her company of bellringers who officiate at all weddings and funerals in Willowmere.'

They were back in the village and he said, 'So what is it to be, the pub or the tea rooms…or your place?'

He was sounding her out, she thought. Wary that she

might have her eye on the vacant slot in his life. She told him coolly, 'I can't see the Hollyhocks being open at this hour, so perhaps just one drink at The Pheasant and then I'll say goodnight, if you don't mind.' She didn't mention her cottage.

'No, not at all.' And where her tone had been cool his was easy as if he wasn't bothered either way.

They had one drink with little to say to each other and James was about to leave her at the gate of the cottage. This was unreal, Lizzie thought as they faced each other in the autumn twilight.

She didn't want him to go, yet neither did she want him to stay, because if he did it would be the beginning of something she couldn't control, and afterwards she would be floundering in all the things she'd avoided so far, such as uncertainty, hope, dismay, all brought about by giving in to the sexual chemistry that was keeping her rooted to the spot instead of bidding him a swift goodnight and hotfooting it inside.

She was about to discover she needn't have got herself in a state. James was turning, ready to go, and saying, 'Some time, if you like the idea, I'll take you along the river bank to where an old water-mill has been turned into a restaurant. That's if you're keen to get to know these parts.'

'Yes, of course I am,' she told him, and asked James if he was offering to play the tour guide out of politeness rather than anything else. 'Why don't we go there next Saturday with Pollyanna and Jolyon after *she* has tried on the blue shoes and *he* has seen where Daisy the cow grazes. It would be more interesting for them than having lunch here, with the rooms being so small.'

'Mmm, we could do that if you like,' he said in the same easy manner, as he took in the message she was giving out. It was clear that Lizzie didn't want to be on her own with him. She'd been edgy all the time they'd been together tonight. Was she afraid that his honourable widower reputation was a front for a guy who didn't miss the chance of a no-strings-attached romp with an available member of the opposite sex when it presented itself?

Thinking that she could at least have invited him in for a drink after giving up his evening for her, she said lamely, 'You could come in for a coffee, James.'

'Thanks, but I need to be off,' he said in a tone that was empty of expression. 'Although Helen is at Bracken House she doesn't like to be kept up too late. I'll see you in the morning, Lizzie. Bye for now.' Then he was gone, striding past the colourful peace garden on his way back to the life that she was envious of in spite of herself.

What had happened? James was thinking. She'd been so cool and reserved and clearly hadn't wanted to invite him in for coffee, though it had fitted in with the rest of her reluctance to be alone with him.

Yet when there'd been just the two of them in the clinic at the end of the day he hadn't been aware of anything like that. There had been a strong feeling of mutual attraction, and if he'd stayed any longer something would have developed between them. But it hadn't been there during the evening and now he was deciding that it must have been wishful thinking on his part.

Olivia Derringham arrived the next morning with some good news that Lizzie was grateful for, after spending most of the night lying awake and wishing she'd acted less like a nervous virgin while she'd been with James. She'd fallen into a restless sleep eventually and had woken up to grey skies and a heavy downpour.

'My husband is meeting the leaders of the primary care trust that controls St Gabriel's next week with regard to a birthing pool,' Olivia said. 'The discussion will be about how much will it cost and how important it is in comparison to other much-needed medical facilities.

'He is going to offer to pay half the cost and that should help to bring about a favourable decision, but he thinks, and so do I, that the trust will want to wait a while to see first how well the clinic works, which could mean some delay. So how does the idea strike you, Lizzie?'

'I think the fact that it is even going to be considered is incredible, and that His Lordship is very generous indeed to offer to help with the funding of it,' she said joyfully. 'I can't wait to tell James!'

'Go and do so now,' Helen said. She glanced at Sarah, who had been looking pensive ever since arriving. 'We'll hold the fort for a while, won't we, Sarah?'

'Mmm, I suppose so,' she said listlessly, and on the point of going through to the surgery Lizzie stopped.

'What's wrong?' she asked. 'Have you told Sam and your parents you're pregnant?'

'Mum and Dad know and they don't have any problem with it, but it's going to be days before I can get in touch with Sam as his troop is out of reach on manoeuvres and likely to be so for some time.'

'Oh, that's a shame,' she sympathised, 'just when you're bursting to tell him your exciting news. *He* might ring *you*, have you thought of that? And you will be able to tell him then, Sarah. Keep your fingers crossed that he will.' Hoping she had offered the young receptionist a little crumb of comfort, she went to find James.

When she appeared in the doorway of his consulting room he observed her in surprise. Gone was the reticent woman of the night before. Her eyes were shining, mouth soft with pleasure, and he wondered what had caused such radiance. He'd like to bet it wasn't the sight of him behind the desk.

'Lord Derringham is going to approach the hospital trust about a birthing pool,' she told him jubilantly. 'Isn't it wonderful?'

'It must be if it can make you look like that,' he said dryly, and watched her delight dwindle.

'What do you mean?' she asked stiffly. 'How would you expect me to look on being told something like that?'

'Exactly as you did a moment ago,' he replied coolly, the feeling strong inside him that Lizzie didn't need a man in her life, she was in love with the job. Which was great, he supposed, and he had no reason to be jealous about that.

But with the feeling of futility that the previous night had left him with he persisted with his downbeat approach to what she'd just told him and said, 'It is good news, but if you remember when the subject came up before, I said we had to learn to walk before we could run.

'It is early days to be thinking of something on that scale, we, and you in particular, have to prove ourselves. The clinic has only been open a couple of weeks and though I have every confidence in you, Lizzie, I'm sure the trust will feel as I do that we need to wait a while.'

'I do realise that,' she said stiffly, 'and so do the

Derringhams, but I did at least expect some enthusiasm from you on hearing that it is a possibility. I won't keep you any longer.' And turning on her heel, she left him to his thoughts. They were not happy ones.

What on earth had possessed him to be such a wet blanket? he wondered sombrely. He was as keen on the idea as Lizzie was, probably even more so as he'd long wanted an improvement in Willowmere's maternity services.

But seeing her all lit up about the birthing pool, which would cost an arm and a leg if the idea ever got off the ground, had made him question what it would take for *him* to make her look like that, and he'd been snappy instead of supportive.

He had a patient waiting so couldn't follow her to apologise, but the first chance he got he was going to say he was sorry. What reason he would give for his abrupt manner he didn't know, as he was in no position to tell her the truth in the face of her attitude the night before.

When Lizzie returned to the clinic Olivia asked, 'Well? Was he pleased?'

'I'm not sure,' Lizzie told her with the chill of his manner still on her. 'He seemed preoccupied and also was at great pains to point out that we need to prove our worth first.'

'And what did you say to that?' Olivia enquired.

'That we all know that.'

'James is a great guy and just as keen as any of us to give pregnant women the best service possible. You must have caught him at an awkward moment. He'll be right as rain tomorrow, Lizzie, you'll see.'

'I hope so,' she replied.

It mattered a lot that all should be open between them, and if she'd done something wrong she wanted to put it right. He'd made a quick departure the night before when she'd wriggled out of having him and the children for lunch at the cottage and had suggested that she take them to the restaurant that he'd mentioned beside the water-mill instead.

Maybe that was what had made him so unlike the delightful man she could so easily let herself fall in love with, and that was the crux of the matter. She was out of practice when it came to romance…and family matters, never having had a proper family of her own. She thought wistfully how Pollyanna and Jolyon were completely at ease with her and she with them. If only she could be like that with their father…

CHAPTER SEVEN

LIZZIE was called out to an imminent birth in the lunch-hour, leaving one of the practice nurses in charge of the clinic, and as she drove to the market garden on the edge of the village where the Dawson family lived she was hoping that this time it would be a son for Will Dawson and his wife, Melanie.

They already had three daughters and the pregnant mum had told her that if this one wasn't a boy they were giving up. Lizzie had delivered each of the girls for Melanie when she'd been based at St Gabriel's, but on this occasion she was only a short distance away when it was time for the birth…

Melanie was strong and healthy and one of those fortunate women who seemed to find childbirth easy, which was often due to the mother's pelvic measure-ments, and if everything went to plan she would be up and running soon after the delivery. Putting the washer on and making a meal as if bringing a newborn into the world was all in a day's work.

Sadly, as Lizzie knew from experience, it wasn't like that with every pregnant woman, and a recent case came to mind where what she'd been expecting to be a straightforward delivery had turned into a nightmare of unexpected haemorrhaging immediately after the birth and had nearly been fatal for the mother.

Fortunately the skill of a surgeon had saved her and Lizzie had seen her recently, looking fit and well with a bonny baby in her arms, but it had been a reminder that there was always the chance of something unforeseen happening in the process of giving birth.

There had been no sign of James as she'd driven off the forecourt of the practice and his car hadn't been there, so she concluded that he was either out on his home visits or having lunch elsewhere, and again she wondered why he'd been so downbeat when she'd mentioned the birthing pool.

Whatever the reason, it had shown her that they were not on each other's wavelengths as much as she'd thought they were, but maybe it was for the best. How often had she told herself that no relationships meant no heartache, and so far it had proved to be true. But that had been before she'd met a country doctor who was every woman's dream man.

It was the same as before when she got to the Dawsons' house. A fast, straightforward delivery for Melanie, but as Lizzie placed the newborn into its mother's arms there was one difference. It was a boy and from the expression on his parents' faces they were delighted that their family was now complete.

'I don't need to initiate you into the dos and don'ts of breastfeeding, do I, Melanie?' she said with a smile for the radiant mother when she was ready to depart. 'But I'll be calling each day for a while to make sure all is well.' And off she went, accepting once again that the ache that was mixed with the pleasure of every birth she was involved with was not going to go away.

The afternoon was well gone when Lizzie arrived back at the clinic, and as soon as she presented herself Sarah said, 'Dr Bartlett was called away earlier. His little boy had a nasty fall in the school playground at lunchtime and he's taken him to St Gabriel's for tests as his head hit the concrete really hard when he fell. He rang a few moments ago to ask if you were back and when I said you weren't he left his mobile number because he wants a quick word about Jolyon.'

'Oh…right,' she replied, dismayed that Jolyon had been hurt but surprised that James wanted to speak to her about it when there was Jess and Helen who would be just as upset about the accident as she was.

She rang him straight away and when he answered he said, 'Can I ask a favour, Lizzie, after being such a pain this morning?'

Yes, of course you can,' she replied levelly, 'and I am so sorry to hear about Jolyon being hurt.'

'Yes, indeed,' he said tightly. 'He's being checked out at the moment. There's a large, soft swelling on the side of his head and one always thinks of a haematoma in such circumstances.

'The favour I'm asking of you is this. They are going to keep Jolly in for observation even if the scan shows no bleeding, as it was some fall he had…and he's crying for you.'

'Me?' she questioned blankly.

'It's all about that damned cow. He thinks he's going to miss seeing it if he's still in hospital, and won't be consoled until you are around to reassure him that Daisy will still be there when he comes home...and that so will you, Lizzie. He's fretting about that too. For some reason you have hit the right note with Jolly. I can tell that he's taken to you, that he feels secure around you, which, knowing him, is surprising in so short a time. You'll have to tell *me* where your magic comes from as sometimes even I don't understand him.'

'You are fantastic with both your children, James,' she told him softly. 'I'll come straight away. I've just been involved in a delivery for Melanie Dawson and have no one else booked in until morning, so I'll be with you soon. I take it that you're still in A and E.'

'You take it right,' he said wryly, 'and don't drive too fast. I'll tell him that you're on your way with a message from Daisy.'

Lizzie didn't drive too fast, neither did she drive slowly. There was a warm feeling inside her because James and Jolyon needed her, though she would have wished the circumstances of it to be different. Maybe one day the resilient Pollyanna would also need her, but sufficient unto the day was the wonder thereof.

When she drew back the curtains of a cubicle in A and E, Jolyon was lying on the bed, pale and tear-stained with a large swelling on the side of his head. James was holding his hand and talking to him gently, and when he saw her he said, 'Here's Lizzie come to see you, Jolly.'

'Hello, there, wounded soldier,' she said lightly. 'I've come with a message from Daisy. She says "Moo" and she'll be waiting for you at my back fence when you come home.'

His face broke into a watery smile and she went to sit at the opposite side of the bed and held his other hand. 'So how *is* everything?' she asked guardedly of James, who was grey-faced with anxiety.

'We are waiting to go down to Theatre. Need I say more? he said bleakly, and Lizzie's heart sank.

'So it's as you thought it might be?' she said in a low voice.

'Yes, that's the score. I've just spoken to Ben and he's offered to assist during the operation, and needless to say the neurosurgeon was happy to have someone of his calibre on his team. He's on his way, and with time being of the essence said he'll go straight to Theatre when he gets here.

'Ben lost a child in an accident. His little boy was drowned in a fast-flowing river, so no one knows the agony of losing a child better than he does, and that is not forgetting that you've been through that vale of tears yourself.'

She didn't reply, just nodded and thought that, yes, she had, but to lose a child that had lived and breathed and had its own special place in one's life must be sorrow beyond compare.

'You aren't going to lose Jolyon,' she said, longing to hold him close and soothe away his fears. 'They will give him back to you safe and sound, you'll see.'

He didn't reply to that, just nodded sombrely and said, 'They're going to have to manage without me at the surgery for the foreseeable future. Fortunately David and Laurel will be back on the job on Monday.' His voice broke and he turned away so that Jolyon wouldn't see his distress.

'I'll stay for as long as you need me,' she told him,

still wanting to hold him close, but not knowing what his reaction would be if she did.

He raised his head and their glances met. 'Thanks, Lizzie. It would be great if we are both there when Jolly comes out of the anaesthetic.'

'And we will be,' she assured him.

They walked beside the trolley as the porter wheeled Jolyon down to Theatre, and Lizzie could visualise how much it cost James to step back at the door and hand Jolyon over to those who were waiting there. But he had no choice and as they made their way to a nearby coffee lounge provided for anxious relatives she said, 'Is Helen looking after Pollyanna?'

He nodded sombrely. 'Yes.'

'And what about Jess?'

'She wasn't there when it happened. Jess is getting married soon and has taken the afternoon off to go and be fitted for her wedding dress. She won't know anything about the accident yet.'

'So are you going to lose her?'

'Maybe. It all depends if she wants to continue. I imagine she will as they'll need the money like any young couple starting their married life. Her fiancé is the son at one of the farms in Willowmere, but there was talk of him wanting to emigrate at one time. So we'll just have to wait and see.' Now his tone was grim. 'The same as we're having to do with Jolyon.'

He sounded so bleak, and before she threw caution to the winds and did take him in her arms Lizzie said, 'I'll get us a coffee. Would you like a sandwich with it?'

'Whatever,' he said absently. 'I feel as if it would choke me but I suppose it's the sensible thing to do.'

A nurse appeared beside them at that moment and said with a reassuring smile, 'Just to let you know that Dr Allardyce has arrived and the operation is already under way, Dr Bartlett.'

'Thank you, Nurse,' he said flatly. 'I don't suppose you can give us any idea how long it's going to take?'

'I'm afraid not,' she told him, 'but as I am sure you are aware, the usual procedure for a bleed of this kind is to drain the surplus blood from the skull as quickly as possible before any brain damage or other dangerous conditions arise, and once that has been done the patient usually makes a quick recovery.'

With a sympathetic glance in Lizzie's direction she said, 'I'm sure that you'll soon have your little one back with you safely sorted, Mrs Bartlett.'

Lizzie could feeling her colour rising at the other woman's mistake and was about to explain, but James was there before her. 'Lizzie is a colleague at the practice in Willowmere,' he told the nurse and it was at that moment Lizzie knew for certain that she wanted to be more than that to him, much more. But the speed with which James had explained their situation to the nurse made it very clear that he wanted no such misapprehensions to be made about them.

Jolyon was in the children's high dependency unit and had just surfaced from the anaesthetic. When he looked up drowsily and saw them standing side by side, looking down at him, he smiled and asked, 'Am I better now, Daddy?'

'Nearly,' James told him. 'You have to stay here for a little while and then you can go home, Jolly.'

'There *was* a bleed,' Ben had told them after the surgery, 'but not as severe as we'd expected. It's been drained. Jolyon will be a bit fragile for a few weeks so keep your eye on him, James, but apart from that he should be fine. He's come out of it very well and I'm delighted for you.'

'I owe you for this,' James told him huskily, and he shook his head.

'No! Not at all. I wasn't the only one in there.'

Ben glanced across to his neurosurgical colleague, who was asking Lizzie curiously, 'So how do you happen to be involved in all this, Lizzie? Have you left us?'

She was sparkling up at him, joyful at the successful result of the operation, and watching her James thought enviously that if she was as relaxed and happy in *his* company then *he* might have something to sparkle about.

After those few moments with Jolyon they were asked to let him rest, and as they prepared to go back to where they'd been waiting they saw Jess and Helen, holding Pollyanna tightly by the hand, coming towards them anxiously.

Lizzie stood to one side as James swooped his daughter up into his arms and smothered her with kisses, and then explained the events of the afternoon and evening. As everyone was talking at once she slipped away and once in the corridor moved swiftly towards the car park.

The feeling of being just an onlooker had been strong back there, she was thinking as she set off for home. James and Jolyon would be all right now they had Pollyanna and Jess and Helen with them. The two women had known his children a lot longer than she had and had earned right of place by their sides.

Ben had been getting into his car when she reached the car park and he said with a smile, 'You can head off for home with an easy mind, Lizzie. Jolyon is going to be all right. There was a time when it hurt like hell, using my skills for a sick or injured child when I'd never got the chance to save my own, but since Arran was born all the bitterness has gone.'

'I lost a child that I was carrying in an accident,' she told him, 'and have the same feeling sometimes when I've delivered a mother of her newborn.'

'Ah! So that's the reason for the bruised look that you sometimes have. You may not know it yet, but your work has brought you to a place of healing. I'm not referring to the village practice, I mean Willowmere itself. Give it time, Lizzie, and you will see.

'It has a tranquillity all of its own without being a dead end. It is where Georgina came to heal her broken heart when we lost Jamie and I was impossible to live with, and now that I'm here I'm just as enchanted with it as she is. So don't despair. One day you'll know it is where you're meant to be.'

'I'll try and remember that, Ben,' she said, dredging up a smile.

As they went to their separate cars and followed each other out of the hospital car park Lizzie thought that it all sounded so easy put like that, but Ben was not aware that any healing of *her* sore heart might be a long time coming and she might wish one day that she'd never moved to Willowmere.

When James realised that she'd gone he was aghast…and hurt. Lizzie had been his rock during what had seemed an endless time of waiting, and she'd kept her promise to be there for Jolly when he woke up. So now had she decided that, having done that, she'd done the favour he'd asked of her?

Jolly needed her, and so did he, but it seemed that now Jess and Helen were on the scene, and she'd glimpsed that Pollyanna was all right, she'd gone home to do her own thing without a word of farewell.

She'd reverted back to her other self, he thought, and the caring compassionate woman who was bringing back to mind the long-forgotten joys and blessings of a good marriage had gone back into her shell.

After Jess and Helen had seen Jolyon, and Pollyanna had observed her brother, wide-eyed and tongue-tied for once, James took her and Helen home, leaving Jess to sit with Jolyon until he returned after putting his bewildered daughter to bed.

'Is Jolly going to die, Daddy?' she asked, gazing up at him as he tucked her in.

'No, Polly,' he said gently. 'He's going to be fine.'

'But we won't be able to go to Lizzie's on Saturday, will we?'

'No, maybe not, but there'll always be another time,' he said soothingly, with grave doubts about the likelihood of it.

Lizzie had given him the message stark and clear and it said, *Don't take me too much for granted.*

As he was about to leave the bedroom Pollyanna burst into tears at the sight of Jolyon's empty bed so he picked her up in his arms and carried her into his own room and tucked her into his bed. Within minutes her eyelids were drooping and as he stood looking down at her he thought about how well the children seemed to respond to gentle, motherly Lizzie.

He'd always been aware that by not remarrying he was denying the children a mother's love. But had consoled himself with the thought that better no mother than the wrong one, and now unbelievably the right one had come along. He knew it, but Lizzie didn't.

By the time she arrived back at the cottage Lizzie was dismayed at the way she'd behaved by leaving James without a word, and her mortification increased at the sight of Bryan Timmins and his wife approaching from the peace garden while she was parking her car.

'Do you know anything about young Jolyon being in hospital?' the burly farmer asked. 'It's on the village grapevine but nobody seems to know much about it.'

He was remembering how the new midwife had called on James to save her from the docile Daisy and had sensed that they might be friendly, even though she hadn't been in the village five minutes.

'Yes, I've just come from there,' she told him, longing to get inside and take a long hard look at herself. 'Jolyon fell and hurt his head in the school playground and his father thought there might be bleeding inside the skull.'

'And was there?' the farmer's wife asked anxiously.

'Yes, I'm afraid so,' she told them, 'but it's been dealt with and he is now recovering from surgery. He was due to come here on Saturday and was looking forward to seeing Daisy, and is very disappointed.'

'Young 'uns set great store by some strange things, don't they?' Bryan said laughingly. 'Who'd have thought that seeing that dozy Daisy of mine would have been such an attractive prospect?'

They were about to move on and Lizzie said hesitantly, 'I don't suppose you could...er...'

'What? Take the mountain to Mohammed? I suppose I could. I've transported cows all over the place in me time, but is the young 'un near a window? An' they won't want hoof marks all over the hospital's lawns and flower beds.'

'I know St Gabriel's well,' she said. 'I worked there for a long time. All the children's section is on the perimeter of the building next to a lane that is a public right of way. If you could pull up on there opposite the children's ward they would all be able to see Daisy.'

'All right,' he agreed. 'When?'

'Tomorrow afternoon all right?'

'Yes, as it won't interfere with the milking.'

'I'll check in the morning that it is where Jolyon will be, and if you don't hear anything different that's the plan,' she told him.

'And will you be there?' his wife asked curiously.

'I'm afraid not. I have appointments at the clinic to deal with, but Dr Bartlett will be with him. Don't mention it to him, though, will you? I'd like it to be a surprise.'

She was hoping that it would be more in the form of atonement for the way she'd behaved in the hospital waiting room earlier. Recalling her conversation with Ben in the car park, she wondered just how obvious her uncertainties were to those she met.

James stayed the night at the hospital in a small suite at the end of the children's ward provided especially for the parents of sick children so that they could be near their little ones night and day if they so wished.

He was still upset at the way Lizzie had left so quickly and as he lay wide awake with Jolyon sleeping peacefully not far away, he was admitting to himself how much he'd needed her by his side on one of the worst days of his life. And she'd been there, until Jess and Helen had turned up. For the life of him he didn't get the connection.

But was he ready to admit that he wanted Lizzie on the good days in his life as well as the bad in the form of a binding commitment. Most of the time when they were in each other's company she was on the defensive and he wasn't sure why. Yet there were moments when they were so in tune he felt on top of the world.

Back at the cottage Lizzie rang Helen to ask if she needed any help with Pollyanna, it being the first time the twins had ever been separated, and when James's housekeeper answered the phone she said thankfully, 'You must have read my mind, Lizzie.

'I'm struggling here with Pollyanna. She's breaking her heart because James and Jolyon aren't here. She was fretful earlier because Jolly wasn't there when it was bedtime and eventually he settled her in his room away from the empty bed. But she's awake again and in real distress. If you could come over for a while, I would be most grateful.'

'Of course I will,' she said immediately. 'I'll stay the night if you like. Just give me a moment to find a nightdress and my coat and I'll be right with you.'

'Thanks for that,' Helen said. 'I'm not as young as I used to be for coping with this sort of situation.'

When she arrived at Bracken House, Lizzie found Pollyanna huddled on the bottom step of the stairs in her nightdress, sobbing quietly, with Helen hovering over her anxiously.

'Hello, Pollyanna,' she said gently. 'Are you missing Jolyon and your daddy? They will soon be home, you know. And until they come would you like *me* to give you a cuddle?'

There was no reply, just a nod and a small hand held out to take hold of hers.

As they walked up the stairs together Pollyanna found her voice and said, 'I was sleeping in Daddy's bed.'

'So why don't I tuck you up in it again?'

'You said we were going to have a cuddle,' was the reply.

'Yes. I know I did.' She opened the small bag she'd brought with her. 'Look, I've brought my nightie. I'll just go and get changed, and we can cuddle up on your daddy's bed if you want to.'

Still subdued, Pollyanna nodded, and when Lizzie returned and pulled back the covers, lay on the bed and held out her arms, the tearful little girl slid into them and curled up against her with a contented sigh.

When Helen came up to check on them some minutes later she found them both fast asleep with Lizzie's arms protectively around Polly, and as she smiled down at them she thought that James must be blind if he couldn't see that the one he'd been waiting for all this time had arrived.

* * *

After checking that Jolyon was all right and had eaten his breakfast the next morning, James went home for a short stay to shower and change his clothes before the neurosurgeon was due to check on his patient.

Jolyon's face was black and blue with the severity of the fall followed by the surgery, and a dressing on his head stood out starkly against the discolouration. But the hospital staff and his father were satisfied with his progress and the young patient himself was gradually getting sufficiently acclimatised to his strange surroundings for James to be absent for a short time.

When he arrived home he found Helen at the cooker and the table set for breakfast but no sign of Polly, and she said, 'She woke up not long after you'd gone last night and was still very upset, but she's asleep now.' As he went bounding up the stairs she was smiling a secret smile.

His glance went straight to the bed when he opened his bedroom door and his heart tightened in his chest. It was true what Helen had said. Polly was still asleep, but she was sleeping peacefully in the crook of Lizzie's arm, with her small fair head resting contentedly against her breast.

Lizzie was awake, watching him with wary violet eyes. Unable to believe his eyes at the scene before him, James thought that while he'd been fretting and fuming at St Gabriel's about imaginary rights and wrongs she'd been there for his children once again.

Lizzie carefully eased her arm from beneath the still sleeping Pollyanna. 'Would you have a spare robe I could borrow?' she asked, feeling a faint flush of colour rise in her cheeks. He nodded and reached into a nearby wardrobe for a silk striped robe that looked as if it was meant for special occasions, and she thought that standing before him in her nightdress surely had to be one of those.

As she took it from him she saw that his glance was on her smooth shoulders and the rise of her breasts under the thin cotton nightgown and it was easy enough to wonder what would have happened if little Pollyanna hadn't been sleeping nearby. But that was why she was in James's bedroom in the first place. There was no other reason she was ever going to be there.

'I was mad at you for disappearing like you did yesterday without a word of explanation,' he said in a low voice as she wrapped the robe around her, 'and then I find that after being there for my son, you have been comforting my daughter. I am truly grateful, Lizzie.'

'Don't be,' she said. 'I've only done what any caring person would do in such a situation and, James, it is I who should be apologising to you for leaving like I did. It was just that I suddenly felt I was taking too much for granted and when Jess and Helen arrived I couldn't see you needing me any more. I wouldn't have left if you'd been alone at the hospital.'

'So that's what you thought,' he said slowly. 'That I was happy to have you around when I had no one else, but once reinforcements arrived you became surplus to requirements. How very selfish that makes me sound.'

'It isn't meant to,' she protested weakly. 'You are the least selfish person I've ever met, and while you're handing out the medals it was just on the off chance that I phoned to check with Helen that Pollyanna was all right. When she said how upset she was I came straight over. We came up here, had a cuddle and she went to sleep in my arms. She was so upset about Jolyon. How is he this morning?'

'Battered and bruised but chirpy enough. I was close by him during the night and didn't leave the hospital until I'd made sure he'd had some breakfast. He was trying to decide if he wants to be a doctor when I left him.' James checked his watch. 'I'm only here briefly as I want to be there when the neurosurgeon comes to check on him. So let's go down and see what Helen has for breakfast, shall we? Then I'm going to have a quick shower and go back. I intended taking Pollyanna with me, but if she's still asleep when I'm ready to go, I'll ask Helen to bring her later.'

When they went downstairs there was the same good food on offer as on the day when he'd sent her to Bracken House for breakfast after the episode with the cow, and Lizzie held back a smile at the thought of Bryan arriving on the lane with his dairy cow some time during the afternoon while she was working in the clinic.

It was a strange feeling to be having breakfast with James, just the two of them in the big family kitchen, Helen having put out the food and then made a tactful exit. This is how it would be if we lived together, Lizzie thought dreamily, though with just one difference. The children would be there to make it a family breakfast and she would love that, the four of them starting the day together, but she knew that James's thoughts were very different. His mind was on getting back to Jolyon in St Gabriel's as quickly as possible, and who could blame him for that?

CHAPTER EIGHT

LIZZIE wasn't wrong about where James's thoughts were and within minutes he was getting to his feet and saying, 'Ben will be in charge of the surgery in my absence, Lizzie. I'll be staying with Jolly for the rest of the day. I'm keeping Polly off school until her brother comes home in view of her distress last night. I really do appreciate the way you've been there for them both and maybe when life gets back to normal you'll let me thank you in a positive way.'

She gave him a gentle push towards the door. 'Thanks are not necessary, James. Don't worry about this end. I'll be around to assist Helen with Pollyanna if she needs me, and Jess will be here soon, won't she?'

'Yes. She can bring Polly to the hospital later in the day instead of Helen, who could do with a rest.'

'What time will Jess be taking her? Not too late, I hope?'

'Er, no,' he replied, looking puzzled, and Lizzie thought he wasn't to know that the farmyard was coming to St Gabriel's. She was going to ring the ward when he'd gone and tell the nurses to look out for Daisy without James or Jolyon knowing anything about it, and as for Pollyanna, the next time Lizzie went to Bracken House she was going to bring her the blue shoes to play with.

When Lizzie had said goodbye to her last patient of the day it was only half past four and she decided to go straight to the hospital to see James and the children, but first she wanted to ask Ben if he had any messages for James about the practice.

He smiled when the trim figure of the community midwife appeared and when she said, 'I'm off to the hospital to see if there is anything I can do, Ben. Pollyanna was very upset last night at being separated from her brother and I stayed the night with her. She was still asleep when I left this morning and hopefully might be feeling happier, but if she isn't it's a lot for Jess and Helen to cope with while James is absent. I've popped across to see if you have anything you wish me to tell James about the surgery while I'm there.'

He shook his head. 'Only that everything is under control, Lizzie.'

'Good. I'll pass that message on.' She paused in the doorway as she was leaving. 'I want to check on any visitors that Jolyon has had when I get there to find out if one of them had four legs.'

'Four legs?' he said blankly.

'Yes, Daisy the cow is due to visit this afternoon.'

'Right,' he said, adding in the bemused sort of tone used by those who thought they have a deranged person to deal with, 'I hope she doesn't let him down.' He grinned, unable to resist getting in on the act. 'Will she be bringing flowers or grapes?'

Lizzie hid a smile. 'I'm not sure, but one thing she *will* have brought with her is a full udder.' And off she went with a sense of purpose of the kind that she hadn't experienced in a long time.

She was beginning to belong, she thought as she drove to the hospital between hedgerows dressed in autumn colours of bronze and gold. To be accepted by the village and its people was a warming thought, but to belong to the motherless ones and their father at Bracken House would be heaven on earth.

She didn't think the children would have any problem accepting her in place of the mother they'd never known, but their father was a different matter. She'd thought it before and was thinking it again. If James had coped without the joys of marriage for nearly six years, why would he think of changing that for a dried-up, childless woman whose heart had been frozen for the last three years and was only now beginning to feel warm again?

When she walked into the ward Pollyanna and Jolyon, who was still looking battered and bruised with a bandage round his head, were playing a board game at a table by the window, with James seated nearby.

'And how is my little wounded soldier today?' she asked softly.

The soldier in question didn't reply. Instead, he said excitedly, 'Lizzie, Daisy came to see me!' He pointed to the lane outside. 'She was just there on the grass with Farmer Timmins!'

'Well!' she exclaimed. 'What a surprise! I wonder who told Daisy that you'd hurt your head.'

When she looked up James was observing her with a quizzical smile and he said, 'I would expect it was someone who is kind and thoughtful and top of the list of people he likes.'

'Is that so?' she replied, not meeting his glance, and went for a swift change of subject. 'So what has the surgeon had to say today?'

'Good progress, he says, and if we promise to see that Jolly doesn't do any chasing around for a while when he gets home, he might discharge him at the weekend and refer him to Outpatients.'

'But can I still sleep with you, Lizzie?' Pollyanna asked, the memory of the cuddles of the previous night still fresh in her mind.

'Well, yes,' Lizzie said hesitantly, 'but don't you think your daddy might want his bed back?'

'I can sleep in Jolly's bed,' James said easily, as if her moving in on a temporary arrangement was no big deal.

'Er, well, yes, then,' she agreed weakly. 'If that is going to make Pollyanna happy.'

It would make *him* happy too, James thought, *and* Jolyon, but he wasn't sure where he, as the children's father, came in her scheme of things. Lizzie's love for Polly and Jolly was plain to see. Would he end up as the hanger-on if he asked her to marry him?

Jolyon had been looking through the window wistfully when the cow had appeared only feet away, and he'd observed it with high delight, while *his* own first thought had been for Lizzie. She would have thought of this and he could have wept at the wonder of it.

The farmer and the docile Daisy had stayed there for some time, with all the children in the ward and their nurses watching as she munched away contentedly on the grass verge of the lane, and when at last Bryan felt it was time to go he waved goodbye and led his dairy cow back to the vehicle that he'd brought her in.

Her visit had been the main topic of conversation between the children for the rest of the afternoon and as James had listened to them he'd wished that Lizzie could have been there to see their excitement.

He had arranged with Jess that he would take Polly home for her tea and then come back to stay with Jolyon for the night again. The nanny had gone home just before Lizzie had arrived, so now there was just the four of them.

'I'll stay with Jolyon while you take Pollyanna home,' Lizzie said, 'and when you come back I'll go to Bracken House again to spend the night with her.'

James was frowning. 'I can't help feeling that we are putting you to a lot of inconvenience.'

'And what else would I be doing at a time like this except helping in any way I can?' she said coolly, not pleased that he might be thinking that was how she was seeing her involvement in the anxious time that he'd been going through.

And upsetting her further, he said, 'Life has been reasonably free from trauma during the years I've been on my own with the children, but at times like this I feel that they need a mother and maybe it is time I did something about it.

'Anna, my sister, filled the gap for them until not so long ago and they were content. When she married Glenn and went abroad with him I employed Jess and Helen, who are both lovely with the children, but Jess has her own life to lead away from Bracken House and Helen is elderly, which is why I never leave the house in the evening until the children are fast asleep.'

As he was about to explain his true feelings, that, no matter what, he would never marry again if the woman in question didn't love him as much as his children, Lizzie didn't let him finish.

Stung by what she saw as a tactless hint that she might fit the bill with regard to his household arrangements she said dryly, 'So why not try a mail-order bride or speed dating on the internet?'

He flinched, groaning inwardly at what was turning out to be a poor attempt at trying to gauge her feelings for him. His timing had been all wrong for one thing, and giving her the false impression that he only wanted her for the use of, when every time he saw her he was more drawn to everything about her, was catastrophic. He was falling in love with her but so far she'd given no sign that she returned his feelings, and he'd been hoping she would open up to him when he'd explained that marriage was in his mind.

She hadn't finished. 'Maybe we've both kept faith long enough, James, without any means of knowing if our respective partners would want that of us. I'm sure that no one would condemn you if you felt the need to take a fresh look at your life. I might try a little speed dating myself.'

As if, she thought as he stared at her in disbelief. She was already wishing she could take the words back and tell him that she had already met a man like no other, who had gently turned her painful, nightmare thoughts about Richard into just a sad memory, and that now she was ready for a fresh start with him and his beautiful children. But James had just made it clear that he didn't see *her* in that way, and if it had to be as just friends then that was what it would have to be.

He took Pollyanna's hand, kissed Jolyon lightly on his bruised cheek and without any further comment in her direction nodded briefly and departed.

James was back within the hour and found Jolyon having his tea with Lizzie watching over him, and the leaden weight that was his heart became even heavier at the sight.

He'd had time to think on the way back from taking Polly home and had decided that a formal apology without any further explanations or misunderstandings was needed, and was hoping that then they might get back to the no-strings-attached arrangement of before.

On the return journey he'd bought her flowers, a beautiful arrangement of white orchids and pink roses to show how much his apology was meant.

When she got up to go he went out into the corridor with her and said, 'I'll walk you to your car, Lizzie.'

She shrugged slender shoulders inside the uniform that she hadn't had time to change and said with the same coolness as before, 'Please yourself. Why don't you stay with Jolyon?'

His glance went to his son, who was happily munching away. 'He'll be all right for a few moments.'

When they were outside in the car park he turned to her and said, 'I'm sorry for being an insensitive clod before. If you'd let me finish you might have thought better of me.' He took the flowers from the back seat of his car and placed them in her arms. 'I also meant to apologise for being so downbeat about the birthing pool. I think it's great that Lord Derringham is on board and you have my full support, too. Whatever you think of me, I can't manage without you, Lizzie. Can't we at least be friends again?'

She was melting with love for him. How could she ignore his plea? She said softly, 'We'll always be that James, if nothing else. Go back to your son and I'll go and see to your daughter.'

Reaching up, she kissed him lightly on the cheek. Keeping his hands tightly by his sides, he resisted the opportunity to extend the moment into something more meaningful and went back to where Jolyon was waiting for him.

Jolyon was discharged on the Saturday, as had been half promised the first time the surgeon had seen him after the surgery, and when the car pulled up in front of Bracken House with James and his son inside, Pollyanna and Lizzie were waiting at the gate to welcome them.

The last few days had been uneventful, with James at the hospital, Jess taking Pollyanna there later in the day and James bringing her home when Lizzie arrived to be with Jolyon. But now it was going to be as it had been before, with Lizzie at her own place and the three of them in Bracken House, unless something unforeseen happened, and James wasn't looking forward to seeing so little of her from then on.

They were back on amicable terms but keeping their distance and he almost broke that rule when he saw the blue shoes in Pollyanna's bedroom.

He was going round the bedrooms and bathrooms, collecting the laundry after they'd all had lunch together, and he called across the landing to Lizzie, 'You shouldn't have let Polly have the shoes. I can tell they weren't cheap.'

'A promise is a promise,' she told him, the memory surfacing of their brief, angry exchange of words at the hospital a few days back. They had made peace when James had given her the flowers, but it hadn't been the same between them.

There were words unspoken that should be said, she thought wistfully, but neither wanted to hurt the other any more, and so they were communicating, but only on the surface.

Pollyanna was tearful when Lizzie was ready to go home and she said comfortingly, 'When Jolyon is really better, maybe the two of you can come and stay the night at my house if your daddy agrees. Would you like that?'

'Yes,' they chorused. 'Can't he come too?'

'I'm not sure,' she said quickly before James could get a word in, and making a joke of it. 'He is very big and the cottage is very small.'

And that puts me in my place, James thought as he listened to the discussion. *Am I ever going to be forgiven for giving Lizzie the impression that I only see her as a mother figure for my family, when I can't sleep for thinking about what it would be like to make love to her?*

The twins were observing him expectantly as they waited for his reply to what Lizzie had suggested, and as if he wasn't feeling that her cottage wasn't *that* small he said easily, 'Yes, of course you can go. You'll have great fun with Lizzie and I wouldn't say no to some time on my own.' That having been decided, Lizzie picked up her small overnight bag and went home.

Sunday was a nothing day. She did her chores, sat around thinking about James and the way she'd avoided any further closeness with him, and as an early October evening presented itself she turned her thoughts to Monday morning at the clinic.

She expected that Sarah would be in a more cheerful state of mind when she arrived as she'd managed to locate the absent Sam back at base from manoeuvres and he'd been thrilled about the baby after the first shock had worn off. He would be home soon and the wedding arrangements were moving along with speed to avoid his young bride showing signs of the impending event on her great day.

Emma was due for a check-up first thing before the tea rooms opened, and Simon was coming with her as he was keen to be involved every step of the way after their hopes being shattered years ago when she'd miscarried for no apparent reason.

They arrived at the appointed time, Emma looking pale and apprehensive and Simon hovering protectively by her side. Her first words when asked how she was feeling were, 'Awful! I can't keep anything down. I feel so sick all the time.'

Lizzie nodded sympathetically. 'I'm afraid morning sickness affects many women during pregnancy, but it usually lessens as the months go by, Emma. Try eating smaller, more frequent meals, and ginger biscuits and ginger tea help to take the nausea away for some women.'

She had Emma's file opened in front of her and said with a smile, 'How about some good news to cheer you up?'

'Yes, please,' said her wilting patient. 'What is it?'

'I have the results of the tests in front of me that I did when you came the first time, and they are all satisfactory.'

'What were they for?' Simon asked.

'A blood test to check for anaemia or rhesus antibodies was satisfactory, and the blood and urine checks I did for diabetes were also clear. So apart from the morning sickness, you are starting off with a clean slate.'

'Let's hope that it stays that way,' Simon said, taking his wife's hand in his. 'Do you think Emma should give up in the tea rooms altogether until the baby is born?'

'Maybe for these first months while she has the nausea and there is the greater risk of miscarrying it would be a good idea, but once the sickness has abated and the tests are still showing clear, there will be no reason for her to coddle herself. Just don't overdo it, that's all. Now, I'm going to check your blood pressure, Emma.'

When she'd done that Lizzie said, 'At this moment you are fine, so go home and stop worrying. Remember, thanks to Lord Derringham, I'm only a matter of yards away if you have any problems.'

As they got up to go Emma said to Simon, 'Do you have a recipe for home-made ginger biscuits in your big cook book? And what was the other thing, Lizzie, ginger tea?'

He was smiling, relieved that nothing scary had come

up during their visit to the clinic, and promised, 'If I haven't, I can soon get them.'

James was back on duty at the surgery, having left Jess in charge of Jolyon and Pollyanna, and life was generally returning to normal, with Laurel and David back from their honeymoon looking bronzed and happy as they took up their respective positions in the surgery once more as nurse and GP.

They called in at the clinic during the lunch-hour to see what the finished article looked like. They'd gone on honeymoon before it had been finished and both were impressed with the facilities it was offering and interested to know that Lady Olivia Derringham was working there on a voluntary basis twice weekly.

When they'd gone James came in and said, 'I've just been back home to check that all is well with Jolly and Polly. I'm going to let Jess take her to school tomorrow. She's happy enough now.'

He was observing her keenly. Lizzie was still staying aloof from him but was pleasant enough, and he thought that the next time he told her how he felt he would make a better job of it, given the chance.

She could feel the intensity of his gaze and asked, 'What?'

'Nothing,' he replied calmly, and went back to his consulting room feeling better for having seen her.

Lizzie kept her promise the following Saturday. The children came for tea and to stay the night. James brought them in the late afternoon and then went home feeling strangely lost.

He wasn't used to having time on his hands like this, he thought. It would have been a good opportunity to have asked Elaine to go over the accounts with him, but he wasn't in the mood for that sort of thing and decided that he would take some exercise, walk up to the moors above the village and back.

The warm colours of autumn were already disappearing he saw as he left the outskirts of the village and the leaves were falling. Soon it would be November 5th and he would do as he'd always done since the children were small, take them to the bonfire on the village green.

It was a special event that everyone who was mobile attended, with the Women's Institute providing hot soup, parkin and treacle toffee in abundance, and this time he was hoping that Lizzie would be with them. The fact that *he* might be the reason if she wasn't was something he wasn't going to contemplate.

He hadn't been sleeping well since she'd slept in his bed and appeared before him in the flimsy nightdress that she'd been in a rush to cover up. His thoughts and desires were making him restless and he had to keep telling himself to get her out of his mind.

She'd made it clear that she wasn't in the market for being a wife of convenience, much as she loved his children, and he had yet to find the right moment to tell her that was far from what he wanted.

He wanted a wife of warm flesh and blood, wanted to give her a child, their child, to make up for the one she'd lost, but he wasn't making much progress towards that end.

It was dark when he got back to Willowmere and as he passed the peace garden and approached the cottage, he smiled at the thought that all those he cherished were sleeping inside.

Lizzie had made them a special fairy tea of tiny sandwiches and cakes with lots of crisps and ice cream, and afterwards the highlight of the occasion had been when Bryan had let them watch the cows being milked in the sheds at the far end of the field at the back of the cottage.

It was lovely having the children, she thought as they settled down to sleep, one on either side of her, but she'd made James feel he wasn't welcome, which was unforgivable as without him nothing made sense. It would have served her right if he'd refused to let them come, and she wondered what he was doing.

Probably having a well-earned rest, she thought wryly, and no one could blame him for that! James must have little time for himself yet she'd never heard him complain. He'd achieved a degree of contentment that she'd never found, but he had the children to give his life purpose and that must have made all the difference.

The white orchids and roses he'd given her were still fresh and beautiful on her dressing table and she wanted them to last for ever as something to hold on to in the confusion of her feelings for the father of the two innocents beside her.

On Sunday morning Lizzie eased herself carefully out of the bed and went downstairs to make a cup of tea before setting the table for breakfast.

As she sat sipping it in the silence she had a sudden

yearning to hear James's voice and picked up the phone, even though it was only half past six.

He answered it immediately and when she spoke he said, 'What's wrong, Lizzie? It's not Jolly, is it?'

'No. Nothing like that,' she told him. 'The children are still asleep and I thought I'd report to base that all is well at camp Carmichael.'

'Right,' he said whimsically, and she could tell he was smiling. 'You do know that it's only half past six, I take it.'

She was contrite. 'I'm sorry. Were you still asleep?'

'Er…no. I surfaced some time ago.'

He could have told her that he'd been longing to hear her voice after a strange night without Polly and Jolly in the house, and that she was the only person he had ever trusted to have his children overnight. As if she'd read his mind, Lizzie was on the phone, assuring him that all was well.

'They are still asleep,' she assured him once more, 'and as it is Sunday there's no rush, is there? I'll bring them back in the middle of the morning.'

'There is no need for you to do that. I'll come for them, and thanks for having them, Lizzie.'

'It is I who should thank you,' she told him soberly.

'Whatever you say, but don't forget that I'm taking you out for the evening some time soon as a thank-you for being there for both of them when Jolyon had the accident in the playground. In fact, why don't we arrange it now? A weeknight would suit me best as Helen sleeps in during the week and will be there to keep an eye on the children while I'm out.'

'Any evening is all right for me,' she informed him.

'I rarely go out after a day at the clinic, unless it's to walk to the beautiful lake near David and Laurel's house.'

'How about Wednesday then? Not too far off. I'll pick you up about eightish. The children will be fast asleep by then and we'll go for a nice meal somewhere.'

There was silence at the other end of the line and he sensed her indecision as clearly as if she was standing next to him.

'Yes, all right,' she agreed at last. 'That would be very nice. I hear voices upstairs, do you want a word?'

'If they're awake, yes,' he said evenly, as if he hadn't just had his enthusiasm lessened for them spending some time together in more intimate surroundings than their usual ones.

She could hear small feet on the cottage's narrow staircase and called, 'Your daddy is on the phone, children, and wants to talk to you.' As she went into the kitchen to start preparing their breakfast she could hear them telling James in excited voices how they'd been to see Daisy being milked, and she hoped he was suitably impressed.

Pollyanna and Jolyon had gone. James had picked them up as promised and the empty silence that usually hung over the cottage prevailed once more.

He'd given her a questioning look when he'd arrived and she'd presumed it was because of her lack of eagerness to be alone with him away from their everyday life, but under their present circumstances she could hardly explain that it was uncertainty rather than reluctance that had been the cause of it.

But it wasn't stopping her from deciding that just for

once she was going to let him see the Lizzie Carmichael that she used to be in the days when she'd loved and been loved in return.

CHAPTER NINE

THE rest of Sunday passed uneventfully for Lizzie. Weatherwise it was a typical October day with a chill in the air warning that winter was on its way, and with it came Christmas, she thought as she did her usual Sunday chores.

It would be her first one in Willowmere, and it would be lovely to be on the sidelines of the children's excitement. But she didn't visualise much cause for rejoicing on her own account. James's intention to take her out to dine would be out of his usual consideration for anyone that he felt indebted to, and when the festive season arrived he would have the friends who'd always been there for him to share it with.

But she'd had a few quiet Christmas times since she'd lost Richard and another one wouldn't be the end of the world. At least she would be spending it in the beautiful Cheshire countryside.

A few of her patients were expecting their babies during the festive season and that would be something to anticipate with pleasure.

When James awoke on Monday morning and went to get the children up, he found Pollyanna clomping around in the blue shoes and as he smiled at her he thought that Lizzie had the knack of getting it just right with his children. He wished she would come up with something that was just right for him, such as responding when the chemistry was there between them. Surely she could feel it, too?

There were times when she was near that his need of her was so great he had to exercise self-control or step into the unknown and risk a rebuff. But he had waited a long time to find someone he could love as much as he'd loved Julie, and could wait longer if he had to, if only Lizzie would give him a sign that she cared, but so far it wasn't forthcoming. But there was Wednesday night to look forward to. Would it bring the answer to his dreams, or be just a friendly meeting of acquaintances?

When she answered the doorbell to him on the night in question James's spirits took a downward turn. Lizzie was still in her uniform.

When she saw his expression she said hurriedly, 'I'm sorry. I was called out to a delivery only minutes after I came home.' She stepped back to let him in. 'Is Natalie Morgan one of your patients?'

'Yes. She and her husband have a bed-and-breakfast place halfway up the hill road. So it was Natalie who called you out.'

'Mmm, it was. She'd started labour and was panicking now the time had come, wishing she hadn't arranged to have the baby at home. As it happened, she didn't. I had to get the emergency services out to take her to St Gabriel's. The baby was in distress and I couldn't take any chances. Do you still want to go for the meal? I need to shower and get changed. It will take me at least half an hour.'

'Go ahead. I've booked a table and will ring the restaurant to explain that we'll be delayed.' As she turned towards the stairs, he added, 'That is, if you're not too tired after working all day and then being called out.'

'No, I'm fine,' she said as a lump came up in her throat. She wasn't used to being fussed over, but since coming to Willowmere James had been concerned about her welfare on other occasions too, and it gave her a warm feeling inside. Even though she expected he would be just as caring for anyone he thought was in need of it. But if she'd been dropping in her tracks she wouldn't have wanted to miss the evening that he'd planned so she climbed the narrow staircase and was under the shower within seconds.

There was no need to consider what she was going to wear. She'd laid the clothes out on the bed that morning and when she came downstairs again Lizzie was dressed in semi-eveningwear. A short, low-cut, strappy black dress with a matching jacket draped over her arm to keep at bay the chilly night if needed.

The long golden plait had been untwined and her hair hung down in a shining swathe on her shoulders. As he took in the effect James saw that there was a question in the violet eyes meeting his and wished he knew what it was so that he could give the right answer. That being so, he said what he was thinking, which couldn't possibly be wrong.

'You look wonderful. Heads will turn when we enter the restaurant.'

He saw her colour rise at the compliment but her reply was flippant.

'Why, because I'm showing some cleavage? I can't remember when last I dressed like this.'

'No, not because of that. It will be because you'll be the most attractive woman in the place.'

Lizzie didn't take him up on that. She wanted to calm down now and take the evening in her stride, but the fact that James approved of her appearance was like balm to her soul.

Tonight she wanted to be a woman that he was happy to be with, not someone the children liked, or the midwife who brought babies into the world, but an attractive and interesting companion, and so far she seemed to have got it right.

A little later, as he watched her sparkle like the wine in their glasses James thought he was out of practice at this sort of thing, and so was Lizzie if he wasn't mistaken.

Their social and sex lives had been on hold for a long time because of circumstances they'd had no control over, and the last time he'd taken flowers to Julie's grave in its quiet corner of the churchyard he'd felt as if she was smiling down on him in gentle approval.

But there was nothing to say that Lizzie was feeling the same way. It didn't mean that because he was ready to accept closure she felt the same. Her gaze was on him over the top of her wineglass and the sparkle was dimming into uncertainty.

'Why so serious?' she asked.

She almost dropped the glass when he said gravely, 'Have you ever slept with anyone else since your husband died?'

'No,' she croaked. 'I've never wanted to. Have you?'

'No, for the same reason, I've thought of it once or twice but that was as far as it went.'

'And?' she questioned warily.

He was smiling. 'I've sometimes thought I was crazy, but I don't any more.' The food they'd ordered arrived at that moment, so talking was replaced by eating, and when it could have been resumed during a lull between courses there was silence between them until James asked casually, 'Will you be staying in the village over Christmas?'

'Yes,' she said. 'I have nowhere else that I would wish to be.' *Except near you*, she thought, but said instead, 'I would imagine that Willowmere is quite something then.'

'It is indeed. You will see for yourself when the time comes. We're having a big party at Bracken House in Christmas week so that we can all be together, Helen, Jess, Georgina and Ben, with little Arran this time, and David and Laurel also with us for the first time. I'm still waiting to hear from Anna and Glenn if they're going to be home for Christmas. If they can't be with us, it will not be the same.'

'It sounds lovely,' she said in a tone just as casual as the one he'd used.

'So do you think you might stop by?' he asked. 'The children will want to show you what Santa has brought.'

'Yes, if I'm invited. I wouldn't want to intrude.'

It wouldn't be the first Christmas she'd spent alone. At St Gabriel's she'd always offered to work so that staff with families could be with them.

It went without saying that babies ready to leave the womb were no respecters of holiday times, so someone had to be there to welcome them when they decided to put in an appearance. Even here in Willowmere there might be a birth on Christmas Day or thereabouts.

'Of course you are invited,' he said stiffly, and because she'd been so downbeat about it added perversely, 'The more the merrier. I know two small mortals who will be most disappointed if you're not there.'

'And that's it?'

'No, of course not! I'll be disappointed too, Lizzie.'

'Then I'd better be there, hadn't I?'

'Yes,' he said steadily, 'you had, but Christmas is some weeks off. The next event in the village is the bonfire this coming Saturday. Everyone turns out for that. The Women's Institute excel themselves with the food on that occasion and the Scouts and Guides help out, with their leaders in charge of the fireworks.'

'Sounds good.'

'Yes, it is.' He was beckoning the waiter over to settle the bill and as she waited Lizzie thought what a strange evening it had been. First the disconcerting question about her sex life, or lack of it, then a half-hearted invitation to his Christmas party, and lastly he'd been describing the village bonfire in terms glowing as the fire itself, like a salesman on a front doorstep.

As they got up to go James had a sickening feeling that the evening had not been the success he'd hoped for, and he was to blame. He'd talked about everything except the feelings close to his heart, and Lizzie must think he was deranged.

She had no idea how she'd been arousing his senses in the smart black dress that revealed the smooth skin of her neck and shoulders. He'd seen quite a bit of her on another occasion when she'd been in his bed, cuddling

Pollyanna, but at the time he'd been too harassed over Jolyon's accident and Polly's distress to take note. However, it *had* registered in his subconscious.

But tonight it was different. He'd been keen to be alone with her and what had he done? Started off by asking Lizzie about her sex life, like some interfering therapist.

Then just as they had been finishing the meal he'd started to eulogise about the bonfire as if Lizzie would never have seen a pile of wood burning brightly on a November night, when all the time what he should have been doing was telling her how much he wanted her in his life…for always.

There was silence between them again as he drove them back to the village and James thought if she asked him in it would be surprising, yet surprising it was.

'Do you want to come in for a coffee?' she asked, standing in the open door of the cottage.

'No,' he replied abruptly, and she stepped back as if he'd struck her, 'but I'll come in for this.' Stepping over the threshold, he took her in his arms and kissed her brow, her lips and the hollow of her throat until she was clinging to him in total abandonment.

'What was that for?' she gasped when at last he let her go.

He smiled. 'It was to make up for the opportunities I've missed tonight, and now I'm going before I carry you upstairs and we let the chemistry between us really take over. Or are you of the opinion that there isn't any, that I'm mistaken?'

'I don't know what I think,' she said weakly. 'My life has changed so much since I came to Willowmere my mind is in a whirl. The only people who have needed me in the last few years have been my patients, for obvious reasons, but now it is all changing and, James, I think that I need you more than you need me. You are surrounded by people who love and respect you, and you must have been happy enough since you lost your wife or you would have done something about it. Do you really want to change all that?'

'What do you mean?' he said stiffly. 'Do you honestly think it has been easy? My priorities have always been my children and the practice. But as you've just said, one's life can change unexpectedly and then it's decision time, but it sounds to me as if you're trying to talk me out of falling in love with you. That you don't want to break out of the safe cocoon that you've wrapped around you, and so you're reminding me of what a good life I've got.'

He sighed, running his fingers through his dark hair. 'Lizzie. It's us I'm talking about at this moment. Think about what I've said, will you?' With that he opened the door and went out into the night.

As the door swung to behind him she leant against it weakly. Why had she got this mania of wanting to be so sure that James wanted her for herself alone and for no other reason? After the way he'd kissed her she should have no doubts on that score, and yet she'd ended up by trying to dissuade him from changing their relationship from friends into lovers.

Now it was her turn to sigh for the complexities of her thoughts as she went slowly up to bed, knowing there would be little sleep to escape into after what had just happened.

* * *

When Olivia Derringham arrived for her Thursday morning voluntary help in the clinic she asked, 'Are you all right, Lizzie? You look pale.'

She managed a smile. Pale was how she felt, pale and pathetic. The man she'd been drawn to since their moment of meeting had offered her a glimpse of heaven on earth the night before, and she'd been dithering like a frightened virgin.

There would be no chance to talk to him alone in the next few days unless she made a big thing of it, but on Saturday after the bonfire she was going to tell him how much she cared, hoping that he hadn't taken her humming and hawing too much to heart. In the meantime there were babies to weigh and mothers to advise on feeding and teething, and for those who were waiting to be blessed with a newborn the meticulous checks for such things as rising blood pressure, diabetes and other complications of pregnancy.

Thankfully, and it wasn't always the case, it was a smooth run and, when lunchtime came she went across to the surgery kitchen to make a mug of tea to drink with the sandwich she'd brought. Hoping at the same time that she might see James.

But as if she'd read her mind, as she was passing the nurses' room Laurel said that he'd gone on an urgent visit to someone staying at The Pheasant who'd developed severe chest pains and couldn't get his breath.

'Yes,' David chipped in from behind her. 'A couple of elderly walking fanatics are booked in there for a few days and it sounds as if the old guy has been overdoing it.' Then he said the same thing that Helen had said. 'You look pale, Lizzie. Are you all right?'

'I'm fine in body,' she told him, 'but the mind is a bit cluttered at the moment.'

'Anything I can help with?' he asked.

She shook her head. 'No, thanks just the same, David. It is something I have to sort out myself.'

The man that James had been called out to needed an ambulance with all speed, he decided when he entered a chintzy bedroom beneath the eaves of The Pheasant. He was gasping for breath, perspiring heavily, and there was froth on his blue lips.

When James sounded his heart it was beating fast and irregularly and he reached for his mobile and made the call to the emergency services, thinking as he did so that it had all the signs of a heart attack except for the frothiness of his lips, which could indicate some kind of poisoning.

The sick man's wife was waiting anxiously beside the bed and when he'd finished phoning she said, 'Is it his heart, Doctor?'

'It could be,' he said gravely. 'All the symptoms are there, including the blueness around the mouth, but I'm not sure about the frothiness. Has your husband eaten anything that could have poisoned his system this morning?'

There was horror in her expression as she listened to what he was saying and she gasped, 'We were up on the tops first thing among the gorse and heather and we saw what looked as if there were some wildberries still around, and as I've often made a fruit tart with them he gathered some and ate them, even though I warned him that they weren't growing as close to the ground as they usually do. So maybe he was mistaken, is that what you're saying?'

'It's possible,' he said with continuing gravity, 'and whatever they were may have poisoned him.'

The screeching of a siren announced that the ambulance had arrived, and as he heard them come in down below he went to the top of the stairs and called, 'Up here, quickly!'

When they appeared he explained briefly the possibility of poisoning from unidentified wildberries, and after giving him oxygen to help his breathing and checking his blood pressure, as James had already done, they carried him quickly to the ambulance and set off in the quiet morning, with his wife ashen-faced beside him and sirens blaring once more.

James headed back to the surgery, glancing towards Lizzie's domain as he went to his room, but he didn't knock on her door, much as he would have liked to. Every one of the events of the night before were crystal clear and every time he thought about her, passionate and unresisting in his arms, he longed to hold her close again, but there was the aftermath of that passion to consider and he didn't know how he would cope if he couldn't have her. She had brightened his life and loved his children almost as much as he did. Until last night he'd seen the way ahead clearly, but Lizzie's hesitancy had shattered the dream and he was going to stay away from her until she was ready to tell him truthfully what was in her mind.

As she got ready to go to the bonfire on Saturday night Lizzie was wondering if James would be expecting her to be there after Wednesday night. She'd spent the afternoon in the nearest town, doing some clothes shopping to take her mind off what she was going to say when she saw him, and the thought kept recurring that it wasn't going to be the most romantic setting in which to tell him that she loved him, with fireworks screeching above, the fire cracking noisily beside them and the children close by, but for some perverse reason she didn't care. It would be easier in a public place, and she wasn't exactly going to be making the announcement over the loudspeaker system.

Dressing in a warm sweater with a thick jacket over it, and jeans, boots and a woolly hat on her head, she thought that her attire was very different from Wednesday night's. She doubted it would have the same effect on James as that had.

When she stepped out of the cottage into the cold night air there were lots of people about, all moving in the direction of the playing field in the park that ran alongside the river bank, and she thought that this was what living in the countryside was all about—a feeling of community, a common interest.

She loved this place, but she loved the man who had held her in his arms on Wednesday night more. She loved his children too, and would count it a rich blessing to be part of their lives. But first she had to find out if James had really meant the things he'd said the last time they were together.

When she arrived at the bonfire there were so many people there that she had difficulty finding him and the children. Sarah was there with her fiancé, happily looking forward to the wedding that had been put forward to next Saturday, and she saw Jess in the crowd with her sturdy farmer's son and wondered if he would persuade her to emigrate like he wanted to.

A voice behind her in the crowd asked, 'Are you looking for James?' When she turned Helen was there, holding a tray of parkin and smiling her welcome for the woman who she hoped was going to be the new mistress of Bracken House.

Unaware of the direction of the housekeeper's thoughts, Lizzie nodded, knowing she wouldn't be heard above the noise, and the other woman pointed to the far end of the field and she saw that James was there with the children on either side of him.

When she was just a few feet away Jolyon saw her and cried, 'There's Lizzie.' And when Polly heard him she let go of James's hand and came running towards her, with Jolyon following at a slower pace. As Lizzie took their hands in turn and began to walk towards him, James watched her gravely.

'Hello, there,' he said in the kind of tone he'd used when they'd first met, and her spirits sank as she thought, *Is this how it is going to be, back to square one?*

But there was no sign of her inner doubts as she called a casual 'Hello' across the intervening space.

'How long have you been here?' he asked.

'Only a matter of minutes,' she replied as the three of them joined him a safe distance away from the fire. 'What a crowd!'

'There always is,' he told her. A firework exploded into bright stars high above them. 'A lot of work goes into it by the Willowmere Events Committee, and it's the same at Christmas.'

She didn't want to be involved in all this small talk, Lizzie was thinking. She wanted to talk about them, and as the numbers increased of those around the fire she was deciding that it hadn't been a good idea to contemplate telling James that she loved him on an occasion such as this.

They could have talked at Bracken House or the cottage, but she'd wanted it to be on neutral ground, and as she looked around her she thought it couldn't be more neutral than this.

As the children watched the spectacle goggle-eyed, James said in a low voice, 'So why are you here, Lizzie? Is it to finish your downbeat comments of the other night?'

'No,' she told him quietly. 'As far as I'm concerned, what I have to say is as upbeat as it can get.' Her gaze locked with his, and she said, with eyes melting with love for him, 'I've come to tell you…'

Her voice trailed away as above the noise of the bonfire a voice cried, 'James! Surprise! Surprise! We're back!' A woman who'd been pushing her way through the crowd, with a man who was deeply tanned by her side, flung herself into James's arms, while Polly and Jolly clung to her skirts, crying excitedly, 'Anna!'

Aware of how much joy the moment was bringing, and that James had forgotten she was there in that moment of reunion, Lizzie stepped back into the shadow of the bushes, and as the cries of delight continued to ring out she slipped away, deciding that such moments were to be treasured by the family concerned without strangers hanging around.

She saw Helen again as she was leaving, talking to

Jess and her boyfriend, and stopped to inform them that Anna was home from Africa, then went on her way with their delighted cries ringing in her ears too. She felt more alone than she'd ever been in her life before.

It had been a repetition of that time in the hospital when she'd been feeling secure in James's need of her and Helen and Jess had arrived and unwittingly brought her back down to earth.

How could she have ever imagined herself as part of that secure, loving family circle that she'd just witnessed? she thought as she sat in her sitting room, staring into space, with the noise of the fireworks in the distance. She hadn't been wrong when she'd told James that *he* didn't need *her* as much as *she* needed *him*.

Lizzie didn't see anything of James and the children over the rest of the weekend, but didn't expect to. They would all have lots to talk about and Anna and Glenn would have to settle in again after their absence from the place where she and James had been brought up.

The children would be so happy and excited to have their aunt back, she thought, which was only right as Anna had put her own life on hold to fill the gap that the death of their mother had left in theirs when they had been only a few weeks old.

From the way she'd greeted them it seemed reasonable to expect that she would want to take up where she'd left off, the only difference being that her sacrifices hadn't been in vain. Anna had at last been reunited with and married the only man she'd ever loved, and it made Lizzie think that James had only ever loved one person too and probably still did, which made how he'd kissed her, and what he'd said to her, seem even more like just a moment of madness.

She was wrong in thinking that James wouldn't notice her absence. As Anna had released him from her embrace to hold the children close in those moments of homecoming, he'd turned to introduce Lizzie to the unexpected arrivals and saw that she'd gone.

He'd groaned silently, saying nothing that would take away the joy of their homecoming for his sister and her husband, but there was the knowledge that Lizzie had been prevented from finishing what she had to say to him, and that was the last thing he would have wanted to happen as it could have been the words he'd been longing to hear.

But instead she'd left the scene as if she'd felt like an intruder, and she would never be that. At the first opportunity he was going to tell her so in no uncertain terms.

He'd waited so long for someone like her to come into his life that he could not afford to lose her, but for the present there was Anna bubbling over with happiness to be back, with Glenn watching over her adoringly, and for a little while he was going to put his own affairs on the back burner until the right moment occurred. He was determined to make sure it wasn't long in coming.

CHAPTER TEN

DAVID TRELAWNEY'S new wife, Laurel, had come into the practice as a temporary nurse on the arrangement that it might be just until Anna came back. Before she'd married Glenn Hamilton there had been two nurses at the practice—Beth Jackson, who had been full time, and Anna on part-time hours because of her involvement with the children.

When she'd gone to work in Africa with Glenn, Gillian had taken her place on a full-time basis, and shortly afterwards another vacancy had occurred when Beth had left to open a delicatessen in the village with her husband, and a very successful venture it was turning out to be.

It was then that Laurel, who had previously been a nurse in a big London hospital, had joined the practice and in the days that followed Anna's return she was anxious to find out what was going to happen.

If Anna wanted her job back on a full-time arrangement, which she might, then she, Laurel, would not be required. Witnessing the other woman's pleasure in returning to the place where she'd put down her roots seemed to indicate that job hunting might soon be on the cards for herself, and she didn't want that.

She loved the idea of David and herself working in the same place in health care and didn't want to have to leave, but told herself she'd known the score when she'd taken the job and would have to abide by it.

They'd had David's friend Lizzie Carmichael round one night for supper and had asked her what she thought was going to happen now that Anna was back, but she'd known no more than they did about what was going on at Bracken House since Anna's return. All she could say was that on the few occasions she'd seen James since his sister's return, he'd been pleasant enough, but had made no attempts to speak to her privately.

David was just as anxious as Laurel about her position at the practice after a week of uncertainty while Anna and Glenn wallowed in the peace of Willowmere after the frenetic pace of their life in Africa, and when he asked James if he knew what Anna's plans were, he shook his head.

'I've been giving them time to settle back into our way of life,' he told him, 'but over the weekend am going to have a sorting out. I'm going to offer Glenn a partnership in the practice, and you too, if you would be interested, David. If Glenn accepts, it will leave Ben Allardyce free to go back to the paediatric surgery he's been missing out on while he's been helping to cover Georgina's maternity leave. If Georgina decides to come back to us when her leave is up, I intend to offer her a partnership too, which should leave the surgery well blessed with doctors.'

'I'd be delighted to accept your offer,' David said immediately.

'Good. But it doesn't answer your question about what Anna plans to do, does it? As I've said, I'm going to discuss it with her over the weekend and should know where Laurel stands in the scheme of things by Monday morning, if that is all right with you.'

When David had gone, James thought there was no one more anxious to sort some things out than he was, but it wasn't all with regard to the practice.

Since the night of the bonfire he'd seen Lizzie going in and out of the clinic a few times and had had to restrain himself from stopping her and sorting their lives out on the spot, but he was forcing himself to wait until the weekend after he'd spoken to Anna and Glenn, and it was not easy.

For one thing, in spite of the excitement of their aunt's return the children kept asking for Lizzie. 'Why doesn't she come to see us any more?' Jolyon had asked one night when the bedtime story had been read.

Pollyanna had put in her plea by saying, 'I love Lizzie.'

Don't we all? he'd thought achingly every time he imagined how she must have felt when she'd disappeared from the bonfire. Come another Saturday he was going to find out once and for all if they had a future together.

It was great to have Glenn and Anna back in Willowmere, but if there was any justice in the world his future and that of Pollyanna and Jolyon was with Lizzie. He just hoped that when it came to question time she would have the answer he was praying for.

After breakfast on Saturday the children went upstairs to play and as Anna and Glenn got up from the table he said, 'Could I have a word with you folks?'

'Sure,' Glenn said, and Anna nodded her agreement.

'I've got a couple of things I want to ask you both,' he said with a gravity that had them both sitting down again.

'First of all, would you be interested in a partnership in the practice, Glenn? You weren't with us long before you married Anna and went away, but it was long enough to know that you are an exceptionally good doctor, as is David Trelawney, the other GP in the practice. I've offered him a partnership too if he wants it and he is keen to accept. So how would *you* feel about joining us on a permanent basis as well?'

There was silence for a moment and then Glenn said, 'I am most interested in your offer, James.' He glanced at his wife. 'And I know that Anna won't object. She tells me frequently that there is nowhere else she wants to live except here in Willowmere. So, yes, definitely, I accept your offer.'

'That's fantastic!' James exclaimed. 'And now it's your turn, Anna. Do you want your old job back?'

'No,' she said. 'As you know, James, I can't have children because of the injuries I received when Julie and I were in that dreadful accident. So we're going to adopt a child, or two if they'll let us, and I'll want to be there for them all the time as they get used to new parents and surroundings. I hope you don't mind.'

'Of course I don't mind!' he exclaimed. 'That's wonderful news.'

'I know that adoption can be a lengthy procedure but while we're waiting I will enjoy having some time to myself, which could mean that I won't be there for Pollyanna and Jolyon as much as I used to be, I'm afraid,' she said apologetically.

'You don't need to worry about that at all, and especially if a certain community midwife agrees to marry me,' he told her. 'I'm in love with her, the children love her too, and she loves them. Her name is Lizzie, short for Elizabeth, Carmichael. She lost her husband three years ago in similar circumstances to how I lost Julie and thinks that I don't really need her because I'm so well blessed with family and friends. So I've got to convince her that her place is here at Bracken House with me as my wife. Wish me luck, will you?'

Anna stared at him in delighted astonishment. 'That's the best news I've heard in years. How can I meet this amazing woman who has broken through the James Bartlett barrier? We're not talking about the blonde midwife who's based next door, are we? I haven't met her yet, but I've seen her coming and going.'

'Yes, we are,' he told her, adding with a smile, 'How many community midwives do you think we have in Willowmere? Lizzie is the one and only at the moment.'

'So when are you going to pop the question?' Anna wanted to know.

'Soon, very soon—today, I hope. She is the only woman I've looked at twice since I lost Julie and I'm in love with her, but first I've got to convince her how much I need her. Lizzie thinks that because I'm surrounded by loving family and friends she'll be on the fringe of things if she marries me. She was beside me at the bonfire when you surprised me, and when I turned round to introduce her to you, she'd gone.

'She's had a grim time in her private life over recent years and is wary of relationships for the wrong reasons, but the first chance I get I'm going round to her cottage to ask her to marry me. So would you mind keeping an eye on the children for me while I'm there?'

'Of course we will,' they chorused, and Glenn said, 'We've got some news for *you*. We've put a deposit on a house in the village.'

'Great!' he cried. 'Which one?'

'Mistletoe Cottage, next to the water-mill.'

'This is going to be a day to remember,' James said. 'I've got myself two new partners, which means I can sit back sometimes and spend time with Lizzie if she'll have me, and you folks are putting down some fresh roots in Willowmere in that delightful cottage. This is simply wonderful.'

By the late afternoon James was beginning to feel that things weren't quite so wonderful. Every time he'd been round to Lizzie's she hadn't been there, and he kept telling himself that if he'd had any sense he should have let her know he was coming. It was a form of arrogance to expect her to be there just because he'd decided to honour her with his presence.

He was turning away on his last abortive visit when he heard a faint cry and stopped in his tracks. It came again and his blood ran cold. The door was locked. He'd tried it a few times and was going to look a fool if he broke it down and then found that the calls for help were coming from somewhere else.

But he wasn't taking any chances, he decided. He'd lost one woman he adored and now the kind fates had brought Lizzie into his life. He wasn't going to lose her too if he could help it, and as the cry for help came again he put his shoulder to the door.

Lizzie was lying in a crumpled heap at the bottom of the narrow staircase and the scene in front of him told its own story. She'd fallen down it.

Her face was twisted with pain and streaked with tears as she cried his name in blessed relief. 'How long have you been here?' he asked gently as he knelt beside her in the confined space.

'For hours,' she sobbed. 'I tripped over the hem of my robe as I was coming downstairs what seems like a lifetime ago, and I can't get up, James.

'I knocked myself out and when I came to couldn't move because I think I've fractured my hip. I've kept drifting off with the pain and then coming back to reality again, and it happened that this time I heard you knocking and ringing the bell. Have you been before?'

'Have I been before?' he repeated gently. 'Yes, I have, my darling. I've been going crazy, desperate to talk to you but without success, and all the time you were lying here.'

Even as he was speaking he was ringing the emergency services and while he asked for an ambulance Lizzie lay white-faced and tear-stained beside him.

His was the name she'd called every time she'd come to. He was the only one she would ever want during good times or bad, and she said weakly, 'I knew you would come.'

He groaned. 'It took me long enough, didn't it?'

'You must have come before when I was out of it.'

'Possibly, but thank God I've found you.'

He'd placed his jacket over her when he'd found her but even so she was shivering from shock and he said quickly, 'Is there a hot-water bottle anywhere in this place?'

'Yes, in the bathroom.'

He looked down at her with all the love in the world in his eyes and said, 'Don't move an inch while I'm getting it.'

'I won't. I can't,' she told him, and he went up the offending stairs like a bullet out of a gun.

When he placed it in her arms she managed a pale smile and said, 'You are so good at taking care of me.'

'I want to do it permanently. That is what I've kept coming round to tell you. Will you let me?'

'Even if I end up walking with a stick?'

'Even if you end up walking with two sticks. Will you marry me, Elizabeth Carmichael? My children and I love you so much. Polly and Jolly keep asking for you. We want you in our lives for always.'

'Do you really?' she said on a sob. 'Then I'd better say yes, hadn't I?'

He could hear the ambulance coming up the road and he kissed her tear-stained cheek. 'Yes, you *had* better say yes, and it will be the sweetest sound I ever heard.'

He phoned Bracken House while the ambulance was on its way to St Gabriel's to let Anna and Glenn know what was happening and warned them that it could be some time before he came back. They were horrified to hear what had happened and Anna said, 'Just do what you have to do, look after Lizzie.'

'I will,' he promised grimly as he held her hand in the ambulance.

It had been nerve-racking, trying to move her out of the small space at the bottom of the stairs without causing further damage to her hip, but the paramedics were skilled in such situations and now she was lying on her good side in the ambulance, with him watching over her like a guardian angel.

An X-ray showed a fracture of the neck of the femur and that luckily the bone ends hadn't become impacted in the fall. An operation would be necessary to realign them and until it was performed the pain would persist and she wouldn't be able to walk. But once it had been satisfactorily accomplished she should soon become mobile again.

The deep cut on her head from when she'd hit the floor in the hall had been stitched, and no bleeding inside the skull had shown up, as it had with Jolyon, so the damage to her femur was the main problem.

As they were taking her to Theatre she said drowsily, 'Go home to the children, James. I'll ask them to let you know when it's over and I'm in the high dependency ward, or wherever else they decide to put me.'

He shook his head. 'Polly and Jolly will be fine. They're with Anna and Glenn, who are most sorry to hear what has happened. I'm not budging, Lizzie.' And with his voice deepening, he went on, 'Never in my wildest dreams did I think I would be proposing to you while you were in a heap at the bottom of those stupid stairs, but I got the answer I was longing for. So I want to ask you now, my darling, how would you like a Christmas wedding?'

'Mmm,' she murmured as they wheeled her into Theatre, and as the doors closed behind her James thought wretchedly that this was a repeat of the awful moment when Jolly had been hurt. He couldn't wait for the four of them to be together in more tranquil times.

* * *

Surgery on Lizzie's broken hip had gone smoothly, the orthopaedic surgeon who had operated told James when he came to see him afterwards. He confirmed that the bone ends at the neck of the femur had been realigned and metal screws inserted to keep them in position. In a few days' time she would be able to walk without pain and return to normal living.

'I was surprised to see Lizzie Carmichael on the table,' he said. 'I knew her when she worked here. What connection does she have with you?'

'We're going to be married,' James told him.

'Really! You must have something special to have captured Lizzie. There were a few guys here who tried to get to know her but she was never interested.'

'I consider myself very fortunate.'

'Yes, I'm sure you do, but we're not going to let you have her back too soon. She was lying injured for a long time and we'll be watching for the effects of shock for a couple of days, as well as making sure she's mobile before we discharge her. If you want to be there for her when she comes round, they've taken her to the recovery unit.'

If he wanted to be there for her! James thought as he strode off in that direction. *That was all he was ever going to want, to be there for Lizzie...and his children.*

When she came round from the anaesthetic and saw him sitting beside the bed, holding her hand, she said weakly, 'Break it to me gently. What is it to be, James? One stick or two?'

'Neither, from what I can gather,' he told her gently. 'You might need some support for a little while but nothing permanent, and when they discharge you,

you're coming to Bracken House where you can be looked after properly.'

'I thought we weren't supposed to see each other before the wedding, that it's bad luck?'

He was smiling down at her. 'All our bad luck is going to be a thing of the past from now on, you'll see.'

She managed a smile of her own and as a nurse appeared at the bedside, about to suggest that he let the patient get some rest, she said, 'I think you might just be right about that.'

By the time he'd got to the door she'd drifted off again and as he drove back to Willowmere through the dark November night the thought of the joy that this particular Christmas was going to bring took away some of the nightmare that the day had brought.

Lizzie was discharged three days later and as she walked slowly up the drive of Bracken House, holding on to James, she could scarcely believe that this gracious dwelling was going to be her home from now on.

During the past three years there'd been the soulless apartment across the way from St Gabriel's, and here in Willowmere the small cottage with the narrow staircase that had been her undoing. Neither of them could compare even remotely with Bracken House, and to live there with James and the children would be bliss.

But first Pollyanna and Jolyon had to be told what the new arrangement was going to be, and the last thing she wanted was for them to be made to feel insecure because of it.

They knew she loved them and they loved her in

return, but not yet as someone who would very soon be sleeping in the same bed as their father. Until they were married she was going to occupy the bed in the spare room next to theirs, and she and James had decided that when the twins came home from school they would tell them about her coming to live with them and the changes that would be taking place at Christmas time.

Helen had made lunch for the two of them and was beaming at them as she observed how James was looking at Lizzie. She would have a perm for the wedding, she decided happily...and a new hat...

Anna and Glenn were nowhere to be seen. They'd moved into rented property at the other end of the village until the purchase of Mistletoe Cottage was completed, so as to give Lizzie space during her first weeks at Bracken House, but it wasn't stopping Anna from being eager to make friends with the woman who had brought her brother out from behind the defences he'd erected since losing Julie.

Jess tactfully disappeared when she'd brought the children home from school, and when they came in and saw Lizzie they smiled but didn't come rushing up to her as they usually did, and she found herself tensing. Had she been taking too much for granted? she thought.

Jolyon spoke the first. 'Which is your poorly leg?' he asked with his usual attention to detail.

'This one,' she said softly, pointing to the leg in question.

'Won't you be able to play with us any more?' was Pollyanna's contribution to the conversation.

'Of course I will,' she told them. 'We'll have lots of fun.'

'Lizzie is coming to live with us. What do you think about that?' James said.

'Is it because we haven't got a mummy?' asked the deeper thinker of the two.

'No,' Lizzie said before James could answer him. 'It's because I love you all and you all love me, but I'll be able to do all the things for you that a mummy would do, and you would like that, wouldn't you? So am I going to get a kiss?'

'Yes!' they cried together, and as they ran towards her James met Lizzie's gaze above their small fair heads and the message was there for all time in the eyes looking into his.

I love you all, it said.

Lizzie had been absent from the clinic for a week and during that time one of the practice nurses who'd been involved with antenatal matters at the surgery before the new clinic had opened had dealt with patients' health checks and problems, but there was relief all round when she appeared once more in her neat blue uniform and with a solitaire diamond ring on her engagement finger.

When she told them the news, there were excited congratulations from all sides and Helen said, 'I've thought all along that you and James were made for each other, but do I take it that you needed convincing?'

'Something like that,' Lizzie told her blithely, with the memory new and precious of how they'd gone to a jeweller's in the town and together had chosen the beautiful ring. Every time she looked down at it on her finger, the wedding they were planning for Christmas Eve couldn't come quickly enough.

While she'd waited for James to come for her on that special day there had been a poignant moment in the midst of her happiness when she'd taken off the wedding ring that Richard had placed on her finger all that time ago. She would never forget him, just as James would never forget Julie, but they were both being given a second chance of happiness and Richard would never want to deny her that.

The news that James Bartlett had succumbed at last, and to the new community midwife of all people, had gone out on the bush telegraph with all speed after one of the expectant mothers visiting the clinic had heard the conversation. When they'd heard the news, all the hopefuls had sighed and wondered what she'd got that they hadn't!

Anna was to be matron of honour at the wedding, Pollyanna bridesmaid, and Jolyon had dubiously agreed to be a page boy. Glenn was James's choice for best man, and the only vacancy amongst those taking part was someone to give Lizzie away.

When the question arose she told James serenely, *'I'm the one who's giving myself to you, no one else, and shall walk down the aisle to stand beside you at the altar on my own as I've been for so long, and after that I will never be alone again, will I, James?'*

'You can count on that,' he told her tenderly, and that was how it was going to be.

The day they had both been waiting for had dawned, and when the curtains had been drawn back at Bracken House there had been cries of delight from everyone.

Snow had fallen during the night and the village lay beneath a smooth white blanket.

When noon came Edwina Crabtree and her friends would send the bells pealing out joyfully over the village to salute the doctors they all knew as friends. After the wedding, the party at Bracken House that was usually held earlier in Christmas week was going to take place, and this time it would be hosted by James and his new wife.

It was all going as planned, and as villagers and guests in the crowded church waited for the bride to appear, Helen, in one of the front pews, nodded her newly permed locks in satisfaction, and Jess, in love herself, prayed that one day she might be as happy as the little family that she had been delighted to serve...

When Lizzie walked down the aisle to the man she loved, beautiful in a flatteringly simple dress of cream brocade, with a pale fur wrap around her shoulders, she was minus a veil, but in her hair she wore white orchids and pink roses, and was carrying a bouquet of the same flowers as a reminder of the day when James had given her the same kind of delicate blooms.

For the groom and his bride it was as if their worlds had righted themselves, and with the small bridesmaid and page boy happily watching they made their vows with the church bells pealing out joyously over the village.

It was evening and the guests were arriving for the party. Caterers had been hired to prepare a buffet. A giant spruce with bright baubles and coloured lights dominated one corner of the sitting room, and beside it Lizzie and James held hands with the children on either side of them.

He bent and whispered in her ear, 'I love you.'

She gazed up at him with happy tears sparkling on her lashes and told him, 'I love you too, James, so very much.'

Everyone came to wish the newlyweds well. Anna and Glenn were there, happy to be home and delighted that James had found someone to love as much as he'd loved Julie. Helen and Jess were also beaming their approval, and Georgina and Ben had just arrived with baby Arran in his father's arms. David and Laurel had come with Elaine her aunt, who was practice manager, and next to them were Beth and her husband, away from the deli for a few hours. Gillian the practice nurse had brought her husband, Lord Derringham's estate manager, and last but not least by any means came the Derringhams themselves. It was as if the whole of Willowmere was there to share in the happiness of the Bartlett family.

Later, much later, when the children were fast sleep and the guests had gone, Lizzie lay in her new husband's arms in the bed that she'd once shared with Pollyanna and said dreamily, 'Do you think we might have a baby of our own one day, James?'

'I think that could be arranged,' he said softly. 'A baby for the midwife who has brought so many into the world, and the doctor who would love to see her holding a child of her own in her arms.'

'And a brother or sister for the two adorable children that they love so much already,' she reminded him.

'But of course,' he said. 'That goes without saying.'

3

MILLS & BOON®